ALONE TOGETHER

Alone Together

Sherrye Henry

Heywood Books

© Sherrye Henry 1982

Excerpt from 'What Did I Have That I Don't Have?'
© 1956 by Alan Jay Lerner & Frederick Loewe
Used by permission of Chappell & Co Inc,
owner of publication and allied rights
throughout the world
International Copyright secured

Published by arrangement with Doubleday,
a division of Bantam Doubleday Dell
Publishing Group Inc

First published in Great Britain
by Judy Piatkus (Publishers) Ltd

ISBN 1 85481 035 9

This edition published in 1989 by
Heywood Books Limited
55 Clissold Crescent
London N16 9AR

Printed in Great Britain by
Cox & Wyman Ltd, Reading

For *Elizabeth*, *Sherrye* and *Emil*
patient tutors, stalwart supporters, loving friends

Friday, August 1

The door stuck in the humidity, or again she had the wrong key, or there were just too many packages under her arms to pop the door open with her hip. Klutz! How could anyone who thought herself graceful be so bloody awkward? Maggie usually stood at her shoulder at a frustrating moment like this, commanding, "Be ept, Mom, be ept," but Maggie was gone. Max too, and thank God. The day had been too hard, the week too demanding, and the promise of time alone too delicious to wish them home.

Ah, it gave. Inside now, lights, look around. Just the usual damage this time, not the hurricanic aftermath she had feared. Into the kitchen: pots in the sink, food-encrusted of course, drips down the fridge. Chocolate again for lunch, kids? The mouse droppings they leave behind. Didn't they know all she needed was a two-minute tour of the place to know what they ate, drank, smoked, who joined them, how rowdy they got, and how late they stayed? Surely mothers were the original detec-

tives and children the sloppiest clue-droppers. Either they don't
mind having their business known or the psychologists were
right—they wanted to be found out.

Still, the final preparations for the trip seem to have been innocent—messy, but innocent. It wouldn't take more than an
hour to follow behind them, cleaning away the vestiges of their
departure, returning the place to home—her home—which
meant straight, clean, without disorder. Was that the key—
without disorder? Maybe she *was* over-toilet-trained, compul-
sive-anal, or whatever the affliction is of being at peace only
when surroundings were in place. Or maybe there were too
many years behind her as a housewife, too many endless days
filled with floor waxes and washing machines. But hadn't she
been a whiz at the job? The accomplished servant every woman
dreams of and can't find. "I still scrub the cleanest tub in
town," she told fellow analysts when the market did not move
as she predicted. Housewife: fall-back position. Perversely, in
spite of the time-consuming and satisfying professional life she
enjoyed, it gave her pleasure like nothing else. Towels folded
and shelved in perfect piles; wood redolent of lemony wax; windows clean of a winter's grime. Anyone who could manage as
pleasant a home, with as little time, and with two teenagers intent upon disorganizing her organization could never be a failure regardless of what the market did—or so she consoled herself. No, damn it, it wasn't her potty training. Disorder in other
people's lives never dismayed her, nor in her own when hired
hands followed behind the slovenly habits around her, though
she had to remember back to prehistoric times when that was
true. Back to the big house in Atlanta, growing up with as
many servants as family members. A kitchen in chaos *then* did
not disturb her composure, nor could she remember ever
plumping a pillow or smoothing a spread. She thought her
demonstrable change in attitude, her inability to deal with confusion must have begun with a subliminal addition to her marriage vows: "Do you take this man, and an orderly house . . ."

Jim used to complain she was the only woman in America who could make the bed in the morning before he was out of it. Cleaning after a husband, though, was reasonable duty; it was the constant jumble of children's belongings, the inconsiderate trailings of their dirt, the thoughtless destruction of their careless hands that she considered the punishment of vengeful gods. She imagined that somewhere, surely, there existed the mother who managed to teach her children that bare dirty feet *did not* belong on white walls while they reclined upside down watching television. And possibly someone had inculcated the message that unscraped plates in the dishwasher didn't give the machine an even chance. And perhaps, just perhaps, there was a mother brave enough to employ behavioral conditioning, who had the determination, upon arriving home late at night and finding a particularly filthy conglomeration of dishes and garbage, to quietly shake her little man or woman awake, push the sleep-dazed body in the direction of the disaster, and say kindly, but firmly, "Clean it up—*now*." Skinner would approve; she always lacked the resolve, and the energy. Easier to whip it back in shape herself, and faster, fury fueling the attack.

Perhaps, the truth is—and she stopped working momentarily as she thought silently what she would never speak aloud—she never should have had children. No, that was too harsh, and untrue. But there was an elusive quality in her motherhood, something missing she found in other women which provided them ultimate satisfactions regardless of the sacrifice. What's wrong with me? she asked herself, the oft-repeated question clenching her eyebrows, producing the familiar uneasiness which made her feel at times unnatural. How could I be more fortunate? For all their faults I can't imagine any children I would trade them for. They're interesting individuals, fine lifegiving people, overflowing with plans and promise with as good a chance as any at happiness, whatever the hell that is—isn't that enough? Why can't I accept the responsibility and simply enjoy them?

Because they are too goddamned messy, that's why, and she savagely swiped the front of the refrigerator. And I'm tired. Down to the bone-marrow weary of twenty-four-hour days, seven-day weeks, fifty-two-week years. But thank you, God, for not completely forgetting me: they're gone. She straightened to rinse her sponge and tuck back her hair, then repented. Virginia, you'll be punished. Retribution will be served and you'll deserve it. That plane will go down in Colorado with those adorable children aboard, and they'll bring you two charred bodies to identify through their bridgework, only, God help me, they don't have any bridgework, and He'll reward you for your wicked thoughts. She sprinkled cleanser over the last traces of their irresponsibility. Still, I've three delectable weeks, twenty-one miraculous days of queenly quiet, in the regal splendor of cleanliness. With my room the same—unbelievable!— when I come home as when I leave. With my clothes untouched, my hairbrush still in place, my tub without a ring or filled with scummy water, my towels hanging properly instead of mildewing in a heap turning the floor white. Three weeks to eat when I want, what I want, to hear my music without the competition of a radio in every room tuned to a different station, to store energy for the onslaught of their return. Virginia, you never should have had those children—and she pulled the gooey strings of their last meal from the strainer. Then, as a flush rose from more than the steaming water before her, a quiet voice inside asked: Then why in God's name are you having another?

The sudden reminder of her pregnancy forced her shaky legs to find the kitchen stool while she gulped at the effrontery, the risk-taking so alien to her methodical, mannered existence. Is this really *the* Virginia Winburn, she thought, six weeks past my last period, beginning to swell again, breasts rounding out to the shape I would have traded my reputation for in the old days—"the most precious thing a girl can own," Mama used to say—can this be true? Can I play out such a crazy unlikely game? Hell, I'm not conversant with the rules. I've never trained for world-class bitchmanship before, much less competed. How can a supposedly sane, intelligent, forty-year-old woman with a dandy job, the major responsibility of two children, and—yes, let's say it for Mom's sake—a good reputation, contradict the ingrained patterns of a lifetime by having another child, *alone?* Sweet Jesus, you'd think just the prospect of cleaning up after the child would be deterrent enough, but a baby! at this point in life, and single!

Her friends, she knew, would think her mad, perhaps in need of treatment. They were urbane and sophisticated and far too accustomed to affairs (heterosexual ones barely raised an eyebrow) and serial divorces and May–December marriages to have their heads turned, but bygod, she'd stir them up this time. Virginia Winburn, pregnant, the Immaculate Conception of the Twentieth Century. Virginia Winburn, who had only recently developed her professional life to the point her friends no longer lit candles for her financial status; who worked for the most conservative, no, the stuffiest firm on Wall Street; who floored the gray-suited stiffs simply by being inside the doors, and absolutely stunned them with her expertise. Virginia Winburn, who was now going to risk all that hard-won gain doing what women have traditionally done to knot up their lives just at the point of straightening them out—Virginia Winburn was going to have a baby. And no one would know by whom. Baby Winburn, out of Virginia Cargile by BLANK. Strange, that her child, *their* child, would be known by the name of her former husband, God knows, least likely to be the baby's father of all the men she knew. And stranger still, of all the men who should have this child, who would be most thankful, who would have the wherewithal to provide for it (Christ, does he have the wherewithal), of all those who would be a committed, loving parent, Michael Strange was the most logical. So perfect for the job he would be a paint-by-number sketch for Father of the Year. He *needed* this child, would *want* this child with a passion she had known only once in her own life—when she had wanted him. And she knew with visceral certainty, as she steadied herself upon the stool, drawing more regular breaths now, remembering her motives, she knew she would use every ounce of her life's force to be absolutely sure Michael Strange would never see, know, or touch his only child.

Having children was one part of life she had never doubted, nor over which she had been able to exercise much control. They simply arrived. Two children within two-plus years, both unplanned—though, truthfully, joyfully received. How often she had wondered: if college graduates like Jim and herself were visited with surprises (not unlike the stork bundles in her earliest picture books), then what happened to really ignorant people? Diaphragms and their 95 percent effectiveness? Bullrot, as Max liked to say. James Maxwell Winburn and his socially impeccable Atlanta bride had given birth just thirteen months after the South's elite gathered on the wide verandas and deep green lawns of the Piedmont Driving Club to celebrate their union, and again thirteen months after that. From that day forward, instead of her having them, the reality was that *they* had *her*, for every thought, concern, speck of leisure time and drop of pleasure was filtered through their requirements, their whims, their demands. Small wonder (when she dared the pain to think back on her marriage) that their joint enthusiasm declined, their dazzle disappeared, their faith in each other's ability to contribute to their partnership evaporated like dew before a murderous August sun. When hard times came, and they dropped like dirt upon the coffin of their marriage, there were no emotional reserves to call on. His were deadened by watching from outside the process, uninterested in participating, yet resentful that he was not the center of attention; hers were consumed from within, devoured by the constancy of their needs. Jim walked out, and the patterns and pride of marriage and hope dissolved. (O timid woman, admit it, you couldn't even leave when the play was over; you had to be ushered from your seat.) But wasn't it predictable then, the way our lives were divvied up? I'll get my freedom of movement, he might have said, and you get the children. I'll gain the ability to start a new life while you concentrate on your God-given role of raising our offspring. I'll devote my energies, daytime, to developing my professional life, nighttime, to my social life, and you may do the same—when you can find some time away from the children.

Once the animosity of the divorce was past and peaceful conversations were possible again, Jim Winburn confessed he missed their life together—not *her*, she was not self-deluding enough to think that cool, distant man could discover affection in middle age—but the certainty that December 25 would bring with it a celebration, that friends would come to eat and laugh on Saturday nights, that a fire would be burning *before* he arrived home. What he really meant, she thought maliciously, was now there was no one to make his nest, keep it clean, and feed the chirping mouths. After all, what, precisely, did he want that he couldn't do for himself? Recently a newly divorced friend had complained to her that it was impossible for him to share custody of his children—after all, he was single, had no housekeeper, and had to work. She stunned them both with her vehemence when she shot back *she* was single, had no housekeeper, and had to work, but she was a logical candidate and he an illogical. Jim was capable of reproducing a home life, had he wanted to, but not once, during their vitriolic legal negotiations, while he battled to avoid guaranteeing a college education, while he insisted on her payment of various categories of the children's expenses, while he carefully listed the furniture and belongings he wanted to take with him, did he ever ask for the children; nor did he or his lawyer suggest, request, even threaten that he wished to be more than a father-every-other-weekend. No, I'll get the divorce and custody of myself, he might have said, and you get custody of the children.

Having her children with her, though, was so much a part of her existence (and when she was less worn down, so necessary to it) that she could imagine neither her present life without them nor a reincarnation. She would have found it impossible to negotiate away their time together and wondered at trendier mothers who were able to kiss their children off for six months of joint custody. She wrapped hers around her with the comfort and familiarity of an old sweater; but even favorite garments wear out, and so were her maternal energies. She found herself counting down the remaining years—one before Maggie went to college, two for Max—when they would be removed from her immediate sight and she could deal with them as Jim did, with occasional telephone calls, clever magazine cartoons, and tidbits of family news passed along to fill their mailboxes.

She often thought it strange that men do not allow children to dictate their lives, nor do they feel guilty when they are away from them. Welfare fathers shamelessly desert children in great numbers—where are their qualms? Married middle-class fathers spend time with their kids as long as it is *after* bowling or their television viewing, after meeting the guys for a beer or sleeping late on the weekends. And unmarried fathers? Connections to their children are as thick as spider's threads. Consider soldiers who traditionally leave war zones deserting tiny progeny of mixed nationalities, and office swordsmen who boast of knocking up the little secretary without any feelings of responsibility toward the baby she carries. And think of all the judges listening to testimony from the most blatant liars who look at the tearful plaintiff before them and coolly deny the child in her arms is theirs. Do they dampen down their feelings toward the extensions of their flesh—or have they little to begin with? For many men children are like room additions to a small house, tacked on when they want them, and lived with only until struck with the desire to move on.

Virginia moved through the silent apartment shutting windows against the city's dirt and heat, closing up still rooms which would not know their occupants for a time, straightening ashtrays and pictures which would hold their place for three full weeks. Here you are, she said suddenly and quite out loud, an unenthusiastic, almost unwilling mother—only your frigging sense of responsibility has kept *this* load from dragging you under—here you are at the end of the road with some degree of relief ahead and you're going to start over again. Who *do* you think you are—Wonder Woman? Easier, kid, to bounce bullets off your wrists and lead packs of Amazons through the jungle than—merciful heaven, am I out of my mind?—start this madness over again.

A mirror loomed ahead—a mirror at the end of the hall which she had begun avoiding the past year. Before, mirrors had been friendly, useful pieces of equipment, pointing out stray hairs and uneven hems, acting as reminders that oftenheard compliments were reasonably true—or used to be. A randy-looking young black, sauntering toward her on the street just days before, had leaned in close as he passed, and said, "Betya were pretty when you were young, honey." She had been, with a face actually more than pretty but less than beautiful. It was pleasant, even for her, to come upon suddenly—until lately, that is. She had regressed to merely attractive now and might remain so for some time to come, but mirrors revealed truths she preferred not to know—lines falling too soon into place, crevices promising even more breaking points—so she approached mirrors squinting automatically, blurring the image to drop the years away. The reality of slow deterioration shook her every day now as if she saw it for the first time.

Virginia stopped before the mirror—at least the hallway was in half-light—and studied the predictable, conservative woman before her, neat with a certain casualness, graceful without artifice. Not bad for a broad your age, she said. Then, instinctively, she performed a motion almost forgotten. It came back to her from past pregnancies like the first swim after a long winter. She turned to the side, slightly slumping her shoulders, pushing her pelvis forward, and stared at her reflected belly. Nothing, not yet. But in there. Something alive and mysterious and needing her, and she was going to have it alone. She would fight indigestion attacks sprawled on the bathroom floor, alone. Massage her own back and get her own drinks in the middle of the night. She would place pillows in strategic places as her girth increased and find ways to complain so that she could hear herself and offer herself comfort. She would time her pains alone, admit herself to the hospital alone, and have this baby by her lonesome. Then she would spend the next twenty years buying for it, planning its future, spotting its problems, dealing with its insecurities, and smoothing its course through schools and camps and teasing playmates. She would teach it to swim and to drive, she would give it tennis rackets and Scrabble games, she would sing it family songs and fight her conscience about how much religious instruction it should have. She would, God help her, have this baby. And she would do it alone.

Being perfect got in Virginia's way. Vaccinated against less than perfection as early as smallpox, it plagued her every living day. Be the perfect wife. Never let family or friends know the perfect couple is in trouble. Never ask for help—or even complain to the perfect husband that changes were necessary. Be the perfect housekeeper with the perfectly wonderful menus that you and Julia Child and a pittance concoct. Be the perfect friend—helpful, consoling, strong, and cheerful. Be the perfect mother. Love them deeply and equally; satisfy their needs, develop their potential. And if you accomplish these tasks, the Great Promise is that all will be yours. Just as she remembered from college exam periods, you put in your time—fully, exhaustively—and you came out with an A. That was it: Life would give you a mark. The World would recognize you had faithfully performed your duty and would reward you. And what is the reward? That the World would acknowledge you had been perfect, of course. Never mind the pleasures you didn't enjoy along the way, the self-indulgences you renounced, the love affairs you skipped, the impulses you squelched, the freedom you never tasted. Straight from Daddy's house to Husband's bed, without a day in between, with controls passed from one man to the other.

Bending under Maggie's bed to extract an empty ice-cream carton and still-sticky bowl, Virginia suddenly remembered and understood: In that picture-book Episcopal church at the altar ablaze with candles, with half of the town looking on, Daddy put my hand into Jim's and simultaneously slipped him all the power, the way you surreptitiously hand a headwaiter five when you leave a restaurant, and Daddy sat down smiling because he had perpetuated their system. And what did I do? I looked at the calla lilies in my hand and the blazing ring on my finger and thought what a perfect wedding.

Virginia pulled up on the bed and sat staring without seeing as she realized that for the first time in her life she was not going to try to be perfect. She would instead be different, even peculiar. Almost past a decent age to have a baby, she was going to raise it not only without a father but without a father's name. She would sully the "reputation" her mother claimed one lived for, restrict her financial resources—not to mention her time and energies—and she would force the conservative, proper world of Wall Street to handle a phenomenon during its business day that it refused to accept in its private life. She would be more inexplicable than the average unwed mother because she was also the mother of two proper, legitimate children. And those children—how could she tell them? How could they understand? What kind of relationship could they establish with a sister or brother they probably wouldn't want, and undoubtedly would feel shame about? What would become of the perfectly open system of communications that she, as the perfect mother, had worked so long to develop?

You know, sister, she thought as she lifted long legs to the coverlet and stretched her arms behind her head, you'd better be damned sure you want to play this game. The stakes are high, the rewards uncertain at best, disastrous at worst. Let's review the bidding one more time.

It didn't begin this way. There was once a clean, pure moment when she wanted what she wanted with no spite attached. There was no need to get even, just a need to get together. Whatever impulses she and Mike had followed separately, whatever queer directional signals they obeyed, suddenly they bumped together like Dodg'em cars and were left dazed by the electric encounter. Maybe she would not—as she had so firmly decided previously—go her way by herself alone. Those self-contained promises of independence had been made not from conviction but from fear, fear that leaning on a supportive shoulder would land her on her ass. How rational, she had decided, when scar-covered, not to consort with those carrying swords. So she played her games as far as possible from the coliseum where showdown matches took place. Married men—safe enough. They satisfied the body's needs, massaged the ego as well as more sensitive places, gave life a melodramatic glow, and popped away just in time, before you depended on them for too much, or before they lost their magic. There had not been many—Virginia stopped and counted silently on several fingers—and never more than one at a time. (Always respectable, even in secretive dealings.) But because they had been such a persistent pattern she was forced to recognize that unavailable men avoided any risk of real involvement and reduced the odds on emotional bloodletting. Take a real chance? Put herself in the path of a serious honest feeling? Too risky, too chancy, and Virginia Cargile Winburn did not take chances. Single available men, even attractive single available men, were subjected to conversation as current, as informative, as argumentative as necessary to convince them she was as resolutely businesslike as they, miles away more disinterested, and absolutely the mistress of her ship. As if with semaphore flags, she signaled her determination to sail both in and out alone. Virginia knew her cover was so obvious it was embarrassing. But her excessively proper upbringing had taught her: They ask *you* to dance. And you don't for a minute let them know you want to. You don't tap your foot to the music to give away your interest, and you never, no you never wink encouragement. Better to walk home tall and proud than ask one of those pimply-faced fellows to dance. Pride builds a lonely house, she thought. How did Michael Strange ever get inside?

Mike was a mistake, an accident. She simply had not been wearing her armor plating that gray afternoon when he walked into the security analysts' meeting. A hotel-ballroomful of economic buzzards were perched waiting for the current wizard of the video market, ready to devour his corporate utterances, hungry to hear an explanation of his phenomenal rise in earnings while the rest of the Fortune 500 moaned recessional dirges. They wanted to hear him name the secret oracle that had directed him to stockpile cash before the Federal Reserve ratcheted up interest rates; and they hoped to discover, somewhere in his speech, the way the Street must go—as had Matterhorn Industries under Strange's direction—in order to revive its prosperity.

The room's hum faded as he entered. The quick and the deadly—that's what this type of man should be called, Virginia thought. For the safety of society in general and the innocent in particular, they should be required to wear ribbons across their chests proclaiming their inordinate desire to wield power, and their determination to pulverize any who did not give way before them. A buzz of anticipation raced around the room as he approached the podium. She arched her neck and raised her chin. First she saw the top of his head and a wealth of hair, then hands cupped to light a cigarette as he walked. He looked neither to the right nor to the left, nor to his cigarette, only up. Up with the wariness of an animal entering strange territory, perfectly on its guard. He trailed aides the way carriers trail escorts. Virginia watched with detachment as this season's living legend (like mushrooms, Wall Street grew heroes overnight) mounted the stage for the number his stockholders paid him so well to do. Handsome devil—if coarse features appeal to you. A sort of craggy quality that would not produce any jealousy in his jock friends at "21" but would draw most females' second glances—and seventh. But it was his size more than his face that struck her. A minimum of six three, he seemed even taller because of the breadth of his shoulders and because he was all one color—dark hair and heavy eyebrows, dark suit and tie relieved by a white shirt that appeared brilliant in contrast, and startlingly white whites of eyes in the midst of a dark complexion that toned his brown pupils near to black.

Virginia watched long enough to see the juggernaut move into place at the podium, then turned to prepared notes and questions which would help her make a call. His presentation, regarded as routine by most analysts in the ballroom, was especially important to her. She had already decided on a strong buy recommendation for her firm because this stock was going through the exchange roof and she knew it; what she did not know was whether the other analysts recognized its potential too, and if she could ready her report fast enough for clients to act decisively before Matterhorn began its rise.

Almost disinterested in the preliminaries, she heard the light greeting, the mildly self-deprecating remarks that drew a murmur of genial response. Winning them over on charm alone, the bastard. She began swinging her foot. For God's sake, on to the projections.

Move to them he did, with a dazzling delivery of facts, statistics, percentages, and confident predictions. The man spoke with no notes, yet never hesitated: the energy crisis and its effect on earnings; the Administration's overdue plans for breaking dependency on foreign oil; the cost-push inflationary spiral and the diminishing ability of the consumer to buy; labor's outstretched hand and the press's closed fist. Skipping around the macro-economic profile of the nation, Strange sketched the business climate with broad strokes, then meticulously painted in Matterhorn Industries' prospects. Disarmingly he outlined past mistakes, admitted callously ripping out companies inappropriate for Matterhorn's overall distribution system, lighted momentarily on discharging unproductive executives, and thoroughly explained an apparently unlikely acquisition. The analysts already knew the parts of the story he did not recount: the broken men who dared to challenge his control; the boards of directors defeated by bruising tender offers; the corporate executives curtly handed walking papers when their numbers were not met. Virginia remembered the old Revolutionary flag with a coiled snake and the words "Don't tread on me," and shivered.

The question period began. "What will become of your midwestern plants, Mr. Strange, if Japan refuses to limit its television exports?"

"When, if ever, do you plan to bring back into this country the profits of your foreign subsidiaries?"

"How long can Matterhorn hold its skimming price on home-use computers before bowing to the competition?"

His answers were measured, to the point. Simultaneously satisfying their need to know and his to impress, for three quarters of an hour he alternately entertained and informed.

"Some claim, Mr. Strange, your colorful, but, ah, adverse publicity lately may turn the buying public off your stock. Have you considered making your peace with the press?"

Trade magazines were dissecting his authoritarian management techniques with a malicious glee reserved for the very successful.

"Make my peace? I'd rather make the deal Adlai Stevenson

offered the Republicans when he said, 'I'll stop telling the truth about you if you'll stop telling lies about me.' "

Appreciative laughter indicated the audience preferred to accept his response, however off the point, rather than force an answer. Virginia felt the session's momentum winding down. She did not enjoy drawing attention to herself in the all-male company, and had hoped another questioner would do her work for her. No luck, dang it. She uncrossed her legs, moved most of her papers to the floor, and stood to be recognized.

"Virginia Winburn, Mr. Strange, from Peabody Slocum."

"I know, Miss Winburn. Congratulations on your recent promotion."

So he was apprised of her appointment as the firm's chief analyst for diversified industries; the man missed nothing. Virginia covered her surprise by glancing again at her notes. "Thank you, sir. My question involves your position within the video-disc market. How will you entice consumers to begin to collect video discs without providing the level of stereo engineering they're accustomed to in audio recordings, and if you do, how will you price your product to keep it within the range of, for example, video cassette recorders?"

"What did Henry Higgins sing? 'Let a woman in your life, and your serenity is through.' " There was laughter again as Strange mockingly shook his head. "Thought I would get away without having to answer that one. If I give you a complete and truthful answer I'll jiggle some delicate ongoing negotiations, as well as show my hand to our competitors, so forgive me if I postpone your question for a later date when that information will be forthcoming."

"You'll bring it to our attention?"

"Count on it. Until then, suffice it to say that if I briefed you fully on our plans I would be estimating a twenty-two percent increase in earnings for next year instead of my usual fifteen percent."

The crowd emptied the room quickly, leaving a disarray of

coffee cups and cocktail glasses. Like a practiced politician,
Strange moved toward the closest exit, aides gathering to form
a phalanx which led him out swiftly, shaking hands as he went,
while he appeared to be leaving quite reluctantly. Virginia
knew the motor of his limousine at the curb was already
purring.

A taxi provided her more traditional transportation back to
Peabody Slocum. While the driver alternately honked and
yelled his way through traffic, she reflected on the afternoon's
performance, mentally beginning her report. Everything she
heard this afternoon reinforced her instincts about the stock's
potential, and indeed, so had everything she saw. Strange had
all the characteristics of a chief executive in the heady days of
the sixties, when glamour stocks surged ahead on the personalities of their leaders coupled with a belief that good times
would be forever. Now optimism was as hard to find in New
York as an inexpensive dinner, still Strange inspired even cau-
tious observers.

Is that true? Virginia checked herself. Were others today as
swayed by his performance, as ready to bet on his team in the
face of the adverse economic climate? How much were her
final impressions colored by his rather charming recognition of
her new position? Why did she now, instead of struggling to review the weaker points of his presentation, recall the strength
of his chin and, surprisingly, the delicacy of his hands? And why
was she wondering if there was a paunch beneath what appeared to be a trim double-breasted jacket, and if he preferred
making love on top?

The office was dark when she arrived. Her right hand, secretary, friend, and supporter, Mary Jennings, had taken the afternoon off for a doctor's appointment, and she was alone. God
must have meant me to be, He leaves me that way so much of
the time, she snapped out loud, silently apologizing to Abra-

ham Lincoln for the paraphrase. A pile of pink slips lay neatly on her desk. She glanced through them even as she hung her coat, hoping there was nothing that could not wait until morning. Matterhorn Industries—and Michael Strange—had bewitched her afternoon, and she intended to wallow in her impressions and begin the report without interruptions. Two partners had called—they could hold—and Rutherford—he couldn't. Stanton Rutherford was more than the ultimate authority of the firm; he was her professional control tower, dispensing information about which way the wind was blowing and in which direction lay the safest approach and landing. She needed his presence even when she knew her way, and she was grateful he was there for her. Shelby Anderson had phoned from Anchorage, Alaska, leaving no call-back number. She frowned at the thought of her missing friend, hopscotching around the world on network assignments, knowing she would not pause in the midst of a harried schedule unless looking for solace or long-distance advice. A call from the chairman of the children's school fair; she had no time to help, but somehow would work it in. Several routine inquiries from clients, and a call from Michael—what's this? She sank onto the desk top as she read Mary Jennings' brief unemotional message: "Michael Strange called." Virginia's eyes darted to the time of the call—a bare fifteen minutes ago, Mary must have been just leaving the office. "He will be at Peabody Slocum 10 A.M. tomorrow on business. Would appreciate a moment with you about 11. Call his secretary to confirm. MU 9-2700."

Virginia reached for a pencil. With the eraser she whirled the telephone dial and was connected by the Matterhorn operator to the disembodied voice of Strange's secretary. When scientists provide robots with voices, she thought, they must use as models the toneless sounds of secretaries-to-the-powerful, who, puffed up with osmotic authority, stand as buffers between the world and their titans. The coldness disappeared as Virginia agreed to the appointed hour, even warmed almost to friend-

liness expressing pleasure on the part of Mr. Strange that short
notice was no inconvenience.

"Not at all, but did he indicate what the purpose of the
meeting was?"

"Yes, Miss Winburn. As I recall, he was interested in a
point you made at the analysts' meeting this afternoon and
wanted to pursue it before he leaves for Europe tomorrow
night."

"That's fine. Tell Mr. Strange I'm delighted."

She was. Not just by the attention from an industry magnate
of his stature, which would not go unnoticed in the chambers
of Peabody Slocum, but delighted to have been right. It was a
tentative confirmation of what she had realized when first
studying Matterhorn's past year's performance, that the cards
Strange had assembled now guaranteed he could make game
and rubber, but if he could incorporate a kind of advanced
technology when he brought out his video-disc machine, he
could do it with a grand slam. The serendipitous morning conference would enable her to elicit the final information to build
her report and back her prediction.

Virginia had a reputation of being uncanny when outlining
probabilities. It was a trait the partners still attributed to intuition rather than expertise, but then men often downgrade
what they cannot understand to a level they do not admire.
They could name it anything they wished as long as they acknowledged she was right. She preferred to think of her presci-
ence as judgment, backed by solid research. In recent years she
had come to trust it, to call on it without hesitation as she
moved from the lower levels of the research department, where
she acquired skills by day and an MBA degree in finance at
night, to an analyst's desk of her own. It was an unprecedented
move in most of the larger firms—analysts were highly respected and some thought excessively well paid, two adjectives
not often used for Wall Street's female employees. Still, it became ludicrously unproductive to continue handing over infor-

mation and recommendations to people whose acumen and ability were less than her own. She first stepped into the area of cosmetic and retail industries—a natural fit, the partners must have thought—but once there overcame their final reluctance about her ability, and in a rush of doubtful excitement that must have also followed the first automobiles up driveways as horses and carriages were sent to the barn, she was assigned twelve major conglomerates to follow as her own.

"If you're so smart, why ain't you rich?" Her eyes dropped to a cheap jigger glass on her desk with a painted inscription, now filled with paper clips. It had been a birthday present from her son. Still a little fellow, Max had rowed himself across a Maine lake from his island summer camp, hoofed it into town, where he bought, wrapped, and mailed the unanswered question.

Well, why aren't you? Her mouth tightened at the thought of her personal torment, financial insecurity. If any subject made her physically ill, it was this. Dying did not hold the terror of being unemployed; hard physical labor was preferable to owing money. As well acquainted as she was with the complexities of finance, she could not apply to her own position the principle of using other people's cash to do your business—borrowing as much as possible to pay back in as long a time as possible. "The least and the latest," the venerable accounting principle which applied to paying taxes, was one she thoroughly understood—for others. Her bills sat on her desk, quivering with a life of their own, reminding her that payment was due and owing. She was the kind of customer charge departments applaud—"You have an excellent payment record with us," her Con Edison bill sang out every month. Like a dutiful child with a star stamped on her hand for a clean plate, she accepted the computer's accolade and rushed in the next payment. Why anyone raised in the security of her financial cocoon could be jolted from sleep at three in the morning because of money terrors was a subject she did not bother to dissect. Understanding the subliminal bases of the problem, she knew, would not change the neurosis. She was simply doomed to a riskless, pay-back mentality boring in its conventionality, pinching in its limitations. She even cheated herself. She "left" five-dollar bills in evening purses, in case she should find herself out of cash some stormy night. She hid a twenty within the zippered compartment of her wallet, then promised to forget it was there. There was a cache of money at all times in her stocking drawer, in case of a family emergency at midnight, and she opened savings accounts at more than one bank and left them untouched, even though their low interest rates lost yearly to inflation, so fearful was she of being without ready cash. "El Cheapo," her children occasionally called her. She had come to hate the sound of her words more than they—"We just don't have the money for that, folks." Such a pusillanimous ring, that phrase. How fainthearted, how depressing. How true most of the time. Still, her careful husbanding (a strange word to apply to her) of resources led them from the slough of economic despond after the divorce not just to solvency but to an acceptable level of comfort. From a near penniless, jobless, futureless newcomer to the outside world, she moved to a respected position within an esteemed firm which valued her services more every year in increasing amounts—and, thank God, in dollars. There was enough saved to cover at least one of them for emergency surgery, and provide a week of skiing or two at the beach. She and the children lived not elegantly, but sure of their essentials, yet in her own mind she was one step away from broke. A timidity not likely to allow her to be rich—sorry about that, Max—though she moved among her affluent New York friends as a regular, accepting herself as one of them in everything but bank balances. Michael Strange's private jets, country homes, lavish public and private existence would never make her feel inadequate, uncomfortable. His publicized excessive charm? That was another matter.

Virginia's meandering mind won out. Realizing she was good
for little more than daydreaming, she gave up the possibility of
any productivity remaining in the day and gathered work
papers to read at home. The job was endless. She could spend
eight hours a day, or fourteen, and she could work seven days a
week and still have more to do, but the pace was manageable—
she organized her time well—and the level of responsibility ex-
hilarating. Picking up her coat, she stooped to look into an almost concealed mirror on the back of the door, a concession
to her sex she was not proud of. What successful man
would . . . ? The thought repulsed her and she snapped off the
light in a gesture aimed at the midsection of her narcissism, and
started out the door, but stopped, defeated by vanity as usual,
and returned for a final check of the day's damage. Fluffing out
the fine brown hair, she studied her face. Thanks for the good
genes, Mom, and the English skin. The lines aren't there yet,
but they soon will be, crossing themselves like spider webs. Not
a bad face, though better these days in a dim light.

If it's true you deserve the face you have by the time you are
forty, hers showed a compassionate, gentle woman who loved
more than she hated and gave more than she took from others.
Not much to say about yourself after forty years. No contribution to mankind, not to the country, nor the state nor the city,
not even the neighborhood, unless you count consistently curb-
ing the dog. No, Virginia, the list of accomplishments takes no
time to read—you never moved the world an inch, and face it,
though you once thought you could fly if you moved your arms
fast enough, you never will. You are simply damned lucky to
have survived. To have recovered a fairly strong sense of self
after an emotionally bruising marriage. To have contrived a
means of support for yourself and the children with no early
warning you would be responsible for the supply side of your
life. To have remained upright when your natural inclination
was to slide under the bed the way you did as a child when
things did not go your way, and cry. Well, Big Mac will have to

resurrect the city and Ronald Reagan the country without me.
She rolled a pink shine across her lips, tipped a soft hat low
over one eye, shuffled her briefcase and shoulder bag into place,
and closed the door behind her. All my victories in this life are
destined to be small ones, she thought. Just give me the
strength, Lord, to keep them coming.

When the office, dark and deserted, was snapped to life at
precisely nine o'clock the next morning, she had already written the major part of the Matterhorn evaluation in her head.
She slipped eagerly into her chair, reached for the Dictaphone,
flipped the Matterhorn folder from her desk, and in one motion dived into the only quiet working waters of the day, before
the telephone, the partners, market quotations, and meetings
broke her concentration. Meetings! She raised her head momentarily, shoving glasses into her hair—Strange at eleven. The
glasses returned to the nose, her focus of attention to the report. No time to think of that now. At least the master knitter
will be here to bring together any loose ends of this analysis.

She immersed herself in the material with a completeness
that shut out sound and peripheral sight. If Mary Jennings had
arrived, she did not see her, but vaguely knew the phone calls
were being diverted to another part of the day. The door remained closed, time suspended, as she organized her impressions into a concise, finely drawn picture of the Matterhorn en-
terprises—dynamic, complex, solid, with an edge of adventure.
A forward-moving corporation that, perhaps more than it
should, bore the imprint of its chief executive officer. Like a
play written for a great star, she wondered how the company
would fare without him.

The buzzer sounded. Annoyed, eyes never moving from the
page, she answered, "Yes?"—flat, preoccupied, as exasperated as
she ever got with Mary.

"But it can't be! Too early, Christ, no, it's after . . . Hold
him there, Mary, I'll come out."

Why was she reaching for her comb, straightening her blouse, wiping the shine from her forehead? This is a business appointment. Why the shaking hands?

The smile was genuine when she held out her hand and ushered him into her office. "Do you usually make house calls on your new analysts?"

"Not unless they're pretty." He had an easy way; he could say anything he wanted, probably, and get away with it (and how delicious to hear a sexist remark from someone you hoped found you attractive). "That's not true," he recanted immediately. "I try to meet all of them, either at their offices or mine. They can't really report the game until they've met the players." He did not sit back in his chair, but remained on its edge, pulling an ashtray into position.

Michael Strange did more than enter a room, he took it over as does a pervasive odor, or a strong light. It was hers before, then suddenly it was his. He took it gently, without attack. If the Indian yogis were right, and people wore auras around them, his was palpable. His words were predictable, as he was a predictable type. The surprise was that he was at the same time spellbinding with eyes that fastened on you as he spoke, that were lit from within when he smiled.

"That was quite a performance yesterday," Virginia said. "I knew you had a reputation for Jack Benny's concern for money matters; I didn't know you had his delivery."

"I would prefer to have his age, but I passed thirty-nine some time ago."

He was forty-eight, if his publicity releases were correct, but looked older. Heavy creases in the face, more apparent at close range, streaked his cheeks like battle scars. Lines around his eyes and marching toward his forehead made you know his face was seldom in repose, but there was a brute strength about his features that was undeniable and a flow of confidence that was overwhelming. His form was heavy, but graceful, an athlete gone soft with the years, though his energy level was as electric as a high school sprinter's. A compelling person, a wake-up call for the senses.

Virginia had no trouble with the small talk of business, or social, even sexual conversations (which was this?). Long, white-gloved Atlanta years prepared her to be with kings or presidents, apartment superintendents, school principals, bus drivers, or tax accountants. She easily moved the conversation back to Matterhorn's prospects, knowing there was a reason for his visit.

"Yesterday you promised to present the facts about your video-disc-machine engineering, once you had them. Don't suppose much has happened since then, has it?"

"No, nothing's changed, but since your instinct was so on target in your question about stereophonic sound, I wanted to tell you, confidentially, what we're planning. You know that Peabody Slocum is underwriting a bond sale . . ."

"Yes, but I don't know if there's a specific purpose involved."

"There is. We're raising capital for a major new manufacturing thrust that will bring some of our lost television production back to this country. Japan won't like to hear it, but we've devised a product that will not only play video discs in stereo— as you know, unlike anything on the market now in either discs or cassettes—but more than that, we'll be able to retrofit, at not too high a cost, older television sets with stereo capability, so the consumer has the choice of going with a totally new system or using old components."

"That's fantastic—for the consumer. But why would you promote retrofitting when your stereo-disc players could induce people to part with the price of a brand-new system?"

"Because I'm stubborn. There are enough people out there who'll buy new sets, about as many as we can produce during the first few years. Meanwhile there's a hell of a lot more who can't afford a total system, who'll be happy to upgrade at a modest cost, and they'll expand the market for discs in general, which we are also going to be producing."

The magician had more than one rabbit in his hat. "Software production?" she asked. "A little out of your line, isn't it?"

"Won't be. That's what the bond issue is for too. We're about to complete merger plans with Cooperative Artists . . ."

"They're almost defunct, aren't they?"

"Yes, that's why they're cheap. They also have a backlog of some of the grandest old movies ever made, musicals from the forties and fifties . . ."

"With tap dancers on aircraft carriers?"

"And chorus girls on stairs climbing all the way to heaven, and Fred Astaire singing while he dances."

"Can't wait. But is there enough of a general market to produce them as video discs?"

"Hope so. They also have shelves of children's cartoons, and the kind of children's movies no one makes anymore, harmless and beautiful, plus—and this is why we're taking them over—a stableful of technicians who are still the finest craftsmen in the business. We're going to turn them loose producing discs of rock concerts, Broadway plays, the Metropolitan Opera, and anything else that will become an inexpensive form of home entertainment. We think we'll make recording companies obsolete within ten years. Who will only listen when they can also watch? That's why we want everybody with a decent TV set to be able to adapt to our new sound."

She looked at him hard, not quite sure herself what she meant as she said, "Very exciting."

He took a moment longer than he needed to answer. "I hoped you'd think so."

The quiet between them could, in one more millisecond, become embarrassing. She knew as he had spoken that his message was important—and could just as easily have been delivered over the telephone. He knew as he spoke that for what he wanted to accomplish he was right to have come in person. She was almost grateful that sounds of unusual activity outside her door interrupted their conversation.

"Excuse me, I'll see what the commotion is."

As she opened the door, the noises became urgent. People were in motion down the long elevator hallway. Mary Jennings was coming toward her in a running walk.

"A bomb threat, Virginia. Gotta go."

"Not another one. This is getting to be a bore."

"No funny business this time. There was an explosion across the street. Didn't you feel a thud a minute ago? The entire area is ordered to evacuate. Emergency stairwells are open. Better get going." Mary was gathering her coat and bag, transferring call lines to the reception desk as a routine measure. There would be no one there to take them.

Virginia turned to find Michael Strange immediately behind her, her coat and shoulder bag in his hand. Gathering her into the protection of an arm as he passed, he moved her decisively toward the stairs, speaking quietly as they went.

"There's always the chance more than one bomb has been put in place. And if one exploded that means fire. Don't want to alarm you, but we *are* eighteen stories above the ground, and there's going to be a crowd trying to get to the street. We should move as quickly as possible."

He was correct. Clattering down the first several floors, there were relatively few people alongside, but as they descended, and the word spread among the various offices, the concrete passageway was thronged. The crowd was orderly, almost speechless as it twisted through the innards of the building, making its way to the ground.

Mike and Virginia joined the dark stain of human beings pouring from the buildings onto the street and sidewalks like a thick, slow ooze of paint from an overturned bucket. Pressure from the rear was unrelenting as those still descending sensed the safety of open air and pushed toward it, panic held barely in control. Jostled and jostling, shoved and shoving, they matched the pace of the crowd to avoid its danger. Mike's arm was under her elbow, gripping her wrist like a sailboat's rudder to steer their course, forcefully directing, unassumedly protecting. His strength, negating any need for her own, was almost incredible; it left her dazed. After years of commanding her own troops through danger zones, it was as if she were playacting not to be in charge, not to be calling out orders, planning strategic moves, responsible for the ultimate safe-home. Relief from duty overcame her like a sudden weakness, making her knees shiver, loosening her control. She could close her eyes and play blind as she used to when she and her brother as children took turns leading each other blindfolded, testing the other's bravery—and she would get past this. She could make no decision—and she would be safe. She could succumb to a dependent impulse, clutch his arm, actually admit her terror—and he would pull her through. She would do none of these things (long ago she became incapable), but the knowledge was comforting. When, she wondered, if ever, did the Michael Stranges of the world long for someone to pull *them* through a crowd?

Mike swerved almost gracefully, planning his moves as he saw possibilities, tightening his grip when people brushed too close. Police cars—and ambulances perhaps?—whined through the streets, forcing the crowds apart. Noise made talk impossible. Around them was a roar of babbling, incoherent sounds, harmonizing with fear, pandemonium produced by sudden death.

Several bodies lay on the sidewalk as if awaiting help, where minutes before they had awaited buses. In awkward positions, faces contorted as in pain though they felt nothing, stamped with fear though they were the least fearful in the street, only the dead were quiet. Like watching television with the sound off, she thought, and turned her face away—too terrible to look, too unreal to assimilate. Even the curious did not stop to gawk. The same New Yorkers who ringed every corner fight and raced to automobile wrecks, who listened to open-air arguments as if they were free entertainments, who delighted in the bizarre and fed on the unfortunate, who never shied away from the bloody, the obscene, the most unpleasant, and who then sauntered on oblivious to what they had seen, these same blasé New Yorkers were moving with one collective motive—to put the bombs at their backs.

Traffic stood in gridlock, luckless automobiles facing each other in four directions, stymied, helpless. Cars backing up behind them added to the din, not understanding the cause of the delay, unaware yet of what they would soon hear on their radios: the bombings, the dead and wounded, the thousands fleeing office buildings.

Mike moved them like the hockey star he had been at college, dodging obstacles, curving past obstructions. "I doubt if it's possible to find my car," he fairly shouted in her ear, "the police have probably moved it on. Even if we could, this traffic's going nowhere. Let's take our chances underground."

With a deft turn, he led them suddenly into a subway passage. Clattering down steps filled with bobbing heads and shoulders, Virginia broke through her passivity enough to reach into her shoulder bag for her wallet and fish out two tokens. By the time they were swept to the turnstiles, she had them ready. Seeing the surprised and appreciative look on his face—the toll booths were mobbed with anxious lines—she dropped them into the slot and smiled over her shoulder as he followed her through the revolving bars. "We're even. Don't expect me to have a limousine; I won't expect you to have subway tokens."

The crowd, artificially thinned out by the barrier of the turnstiles, proceeded more calmly down the next stairway to the train platform. "When was the last time you were on a subway?"

"I've ridden enough of these filthy cars in the past so I'd sell my soul to the bitch goddess Success to guarantee I'd never ride another—except in the midst of a bombing. If I have any guilt for living the affluent life—and I have—it's not because I no longer ride the subways."

Mike's last words were almost lost in the roar of an approaching train. Once again he was half at her back, moving with the throng, pushing her through the doors toward an overhead grip. People flowed in behind them until, jammed together like an upright box of matchsticks, there was room for not one more. Then he too came, forcing the doors to open one last time and the passengers to moan in discomfort.

It's queer, she thought. As a rule, we abhor the touch of strangers, recoiling if we are tapped on the shoulder, flinching if an elbow comes too near. Yet we consent to stand in the subways pressed against one another's bodies in the most intimate way, fitted together like jigsaw puzzles; at the same time we acknowledge feeling nothing. How different today . . . The nameless creatures next to her were stone, they did not exist as individuals. But the man who brought her there, whose body was also crushed against hers, whom she had met barely an hour before, reduced her to intense embarrassment.

As if reading her thoughts, or having similar ones of his own, Mike shifted away slightly, edging his shoulder around hers, turning so his hips moved behind and to the side of her. Virginia felt an enormous urge to lean back; especially she wanted to rest her head on his shoulder.

The doors opened and closed, opened and closed. More left the train than entered now. The passengers separated as they were given space, but she did not move away when she could, nor did he take his hand from under her arm.

"Off here," he said as the train screeched into another platform. She willingly followed his lead, totally in his control. "I know this area. Haven't been here for years. Little Italy starts a street or two away, and there are more restaurants per city block than Rome has Catholics. How about some lunch to calm the stomach?"

Mulberry Street, wonderfully garish with its year-round

Christmas decorations overhead, wonderfully peaceful in contrast to where they had been, was like a foreign country one revisits after years away. They pressed their noses against glass windows, strolling down the street, comparing white-tiled floors and beamed ceilings, etched-glass doorways and mahogany bars, arguing gently about which clam bar was the site of a notorious Mafia chieftain's murder several years before. Finally deciding, then laughing, changing their minds at the last moment, they opted away from any further violence and entered another.

The quiet inside—it was early yet for lunch—washed over her like a shower. She had not realized how much perspiration the fear and flight had produced. The semi-dark and hushed tones were calming; the world was moving again at a pace she could understand. She slid onto the banquette as the maître d' pulled the table away, and was pleased to see Mike did not follow, but took the chair opposite. Good—a talker. And who'd want to sit beside this face, this strong, active, open face, and not be able to see every eyebrow twitch?

They were handed menus, which both automatically lay aside.

"Does Soave suit?" Checking first for her consent, he directed the waiter, "Bring us a bottle, please."

"Well, that's it for any more work today." She shrugged her shoulders, lifting her palms in a gesture of surrender.

"We've had more than our share." He lit a cigarette and expelled a long deep breath.

"You're as relieved as I to be out of that."

"Moving away decisively," he said, "I discovered long ago, is far more difficult than decisively moving ahead. Going somewhere is predictable, sensible. Retreating—besides being against my nature—is backing into the unknown blindfolded. And to tell you the whole truth, I haven't heard a bomb explode since the Korean War. Seems all the old fears I thought were buried are about an inch from the surface after all. Certainly never expected to resurrect them in New York."

"Why not, Mike—may I call you that? Fear is the most pervasive emotion in the city; it throttles you. Makes you afraid for your handbag walking down the street at high noon. Makes you wonder if your apartment's been ravaged just because you had the stupidity to leave it, or if your son's been carried off by a male prostitution ring."

"But those fears are, for the most part, without basis." The waiter poured an inch of wine into his glass. He sipped briefly and nodded him away, taking the bottle and filling her glass, then his. "To all your fears being baseless," he said, raising his glass.

She drank with him, but would not be deterred. "New York forces you to be afraid of what you don't want to understand, what you don't want to see. Bag ladies that lie in their urine, screamers that yell profanities as you pass. Have you seen the great god Thor with his buffalo horns and fur cape in front of the ABC building? Or the crazy who drums gutters in Times Square keeping time to imaginary music?"

"They're all harmless, you know."

"Not to eyes glazed over from the other wretched, diseased, unstable people we have here. I think the country's walking wounded have decided New York is their personal hospital ward—only they don't know we ran out of medical supplies and personnel years ago. There's an old woman, Mike, who lives on my block—at least I think she's old, and I think she's a woman —who wraps her face and head in nylon stockings and sticks more of them up her nose. She wears layers of heavy clothing, even in the summer, and walks in half circles around you on the street—afraid she'll be contaminated, I guess. She scares children worse than a Halloween witch, but you should see *her* quake when the transvestite prostitutes slink out of their sleazy hotel—right on my beautiful block with the museum on the corner and the park across the street! They come out at night like bats, ugly and malformed, as if nature made a mistake and can only stand them in the dark. Don't look at me like that,

Mike. I don't know any part of the city free from freaks and criminals and crazies now unless it's the short path between a limousine and a protected doorway. If you so much as head to the corner newsstand, the city socks you in the eye with its troubles."

"But that's always been a part of New York."

"Not like now. It used to be the price of living in this city was rudeness, sometimes loneliness, high taxes, the fear of dying here . . . but now . . ." Virginia took a deep drink of wine. "Do you know anyone who hasn't been robbed? How long has it been since you heard a horror story? A few days? A few hours? In the lobby of my building a woman had two fingers chopped off last week by a mugger. Yesterday we locked all the ladies' rooms after someone was attacked. Today the building was bombed. I have no war experiences, Mike, but I know what it's like to live with fear, and so do my children at the grand old ages of fifteen and seventeen. Max refuses to go alone for a quart of milk any hour of the day—of course, the little bugger knows a good excuse when he has one—but he's been robbed on his way home from school three times, once at knifepoint. That's a lot for a kid who hasn't grown a whisker. Maggie, so far, has gotten off free, except for a couple of sickees exposing themselves on buses, but for how long? And how do I protect her from what's coming?"

Virginia stopped abruptly, breathing hard. She was angry—no, furious—at the morning's maliciousness, the day's indignity, but now she began reeling her emotional lines back in. They were playing too far out before a man who was little more than a stranger.

Mike realized she needed recovery time and gave it to her, toying with his spoon, making patterns on the cloth. Then, quietly, he asked, "Why do you stay, Virginia? Why don't you get out?"

Looking into the calm, strong eyes before her, she knew she had revealed more than one forces upon a new acquaintance,

but it was too late to turn back. She groped for her own understanding.

"Because I've come to care," she said. "New York used to be,
above everything else, synonymous with 'exciting.' Now she
stands for 'needy.' She reminds me of an old dog that shows up
on the back porch, once beautiful, powerful, active. Now she's
sick and tired and the world is throwing tin cans at her and
kicking her around. She's disreputable and grimy, pleading for
a handout, and I can't turn my back on her. Someday I may,
but I hope it's when she's in better health and I can leave without feeling guilty. Besides"—she leaned back on the banquette
and managed to chuckle to break the intensity—"there's the
problem of supporting two children who've a habit of eating
regularly, and who've discovered the fun of charging on Mom's
Bloomingdale's plate. Until Wall Street moves to the sun belt,
or until Max and Maggie learn to support their mother, we're
one white middle-class family that won't fly to the suburbs."

"I don't know, Virginia. I never had children of my own—
unfortunately we couldn't—but if fear in the city's so paralyz-
ing, wouldn't the suburbs be a healthier environment? How
can you afford *not* to take them away?"

"That's a question we working mothers ask ourselves every
day, Mike, especially because we can't offer our children what
we took for granted—for instance, a house that holds a crowd
of friends. Mine was Atlanta's Grand Central Station, always
stuffed with kids having a go at the pinball machine, necking
to the Platters, jitterbugging to Bill Haley and the Comets,
chugging Cokes, licking Sugar Daddies. Our driveway was permanently zebra-striped from cars scratching off. Poor Mom—
there were always broken forty-five records and Lucky Strike
butts all over the side porch when the group left, but she'd
sweep them up, and the dried food to keep the ants away. And
she'd replace the stepped-on Ping-Pong balls and refill the
fridge before the next invasion. Then we'd turn the ceiling fan

on again, lower the blinds against the afternoon sun, and while away another day.

"My kids? They don't have their friends in much—and then, just one or two at a time. The apartment's small, and you can't step outside to see the sunset or tell secrets or smoke illicit cigarettes. In my day, we girls would gather in each other's bedrooms and smush potato chips in the bags and lick the crumbs off our hands while we talked about sex and read *True Confessions* magazines. Those were long, giggly, perfectly silly, perfectly wonderful afternoons—cocoons of friendship and lassitude. For my children it's a major undertaking to visit a friend's apartment—calls when they arrive, again when they leave. They're monitored every moment of the day *because* I'm working, and because, if they get in trouble, I'm almost unable to help them—as if keeping tabs on them is a kind of protection, when they and I both know it isn't. I worry about my children in a way my mother, who spent her afternoons reading novels and listening to our voices under the window, never did. And worry isn't the only price of working. I know all I can't give them—affection when they want it, not just when I have time for it; unhurried mealtimes; languid afternoon ice-cream stops on the way home from school; Halloween costumes cut out on the floor. Maybe those things don't make a happy child or guarantee a decent adult, Mike. Maybe I'm feeling guilty, or maybe I'm just scared and taking stock because of the terror this morning, but sometimes I wonder what will become of them and what, in the postmortems to come, they'll think about a mother who loved them before and after office hours."

There was a long pause. Mike swirled his wine, watching liquid patterns through the glass. "Your appearance is deceiving, you know. You look so capable—almost formidable, totally in control, yet you're obsessed with fears, real and imagined. One would think you'd be crowing about your professional success. Instead you're castigating yourself for what you've accomplished. You remind me of the boys in my generation who wore knickers one day and were given a pair of long pants the next. We didn't look like kids anymore, but we didn't know yet how to begin to act like grown-ups. You hold down a terrific job, I assume you make a fine living, probably have great children—and you reward yourself by worrying about what *hasn't* happened."

"Stupid, isn't it?" Virginia suddenly regretted her outburst.

"No, don't back off now." Mike perceived her discomfort. "It's because you're new at the game, so you're writing contingency plans just in case you lose. My mother used to say, 'Don't bring down trouble on your own head.'" His smile was dazzling. "Now there's a woman who worked all her life, and turned out a pretty decent offspring."

"Who never has any fears?" she asked.

"Only that I won't win big enough. I have to remind myself not to try to reach up and grab the North Star—that it's only there to steer by."

"Suppose you don't win."

He looked at her as if the suggestion were an impossibility. "Then I'd start all over."

Virginia leaned back on both hands, open-mouthed in awe. "Mike, your confidence absolutely stupefies me."

"Oh, c'mon. Half of always getting what you want is, when you can't have something, deciding you didn't want it in the first place. There's a lot of bluff involved, simply fooling yourself. Take you, Virginia. I spotted you in the crowd yesterday at the beginning of the presentation and saw a sensational face— so I made all my best points in your direction. Then you stood up and I liked the rest of you, too. So I made up an excuse to meet you this morning, since I was going to be in your house anyway, to see if you'd like what you saw. Now, if you don't, I'll think of half-a-dozen reasons why you weren't as good as you looked. Either way, I won't lose—though I think winning *with you* would be a hell of a lot better than winning alone. Besides, I trust my intuition. Some of my best decisions have been

made on a hunch—though if you tell that to my board of directors, I'll be back coaching hockey at Boston University. Now,
here"—he handed her a menu—"feed that beautiful face. I'm
much easier to take on a full stomach."

That very moment she was aware her life had changed,
veered from the predicted, streamed off sideways like P-38
fighters in the old war movies, hurtling under power, but moving too swiftly to redirect. She had, in a morning, begun to
transfer control of her life to another. She handed it over the
way you would give family silver to a burglar, piece by piece.

There are remarks one slides by, and feasts on later. Virginia
perused the entrées ferociously, glancing over the list several
times before she realized she was not connecting with the
printed items. Later she would remember the ease—almost
slickness—of his words, and their stunning effect. They dis-
armed her then as they would disrobe her later, that same afternoon, when the model of a bourgeois mother, who had not cast
a wayward glance at work or play since college, who *still* would
not ask the boys to dance and who spent lonely moments in
payment, the same reasonable, practical, yes, square woman, always in control, wasn't.

The afternoon taught her a truth about herself, her strongly
moral self. She could resist any advance, however attractive,
that was ambivalent and equivocating. Any suggestion—like
southern declarative sentences, lilting to a question at the end
—which left the decision to her produced an automatic negative response. But Michael Strange left decision making to no
one.

"We'll go now," he said later. Of course. "I'll call my office
and cancel out the rest of the afternoon. You do too." Certainly. There was no question in her mind because there was
none in his. Perhaps the need to be pursued, ordered, overcome
was biological. Why else was the act of capitulation so comfortable for a woman who had fought wars of independence—and
thought she had won?

Virginia slipped off her bed in the darkening room and angrily switched on the light, glancing at the bedside clock. The perverse hands moved too swiftly. Didn't they always when she ran her tapes of Mike? Endless tapes in living color, in the library of her mind, ready to be rolled through her memory, reliving what she needed to forget. No, by damn, I will not replay that afternoon. I will not regress to that state of emotional dependence when his every goddamned touch was right for me. When sliding next to him—him, a near stranger!—was the most natural act of my life; when his smell and taste and strength and wetness were as familiar as if I had known them always, and his shoulder the perfect pillow for my head.

He made the first act of love so easy. She had taken off her clothes before, with fear and trembling, wondering how other eyes would find her, other hands would judge the feel of her. She had stood before clothed only in inadequacies, quaking for a glance of approbation—but not with Mike, not that afternoon, when there were just the two of them and time to discover what their instincts led them toward: they were an elemental fit, a circle closed, a force of nature unleashed by union. There was no memory later of performance, or prowess—the tricks one uses to disguise the imperfect—or even of motion. They needed simply to be joined, as close as possible, as long as possible.

"Jesus!" Virginia cried out loud to an empty house, then thought, disbelieving: I did it. I played the tape again. When is enough, enough, Mike? You're the past. Can't I have the future?

Tears rolled down a suddenly ugly face, drawn to fierceness, tight-lipped with anger. The newly broken woman, doubled in pain as if she had taken a fist to the belly and bent in agony, fought to move past this moment as she had moved past others. Slowly she stood erect, smoothing away with the heels of her hands the frown that paralyzed her forehead, and said again to the emptiness, "Besides, the best babies have serene mothers, and this is going to be one terrific baby."

For Virginia, the sweetest part of having children was the years of babyhood—like having dessert served first. Except for labor, which was confined to a series of contractions three minutes apart before the long syringe arrived, she did not experience real pain. (She felt guilty but grateful later that ideas of natural childbirth were not too prevalent in her childbearing era —guilty that drugs may have affected her newborn, grateful she was not tested by their absence.) Except for the indignities of the hospital, and the incapacitating days afterward, babies were blissful. She remembered perfectly, even today, the imprint of hairless heads plopped helplessly beside her jaw as she carried weightless bodies from bed to bath, and the special smells about them, whether baby powder, which meant clean, or acrid droplets of regurgitated milk, which meant clean up. She loved the long skinny feet that jutted akimbo as she changed their diapers, the blown-out belly buttons after a full bottle, the ridge-like gums clamping on her knuckles, making way for unseen teeth, and perhaps most of all, the spiderlike fingers closing around hers with surprising strength. She fussed over them endlessly, changing daygowns to nightgowns, tiny sweaters to zipped-up woolly containers. She made excuses to pass their door while they napped, usually unable to resist slipping through to touch their upraised padded bottoms—her frogs asleep on rubber pads. She was unafraid of them or for them, handling them like a wet nurse as soon as they were hers, never fearing she would drop or hurt them, though occasionally she took chances. Driving to her mother's for the usual Sunday dinners, she often lifted Max from the security of his car seat and, monkeylike, sat him on her lap, small arms spread out on her belly, head dozing on her rib cage, and with one hand on the wheel held him close. Connected. That is the way she felt about her babies, enveloping them while they grew inside her body, still connected to them while they were little. It did not last long. As they grew out of the state of total dependency, so her predilection for absolute gentleness fell away. In direct proportion to the noise, tears, and squabbling which arose in increasing amounts as her toddlers moved to childhood, she became more weary and impatient. Conscientious she remained, but her charges became duties rather than delights. The endless mess they created, the squealing voices, the clutching hands, the needs they forced her to meet chipped away at her equanimity and fueled her discontent. Their illnesses brought strange blessings. Struck so frighteningly fast, they regressed to babylike helplessness and squeaked through sore throats and fevers their need for her. Then she would sit for long periods stroking their foreheads, singing them back to sleep and health. Once Maggie was gravely ill. While teams of specialists disputed symptoms they did not understand, Virginia reduced her world to that one room, that single child. How single-minded she became, how simple her life, and with what she knew was her own determination, she accomplished what the diagnosticians could not and brought the girl back from danger.

She loved them best when they slept, she thought, with an indescribable tenderness. She often stood at night over their peaceful forms and wondered at her earlier feelings in the day when she had considered infanticide, or at the very least, gagging and locking them in a dark closet.

Even childhood's days were numbered, though. Virginia developed new interest as, chameleonlike, they exchanged youthful colorations for those of young adults. Far from fully grown, still they transmogrified to individuals, with ideas and arguments and reason governing their actions rather than merely impulse or instinct. She could squint her eyes and envision their adult faces; there were indications about their bodies of final shape. Their tears came not from stubbing toes or crankiness, but from disappointments. Pleasure derived from accomplishment rather than Christmas presents. Her days were

different then, unpredictable. The outside world of school and
friends, opposing teams and dancing classes brought along
problems to solve and share. She became a mediator, a negotia-
tor, a teacher of morals and precepts—so much more satisfying
then scraping Play-Doh off the playroom floor, or settling
disputes that began, "Mommy, Max just . . ." or "Mommy,
Maggie says . . ." Virginia was turning in a good job of mothering again, and liked the work.

Now, puttering around the house, picking up the last of their
dirty clothes, checking under beds for empty bowls, crusty with
dried cereal, closing the desk and bureau drawers (Maggie's
philosophy: "Why shut them when you are just going to open
them again?"), Virginia smiled away their dereliction of duty.
My obstreperous two, she thought, M & M's that melt in my
heart, not in my hand, where would I be without you? Damned
lonely, that's where. For three glorious weeks I'm on vacation,
but please, God, after that give them back to me.

They had been her strength these last five years after the divorce. Strange, to draw stamina and endurance from small children who had so little of their own, but they had been her
champions. Not as opposed to Jim's, just as opposed to Fate or
Fortune or whatever demon was dragging in the next challenge.
They evolved a kind of cheerleading mentality—you can do it,
Mom!—when she was not so sure herself. Not sure at all she
could earn a living for them. Atlanta educated its daughters to
understand ideas, but did not inspire them to create systems. It
taught them instead of a trade or profession that they would be
protected, cared for. It asked in return that they pitch in babies,
emotional support, dinner parties, well-decorated houses, edged
lawns of thick grass, and—always—respectability.

But the James Winburns had been more than respectable,
they had been golden. More handsome as a pair even than each
was separately, they made their way up the easy way, gliding on
an exceptional combination of looks, brains, family position,
and not one infirmity. Neither of them was orphaned, or poor,

or brought up by a drunk parent or a brutal one. Neither had been victimized by child abuse or incest or dishonor from a criminal relative or a crazy one. They lived blessed days without being particularly aware or grateful—they thought it was their due.

Almost in their lack of struggle, they found one, and they divorced on the grounds of putting each other to sleep—like the inhabitants of Sleeping Beauty's castle, she thought, with thirteen years of vines creeping around their marital walls, locking them inside together. But hold on—she reversed her mental field—you've forgotten the rage and pain, and the cruelty. Snoring didn't put bruises on my arms, his fist and my lack of affection did. Sleep didn't drop me into severe depression, his selfishness and my discontent did. Virginia, girl, if it wasn't a marriage made in heaven, it was a divorce concocted in hell.

Remembering was a luxury Virginia seldom indulged. After five years the bruises on her psyche, if not her arms, were still to heal. Her best defense was an amnesic one while she performed routine duties. Just as now she stopped herself from tasting the individual ingredients of their coming apart, and instead concentrated on the items she was removing from the fridge which would become a dinner for herself and Shelby Anderson. God must have known we women were weak, she thought, She provided such strong friendships to see us through.

Butter, Parmesan, parsley, cream. Shelby had become an essential element of every problem's solution. Through two decades of non-judgmental friendship, regardless of how perplexing her situation, how numbing the alternative, her quandary's quagmire was never so deep or wide that Shelby wouldn't slog through, hitching up hip boots of concern until she located her friend in the muck and led her back to shore. Of course they never reached the bank, for then it would be Shelby's turn for help and Virginia would wade back, stretching out her arms and calling words of support. Concluding that female friendships feed on trouble and disaster, they recounted the various episodes over the years, embroidering each tale for friends and family until it became a kind of morality play. They knew how fortunate they had been that, so far, when one was down, the other was up—at least enough to perform emergency rescue measures.

Pasta, salami, lettuce, watercress. Virginia whipped mustard into wine vinegar and grimaced. Shelby would have her job cut out for her tonight. The two seldom had difficulty understanding each other's motives; this time she would push her friend. She depended upon Shelby's common sense, her intuitive reflections, and saw herself more clearly through Shelby's eyes, but she was afraid of the reflected image that would be there tonight. Still, as always, she wished her early, eager for her company.

Virginia wiped the counter after each step of preparation. Compulsive woman, she reproached herself, topping spice bottles and putting them away, swishing out measuring cups and utensils, but knew she could not possibly proceed until all was cleared away. She was as rigidly neat and predictable in the kitchen as she was in life, resenting her old habits, at the same time absolutely unable to break them.

Reaching for voluptuous beefsteak tomatoes, she sliced them competently onto an old ironstone platter, topped them with rounds of purple onions, and fluttered fresh-cut basil over all before adding vinaigrette dressing and moving the dish to the old pine dining table. The simplest objects most delighted her, particularly when placed together to form a symphony of color and texture, as now, when the mellow wood brightened by candles in etched Victorian glass complemented the pure reds and yellows of a bowl of zinnias and was surrounded by straight-backed chairs with natural rush seats. Large checked napkins lay beside classic sterling silver, uncluttered by mats or cloth. The scene was a reflection of the woman who composed it, a combination of old and new, with taste and without frills, colored strongly by tradition. It was generous, openhearted, expectant.

Before Virginia saw Shelby, she heard her, still in the elevator, talking as usual, as if it were always her obligation to entertain wherever she found herself. The elevator man laughed appreciatively as Shelby stepped toward the open door, where the friends hugged and kissed with a strength of feeling which belied the fact they were together often and talked daily. They greeted each other with a special smile reserved for initial meetings—a smile that took nothing for granted about their abiding friendship, but indicated with fondness what need not be put in words. They always took the time for it.

Still holding shoulders, they fluttered through their first moments making clucking noises of concern and sharing compliments.

"You all right?" Virginia asked.

"Um. You?"

"No more jet lag?"

"Slept it off. The whole day's disappeared. I'm feeling fine, though you may have to throw me out about five A.M."

"Well, you're looking good. Interviewing a Nobel Peace Prize winner brings out the best in you." Virginia led her into the apartment.

"Oh, I was properly awed, and he was inspiring, but Frenchmen always think women should be doing something other than a job, and he couldn't decide which he resented more, listening to my French or being forced to speak English. I was happy to get out of there. And by the way, I never want to hear again that I'm 'looking good.' I've decided there are just two ages, young and looking good. Never heard the phrase before I was thirty."

The women often talked of age, and looks, and compared trivia, such as haircuts, makeup techniques, and department store purchases. Though they shopped alone and made decisions independently, almost uncannily they seized upon the same idea, or garment, or new shade of nail polish. Both wore clothes easily and picked gingerly among the latest fashion offerings, preferring to add a new favored item to old ones, and recombining and recycling rather than imitating a designer's runway model. They had neither the money, the patience, nor the inclination for it. Both also prided themselves on breaking away from the vapid side of their former lives, when clothes occupied their attention on a level just below husband and children and just above dinner parties and gossip; still, they regressed to these subjects naturally and enjoyed them. Just as they did stories about people they knew and anecdotes about their children and their maids and co-workers. Out in the real world, conquering careers and building images, with invisible Superwoman sashes angled across their chests, they were the New Women. When the door closed and they had a glass of wine in their hands, these two old friends of twenty years had not changed much at all, except that now they moved from the superficial to the substantive with the ease of trained show jumpers changing leads.

Virginia led them into the living room, picking up glasses from the table, handing Shelby a wine bottle as she passed. They sank into comfortable chairs at right angles, pulling up their legs under them, and picked up what was for them less the beginning of a conversation than the continuation of life's narrative.

"So, was Renfield properly appreciative of your piece? Or is he still cracking his bullwhip?" Virginia asked.

"Do you know, I've finally figured that man out, I actually know what he wants. It isn't enough that we produce the highest-rated documentaries on the network, and it isn't sufficient that when the reviews come in, I usually win top praise. It'll never be enough, because I'm not properly grateful."

"Grateful," said Virginia, "why grateful? Sounds to me like he's going to have your ass one way or the other. Such ridiculous abusive behavior, screaming down the hall, shaking you in the edit room, sarcastic memos, derogatory remarks . . ."

"I'm not sure I can take it anymore either, and he doesn't show signs of tiring. The guy has worn out both my patience and energy. I drag up the steps to work now, duck into the elevator before we meet, sneak into my office like a thief. Here I am, a grown woman, avoiding my boss like I used to hide from my dad after staying out too late necking and drinking beer."

Virginia spread a cracker with Brie, added a slice of hard salami, and passed it over. "I *know* what your father thought you were doing, but why does Renfield turn into an active volcano?"

"I told you—I'm not properly grateful. Look, let me sketch this fellow for you. Unfortunately, he's an archetype in our business, pompous, arrogant, power-crazed—yet eminently capable. He has an ego as large as the Goodyear blimp, and he can match it for hot air, yard for cubic yard. There isn't a story he can't find and cover better than anyone, and he has the ratings to prove it, so as far as the network brass goes, he gets anything he wants. And he wants everything. You should see the sports car he rents on the company—slung so low you need a shoehorn to get in it. His expense reports are abominations, filled with lunches and dinners to lure the youngest, skinniest blondes to bed, never mind the wife and four kids at home."

"But so what, Shelby? What difference does it make as long as his long arms don't reach in your direction?"

"They wouldn't dare—and they don't choose to. A man like that needs compliance and praise and catering to. But I need them too—too much to have to pretend to soothe the ego of a conceited, maniacal tyrant. Him and his Gucci shoes and belt buckles! You know, Virginia, an ego is recognized by the status symbols it keeps. This is a man whose initials will never be enough, so he buys everybody else's—BB, V, YSL—the man looks like a bowl of Campbell's alphabet soup when he's dressed."

"So he's hung up on going first-class. He takes all of you with him, doesn't he?"

"I'll say. When he throws a production party, it's bacchanalian—filets, lobsters, champagne, baked Alaskas. And when we're on location, it's deluxe accommodations, no linen-closet hotel rooms for us. But in return, for all his glad-handing company largesse, and for the munificent salaries we are paid—and I do get a princessly wage—we are to be oh, so very grateful. He really wants to be the Godfather handing out favors, with us touching our caps in the hall when we pass. If I could just learn to drop to one knee when we meet and lick his outstretched fingers, he'd adore me. Instead—you know—I think he's lucky to have me at any price. I save my thank-you's for the people who work under me, not over me, and expect roses on my desk every Monday for doing a hell of a fine job."

"But that's a standoff; you can handle it. Just keep ducking into doorways if you don't want to play the game." Virginia rose and beckoned to her dinner guest. "Come. I'll further upset your stomach with some cold pasta and a salad."

Shelby followed her back to the dining room, talking as she went, poured them each more wine, and lit the candles while Virginia brought in the pasta and a round loaf of hot Italian bread. "I can't, babe. How do you keep going to work every day in a poisoned atmosphere, where no matter how well you do you never hear it, and when, in addition, you are subjected to the most juvenile forms of harassment?" Shelby unfolded her napkin and threw it into her lap. "Niggling things, like assigning me to the biggest fart of a cameraman at the network. No one else will work with him and no wonder. He takes the shots he wants, regardless of what he's told, and he futzes up those. He loses film, or forgets to bring enough. He gets lost going to assignments or coming home—drinking plenty of beer along the way—and stops his crew on the minute for breaks regardless of the situation." She hesitated long enough to hold up her plate as Virginia ladled out pale rosettes of tortellini

bathed in pesto sauce. "If I were interviewing the President of
the United States, and he were showing me the bush in the
Rose Garden under which he had buried illicit campaign con-
tributions, so help me, that fellow would look at his watch and
break the crew for lunch. And even though Renfield knows I
can't deal with incompetence, he assigns him to me every
chance he gets."

"Complain. Go over his head, or go to him and ask him to
stop."

"None of the above." Shelby ran her fingers through her
short dark hair in agitation. "You can't complain above him. I
told you—he's the crown prince ever since the program broke
into the top ten. And I can't talk to him—don't you understand? He resents me for being *good* and for not kowtowing.
No. What he wants is for me to quit. It would be difficult explaining why he fired me—I'm too valuable a property—but if I
quit . . . Then it would be out of his hands. He could shake a
doleful head and say what a shame to lose her."

"What a shame for you to lose that job." Virginia shook her
head in consolation.

"I know. But scary more than shameful. Why is it that we
women, regardless of how well we do our jobs and how successful we are, have a fear of firing so deep-down it mixes with our
bone marrow? 'Zipless pluck' I call it, with apologies to Jong.
You see, in spite of my ratings and reviews, I'm not at all convinced I could do it all over again tomorrow, much less at a
new place. And if I did relocate, there's little chance of pulling
down my same pay, and I've become quite attached to having
money at the end of the month and taking the children away
on vacation during their spring break. Still, I know the time
has come; I'm starting to look around. I have to get myself out
of there before he finds a pretense to do it first."

Virginia slathered a hunk of bread with sweet butter. "I
can't believe I'm hearing Shelby Anderson, Emmy Award-win-
ning reporter, whom lawless rednecks have shot at, who's battled the Mafia and lived to tell the story—even Mike Wallace

respects her work—and Shelby Anderson is going to be driven away by a first-rate producer and a second-rate human being."

"That's not the whole of it, Gin." Shelby was suddenly thoughtful. "Maybe it's just time to repot. I've worked my way up to feature reporter, sure, but it's taken me twelve long years to do that. Here I am now, over forty, schlepping around the world every time a crisis breaks or a scandal develops. I'm the best-informed person I know about the widest number of things in the shallowest fashion imaginable. I take on corruption in the Alaska pipeline, handle that, move on. Consumer fraud in the credit card companies, move on. Rodent droppings in federal school lunches. What's next? How can I do this for another ten years? Ace reporter at fifty? Ridiculous. Just as I've never understood how people with diminutive names get to be adults and still call themselves Cookie or Trixie. In my family —true to southern tradition—I have an uncle who was called Son when he was a boy. Now we call him Uncle Son. Can you hear what his grandchildren call him? In the same way, how do I keep on reporting what other people do, and watch my own life slip by without doing something myself? Broadcasting's a passive occupation. We depend on others to be outrageous or adventuresome or corrupt or inspirational. We're simply the conduits, pipelines that carry information about people who change the world to others who might. Don't let this get around but it really isn't grown-up work. A lot of it is schlock and hype. We all know the tricks to titillate—ways to make people seem more important than they are, or situations more fearful. Listen, if I were doing a story on community residents who live at the base of a nuclear plant, and I took my camera crew out for MOS . . ."

"What's that?"

"Man-on-the-street interviews, opinion polls based on no research and less data. . . . And if I talked to fifteen straight people who yawned in my face and said they hadn't even noticed it was there, and then I found a crazy who was ready to throw himself into the reactor, guess which I'd use? And I'm one of the more responsible reporters working. A lot of it's just a game. We force ourselves on people in tragic circumstances, like families of accident victims, and what does the camera do, remain at a respectful distance? Of course not. We zoom in to record every tear and miserable gulp. Do you remember my recent story on euthanasia? I heard about a mother out in the Midwest whose son was in a coma, hooked up to life-support machines, and I flew like a buzzard to be there when they turned them off, only she fooled me, that brave strong woman. At the last moment she refused to let the doctors or the hospital staff do to her son what she herself had ordered. I watched her walk into that child's room, all alone—you remember she was a widow with a couple of other children at home, without enough money to take care of the healthy, much less a vegetable in the family—she walked into that room and pulled that plug herself, and stood there until she was sure her son was dead, holding his hand, rubbing his forehead, talking to him. I could hear her through the open door. And when everything was quiet again, and she was sure it was over, she walked back out into that hallway where all the doctors and nurses and reporters were waiting, and there I was, camera rolling, ready to shove my microphone right under her nose and ask her what she felt, or some other inane crap, and she looked at me . . . I'll remember that face the rest of my life . . . jaws set, features steady, you couldn't see her eyes for the tears. She looked at me as if to say, 'After what I've just done, what's left to say?' Gin, I put that mike away, stepped aside, and after she passed, I cried my eyes out. I also lied to Renfield and told him I hadn't gotten to the hospital on time. I tell you, I'm sick of the exploitation the media are guilty of, and equally sick about the way we allow ourselves to be exploited. Got a story on the latest jiggle girl on TV? She can't talk? Never mind. We'll shoot around her, edit in other people's remarks, and make her look so delectable we produce a new plastic queen overnight. Show her as she is—her empty head, the coke she toots before the cameras roll, the vulgar remarks to her bearded lover in his

Jesus sandals? Not on your life. The country wants a heroine; we manufacture a heroine."

"Shelby, you're exhausted; you need a vacation." Virginia squeezed her forearm as if to inject it with fortitude. "Every job has its drawbacks, but few have the advantages of yours. You've money, celebrity, a chance to make a difference in people's lives. You uncover the unscrupulous, reward the virtuous, bring information to people who wouldn't have it otherwise. That's a gift—and power too. Don't be so fast to let it get away. Besides, I enjoy having a famous friend. I'll write a tell-all book about you someday—your love affairs and nefarious doings—and pay my way into an old-age home."

Shelby threw off her depression. Her moods changed as quickly as seashore breezes. "Well, I'm sorry I haven't lived any chapters recently. I think my pipes may be frozen. How about you, babe? Any sizzling tales for your closed-mouth reporter whose recorder is running under the table?"

Virginia leaned back in her chair, dropped her fork lightly on her plate, and dabbed her napkin at the corners of her mouth. A languid smile spread slowly from the inside out across her face. "I'm pregnant, Shelby. I'm going to have a child." She said it very quietly.

Shelby looked up, startled, from her plate. "I'm sorry. Oh, how awful for you. How did it happen? No, scratch that, I've had enough scares myself. What will you do? When? How can I help you? I know the clinic connected to Planned Parenthood, the one on South Park. It's supposed to be terrific, fast, accessible . . ."

"No, thanks, babe." The smile widened to a grin, frankly cheerful, almost wicked. "I really am going to *have* this child, in just about seven months."

"Who's the lucky guy? When's the wedding? What a way to tell me— Mygod, I didn't even know you were seeing anyone. I thought, ever since you and Mike . . ."

"You're right, ace, as usual. There isn't anybody else. It's Mike's child."

"But you broke up months ago. When? December? Around Christmas? Are you carrying on behind my back, or are you already married? What *is* going on here without my permission?"

Virginia's laugh was deep in her throat. "Nothing's going on, or will go on, and this is—and I'm underlining it—just between us. No one knows, the children, nobody. I could hardly believe it myself, those first unmistakable signs, the druggy midday sleepiness, the nausea in the back of the throat. Then I began to fill out the wrinkles in my bra and I *knew*." She laughed again. "The acid pregnancy test. Of course, I made the ritual runs to the bathroom, a dozen times a day, stripping down my pants, praying to heaven I'd be forgiven for my sins. Then I thought it must be my age. Maybe the ghost of menopause future was leaving me a calling card and a promise to return. But the days began to add up, there were the usual hunger pangs, the catnaps, then I fell asleep on my desk one day over a vitally important report, threw up the next on beef broth, and I knew."

"But are you sure? Have you been tested?"

"Oh, yes. I took a specimen into the lab, and a frog—somewhere—and I are pregnant."

"Have you told Mike? What did he say?"

"I told you. Nobody knows, least of all Mike, and I've no intention of telling him, now or ever. There's no reason for him to know, and I couldn't handle the complications."

"Look, pal, it's all right for the frog, but you're forty—babies are born deformed to women our age. You're unmarried, with little behind you in the way of assets, and you support two extravagantly costly children." Shelby's voice rose to a near roar. "What do you mean you won't tell him about his child?"

"It isn't his child, Shelby, except by accident. He didn't want it, or even consider it possible. You know he always thought he was infertile. He put his wife through every imaginable test, but the doctors said it was he who couldn't have children. Something about the sperm count. We never even took precautions. He'll never suspect and I'll never tell him. If I did, I'd have to deal with him at close range and I can't take that. I'm not strong enough."

"You were obviously at close range not too long ago," Shelby interrupted.

"Yep. I get weak every once in a while, but the break last Christmas really was final. I had dropped to number three or four on his preferential list, and number one—the redoubtable Deena Woodard—had taken a giant lead. She's available to travel whenever he wishes, she's as conservative as he, so I'm certain they never argued about politics, and she seems to enjoy his jock friends, which you know I never did. She has several legs up on me and two around him. I couldn't take the competition, so the lady quit the ring. No fight, no contention for the title. Just hung up my gloves and walked out with pride intact, but no trophy. He didn't seem to miss me, though he called often, from other states and other continents. And sent postcards from places we'd been together. Used to double me up when I found them in the mail. But I pretended indifference—since I knew I had lost—and made chitty-chat, as Max says, when he called. And every so often, when he decided to work me in, we'd spend an evening together—because I couldn't say no. We'd go to one of his favorite watering holes. I'd drip perspiration all through the meal while we talked annual reports and proposed mergers, children's boarding schools, and his problem keeping a chauffeur. Then, over our third cup of coffee, he'd look up suddenly in that startled way he has and say, 'Want to go back to the Carlyle?' I'd nod and we'd leave the restaurant as casually as any old married couple. Back in the limousine, we'd hold hands across the big back seat and talk about the Administration's incompetence. Then he'd send the chauffeur home, and inside, we'd fall into each other's arms like a couple in wartime when the soldier gets a furlough before being sent overseas. Always as if we'd never have another moment together—or that's the way I felt. Then I'd put my clothes back on and smooth away the signs of him and make up my face. He'd take me home and say as I got out of the cab,

'I'll call you this week.' But of course he never did. It would be several weeks later, or months, and we'd go through the charade again."

"Didn't you ever really talk? Didn't you ask why he continued to come around, and why your time together was so special —I believe that's what you're telling me—if he cared so little for you? Didn't you ever tell him how you felt, regardless of whether those feelings were returned?"

Virginia looked hard at her hands. "No. Wouldn't have made any difference. You can't talk a person into loving you, and he had just moved on. I spent my time wondering about my own lack of control and his lack of heart. And I tried to blot him out. I recounted the myriad reasons why he was wrong for me—his shallow emotions, or so they seemed, his egoistic need to be the center of every circle, and his overwhelming personality. He was like a giant tree that threw a mighty shade but took my sun away. I would have been stunted in his shadow. Actually, our last time together marked our first honest conversation since the breakup."

"What did you talk about?"

"Regret mostly. He said he'd found no way to fold me into his life. That my independence was really based in insecurity, I hid myself behind it and was afraid to let go and trust. That I had been so emotionally battered by Jim Winburn that all men were rotten in my eyes and he was weary of continually justifying himself. There's a lot of truth there."

"What did you say to him?"

"I said my lack of trust was borne out by his lack of staying power. That I always expected him to move on, like a crack passenger train that streaks into a station already bursting full, with doors opening and closing almost at the same time. He said that regardless how long the doors are open, a train can only come and go. The passenger must decide to make the trip. And there's some truth in that too. But there was too much distrust on both sides, we both knew it. Even that night, when we made love, I was careful to tilt my head back so the tears ran into my hair and he wouldn't know how miserable I was."

"Gin, you love this man"—Shelby's voice was soft but her exasperation was keen—"but your insane pride and fear of rejection won't let you reach out for him. Hell, use this baby, if you're so determined to have it, as a way of doing that. Didn't you tell me that Mike Strange's major regret in his storybook life is his inability to have children? And haven't you just admitted your unwillingness to commit yourself was a major factor in his withdrawal? Give him what he wants—a devoted wife and an heir, in one package—and get what you want—him, and a small fortune to go with him. Jesus, what a match." A wicked smile cracked the corners of her mouth. "What shall I wear to the wedding?"

Virginia was too uncomfortable to respond. Her countenance became more morose by degrees, like a thermometer dropping. "You don't understand, not fully. He doesn't love *me*, Shelby." She hit her chest with her fist. "He can't commit himself to *me*"—she thumped her chest again—"so what am I to do, use my baby as a taxi ride to easy street? That's not just dishonest, it's degrading, and mortifying that you'd suggest it."

"Oh, can the self-righteous nonsense," Shelby broke in furiously. "I'm not suggesting that you marry the man for his money, just that he happens to have plenty and would adore spending it on you and little Mike."

"Perhaps on both of us." This time it was Virginia's voice that was raised. "But not just on me alone. What am I—a breeder cow? The prize bitch? Good only for offspring I carry full-term? Perhaps he should wait till I deliver before he marries me. God Almighty, through the ages women have been worth little more than the children they produce for men to hang their egos and their property on. Wombs for hire in return for security. I won't have a baby to perpetuate that system!"

"Good. Then don't have it."

"I have to. There's no other way."

Shelby threw down her napkin. "Of course there is. It's called an abortion clinic. It's also called sanity. How can you seriously think about raising this child alone? You'll be sixty when it graduates from high school, and you'll spend the next twenty years wondering how to support it once Peabody Slocum drops you from its employment rolls."

"I'm not so sure of that."

"Yeah? I've a mental picture of those pin-striped suits holding an office baby shower. They'll get rid of the embarrassment of an unwed mother almost as fast as your socialite friends drop you from their guest lists. What makes you think you can flout the conventions and values of your social order and pay no price?" Shelby calmed her attack. "Besides, Gin, what's the point? You have two fabulous kids—enough, you're a fortunate woman. They're almost out of the nest. I've watched you brushing them off the branch for the past couple of years even before their wings had feathers. Is this any time to begin it all again, waiting on line in pediatricians' offices, scouting nursery schools, dyeing Easter eggs? Have you forgotten all those years of pushing swings in the park, being home every night for tuck-in bedtime stories, spending Saturdays at the zoo or yet another boring museum? When is it your time? Haven't you earned that? Time for a marvelous man who deserves you. Not a Michael Strange who's more interested in his stock specialist than his lover. Not an immature gadfly who—what is it they say?— way down deep is shallow. A moral manly man, someone whose gilt is fourteen-karat. You've the last third of your life ahead, to love and learn and grow, why throw that away on . . ."

"A child? A person? Part of me?" Virginia broke in. "Half this child is Mike, Shelby, but the other half is me. If I could think about killing his half, I couldn't do it to mine. Now this may sound melodramatic, but I'm its cradle, its protection, with the sentence of life or death in my hands, and, Shelby, I'm no executioner."

Suddenly, violently agitated, Shelby leapt from the table and strode stiff-legged across the living room, coming finally to lean her forehead against the window as if to drain away the cool.

Virginia stared, momentarily startled, then followed her friend, touching her shoulder from behind tentatively.

Shelby brushed her hand away as she turned. "Then have the child. You'll be carrying out your own execution—by killing your future." She started back across the living room, swinging her handbag off a chair as she passed. "But if you really want to commit suicide"—and she pointed to the window where she had been standing—"just pop up over the balcony. It's quicker. Thanks for dinner, pal. I'll call you tomorrow."

The door slammed. The room was suddenly so empty even the oxygen seemed to have gone out of it. Virginia felt a chill of solitude on the warm summer evening. Her decision was based on a tight intact circle: her children, her parents, her closest friends, her baby. No, not totally honest. Her decision was in order to *devise* a close circle. Forcefully struck with the simple truth, Virginia dropped heavily into a chair. Living alone since her divorce had closed doors of opportunity rather than opened them. Free to do anything she wished with anyone, she was able instead to do less. Available for any relationship, she locked herself away from almost all. She had discovered that independence, precious after years of an oppressive marriage, had its joys, but brought along its companion, Isolation, and forced him uninvited into the party of her life. Isolation—who hugged hello and took her breath away. Who sipped her discontent and vomited it in her lap. Who became a cloud of smoke making it difficult to find her way, closing her off from others.

Before Mike she had been despairingly lonely, traveling cyclically to the dark side of the moon, desperately fighting off attacks of depression that left her emotionally numb and that no amount of activity or determination dissipated. The lack of a central figure in her life so impoverished her emotionally she suffered a spiritual malnutrition that left her weak, hungry for contact, unsatisfied by groups of people. The greatest number in her case was one and she was farthest away at zero. Shelby often admonished her for being too choosy, as if she were still eighteen with a ten-year spectrum of young Atlanta bucks to pick from, but she rejoined, "If you are used to Mozart, how do you settle for punk rock? How do you change the standards of a lifetime because a commodity is in short supply?"

It was. In her generation the good men were married, or divorcing and moving immediately into encircling arms pre-selected before their breaks. Left over were the cripples—homosexuals, neurotics, alcoholics. They drank too much, and bounced from bed to bed, paying psychiatrists to justify their aberrations. Virginia tried to keep company with the healthier, but found even them unacceptable. Since she did not hide her feelings well, they did not call her often.

Except for seeing a few close friends, and the sprawling city's social life made that difficult, she usually went to dinner with these men before or after typical New York affairs that specialized in names and reputations but were devoid of friendships or feelings. They were attended by some who arrived in limousines and some who wished they had—crowds of acquaintances who knew each other from similar functions. As the invited were mostly men of prestige and the women who accompanied them, the ritual gathering and separating consisted in the main of giving and receiving recognition, so that all could return to neighborhoods where they knew no one on the street, and hotel-like apartments where they knew no one in their building, and feel that they belonged. They would send each other Christmas cards and invitations to impressive parties, and perhaps attend each other's funerals, but they would be unlikely to call if there were a divorce in the family or if a child became gravely ill.

Very occasionally she met a person who gave her hope, the bank executive, for instance, who seemed such a perfect fit. He was newly divorced, and his children were the ages of hers with many of the same interests. Their family backgrounds were similar, as were their political preferences and the kind of music they enjoyed. They shared a fondness for furnishing houses and spent tranquil hours rummaging through antique shops and country auctions. His eye was even faster than hers at discovering value beneath grime or under an extra coat of paint. He was young too, almost her age, yet did not prefer the company of much younger women and she liked that. He was almost a man to spend a lifetime with, almost—but he could not have sex with her. His easy arousal sank away to nothing once they were in bed. She accepted the blame without being asked. It was her strength and independence, he said, that made him feel ineffectual, unnecessary. But those are the traits, she answered, that you claim to find most attractive in me. Ah, that's the irony, he said.

They continued to see each other, but always during the day. Once at lunch he described with much laughter the twenty-six-year-old who picked him up at P. J. Clarke's, who took him to his own room to bed him down, then without consultation had her telephone line switched to his house and arrived with all her clothes to stay. He married her soon after.

Virginia missed his exuberant, optimistic company, and the opportunity he had almost represented to rearrange her life. The world walked, she knew, like Noah's animals, two by two, whether old couples steadying one another down the street, young ones rubbing against each other in the park, homosexual lovers oblivious to the stares of a different world, or married couples in restaurants sitting without touching or speaking but, still, together. To be One in a society of Twos was to be different, out of step with life's rhythm. Though she did not dwell upon it day to day, involved as she was in a vigorous, satisfying routine, she felt on the whole diminished by not being part of what seemed the more natural way.

After a while she drifted into celibacy. At first she did not greatly miss a physical relationship; then she had difficulty remembering what one had been like. She found new meaning for the words Alone and Loneliness. Alone had been desirable after a hectic weekend, when her life was full of someone else, or before the busy holidays. Then she smugly prided herself on her ability and desire to be Alone. To pile up on her bed surrounded by pillows, books, articles scattered around, her precious music playing, a telephone nearby. She sank into hours of seclusion, retreating from harassments, rebelling against interruptions. Now she knew Loneliness was Alone attenuated, stretched in time until there was no relief. Loneliness was having no hectic weekends behind or ahead. It was the empty glass in her hand once the crowd was gone and only Isolation stayed to keep her company.

Virginia was not without a sense of martyrdom, and dwelling on loneliness became dangerously, indulgently self-fulfilling. However highly she valued herself as mother, friend, businesswoman, her self-esteem dropped below the safety mark when she judged her desirability, and all the alarm bells and flashing lights that accompanied an ego in free fall were unable to motivate her to rescue it. She might have sought a psychiatrist's help, but it was her way neither to admit weakness to a stranger nor to put her fate in another's hands. Shelby was her source of greatest comfort, though her empathy and patience were limited by her own aggressive ways with problems. Shelby would never wait in suspense for a man to call; she would make the first contact, and if she were rejected it would be because of his poor judgment, never her intrinsic worth. In the face of such self-assurance, Virginia did not dwell upon her quaking confidence.

So how did she know about the balcony? Virginia thought, looking again toward the window. But for God's sake, I was never really going to . . . Still, I thought about it, she admitted. Wondered how far down it was, whether it hurt when you hit, and how much of a mess there'd be to scoop up and haul away.

She also questioned her right to be that selfish, depriving her children of their primary parent, and wondered whether they would wonder, at depressive periods in their own lives, if they would do the same. She even considered killing herself without leaving justification, she remembered, but wasn't selfless enough to go without explaining why.

She pulled herself heavily from the chair. She knew so many lonely people—why didn't that make it easier? she thought, walking back to the littered table. Still, death-row prisoners find little consolation in knowing that others on the cellblock share their fate. We lonely ones should be able to help each other through, but we've no spirit or energy left, and we're old before our time. It's easier to think about not living at all than living half a life.

Virginia piled the silver on the dishes, dishes on the bread tray, brushed crumbs onto all, and turned for the kitchen almost in despair as she considered her alternatives. One more dinner party or cocktail hour, shoulder to shoulder with the contented, arguing Soviet incursions into the Third World or the way unions are ruining this country while tears gather behind the eyelids was simply unacceptable—and unavoidable. Next to that, quitting seemed eminently rational. No, she had never been really close, but each time she considered the option she died a little, chipped away at her soul like a small-town whittler hunkering in the town square, pulling against the wooden knob until the sun goes down and there is nothing left at all.

Maybe Shelby is on to something, she thought, putting the refrigerator items back into the cold. Maybe she *had* found a way to close herself off permanently, make herself unavailable for what she thought improbable anyway. If it was difficult-to-impossible to find a man willing to play foster dad to teenagers, who in heaven's name would take on a fatherless child?

Running water over the stacked sink, she thanked God she had dishes to do, comforting dishes. In a way, she thought, women are peculiarly blessed, because in time of crisis, or when death arrives, or illness, we still have dishes to do—one thing at least we know we can handle.

Saturday, August 2

Saturday was the week's beast of burden, carting and hauling the chores, repairs, shopping trips, and service errands that Virginia ordinarily had spread from Monday through Friday before she began working. When she was forced to crush them into labor's leisure hours, she discovered a working mother's foremost dilemma was not inexperience, or lack of assertion; it wasn't fending off her boss's advances or feeling guilty about her children; nor was it competing with men for equal pay and promotions. It was finding enough time. She fought for it in quarter hours, rationed it among her priorities, and resented mightily people and things that robbed her of her due. "Don't spend my money for me or my time" was the angriest proscription she hurled at her children when laziness added their undone obligations to her own. She looked everywhere for time and found it in pieces. Time on the telephone became time for a manicure. Waiting for meetings to start became list time—Christmas lists, grocery lists, lists of errands and calls. Then lists of the lists. Like money owed, she committed her future time before she got it, and like a bad debtor, always owed more than she would ever have. When she first went to work her friends asked how she managed the house, the children, the job, and an occasional dinner party. She spared them the details, but she knew. Mostly she gave things up. Silver objects requiring polish were removed from tables, bagged in plastic, and put away. The number of house plants was significantly cut back—watering came around too often. Sheets weren't changed as religiously, blouses were worn "just once more" before pressing, shoes down at the heels were pushed to the rear of the closet instead of the repair shop. She no longer comparison-shopped, shopped the sales, or shopped much at all. The supermarket, linchpin of her Saturdays, was also the source of a future bleeding ulcer, she knew, as she stood in weekend lines for as long as it had taken her to fill her basket, losing her patience and her time. Cooking changed too. In the old days, she and Julia Child repaired to the kitchen to produce soufflés and sauces and answers to all kinds of emotional problems. It was a form of therapy. Now she organized mass-production lines turning out casseroles, turkeys, pots of split-pea soup, food that would feed twice, or freeze, or slice and serve again. Mostly, though, she found time by giving it up. Job work was over at five; home work lasted as long as she managed to stay up, so free time died a natural death. "Whiling away" was a phrase no longer required in her lexicon. She reserved her greatest envy for those able to indulge themselves with books and music, long catch-up telephone conversations, or simply doing nothing. To be idle—blissful. To be bored—heavenly. To burn her lists as rebellious students burned their draft cards— the act of ultimate defiance.

But today Virginia lay abed, her Saturday sliding past the hands of her clock, not concerned with present time or the lack of it, but with future time, and what it held for her and her child. She had awakened stinging from the sharpness of

Shelby's words and for the first time fiercely protective about the tiny life she harbored. Somewhere inside she imagined miniature waves of gratitude and affection. Her fingers, stroking her stomach, picked them up like a receiver set and returned signals of protection and reassurance. No one gets at you except through me, she thought belligerently. But maybe it's time to pull the wagons into a circle and call for reinforcements. She reached across the pillows for the phone.

The first call, affecting her future, requested an immediate nonstop reservation to Atlanta. It was still home despite the many years away, and it was there she hoped to die. Not that she cared a great deal about dying there. It was simply that New York seems so involved with the business of living, so busy, so impersonal, it was unlikely to properly mark a death as important to her as hers would undoubtedly be. She had always felt she was living out of a suitcase in the city, and never lost her sense of surprise when Max and Maggie called it home. In contrast, she saw herself just passing through, a traveler without a fixed date of departure but with a return-trip ticket in her pocket.

The second call concerned her present. It was to Shelby.

"Ready to deal with me again? I'm going home this afternoon, leaving from La Guardia at six. Have lunch with me and help me get my head straight."

The sweet honest voice she expected was there for her. "You're on, Gin, though you may have to work your magic on me first. Something kept me awake most of the night and it wasn't your pasta. Here I am in the communications business and I'm neglecting to report the full story. Let's rent a table for hours somewhere and plan the rest of our lives."

"Gino's? O'Neal's?"

"Too noisy. Make a reservation at Café des Artistes—in the back where it's quiet. You know the captain, don't you? Spilling one's insides is more conducive in a lush setting, and if

you'll drop a little dirt on your Wall Street bandit-colleagues
I'll put it on the expense account."

"One o'clock?"

"Perfect. See you there."

The third call involved her past.

"Mom? I'm coming home."

Knowing she interrupted little in the restricted daily lives of
her elderly parents, Virginia expected and heard the pleasure in
her mother's voice. "I'll be on the Delta flight that arrives at
eight oh-five and I'll find a cab. . . . No, don't even think
about coming to the airport. Has Dad made enough of a men-
ace of himself to have his license revoked? . . . Well, he
should turn it in for the protection of society. . . . What? . . .
No, don't you dare. You know you're night-blind. I'd rather
think about you two battling to the death over a backgammon
board while I ride in safety. . . . No argument now. Tell Leslie
to leave my boiled custard in the icebox. I'll see you soon. . . .
No, everything's fine, Mom. It's just that the children are with
Jim in Colorado, this town is steamy and grubby, and I miss
you. See you tonight. . . . Love you too."

The Idyll was over. Aware again of the imminent passage of
time and mentally forming a list of priority preparations, she
threw back the sheets and pitched herself into the day, packing,
pressing, rinsing clothes, organizing. She wrote notes to the
children, the cleaning woman, her neighbor who would water
the plants and collect the papers. She called the maître d' at the
restaurant, and her secretary to explain her Monday absence.
She paid the most pressing bills and cleared her desk of incom-
ing mail. She sorted files and reports for airborne reading, and
in between she bathed and dressed, blew her hair dry with a
machine and her nails with her breath. She played a game
against herself while making arrangements like these when it
seemed impossible to complete everything. She churned
through her lists at high speed, knowing the odds were against

finishing, but bet on herself even as she added details to each job so it would not only be completed, but accomplished perfectly. She usually won, as she did today, panting a bit but double-locking her apartment door with the satisfaction of order within and nothing left to do but close her luggage for the ride to the airport.

At one o'clock she passed the restaurant's leaded windows, boxed with blazing red geraniums, the only living things around happy with the August sun. Once inside, momentarily blinded, she scanned the busy room for Shelby and found her talking, as usual, or rather entertaining the captain, a busboy, and a pair of waiters. Most people found her irresistible, drawn to her energy, her frankness—which could occasionally be appalling—and her extraordinary sense of fun. She threw off light like a Fourth of July sparkler, and attracted as much attention. Virginia often felt pale beside her, almost bland. Though physically she was as attractive, she could not match her wit or style, which she admired as much as Shelby respected her competence and strength. They were oddly but fortuitously matched, and nurtured the friendship; they kept each other in a privileged place, protecting their time together and their confidence. They had never discussed only those things they could not remember or had yet to experience.

Yet today Shelby had a secret, so closely held it was making her ill. She needed to give it up as one longs to vomit an indigestible meal. When both had ordered bloody marys, unusually subdued, she bent over her service plate as if over a toilet and held her head in her hands.

"I've a confession to make. Fast."

"Jesus, you look like you killed somebody," Virginia said, concerned.

"Sort of. I had an abortion once . . ."

"You?"

"Um, back in the Dark Ages, which is the reason I shot out of your apartment last night. I'd managed to forget it—I suppose the operative word is 'repress'—until our discussion, then it all came crashing back and I needed room to remember and relive. It changed my life, so I want you to know about it before you make a final decision."

"When was it?"

"About six months after that miserable trial and divorce. I spent my days cataloguing mounds of unpaid bills and talking the telephone company into turning the phone back on. Good ole Ned wasn't the heart of generosity."

"I remember. And all that money. Why didn't you appeal? Judges provide for destitute women and children, you know."

"Are you kidding? And fight any more battles in court that I couldn't handle in person? And in *those days*? That was back in the middle sixties when women thought liberation referred to prisoners in concentration camps—come to think of it, that's an accurate description of my marriage—when you were considered frivolous at best, certifiable at worst, to give up a good man, in quotes.

"Anyway, I was broke, shunned, scared, and might have cracked if I hadn't been having an affair. My lawyer, who was standing up to Ned, was lying down for me, thank God. He kept me sane, and somewhat aware I was not an untouchable with the modern version of the Scarlet Letter across my forehead—D for divorce. Can you imagine what people would have said if they'd known about us? Then, of course, I got pregnant."

"Before abortions were legal anywhere," Virginia prompted.

"Except Switzerland. And I couldn't have bought a plane ticket to Chattanooga. I've no words now to express my panic then. There was no way I could have the baby and no way I couldn't. My brain stopped. Thinking was impossible because the problem was incapable of solution, and my guilt was so enormous I couldn't have told anyone—my mother, my sister . . ."

"Your lawyer?"

"God no. It never occurred to me that it was either his fault or his responsibility. If the sentence was hanging, only one of us deserved the gallows—guess who? And there was more. I thought he'd think me somehow unworthy, irresponsible, a troublemaker. He always left birth control to me—I can't remember his ever mentioning it."

"How many of them ever do?"

"Finally I turned to the only person I dared confess my sins to—my maid. She was an old colored woman who had taken care of the children since they were babies. I trusted her, and knew there wasn't anyone she'd tell who'd make any difference, and I figured her folks dealt with the problem more than my very polite society, and sure enough, she set me up. Gave me an out-of-state telephone number . . ."

"You didn't." Virginia started to sip her drink but put it down, already anticipating the horror of what she would hear.

"What would you have done? Of course I did. My people would rather have had me abort, as long as they didn't know about it, than bring up a fatherless child. Doing away with the baby was illegal, but having it was worse, it was immoral, not to mention impossible in my financial state. So I gathered every cent I could, even robbed the children's Easter boxes, I'm ashamed to admit, and drove myself and five hundred dollars down to a town in Mississippi so small it was just this side of a 'resume speed' sign. I found the only gas station in town—the kind with the big red Coke box out front full of icy water and Spur Colas and all the locals on the stoop with shotguns in their laps eating Moon Pies. I asked for a couple of gallons of gas, as ordered, and pretended to make a telephone call from the outdoor booth. Then I heard footsteps behind me, and a voice telling me not to turn around and to follow when his blue pickup truck left the station."

"Shelby, stop. I can't believe you were so foolish."

"Desperate is the word. I followed, all right, shaking so hard I could hardly hold the wheel. He led me to a scrubby motel—

the old-fashioned kind before Holiday Inns, with small cabins spaced out like teeth with gaps in between. The truck pulled up to one and I followed the back of the man—never did see his face—up to the door. He opened and closed it in one motion and suddenly I was inside with another man. The light was so dim I couldn't see his face either, but I heard his voice— oh God, will I always remember that voice telling me to take off my clothes and get in the shower. By this time I was sobbing in sheer terror— I could have bathed in tears. I showered, wishing I could drown in that scummy little cubicle rather than face him, but I did it and he did it. A stranger in a dirty T-shirt cleaned me out of babe and money and sent me back down the highway socially presentable again and half dead."

"Why? What did he do to you?" Virginia's face was as bloodless now as her friend's was flushed.

"I hemorrhaged badly. The turkey stuck something through my womb."

"God, Shelby, poor girl, all alone. Did it hurt?"

"The pain was manageable after the abortion—except for the wound to my psyche. During? I still can't talk about it, so let's don't. If that guy got off on torturing women, then his sadistic plate was full that afternoon. The drive back is a blur. Like a horse going back to the stable, the car brought me home, but I lost so much blood I don't remember anything. Somehow my sister was there bundling me into the emergency room, and I woke up a lifetime or two later pieced back together. Fortunately I didn't want any more children."

"How awful for you."

"Not entirely, and that's why I've put you through this soap opera. The abortion *was* horrible. I felt like a political prisoner, shackled and tortured, who's released and warned if she ever mentions what happened they'll come back and do it all over again. So it was years before I could talk about it. But, Gin, not only was my life spared after that punctured uterus healed, so was my future. The abortion after all was a reprieve, a governor's pardon delivered at the eleventh hour before sentence was carried out. I, Shelby Anderson, got the right to live again without another child, for which I had neither the energy nor the time nor the money, and without the weightiest baggage one carries in a small town—shame."

The restaurant glittered and chattered around them, waiters slid by each other with steaming dishes, newcomers scraped their chairs under them and reached for menus. The two friends inclined their heads, sharing hurt and understanding silently as two devoted women do who would gladly bear each other's pain. Virginia often wanted to rewrite the old refrain to "She's no burden, she's my sister." Hiding no infirmity, spelling out every weakness, each was available to the other when Need arrived, or Anguish or Anxiety, for it was misfortunes that bound them close and allowed each to share the other's happinesses, when they came, as if they were her own.

The waiter's interruption was welcome, diverting their attention to puffy brioches alongside softly scrambled eggs and Scotch salmon and salad plates filled with endive and walnuts. They traded empty cocktail glasses for white wine, and pushed their food around looking for a way to renew the difficult conversation. Finally putting down her fork to squeeze the hand that had so often symbolically held hers, Virginia asked, "Then why so miserable? You did what you had to do. It worked, you're alive! What demons still hold you?"

"None—except those in my head." Shelby looked up from her food with tear-filmed eyes. "Occasionally I count on my fingers the years we haven't spent together—November would have been seventeen. I imagine life with another teenager around the house and mentally buy presents for one more. I wonder what kind of face it would have had, and personality, and whether we would have gotten along, been close. You see, I gave the child up physically, but it's always been a part of me. Just won't go away."

"Shelby, you just argued my case before the jury—brilliantly!

And won! Don't you see, that's precisely why I can't lose this child."

"Hold on," interrupted Shelby, suddenly infuriated. She rose to address the bar again. "Don't twist this present discomfort, remembering a nasty time in my life, to suit your predetermined conclusion. *I don't want that child back.* Sure there are memories, of course there are regrets—something in me will always be a little in pain, like a cracked bone that healed wrong. But the rest of me functions beautifully. I'm stronger, happier, better adjusted without that child, and totally without guilt. I've done my bit to repopulate the earth—three human beings of quality the race can be proud of, but my God, I could have had what, twelve, fifteen children? Reproducing isn't all I'm capable of or all I choose to do. There are too many other possibilities for me—and for you, Gin, and here you are about to throw away . . ."

"The baby and the bath water? No one's forcing me to do this. Your curse is my blessing. I'm just as supportive of your choice of abortion as I want you to be for me not to have one. Remember those women in the early seventies who signed the manifesto claiming they'd had abortions? Heroes! Some who signed actually hadn't, but all of them were willing to draw the fire of the opposition to make it a legitimate act of rational people. Christ, what that must have taken! Look how difficult it is for *you* to tell *me* after all these years. Believe me, I'm grateful for the ability to choose, but this is what I want, need, must do. Don't pity me, just help me face the craziness ahead. Help me."

Shelby looked at the eyes before her inspired with purpose and determination, and in a sudden burst of resignation, nodded in agreement. "And you won't reconsider and . . ."

"Tell Mike?" The women often finished each other's thoughts. "Be honest. Do you want me to tell him because you think it's fair, or because you secretly hope it will bring us back together?"

"All right. I'm more concerned about you than him. But there's more. If you insist on upsetting the stability of your life and your children's, then he must be forced, not allowed, *forced* to help. You can carry it in your stomach; let him carry it on his back."

Virginia hesitated to explain to Shelby what she found so impossible to understand herself. She bought time. "Let's go. People are piling up for tables, and we'll have to eat our napkins if we stay any longer. We can talk going home."

Signaling the hovering waiter, who gratefully took her credit card, Shelby led the way to the door, waving to friends and nodding to strangers who recognized her. Virginia strolled in the wake of the broadcaster's fame almost maternally proud. Even when her friend went unrecognized, the two usually attracted attention, matched as they were like a pair of carriage horses with similar size and coloring and an almost palpable sense of identity. Ambling down Central Park West, arm in arm, oblivious to the stares of passersby, they continued shaping their lives.

"You're impossibly stubborn, you know."

"That's a plus. You didn't say stupid. Shelby, why should Mike know? An active sperm count doesn't make you a father. He didn't ask for this child, or want it, or expect it . . ."

"Nor did you."

"Not true. Ever since I fell in love with Mike I dreamed, fantasized really, about having this child—being the only woman who could miraculously give him what he wants. Having part of him in part of me—the ultimate connection—but he doesn't feel that about us, or about a child of ours."

"How do you know? Give him a chance."

"It's too late. Once, perhaps . . . not now. He cares more about his latest merger, his golf stroke, and two or three girlfriends—in that order—than he does about me. You know how unhappy I've been without him, like a dog tied outside a grocery store miserably searching for the one face that matters. I need to be unleashed from the pain of watching for him in every crowd, for his car in every traffic jam, hoping every telephone ring is his. I want loose, free to remember our magic times together instead of the tortured ones, and I won't be until I make up my mind that we're really finished."

"But the baby . . ."

"The best thing Mike ever did for me—the crowning gift."

"Stubborn *and* stupid. All those millions . . ."

"I make a good living, not sumptuous, but adequate. I'm smart, experienced, healthy, with thirty years or so before I join you in that rocking chair on the porch, and I know I can provide for this child."

"Just occasional help, rock-head? A good nurse? Braces? A guaranteed education that includes graduate school?" Virginia's mouth drawn thinly across her teeth stopped Shelby again. "Your mind, made up, is as hard to dent as a wrecker's ball. O.K., I give up."

"Thanks."

"You're welcome."

The four long legs traveled a block in step before Shelby continued. "Ironical, isn't it? We've worked so hard for recognition, for success. You went to graduate school at night, holding down a full-time job and taking care of two children. I called mine from around the globe feeling guilty, but working my ass off on crappy assignments to finally get the stories I want. Now you're financially secure, and I've a recognition factor any politician would envy, and we're both throwing away what took such effort to accomplish, I because of a shit-heel employer, you because of a shit-heel lover. Can you imagine a man who worked as hard as we have doing what we plan to do? No wonder women aren't presidents and senators and chairmen of the board; we're so easily diverted."

"By human considerations, though, by matters of the heart as well as the mind. By the quality of our lives as well as the quantity of our money."

"Maybe. And maybe that's one more cop-out we allow ourselves when we can't make the pieces fit."

"But we do what we have to do," Virginia said.

"Yes, we do what we have to do," Shelby said.

Over the years, so many of their conversations had ended with the phrase Shelby insisted should be etched on her tombstone. Translated, it explained that the decisions they made, even the apparently irrational ones, were a balance of available options, and included the cost of doing business. Virginia knew the price of her most recent one would be high, but had yet to understand the full toll she had imposed upon herself.

As a summer storm swirls upon a languid afternoon, Virginia's travel schedule suddenly interrupted the quiet pace of the day, sending her scurrying for bags and cab, waving promises to stay in touch. She departed stronger than ever, almost self-righteous about her decision, unlike Shelby, who turned toward home worried and pessimistic, concerned about what she thought was an ill-considered, perilous course. Hands in pockets, chin to chest, she kicked objects in her path as she made her way across the park to the East Side, brushing aside children who skated too close with a brusqueness she realized was an angry reaction to the wasted life Virginia had chosen. Two Puerto Rican teenagers slouched by, odorous of marijuana, dragging a portable radio half as large as a suitcase which deafened all who had the misfortune to pass by. Shelby snarled aloud what others silently thought but dared not say: "Shut the fucker off; it's against the law!" She had few restrictions on what she said and to whom. A sudden spitting tension rose among the three, a city phenomenon repeated thousands of times a day between different ages, classes, ethnic groups. Though New Yorkers remained poised for combat and were easily goaded into battle, generally women knew better than to pick fights which could cause them physical harm—and so did Shelby. But today she found herself striking out at what she disliked and saw a possibility to change, unlike Virginia's utterly senseless idea of becoming, at her age and station, an unmarried mother. The kids snarled threats in return, but produced no more than an elementary match in obscenity. Shelby had bettered many far more adept than they at hurling epithets. Disengaging, she continued across the park, searching for rationalizations which would take away her fears. The walk did not restore her equanimity, nor did the refuge of her apartment, once she closed the door, afford serenity. Uncharacteristically for the early hour, she poured a stout drink, added ice cubes, and sat in the lowering darkness nursing a sense of impending disaster. It was unlike Shelby to meet defeat on a referee's decision without first swinging a few punches. By the time the summer dark forced the sunset below her western terrace, she was not at all sure the fight was over.

By contrast, Virginia left town on a high. Having defended her vital secret against Shelby's formidable arguments, she was more convinced than before how straight was her duty, how pure her choice. She envisaged a sort of aura enveloping her, a white light proclaiming the justness, the virtue of what she would accomplish—the baby she would bear against giant odds and raise in the face of community opposition.

Her exhilaration existed partly because she mistakenly believed she had brought Shelby around to her thinking, and partly because of the multiple bloody marys, which, by the time she had buckled her seat belt and was lifted toward the very sky into which Shelby stared so regretfully, wore off enough to drop her mentally back to earth. A single point nagged, picked at her brain, something she thought about during her manic explanation to Shelby why Mike should not know his child; what was it now, where had it appeared in the conversation, why had she been loath then to stop and examine what she knew, like a body buried without identification, must later be exhumed and reexamined? Her mind hung as suspended as the plane, searching without direction, until suddenly it was there, the question she did not want to recognize or answer: Was she doing this to punish him? Was this her way of getting even?

Appropriate to have to consider this on a plane, she thought. So much of what they were had been interconnected by machines—airplanes, telephones, telegraphs, telexes. They were the modern technological couple, moving from coast to coast, across seas and international datelines, to find hours together, braving bad weather, time zones, and unbending schedules. They managed it cheerfully, he more than she because of his limitless energy, which allowed him to inspect California operations for a twelve-hour day and still be as fresh when he met her 3 A.M. plane from the coast as the carnations he thrust on her, then crushed in a welcoming bear hug.

Mike operated on an inner life-switch—the world's on, the world's off—and when he darkened his corporate lights and brought their private time into focus, nothing was allowed to intrude. Their needs were supplied effortlessly, silently, by invisible assistants who hired cars, dispatched tickets and luggage, alerted boat crews, made dinner reservations. Hungry for each other, their most difficult choice once together was between loving conversation and conversational loving, for even as they made love, they talked, unable and unwilling to cease explaining the essence of their separateness and the wonder of being together.

Intimate moments with Jim Winburn, even at the start of her marriage, had been silent—functional, predictable, and quiet. Had they married later in the sixties they might have devised less restricted responses to each other buoyed by the national wave of permissiveness, but left to their own imaginings, they were a bloodless, passionless couple. His lips met hers in a thin hard line; she never knew his tongue. She thought men made the rules, so it was not her place to suggest this way no, not there . . . there . . . with your fingers . . . wait, not yet

. . . I'll tell you when. She never said a word, and he kept his silent counsel. He stopped using the word "love" before their first year was finished.

Virginia knew she had been different—better—with other men after her divorce and wondered if Jim looked back at her, after surely experiencing more spirited passion, as a sexless woman, incapable of lusty pleasure. With Mike, it was as good (and she was as good) as she could have hoped, and more than she had expected. His talking helped. Joking sometimes, she found herself in the ambiguous situation of belly-laughing with her pulse racing, or having love-words nuzzled into her ear along with his tongue, he stroking her and finding pleasure and telling her, and then telling her when he felt himself coming and then telling her how he felt as he came. Mike demystified sex and made it easy, feeling no pressure to perform and applying none. He never cared which of them had an orgasm first, or if one of them didn't—and occasionally that happened to Virginia when there had been a lot of sex or when she was tired, or because of reasons she did not fully understand. But those moments too contained a degree of wonder, just holding him, feeling his weight on her. There were times when they dropped off to sleep wrapped around each other, him in her, content in their closeness. There were even times when she simply was not as interested as he and found herself barely participating, making mental lists of tasks ahead, but guiltlessly. His easy way allowed her that, just as his enjoyment in every part of her permitted her to drop the last mental towels of modesty and afforded her the purest pleasure, intense as any orgasm: the simple joy of pleasing him.

God knows, he wasn't perfect. He picked his nose occasionally when he thought no one was looking, and insisted on being the center of a crowd of two or twenty. She, in thorough enjoyment of him, abdicated the role of dual conversationalist and learned to nod at appropriate times to support his extemporaneous performances. She thought he sometimes wore bronzing makeup, though she wasn't sure and didn't care; he may have rinsed his hair a time or two, but so what? He was a handsome man who otherwise neither fought the passage of time nor dwelled on it. If he showed the raggle-taggle of insecurities left over from an earlier age, she owned a number too. Love equalized their defects and made them unimportant.

As naturally negative as she was, he was obstinately optimistic. They were walking along Fifth Avenue once, just before Christmas, holding on together against the cold, making their way past ostentatious windows beckoning shoppers inside with sumptuous displays. Moving slowly through the holiday rush, with no more demanding task ahead than deciding at what point spirits should replace spirit, they angled across the street to stroll past the glittering angels lined up as guards before the great Rockefeller Center tree.

"It's somewhat fake, you know," she said, arching her back to look up to its highest point. Guy wires thick as saplings tethered the giant spruce to four adjacent buildings. Barrel stays large as mill wheels encircled its base. The evening breezes flapped its branches like wings of a dark pterodactyl straining to break away.

"That? How could that be fake anything?" he asked.

"Well, it's Canadian, for a start. You'd think the country's largest Christmas tree could be grown in the U.S."

"Oh, the holiday has no boundaries," he said.

"And a lot of those branches are added. They didn't all grow that way."

"Oh, yes? Let's take a look." He moved them closer to the tree, directly across the rink where skaters carved icy circles. Workmen could be seen climbing near the mighty trunk, arranging strings of lights.

"Know what?" he asked. "The star's crooked. Doesn't matter if they add a branch or two—fills it out—but we can't have a crooked star."

"It does lean to the left," she agreed, tilting her head to match the star's center point.

"Have to do something about that," he said, grabbing her hand and starting toward the sidewalk around the rink.

"Do what? Must be fifty or sixty feet off the ground."

"We'll see. Can't have a crooked star."

Mike hurried them to the tree's base, where he stopped a workman climbing out of the innards.

"Hey, fella," he called to him. "The tree's great, but the star's crooked."

Virginia hung back, shaking her head at his impulsiveness, saw the wary look on the stranger's face, and knew without hearing his response that just minutes away from quitting for the day he was not interested in anything which would keep him in the cold. Still, he had never met the infectious enthusiasm of Michael Strange. Before her amused eyes Mike urged him out from under the branches, turned his eyes toward the top, then talked him back to the Fifth Avenue sidewalk where they had first detected the flaw. Watching the pair through throngs of sightseers, she saw only the workman return, half jogging, then clamber over the wooden fence at the bottom and begin the arduous climb up.

The thin winter sun was gone now, turning the city dark even before stores closed and offices emptied. She stood shivering in the wind watching the rescue mission. The workman, as close to the tip as was safe, struggled with connecting wires to readjust the star, looking out to the Avenue occasionally for his marker, who was waving his arms in direction. Finally both of Mike's hands clenched above his head in an athlete's sign of triumph. The tree climber began his cold descent and Mike returned to meet him as he dropped to earth; they threw arms around each other's shoulders like victorious teammates coming off a playing field.

Mike believed in himself absolutely when called upon to improve momentary imperfections; Virginia was generally too cynical to try. Yet Virginia's patience in attempting to resolve longer-lasting personal problems was beyond his capacity; he did not have an admirable record. A Catholic, he had been married for twenty-two years, but his wife was dead now from a lingering muscular deterioration which years ago had removed her to private thoughts and solitary days. They had been childless, so she shrank in a wheelchair alone as he sped around the business world in private jets and limousines. They had long since ceased to care for one another, and played out their roles as society demanded. She drooped away to death without complaint, with drunken fits occasionally to expel the pain. He hired nurses, conferred with doctors, and played the part of attentive husband during the rare moments he was home. She was not so much a concern of his heart as one more detail in his controlled environment, handled by functionaries, cared for by medical payments. Michael Strange, cruel as it was, and long before she died, had moved on.

To what? To a series of nameless, faceless women, who never unpacked their bags, to whom he made no promises, and who asked nothing more than what they had to give—an ability to make the moment or the night or the weekend come alive. They seldom felt cheated when he left, though most were sorry to see him go. Unlike other commanding men who had the power to order up variety, he did not use drugs to produce his highest times and his sex was straight—adventurous, but without perversions. He made the rounds on two continents pretty thoroughly, and was seen with recognizable faces—a magazine editor, an established high-fashion model, assorted film actresses. He did not require well-developed minds in his recreational partners, but neither was he often in the company of dummies. His criterion was someone to make him laugh, to divert his mind.

He invariably appeared at business functions alone, earning the concerned glances of colleagues' wives who knew his wife was terminally ill and blessed him for his patience. They clucked and cooed around him, patting his sleeve as they asked about her, and were thankful his smile never faded as he responded with hopeful statements. He reserved his numerous women for nights alone, at elegant out-of-the-way spots, and later at the corporation's hotel suite. There was no attempt to hide them, nor did he expose himself unnecessarily to adverse publicity.

But nothing stuck. Virginia wondered why one had not been more special than the rest. Romantically, she would have preferred attributing his attitude to loyalty to a dying wife, but why should she subvert the truth when he refused to do so?

The day she died, several months after Mike became a serious factor in Virginia's life, a secretary called to inform her of the death. She was on a list methodically, efficiently being notified according to prearrangements for the emergency. By the time she heard and was able to call him back, his grieving, if there had been any, was over. She was seated at the funeral—again, according to plan—several rows behind where she watched him, too elegant for the rest of his Italian kin, moving his relatives in and out less like a mourner than a politician who had gathered the faithful for a difficult concession speech.

She was not on the list for the burial service or the wake, so did not see him again until the following evening. Had he removed her from his life at a complicated time because she was superfluous, or had he handled the situation with tact? Was he protecting her and them from criticism, or were his emotional gears in neutral, needing nothing from her in the way of comfort or solace? At dinner she tried to probe his deeper feelings, but noncommittally he changed the subject.

Later that night, undressing in the hotel suite, Mike threw his wallet on the bureau along with change and various slips of paper. He hesitated, then retrieved one, unfolded it slowly, and passed it over. The writing was quivery; the paper unsigned: "I wish you'd miss me when I'm gone, you rascal you."

"A paraphrase of the old song. Must have been drunk when she wrote it," he said without emotion.

"Sounds like a suicide note—as if she knew she was going to die."

"She may have taken pills."

"*May* have? Don't you know? What did the doctors say?"

"I didn't ask, they didn't tell me." Mike stripped off the rest of his clothes. "Come, let's go to bed."

"Don't you want to know?"

"The only thing I want is to make love to you." He pulled her down beside him, and though she went through the motions, she remained unaroused. He was rougher than she ever remembered him and when he finally peaked she was grateful he was through. She lay beside him frowning into the darkness, trying to remind herself that the man she loved had experienced a traumatic time and needed her understanding, but a warning bell kept ringing in her mind, telling her that she and Mike were different. They valued connection and loss in different currencies, and if she put too much store in hers, his was undervalued.

How did they give each other up? They didn't really. Their separate boats began to drift away and neither extended an oar before the other was past reaching. There was pride involved— too much. He was accustomed to submissive obeisance from his staff, if not adoration, and persistent courting from the media, hopeful politicians, and purveyors of charitable and social causes, not to mention female acquaintances of all ages. She, in turn, had never fought to get or keep a man's attention. They felt the first distance after a series of ideological discussions— not arguments, never arguments, just differences of opinion.

"Men are exploratory creatures," he said. "We're dogs, peeing on every bush and hydrant, marking our territory, sniffing for a bitch in heat. It doesn't mean anything substantively, really, our sexual meanderings. What counts is where home is, and who's there."

"What do you think of women like that?"

"Women aren't like that—except an aberrant few who sell themselves on street corners or work massage parlors. Women must feel an emotional connection before sex is attractive to them."

"And men are naturally rogues?"

"Right. It's biological."

"And women have only monogamous blood running through their veins? Suppose it's cultural, and we newly liberated women who have been set such an example by our admirable leaders begin to experiment, to dabble with all those studs leaving their scents around. How would you feel if you paired up with a woman who thought and acted as you have in the past?"

"I'd walk out. I wouldn't ask a question or listen to an explanation, and if you think that's a double standard, let me tell you now you're right."

"But you're basing your reaction on the old order, when all the men you knew did what they pleased, then went home to women who pleased only them. Maybe there's a new day a-breaking. Many of the young women today seem to have few of the inhibitions of our generation. They have a go with a guy when they feel like it, without guilt attached. Those young women are going to be married one day."

"Good luck to the guys that get *them*."

"Exactly. But suppose they're in the majority, and a man doesn't have much choice, just as girls haven't had much choice in the past if they were looking for a one-girl guy."

"If it comes to that they'll have to accommodate each other."

"But what about the children, Mike? When women behave sexually like the men they marry—having one-night stands on out-of-town business trips, or making it with a fellow at the office, or getting into longer affairs on the side while they live out their married commitments—how are husbands going to know for sure when the babies arrive whose they are?"

"A man would know his own child."

"Come on. Unless you're white and the baby's black, or vice versa, how's a man to look at a newborn child and know if it's his? His wife would never tell. And if she's behaved like a good many men I know, she'd have a tough time being sure herself."

"What's your point?" he asked.

"That double standards don't work anymore. And men who think they do are going to be the losers."

"Men are already the losers, aren't they?"

"How's that?"

"We used to have two major functions in life. We were the hunters and the foragers—in charge of *production*—and the propagators of the species—in charge of *re*production. Now women are out making their own living, so who needs us anymore? And they have their babies when and with whom they wish. Married women have other men's babies, single women have babies, even lesbians have themselves artificially inseminated so they won't be soiled by a dirty male. And those who don't *want* babies get rid of them, whether their husbands or partners want the children or not. That pretty much leaves us out, doesn't it?"

"Are you blaming this on the new freedom that women have in making choices?"

"I'm not blaming anything on anyone. I'm saying that if women want to be so goddamned independent that they'll have other men's children instead of their husbands', then they deserve men who fuck around."

"And I'm saying"—and by this time she was quite angry—"that if men are feeling hostile toward women today, it's because they taught them too well. Lucky for the race there're enough straight-thinking men and women who'll match their priorities with their values, have each other's children, and raise them to be decent, loving parents too. But they won't be people who practice a double standard—whether they are male or female."

Though Virginia did not consider herself archetypically the "new woman," because of the nature of her responsibilities she was. And Mike, though he consciously tried not to be representative of the "traditional man," because of deeply ingrained beliefs he was. Both, if asked which was more important, to be together or to be right, would have chosen to be together, but in practice each controversy—since it was not a measure of their affection for each other—became a wrestle of wills, a justification of attitudes, and neither was adept at compromise. Mike had no need to be, in his professional or his personal life; Virginia remembered compromises during her marriage springing from a lack of self-confidence and an inclination to be dominated. She was determined not to repeat her mistakes, and so made new ones. The wranglings took their toll.

"It's the law of the land now, that's all there is to it," she said, speaking of the Supreme Court's landmark decision on abortion. "There's no issue anymore."

"Just because those nine monkeys spoke, do you think the question of abortion is settled in this country? Think again. First, you give me another nine men—and women!—and I'll give you another decision, and that can happen—half of them ought to be retired anyway. But second, tell me how a learned opinion written in bloodless legalese is going to influence the most closely held, fundamental beliefs of people who think they've enough information to make up their own minds about this one?"

"But this decision is in line with a profound cultural development which involves the equality of the sexes and women's participation in a wider world. It is a natural progression . . ."

"Are you sure it's progress? To allow *individuals* to make judgments that affect future generations? We don't allow individuals to decide who's going to fight our wars, who should be committed to asylums, who's going to get the death penalty. There are some issues that transcend one person's opinion, and abortion's one of them."

"You sound like a parochial Catholic."

"Or like a person concerned that the best of our children are going to end up in slop buckets while the least bright, the least able of our population reproduce themselves into the majority."

"Now you sound like a racist."

"A realist. And people like me who give a damn are not about to abdicate their beliefs, religious or otherwise, because people like you say there's no issue anymore."

Virginia was lacking something, and knew it—the commitment to keep a man happy. She had been carefully taught, as a girl, to handle a man like a valuable racehorse, to curry and comb him, feed him and bed him down in sweet-smelling surroundings, keep his spirits high, his temper level. Then when the moment of testing arrived, to send him out with every ounce of energy fighting to win, barreling ahead for glory and rewards; or, if he lost, to bandage him physically and emotionally to run another day. Virginia knew. Once she too had practiced the oldest of female arts, but now she was tired of the effort and looking for stroking herself. She was hungry for the injections of confidence and inspiration she had so freely administered to another, and there were none from Mike, not because he parsimoniously withheld them, but because he did not realize she needed them too.

Virginia's mother also taught her, long before, to predict how a man would treat a woman. "See him when he's angry," she said, "and watch how he treats his mother." She should have added, in Mike's case, "and how his mother treats him." Mike's mother was dead now, but her physical presence lingered like strong perfume once the wearer has left the room. Her only son fulfilled all her expectations. He was worth the penury she endured after her husband's early death, before success or perseverance had ensured his family's future, when she stretched out a living selling sheets and bedspreads and used her department store discount to clothe her son and daughter and buy their scanty Christmas gifts. He repaid her efforts early on as a remarkable scholar and an athlete, and earned a scholarship at Boston University which made them proud. Living at home and working in the evenings to augment their income, he graduated in three years with honors and a reputation as a fiercely competitive captain of the hockey team. Though professional scouts would have wooed him away, he and his mother were of one mind about his future—even about his name, which he modified after high school to subdue his father's Italian and her Irish heritage: Michael Francis Joseph Stranieri gave way to an assimilated Michael Strange. (Later, Matterhorn's top management would refer to him during difficult corporate negotiations as "Strange, Stranger, Strangest," his volatile nature swinging from stormy to placid to murderous depending upon the state of things; and the part of the press mindful of his early beginnings would dub him "the Boston Strangler" when he successfully overwhelmed yet another resisting company.)

As son and mother dreamed, the Harvard Business School accepted the new Michael Strange enthusiastically in light of his grades and recommendations with no idea of the recent cultural transition, and no awareness of the sacrifice in the deteriorating Victorian house nearby, where a woman grew old early pushing herself and her grown daughter to the edge of exhaustion to provide for her golden boy's education. Not from a sense of martyrdom, but from love, the women shoved their favorite through the only pipeline of success they knew with an atavistic sense that their survival too depended on his advancement.

Mike did not disappoint them and never forgot the debt. His mother he loved unreservedly, as one returns total affection honestly given with no strings attached. Whatever his hour of return to the three-storied house, turreted and gabled, he looked toward the end of the cul-de-sac on which they lived and found his mother standing at the landing window watching for him. She was his beacon home. Long after he was married, he would make the journey regularly to the house at the end of the street and without fail, as his limousine turned the corner, he would see her shadow in the bay on the second floor.

When she died and he buried her—his wife neither willing nor able to attend the ceremony—he returned to the house for the first time without her at the window. He wandered about that night, at home but not at rest, searching for a remnant of her to keep with him, hungry for the comfort she had always provided. Finally, in his restlessness, he came himself to stand at the window looking out, and placing his hands on the sill where his mother's had so often rested, he found her prints, marks, rather, of all the years of waiting. He spaced his fingers out where hers had been and cried. The next morning, with cloth and cleanser, he tried to remove them, but could not, so he forced his sister into ownership of the house by offering to pay all her expenses if she would move back into the only home they had had as children. Whatever the young woman really wanted to do, as she had a family to raise she had no financial choice but to become owner-resident and provide the homecomings several times a year for her brother, who customarily arrived, briefly kissed his various nieces and nephews, drank a glass of wine, and left—after standing for quiet moments at the second-floor landing.

Virginia found his dead mother too much competition. Her love had been too total, too accepting; it left no room for disagreement or for change, and Mike, exchanging it for Virginia's, could only be disappointed. As the discordant evidence of incompatibility accumulated, since he was a pragmatic businessman who knew you did not ask one supplier to fill all your orders, he began to look around.

Lord knows, Mike's search was not in the dark. Deena Woodard all but lit flares to attract his attention, and Virginia virtually pushed him in her direction. When Mike bought a table for the annual Hearts and Diamonds Ball at the Plaza, one of dozens of the city's opportunities for the rich and elegant to gather for charity and camaraderie, he asked her to help him entertain several of his board members. She begged off, knowing the evening was mainly business—he did not actively need her —frankly preferring a catch-up evening away from him and with the children. It was a mistake. Deena Woodard, who had discarded one husband and buried another, growing progressively wealthier as she did, knew a house unattended was ripe for the robbing. As chairman of this year's ball, she was also privy to the guest list, and when she saw Michael Strange, recent widower, at the head of a table filled with men and their wives with no obvious escort for himself, she rearranged his life along with the seating chart by simply moving his table next to her own, directly under the bandstand. For an ingratiating woman, as socially accomplished as she, the rest was easy. While Virginia sighed with relief to be free of the noise and crowding and customary filet mignon, Deena table-hopped to be sure her paying guests were comfortable, starting and finishing her rounds with Mike. While Virginia managed to give herself a pedicure and move out-of-season clothes to the hall closet, Deena charmingly insisted no man should be without a dancing partner and led a willing lamb to Slaughter on Fifth Avenue. And long after Virginia turned out the light with only the vaguest sense of guilt for having ducked out of a boring evening when she knew Mike really wanted her there, Deena had accepted a dinner invitation from him which she hoped would be even more personally successful than the brilliant evening over which she had just presided.

Any man would have been vulnerable to such a professional selling job because Deena Woodard believed in her product. She had been a truly pretty girl and, with careful daily maintenance amounting to almost a full-time job, she managed to look far younger than her forty to forty-five years—the actual number long ago deleted from the record as non-essential information for anyone but herself. Her body was rigorously dieted, pummeled by massage, denuded by hot wax, and soothed by cool creams. She would not answer the door without her perfume on, and in every part of her small-boned body she felt *feminine*, so when she fixed her large, admiring eyes on a potential customer she was confident of a sale for at least a trial period.

It was actually some time before Virginia knew there was a Deena in his days and nights, not until she absentmindedly skimmed a *Daily News* gossip column which chronicled the livelier activities of New York money. Mike's name appeared in a list of dinner guests who "gathered in delicious Deena Woodard's elegant Park Avenue apartment" to welcome a peripatetic countess on her continental rounds, and though they were not listed together, by the simple process of matching couples, it was evident the hostess had paired herself off for the evening with the "boyishly handsome Matterhorn magnate Michael Strange."

Virginia was not a jealous woman by nature, but curious she was. Habitually indirect, she did not confront Mike with her suspicions, not even when he called the morning of the article's appearance, giving her every opening to ask about what he knew she had read. Instead she asked around, a friend or two, who would be sure to know. The answers were not comforting. "A good-looking girl," they said. "A terrific body," they said. "You'd like her," they said. No, she "didn't do anything." But she had a house in Palm Beach where she spent the winter, and another in Bermuda. A "big organizer," they said, of the American Croquet Association, and the partner everyone wanted, as she generally was found in the semifinals and often accepting the winner's cup.

When Virginia finally met Deena—it was after she and Mike had made their final break—she understood why he had been attracted to her. She resembled the perfectly groomed croquet lawns on which she competed, lush with the controlled growth only expensive fertilizers and insecticides can produce, with edges clipped as meticulously as if with manicuring scissors, where no weed would dare to sprout. No wonder she had taken up croquet. Her thin hips were perfect for the tight white pants, her tiny feet adorable in the white shoes which danced graceful little jigs when she socked her opponent's ball out of bounds.

The game was not the one Virginia remembered children playing on humid Atlanta evenings before the fireflies appeared. It was a strategic match of will and daring requiring more than skill with the costly hand-crafted mallets. To win, players had to be able to foresee the outcome of their actions six or seven moves away, and had to be prepared to rout an opponent decisively at any point in the play. Deena must have thought Virginia a pushover, because the occasional evenings she spent with Mike at first, admittedly innocent, escalated to intimacy without the apparent presence of another interested party.

Where was Virginia? Busy at work, waiting for the phone to ring. Answering when it did as if nothing was amiss, making a date ahead as if Tuesday or Thursday made no difference, whatever was more convenient for him, then wishing the days away until the time came to be with him, desperate to be with him. Keeping her conversation light, avoiding the peril of asking what he was doing on the days she didn't see him, holding him at the end of the evening in their closest moments when she had a reasonable opportunity to admit her fears but even then veering away from the truth.

"Anything on your mind?" she asked, curled in the half-moon of his body. "You seem distant."

"No. Just wish I were as thin as I am spread. Too much going on, too little time," he said, drunk with drowsiness.

She waited much too long before she replied in a quiet voice, "I know," but he was already blowing sleepy puffs into her ear.

By Thanksgiving she should have understood the situation, even without being told, but blinded by the continuity of their time together—even stretched as it was to fewer meetings, farther apart—and not wanting to face reality, she threw herself into holiday plans as if there were everything to celebrate. One night in mid-November he brought charts to her apartment, and with the children at their feet they laid out a zigzag course through the Exumas. After he had gone she suggested sneaking a turkey on board to surprise him. Maggie embroidered the idea to include a fully trimmed Thanksgiving feast, and it was all she could do to keep Max from baking pumpkin pie that evening. Instead they dug out tennis shoes from packed-away summer clothes, and T-shirts and bathing suits, and almost every ensuing dinner conversation one of them had another suggestion for excess baggage—a Scrabble game, fishing gear, a handmade kite to fly off the rear of the boat.

Two days before departure, even as they were piling duffel

bags by the front door, Mike canceled the trip. He had planned to go to Japan right after the holiday anyway, but was called away early. He knew the kids were disappointed, but promised a longer, better trip at Christmas.

The children were devastated by the news, but the young often are unable to rate a future benefit on a par with a present one. Virginia soothed their disappointment, underscoring his promises. She herself was hardly concerned. After all, she traveled with him often and, truthfully, relished the idea of a few quiet days at home, knowing—as adults do—that postponed pleasures are often sweeter.

Max and Maggie were restless during their long weekend off, and complained of nothing to do, but Virginia knew their enthusiasm would return as soon as Mike brought details of the Christmas excursion. In the meantime, she caught up with her bills, cleaned the kitchen cabinets, and took the books out of the shelves in the living room before the painter arrived. She was unprepared for the picture in the Saturday *Times*. The American croquet team had beaten both the Australian and Bermuda teams on the Palm Beach court of Deena Woodard, and spectators who had quietly stood at the perimeter of the afternoon's match noisily toasted the champions during the post-tournament party. Mrs. Woodard and her winning partner were the center of a circle of admirers, the most demonstrative of whom was Michael Strange.

"A fella just can't have any privacy, can he?" she said. Why didn't she leap at him, claw him, beat her fists against the tanned face across the table?

Mike took a long, thoughtful drink of scotch. "Look, Ginny." He reached across the table for her hand, but it was as limp as a newborn puppy and he put it down again. "Don't make a big deal out of it. I *did* have to go to Japan, and when the Palm Beach invitation came, I thought why the hell not spend a night or two in Florida on the way. It was a fun crowd and I got a little sun. It has nothing to do with us, and frankly, that's all there is to say about it."

She looked at him hard and wondered what it would feel like to grab his hair at either temple and smash his head against the banquette.

"Whatever you say. . . . What looks good to you?" she asked, looking down at the menu to stop the coming tears. "Have you tried the lobster here?"

Later, when she silently castigated him for a lack of emotional depth, she also beat up on herself for an unwillingness to fight for what she wanted. A goddamned female victim's mentality was what she had. If called to execution during the French Revolution, she would have driven the cart to the guillotine, placed her head on the block, and signaled the executioner, and if possible she would have mopped up the mess afterward. But she could not confront him, would not speak of her anguish—and thereby knew herself to be a weakling. She also knew you cannot demand loyalty and steadfastness and all the rantings she was incapable of would never, in the last analysis, stop him from doing what he wanted to do.

After dinner Mike gave his driver the usual instructions. "Take us to the Carlyle, Joe."

Imperceptibly Virginia shook her head, and quietly, without realizing the extent of her refusal, changed the course of the car and her future. "No, I want to go home."

Mike hesitated. He waited the way a parent waits for a child, under an icy stare, to repent a particularly silly position. "Take Mrs. Winburn home, Joe," he said finally, and turned cold eyes to the city flowing past his window.

At her apartment he walked her to the elevator. Rendered mute by the things he was not saying to her, deafened by thoughts she could not speak to him, she turned to meet his impenetrable defenses. He was the fortified castle on high ground—the wall high, the moat deep, the drawbridge pulled up tight.

"Anything more you want to say?" he asked matter-of-factly.

"No, except I wish it hadn't happened. I wish you cared more. I wish I didn't hurt so much."

"I told you, it was an unimportant weekend. Frankly, I think you're being childish. I'm sure you'll think it over in the morning and know I'm right."

"Regardless of how much I think about it, Mike, I can't change the fact it *did* happen, or that you find it such a minor incident. You know what's honest, what's fair—you don't need to hear that from me."

"Look, Ginny, no promises were broken, nothing's changed. You mean as much to me as you did before I left—I just had a good time with a friend at a party out of town." He leaned his shoulder against the wall with his hands in his pockets. "That's all."

"You didn't break a promise, because we haven't made any." She thought the obvious needed saying. "You're free to do anything you want to at any time—and so am I. That's why what we do *is* so important. And why I won't feel differently in the morning."

Neither of them moved an inch toward the other. "It's easy to throw hand grenades, Ginny. It's hard to catch them."

She touched his cheek briefly. "Goodbye, Mike."

The stewardess interrupted her reverie, pencil poised, smile in place. "Which would you prefer, chicken Florentine or the New England boiled dinner?"

Virginia chose on the basis of which the airline chefs could damage least and swore again never to leave home without packing a decent meal. With relief she returned to her thoughts and to one substance airlines had not yet found a way to sabotage—straight vodka.

If it was so clear that she and Mike were inappropriate partners, then why the bitterness? Why the satisfaction of knowing that though she clearly wanted the baby for positive reasons, she wanted it also, perversely, for what it might have meant to him?

In the closing weeks of their affair, before she realized that initials in his ever-present daily calendar referred to other women, she had entertained the most preposterous of ideas—that she indeed would have his child. It would be a sort of miracle birth; she would pop the news with the thrill of an exploding champagne cork, and they would celebrate the wonder of their union and produce the unproducible. Now that the miracle had happened, she could not say where desire for the child ended and the need to prove that she could do what no one else had done began. Because she was honest with herself if not with him, she knew the feeling of superiority it gave her was real, and it was cruel.

The plane was rumbling low over a familiar spider's web of major streets, lit by an endless succession of tiny headlights moving through the dark. She pictured her beloved destination below, a comfortable, spacious home, too large now for just the elderly pair who used to fill it with summer gatherings, debut parties, holiday reunions. Once, she remembered, the house held a hundred teen-aged girls on a sleep-over, their pillows and blankets spread on and under the dining table, up the double staircase, on rugs and furniture in every conceivable position. Wooden cases of Coca-Cola, stacked outside the back door, delivered earlier that afternoon, were emptied level by level. The restaurant-sized refrigerator, crammed with whole hams and turkeys, giant bottles of mayonnaise and mustard spreads, stood open most of the night; the contents were dripped fairly evenly around the house. Outside a platoon of boys waged guerrilla warfare on doors and windows closed by Mrs. Cargile's curfew, and horns blew through the night as crowded cars made forays up and down the winding driveway. Except for a screen blown away by a firecracker, the night passed noisily but with no major casualties. Virginia wondered later at her mother's forbearance and good humor, which was a constant, and her efforts to accommodate her daughter's wishes.

Tonight she would turn into grounds lit as if for a reception. Her parents would still be dressed, well past their usual hour to retire. Her brother would be present, called to welcome her home. The cook would have left her favorite brownies layered under foil, her childhood custard cold in the refrigerator. There would be flowers on her night table; her bed, more naturally inviting still than any she had known, would be turned back.

There would be tears in her mother's eyes as she reached to embrace her taller daughter; her father would fold her into his arms with a tenderness and pride she had felt from no other living person. With an arm around her waist, he would walk her into the comfortable library, windows open to the garden and the cooling evening air. She would hear his usual complaints about the business not making the profits it should because of government interference and the goddamned incalcitrant Democrats. She would nod and hold his hand and while she listened look around at the gleam of polished woods, the soft light on Chinese porcelains, the dark bindings of old books. It always amazed her, when she came home, how ordered the world was there, how stable and protected and unchanged. Her mother would find an excuse to lure her away into her bedroom, all pale blue silk with gauzy curtains softening the windows, and she would hear again the endless grumbles about her father. . . .

"He's slipping, Virginia, just slipping away. He's not the same man we've always known. Can you imagine your father wearing a shirt and hanging it back in the closet—hiding it—so Leslie can't find it for the laundry? The same man who once insisted on changing his shirt several times a day!" Virginia never argued, or defended her father. Her mother was looking not for answers but a sympathetic ear.

"He rattles around the kitchen at six in the morning, banging cabinet doors to wake me up so I'll fix his breakfast, and if

I don't, you should see the mess he makes. . . . Never mind his diabetes, he puts sugar on everything, and barely eats his dinner, just dessert. What *will* I do with him? Just yesterday I found him on the roof—eighty-one, and on the roof!—cleaning out the gutters. He doesn't want to spend an extra nickel now if he can help it, and this is the man who always carried a roll of hundred-dollar bills! Now I know you don't like to hear me talk about your father, Virginia, but if you were just here to see . . ."

The litany rarely varied. Her parents' complaining remarks about life and each other were a prewritten script, repeated at every visit as if she had not heard it before. At each recitation she listened as if she never had, and made the commiserating noises they expected.

This time she did not really listen. Instead she watched the loose skin shiver beneath her mother's chin and her thinning once-gold hair reflect a silver light. She stared at puffs newly formed beneath her eyes and needlelike lines pointing toward her lips. She nodded to move the grievances along and wondered why her mother did not complain instead that her classic English face had developed ridges and hollows and her perfect skin the defacing marks of age. Why she did not rail about her loss of strength and the end of her life which stood so blatantly before her now. Virginia was grateful the reasons for her mother's distress were so answerable.

"You won't believe what he did yesterday—out behind the tool shed, where we pile wood. He stood where he thought he was out of sight lifting a log so heavy it would have knocked him out if he'd dropped it, over and over above his head till I was sure he'd have a heart attack, his face was so red. Eighty-one, Virginia . . . you have no idea what I go through . . ."

Her mother's gentle voice pursued her recriminations, scarcely pausing to place a comma between items, as if welcoming the chance to present the official list of his offenses to an empathic magistrate.

When had roles reversed, Virginia becoming the parent, her mother the child? Somewhere back in the teens when an adolescent overshot her mother's tiny frame, and her mother let go the hand of the child and accepted a supporting arm under the elbow. It was there still. She drove her mother's car pools, chose her elegant hats, planned her menus for dinner parties—and waited for the inevitable applause. Confidence placed in her judgment was so complete she found no reason to doubt it herself.

Even now she handled, long-distance, her mother's health problems and her relationships within the family, and mediated her father's obstinate ways. "You're the only one who can do anything with him." The often-repeated statement obliterated the truth, that her mother declined to challenge him or attempt to change his mind herself—why should *she* do battle when Virginia was available as surrogate soldier? Because her father was a reasonable man and held none of the resentments against her that he reserved for his wife, and because there was enough unquestioned love between them to negotiate any superficial lack of understanding, most problems were concluded in a way that left neither feeling exploited.

Virginia had been a novelty—the first female born to her father's family in three generations—and he relished her company, singling her out for day trips to the family farm, where they crossed the cotton rows, stooping occasionally to crumble the earth to test its moisture. She tripped along behind as he traversed pastures counting every cow, checking the newborn, and listened as he added the clusters: "Fifteen and thirty-two, that's forty-seven, and six is fifty-three. Twenty-three more in the bottoms, that's seventy-six, four in the feed lot is eighty, means we're missing two." And they would retrace their steps until the strays were located, examined, and smacked on the rear in greeting.

He was a possessive man about his earth, his animals, his business, his girl-child. His wife was the glue that stuck his world together, but she was not of it—necessary, functional, but not prized like his daughter, who without effort won the acceptance her mother never achieved. "If you had only been a boy . . ." He would shake his huge head in regret and she would shake hers as they wordlessly pictured the partnership if only the family sign could have read "Cargile and Daughter."

The son he wanted was not the son he got. Perhaps because of a stubborn insistence on dominating his kingdom, there was no room at court for an aspiring prince. Everett Jr. was the recipient of a father's name and jealousy. The more the father resented his wife's attention to her firstborn, the more he pushed his son away. The tiny boy was punished—instead of his mother—for the slightest insubordination; was beaten—instead of his mother—for the tiniest sign of rebellion. Father and son grew apart as the child grew up until there was nothing left between them but the woman they had fought over, a father's guilt, and a sister who received the approbation the son would never know. Brighter than she but not as political, more needful of affection yet less appealing a child, he ground his rejection inside and spewed out hateful behavior. He could not attack his father physically (though years later the men, mirror images of one another, squared off, the fine Kerman carpet for a ring and two hysterical women for referees trying to call the fight before real damage was done), so instead he taunted his sister. Once she kept a pet, a field mouse rescued from the swimming pool which would have drowned had she not swished it ashore with the flat of a broom. She converted a packing crate into a cage, covering the top with screening, and built a cart of playing cards for Mighty Mouse to pull. Sometimes she tied her mother's needlepoint yarn in a bow around his neck and walked him on a leash. She brought Mighty scraps from her dinner plate each night and let him run beneath her covers when her mother turned out the light. One day Ev Jr. walked in as she was changing the grass in the box and picked up Mighty by the tail. "What's this nasty animal doing on the floor?" he said. "Watch, everyone, what we do with filthy things," and he flushed him down the toilet. She grew to hate him early on, and even when she was old enough to understand why he acted as he did, she found him hard to forgive.

Everett Jr. paid his father back. He did not finish college or go into his father's business or remain single until he had established himself. He did not even remain entirely sane. His nerves gave way at the same time his strung-out franchise operation collapsed, bringing to family friends who were unfortunate investors losses so heavy that his father's humiliation was complete. The breakdown allowed the son to return to his most comfortable position, clinging to his mother for protection again while he raged at the absence of his father's acceptance. Virginia marveled at the reestablishment of old patterns and secretly admitted the fortuity of her husband's transfer, which placed her 1,400 miles away from daily participation in the melodrama of their lives.

"Let's join your father and Ev Jr. in the library," her mother said, "or he'll think I'm talking about him behind his back."

Where would he ever get that idea? Virginia mouthed to herself as she picked up their coffee cups and followed her mother's delicate step down the oriental carpet in the hall past portraits of herself and Ev and a gallery of grandchildren's baby pictures in matching frames. Soon an addition would hang there. The cups suddenly rattled in her hands; she had to tell them now and she shook with stage fright.

Virginia had not experienced a fearful moment in front of her parents since her father discovered her in a lie at the age of sixteen when she disobeyed orders and spent a weekend at the University of Alabama. Then he stomped and growled as she quaked at his fury, vowing never to repeat the sin. She meant it. The price of detection was more than she was physically able to pay—shaky mouth betraying her, legs giving way beneath her weight. It was far easier to live virtuously, so the

temptations of her teen-aged friends held no appeal. Steal the
car? Drink liquor? Slip out after hours or date the gas station
attendant—and have *him* find out? She knew, as a small child,
that God watched her every move and knew if she stole a quarter from her mother's purse or a lipstick from the dime store;
and she was certain that her father, like Superman looking
through walls, had X-ray vision into her mind. Now, a middle-
aged woman, experienced, self-assured, mature, she entered her
father's library and felt a puerile desire to flee.

Virginia met his doting eyes and looked away, making an
elaborate act of rearranging needlepoint pillows on the deep
sofa. He and Ev Jr., standing by the mantel arguing choices for
the coming season's football teams, broke off their conversation
when the women arrived. Ev pulled up a Hepplewhite chair;
her father sat next to her, as he always did. He could hear her
better and touch her arm or knee with his index finger as he
made his points, but mostly he liked being close so they could
monopolize each other. His hand folded over hers, she
squeezed it, inhaled audibly, and in a voice that sounded half
an octave higher than usual said, "You may wonder, my dears,
why I've brought you all together. . . ."

Open-eyed faces turned in anticipation. No, Mom, I can't
announce a marriage to a prominent, successful churchgoing
Protestant—though that's what you hope to hear, Virginia
thought, looking at her trusting face. And no, Ev Jr., I can't report I'm a failure and slinking home for resuscitation, though
that might bring you comfort. And, Dad, I've no partnership to
discuss with you, no praise from Wall Street wizards.

She opened and closed her lips several times, wet them, bit
them, forced a smile, and said it: "The old girl's going to have
a baby!"

The same look appeared on all three faces: confusion. Had
they heard? Did they understand? Virginia embellished the
news with forced enthusiasm. "Can you believe *that*, a baby—
at my advanced age? Well, why not? Since it's the one thing I

do with unqualified success . . . and it's been too long now without a little one in the family . . . someone has to make baby-sitters out of you two again." She was rambling, rather madly. "Time to get the old cradle out of the attic. Do you suppose we still have sheets to fit, Mom? Or shall we have some made?"

Her father interrupted her ranting, quietly smiling through his perplexity. "Are you telling us you're married, honey? To whom? Do we know him?"

"Will you move back to Atlanta?" her mother asked, suddenly hopeful. "Have you told the children?"

"Hey, Virginia"—Ev's heartiness overrode his parents—"that's one way to get attention . . ."

All three were talking over one another, surprised, not comprehending. It gave her a moment to control her breathing. She untangled her fingers from her father's, and with both hands covered her eyes and rocked gently in place.

"No . . . whoa"—laughing again—"who said anything about marriage? I'm just bringing you glad tidings about something that will arrive next spring along with the tulips. Everyone's going to have a new name on their Christmas list, so see that you give lavishly . . ."

Confusion turned dark with disbelief. "Darling." Her mother fumbled for the words. "Are you saying you will not *be* married? Or that you haven't *yet* married?"

"There won't be any marriage, Mom."

The room was stunningly quiet, until her mother broke the silence with almost a whisper. "I'm not sure I understand that. How can you have a child without a father? Who *is* the father? This sounds like some terrible April Fool's joke . . . I don't know whether to laugh or cry."

Virginia reached for her mother's hand, but it remained lifeless at her side. "I knew this would be difficult for you, Mom, that's why I wanted to come home to tell you. It isn't easy for me either, but I'll try to explain without going into a lot of needless details.

"The father's a wonderful man—who meant a great deal to me. You don't know him, but"—an ironic smile—"believe me, you'd approve. I found I was pregnant after it was all too clear we'd never work out a permanent relationship. Oh, hell—how I hate the word 'relationship'! So clinical, and it doesn't describe what we were—or almost were—to each other and covers up the disappointment—the misery—I felt when it was over. But it *is* over, and I'm pregnant. That leaves two choices, doesn't it? To have the baby or not to have the baby."

"It leaves only one reasonable choice," Ev broke in gently.

"That's the practical approach. I thought that too at first, and almost 'disposed' of the problem, as they say, which is another clinical expression for almost getting rid of Maggie and Max's brother or sister, my child, your grandchild, another member of the Cargile family, a human being, a child with a life now and a future later. A person with dreams and possibilities who'll someday raise his or her own family. Who may save a stranger's life, or change our country's history or the way humankind thinks or acts. Who *knows* what this child's life will mean to others, or what vast scheme would be upset without it here? Cosmic thoughts are too much for me. I have to reduce the situation to a level I can comprehend. I want this child. Because I loved its father and because I already, in the most profound way, love it too."

Her mother's voice was just as remote. "But alone, Virginia? How can you have a child alone?"

"Don't you think I've considered the repercussions? Forgetting the social implications, I expect the physical and financial obligations alone will be formidable, but when was anything of value easily come by? Mag and Max have been the greatest joys of my life—and the greatest burdens. Should I not have had them? Why shouldn't the next twenty years be better *with* this child than without it—whatever the sacrifice?"

"But what will be its name? Winburn? It's not Jim's child. Cargile? It's not your father's. What do you tell our friends? How can it be baptized at church? I wouldn't know how to write it into the family Bible . . ." She had begun to cry softly. "It's the shame, Virginia, the shame of it . . ."

"Well, the family can handle a little shame." Ev spoke over his mother's whimpers. "After all, it's dealt with me on occasion. But aren't you taking on more than *you* can handle?"

"Raising a child—under any circumstances—is problematical," Virginia answered, searching desperately for the right words to calm their fears. "You need a strong heart and lots of luck. But the petty details, Mom, are as unimportant as the color we paint the nursery. It's what kind of person that child becomes, what kind of chance it has in life—that's what's important! This will be *my* child, whatever its name, and your grandchild. As for the Church, your blessed Jesus made quite a name for Himself and there's been some question about *His* paternity too."

"That's not funny."

"Well, I meant it to be." Virginia tried to lighten her mother's mood. "I don't want you looking only at the difficulties this child will bring and not see the delights. Heavens! When Maggie was born Jim and I didn't have an extra nickel! We never would have had her—or Max—if we'd waited for the perfect moment. And what was I thinking of—having those children so close together? But, Mom, is there ever a perfect time to have a child? When there are no problems? Dad, darling, help me now. As much as you love babies around the house, aren't you pleased to know there's another coming?"

Her father, as usual, had remained impassive during the emotional outburst, leaving the infighting to the troops. As General he would dispense final commands and ultimata in his own time; for now, he wished only to express his bewilderment.

"I can'ta flabbaflotto seea . . ." He squeezed shut his eyes, gritted his teeth, and began again. "How can yaba flibbatobba soma . . ."

"Dad!" Virginia sat back and looked at him aghast.

"He's doing it again, Mom." Ev leaned forward in his chair as if to catch his father.

"Dad!" she repeated, disbelieving. "Mom, what's the matter with him? Dad? Say that again!"

The aging but strong gentleman, grabbing for his dignity once more, turned to look his daughter full in the face with clear, purposeful eyes but spoke again in horrifyingly undecipherable language—phrases that sounded as if they should be real but weren't.

"Don't youcanorama shabba donna . . ." His fists doubled on his knees.

Virginia flinched visibly, recoiling from her father, who sat so close looking desperately at her now for understanding. As he recited his gibberish he was absolutely aware he made no sense. Despairing, she looked to her mother for explanation but found only terror in her face too.

"It's happening again—another spell. Ev Jr., what do we do?" she said softly, staring at her husband but not touching him.

Face alert, the man continued to babble, gesturing strongly as if to force comprehension from his audience. Ev, speaking about him as if he could not hear, explained to Virginia, "This has happened before, several times, we don't know why. He seems to be off in his own world, speaking his own language, wondering why we don't understand him."

Virginia screamed suddenly at her family. "He's having a stroke, can't you see?" She leapt from the sofa, almost overturning the coffee table, cups and ashtrays spilling to the floor. She dived for the telephone across the room, yelling over her shoulder at Ev to pull his car to the door and at her mother for the number of their long-time family doctor, then seeing the traumatizing effect of her own hysterics on her mother, caught herself, calmed her voice, and asked again, almost icily, for the number or street address.

"Iroquois, Natchez, I can't remember," her mother answered, nearly catatonic.

The indulgence had been momentary. Virginia's feeling of being dependent, protected, and cared for in her childhood home faded in the emergency, and spinning back up to speed, she found herself once again in charge. She established with an information operator the numbers of the doctor's home and answering service while clinically watching her father flail away at some hidden mental impediment, some impassable obstacle that blocked his ability to communicate. Her fingers shook slightly, but she resolutely dialed first one and then the other, giving orders in between for her mother to pack a few necessaries and her father to rest quietly without moving. Years of giving commands made them her willing functionaries. By the time she finished speaking to the doctor, Ev had the car at the front of the house, her mother had an overnight bag, and she had her father in her arms, protesting still in fluttering language, at once embarrassed and submissive, surprised and frightened, but grateful for assistance, knowing the infirmity was beyond his control.

The race to the hospital was against a stopwatch clicked on without warning or announcement, and ticking now with no clue when it might abruptly stop. As Ev hurtled through empty streets, Virginia heard from her mother how often the affliction had come upon him recently, and how temporarily incapacitated he seemed. Virginia had no medical education—none. But she recognized changes so severe, so inexplicable they could not be attributed to age or brandy. Her father, erect beside her in the car, was apparently healthy to the eye, but behind the controlled, intelligent face devastation was soundlessly wrecking his brain.

The race ended at the emergency room. Because of the doctor's call, a stretcher was ready, attendants on alert, and incredibly complicated paraphernalia so alien to the average experience there to receive and swallow up a strong-willed, indomitable man who had never recognized physical incapacities in himself or anybody in his family. He had signaled away her own minor complaints with simple statements: "You do *not* have a headache," "You may *not* let yourself have a cold," as if denying were all that was necessary to conquer the body's fragility. Indeed, for him at least, it generally was.

Now humans gave up and machines took over. Three members of a family who had performed every imaginable function for the fourth over a span of fifty years were suddenly useless, inadequate—unless prayers made a difference. Silent hours of the night settled in upon the hospital, a ship of misery, full of unwilling passengers sailing for their very lives. Doctors and their tests, needles, sedatives, and anti-clogging drugs became the new determinants of his fate. A seemingly strong, healthy individual was suddenly prone, spouting tubes, useless as an automobile hoisted on a rack above the ground with no assurance at all repair was possible.

The night was long but merciful. Morning allowed the possibility of surgery, if the blockage could be discovered in time, which would restore oxygen to his brain and him to life again, for Everett Cargile was barely alive now, the deathblow restrained by miracle drugs and the force of their combined will. "It isn't his time," Virginia whispered to her mother during the early-morning watch. "I'm not ready to lose him yet."

Wrestling the angel of death to the ground drained the watchers' life forces too. Three exhausted but grateful people left the hospital in the first gray light, holding each other for strength, feeling the precariousness of their own existence as they contemplated his, going home to find clean clothes and renewed hope before returning to the ultimate battle for his life.

In the car her mother's voice was so soft at first she did not comprehend the words. "The stroke, Virginia. You brought it on, you know. He just couldn't bear your dreadful news."

Thursday, August 14

Long after her return to the city—after the suspenseful CAT scan; after the terrible moment holding her father's hand perhaps for the last time, wishing him health and pledging him love while attendants separated her from the stretcher; after hearing her father whisper as he was wheeled through the swinging doors, "All good things come to an end"; after tears of fear and then of joy, anxious hours monitoring intensive-care machinery, reports from doctors, sudden appearances of friends; after hot champagne in paper cups, short fitful nights of sleep; after all the things one does in a crisis and later remembers—what Virginia brought away were her mother's words "your dreadful news."

Her New York life had shut down for twelve days. As if in punishment for being away, the city beat back at her from the first moment home. The carousel circled endlessly before careening baggage toward the weary travelers; the queue for taxis was a penance in the summer sun. Her jolting cab seemed

to play Dodg'em in reverse along the parkway, hunting potholes at maniacal speed. Watching the filthy roadside flash by,
Virginia imagined the disillusionment of first-time visitors who
saw the city's back yard before they found the front door. The
Triborough Bridge's high-reaching scallops reminded her of the
grandeur of New York, but when she turned left to see the familiar saw-toothed skyline, thick fetid air obscured the view.
Eight million people, she knew, had awakened to radios and
television sets announcing: "The air quality today is unacceptable," as if the telling allowed them the option of leaving
their noses at home. Traffic snarls produced the usual drivers'
obscenities, always more numerous when heat and humidity
oppressed. She closed her eyes and leaned against the hot plastic, sweat rolling down her back, until a final jerk brought the
rattling auto to a blessed stop.

"Welcome home, Mrs. Winburn." The doorman lifted her
luggage from the trunk and led her through the midday quiet
of the lobby. Her heels clicked across the tiled floor.

"Any mail or packages, Carlos?"

Carlos appeared not to have heard, intent instead on attracting the attention of a man drowsing on the lobby sofa, a magazine lying limply across his knees.

"Carlos . . . ?"

"Oh . . . yes, a pile of 'em. I'll send them right up." As they
passed he made eye contact with the man, who barely nodded
in return. "And how was the trip, Mrs. Winburn?" He spoke
rather loudly, emphasizing her name as he placed her bags in
the elevator.

The elevator operator, in turn, lifted them through the last
portal of her journey and she was home. She walked across the
stifling living room—almost shabby compared to where she had
been—and flicked on the lifesaving cool of the air conditioner.
Glancing out the window, she again saw the magazine reader,
this time on the sidewalk thrusting money at Carlos with one
hand while flagging a cab with the other. Something made her

stop and watch until he drove away, something about his haste and about his face which was—what?—familiar.

The apartment was musty, her mail in heaps, flowers long dead in their containers. Her plants cried out for water, the answering machine was clogged with messages, her clothes required unpacking and separating for laundry and cleaning. Her sense of order was in wild disarray, so many chores competing for attention; nevertheless, she paused briefly as if to cross herself and say out loud, "Thank God the children are still in Colorado."

She made an obligatory call to the office, though she had been in constant touch during her absence, and was assured Peabody Slocum continued to function somehow without her and would until tomorrow; then she waded into the tasks around her, culling, sorting, putting away, cleaning out, beginning again the interminable lists that organized her life.

The ring of the apartment intercom was an unwelcome distraction. "Damn." Dropping the lid of the washing machine, cranking the dial to start it, with the other hand she lifted the phone from the kitchen wall. "Yes, Carlos?"

"Mr. Strange is here to see you."

She didn't answer because the announcement had no reality. "What's that, Carlos?"

"Mr. Strange. He's coming up."

The phone went dead. She stood foolishly holding it as if for clarification, realizing nothing except that her blood seemed to have dropped toward the floor. In sixty or ninety seconds Mike would knock at her door. Impossible. Three-thirty on a Thursday afternoon. For godsakes, why? No, too much. No preparation. She needed time before she could be with him, time to put up her defenses, to mask her insecurities. It was a mistake. She had misheard.

He knocked.

"Mike!" The sight of him always thumped her breath away.

"You all right?" He barely grazed her cheek as he leaned to

kiss her, hardly hesitating as he walked to the middle of the room and turned. "Your dad's going to make it, isn't he?"

"Yes, we had a miracle. Thanks for the flowers—they were glorious. The arrangement was so huge it could have covered a coffin—thank God it didn't have to." She felt small as he passed by, remembered she was in her house slippers and hated them, also a wrinkled shirt and jeans and her hair was behind her ears; then remembered it didn't matter anymore how she looked to him today or any day. "What in the world are you doing here?"

"Just checking on you." He looked at her curiously. "Wanted to see how you are, if there's anything I can do."

"Come on now. The entire electronics industry comes to a halt if Strange goes to pee. What's up?"

Mike dropped into the largest armchair in the room and pulled a cigarette and lighter from his jacket, but looked up suddenly and asked, "Mind if I smoke?"

"Course not," she said, surprised at a question he had never asked before.

His gold Cartier lighter clicked and he sucked in heavily. "What do you have to drink, any coffee made?" Even in her living room he was preeminent, taking it over as naturally as he did his boardroom.

"Just made some iced tea. Will that do?"

The welcome moments in the kitchen allowed her to collect herself as well as their drinks; the unexpected sight of him had drained away her control. She was suddenly as vulnerable with Mike there as in the past and realized how emotionally unprepared she was for spending the rest of her life without him. At the sight of him, her resolve grew mushy. She found it hard to remember the pertinent cause and effect that put such distance between them: that because she was to have his child and he must never know, she was consigned to Solitary, which was eternity without his company. Perhaps, even as she reminded herself, she did not believe it was true.

Unwilling to trust the steadiness of her hands, Virginia placed the wicker tray before him in such a way he had to take his own glass, then sat on the opposite armchair, threw one foot across the other knee in the most nonchalant manner she could manage, began rolling up the sleeves of her shirt, and asked again, "So what brings you here?"

Mike picked up his glass, put it down again, and reached for a cigarette though one was burning on an ashtray before him.

My God, she thought, he's nervous too.

He leaned so far across the coffee table toward her there seemed almost none of him left on the chair. "I want to talk about the baby." His face was without expression but his eyes were shiny-bright.

"What baby?" Virginia sat frozen, stunned.

"Shelby told me. Our baby." He half stood as if to start toward her. She held her arm straight out before her.

"Stay there, don't move. Shelby told you *what?*" Stall, delay. Don't panic.

"Thought you'd never get home. Did you see my man downstairs? He's been on watch here twelve, fourteen hours a day . . ."

"Of course! I knew I knew that face."

". . . waiting for you. And for the last few days I've kept your boss, a bank president, and the entire corporate management of what I hope is our next acquisition on hold so I could be here as soon as you arrived." The unruffleable was ruffled. Talking fast, tripping over his sentences, gesturing widely with his hands, Michael Strange allowed a smile to stretch his face which would have perfectly suited the owner of a team that had just won the World Series. "And I'm the happiest guy in America."

"Now hold on, Mike."

"Hold on, hell. We've got too much to do." He was expansive now. "Have to plan the wedding, we'll need a new apartment, big enough for us and your kids, the baby, a nurse, I sup-

pose, as well as my couple. God, I can't count, is that six or
seven bedrooms? We have to decide how to tell our friends,
whether we want a party . . ." He was pacing the living room,
counting the chores on his fingers. "And we should plan a trip,
something wonderful to celebrate, if you feel like it." He suddenly stopped, contrite. "But I haven't even asked, how do you
feel?"

"Mike, please, I'm in shock. Sit down and tell me again,
slowly. Shelby told you . . ."

"Simple, that we're having a baby. She didn't want you carrying all the responsibility alone, not knowing how to tell me,
so she did what any friend would do."

"Fool."

"C'mon. Don't be mad at her. If we had any sense we
wouldn't need intermediaries, but we'll fix that. She's done us
a favor, shortcutting a lot of unnecessary complications we
haven't time for. I can reschedule some business trips as soon as
I know when you can get away and when we can be married."

"Us, married?"

"Of course, us married. You're sure, aren't you? About the
baby? Want to wait for another confirmation from the
doctor?"

"And if the report comes back negative—it was all a mistake
—the wedding's off?"

"Well . . . is there any doubt?"

"Answer the question," she demanded. "No baby, no wedding, right?"

Mike knew better than to say anything.

"Should I have the doctor sign an affidavit? Want it nota-
rized? I could send it over to your lawyers before we get a license."

"Ginny, don't." Mike had not anticipated the conversation's
turn. His game plan had called for the shock of surprise to
wither away residual disappointments he knew held over from
their breakup. She wouldn't expect a suggestion of marriage.

He even surprised himself when he first thought of it, considering the way they had ended. He wasn't a man who accepted rejection, even with cause, and had preferred to punish her by walking out rather than alter his behavior. The way he was, goddamnit, or not at all! Had his mother ever expected him to change? Didn't his enormous success prove his way won out? But he knew her resistance ran deep, and would require a solution carefully balanced between pragmatism and idealism if he were to claim the prize—incredible! unexpected!—of his own child.

Then, the more he thought about it, the less marriage seemed a tactic from which he could retreat to the more likely position of distant, supporting father figure, and the more it became an idea that suited him—no, *pleased* him. Sure, marry, why not! They'd work out their differences. He'd have to learn to deal with her intractability—hell, old-fashioned stubbornness—but he could do that. Probably wasn't the easiest fellow to get along with himself. Yes, marriage. Answered all the needs, would be the best gift he could give the newborn, and would be the perfect method of shortcutting her reservations.

But the plan wasn't working now . . .

"That's the deal, isn't it?" She nodded her head as if with new comprehension. "It's a contract: I give you a baby, you give me a ring. Where do I sign, Mike?"

"It's not a contract, it's a proposal."

Virginia laughed softly. "Is that what proposals sound like these days? No more bended knees? No protestations of love? No discussion of fidelity? Suppose the baby's born dead, or deformed, is the contract voided? After all, you know the law—no consideration, no contract."

"That's unreasonable. We're two adults who know each other very well, not kids who met a couple of weeks ago who think life and romance is what they see in the movies."

"Maybe I am being unreasonable"—she lowered her voice, which had risen a note with each question—"because I'm not following you, so explain to me again why you and I should get married. I don't remember coming to you with such a request. Nor have I asked for any help in raising my child."

"*Our* child. And you shouldn't have to ask. It's yours by rights."

"Suppose I don't want it."

"But that's ridiculous." Mike sat back fully in his chair, taken back by the unexpectedly hostile reaction to what he had convinced himself was not only the most desirable option but, indeed, their only option. "You can't bring up a child alone, it's too great a burden, and why should you? Here's a father— Jesus, I never thought I'd be able to use that word—who can't wait to walk the floor at night, or whatever the hell it is that fathers do, who wants to change diapers and warm bottles, push a carriage in the park, buy a football, begin a collection of children's books, enroll him in the best schools—now! so there's no way he won't get in, buy a gymnasium, goddamnit, if that's what it takes—and start right away to give him a sister. Hell, let's have four, eight, twelve. Whatever the traffic can bear—or the mom. But let's get this child started off right, and that means with two of us taking care of him."

"That's not the way I want it."

Mike stared at her. "What do you mean?"

"I mean any child I have, *I* have. And take care of. Alone."

"Without a father?"

"Without outsiders in my life."

Mike still didn't understand. "How can you call me, the father of your unborn child, an *outsider*?"

"What else, Mike? Where've you been the last six months when I was blue, or sick, needing advice and comfort, or just looking for someone to take a walk with? I talk to my butcher more than I talk to you, and come to think of it, he makes more of an effort for me. I'm not punishing you for not being around; there wasn't any reason to be. We don't mean to each other what we did, so you were justified in being distant, it was honest and defensible. What isn't is this crass and highly demeaning attitude: now-that-you-are-pregnant-honey-I'll-make-believe-I-care."

"When have you and I not cared about each other, Ginny? Was the baby conceived in anger or bitterness? Without affection? Sure, we've had our differences, and we've pushed each other away. You had reasons—I prefer to call them insecurities—to keep your distance, and I've always had a tendency to move on when things didn't go my way. But there's something new to consider—the whole is more than two parts. We're three people now with a natural bond that transcends petty differences. You and I have a responsibility to each other and to the child, each of us bringing to the deal what we can deliver. You can deliver the child, and give him love, counsel, strength of character. I can give some intangibles too, but I can also offer plenty of financial security and the emotional security that comes from having two parents in the home. I want that for this child, Ginny, a stable home based on the best we both have to offer."

"A stable home—based on a business arrangement? How healthy an atmosphere is it when a father is jetting around the world with God-knows-whom, keeping in touch with his wife through his secretary? You don't want a wife, you want a nanny. This isn't a love child; this is a corporate merger. No, thanks, Mike. Not for all your respectability, all your money, all the stability you have to offer." Virginia lowered her voice, which had risen to a strained pitch again. "Funny. Once there was a time when women got married *just because* they were pregnant. Now I'm saying I can't marry you *just because* I'm pregnant. Seems we've come a ways after all."

Mike stood, his brow knotted in frustration. He was too competitive to lose easily, especially before he had tried every strategy. She watched him slowly circle the room, tapping the bookcases absentmindedly as he passed, stopping to rub an infinitesimal ash into the rug, his hands in his pockets, his jaws grinding. The ticking of the Victorian mantel clock was suddenly the loudest sound in the room.

He sat on the arm of her chair. "Ginny"—touching her gently under her chin, turning her face to him—"I haven't been for you what I can be. Now I have reason to be. Give me the chance to prove that." His huge head moved toward hers, but she stopped it in mid-descent, almost frantically. She knew she could not handle his affection. His anger, yes, and his capacity to overwhelm. His brutal self-interest. But not his affection.

"You'd better go, Mike."

"Suppose I said I'm not ever going."

"Please leave, Mike. This discussion never should have been held in the first place. Thanks to Shelby, we are putting each other through misery—at least, that's what I am feeling."

"Let me tell you what I am feeling." Mike moved suddenly to the sofa, which was placed at right angles to her chair. Their knees touching, he took both her hands in his with a fierceness reflected in his words.

"I'm far from certain what I want most of the time. I'm as wobbly as a seesaw, coming down first on one side, then on the other. I want to be head of the largest communications conglomerate in the country, then I want to hide away and write a book, or run a foundation, or buy a small ailing business of my own and bring it back to life. I like the notoriety I receive from *Business Week* and *Forbes*—and I want my privacy. I want to make another ten million and I want to chuck it all and live a simple life on a mountaintop. I am riddled with ambivalence—most of the time. But not now. I want to be a father to this child and a husband to his mother more than anything I have wanted in my forty-nine years. I wasn't much of a husband before—but there was no anchor for my ship then. I got damned little encouragement—and we weren't a family. Have you any idea what it takes out of you to admit that you cannot ever do what everybody else takes for granted? The frustration of always listening to other people chatter about their children while you're locked out of the conversation? In a way, I know how the 'coloreds' felt in the South, told to drink out of other water fountains, to use other toilets. It has to do with being different, not good enough, not quite equal. Now, because of you, and because of what we have together, that's changed."

Mike had a way of looking at people, using their eyes as windows, so he could see right into their minds. Virginia, feeling her resolve slipping, knowing how vulnerable she was to this forceful man, reached back hard for the pain she had lived through the past year, and more, for the bitterness she had felt at his neglect. He had the power to inflict wounds that would not heal. She needed to remember now, and she did.

"I'm sorry, Mike, terribly sorry you've never had children of your own, both for your sake and the sake of kids who would've had a great dad. But you can't have my child without me, and the truth is—if you'll face it—you want the doll, but not the package. And as much as I agree that a child is better off with two parents, if possible, I can't give this child a father without marrying a man who doesn't really love me, and I've come too far, Mike, finding out who I am and what I want—and what I need—to settle for less. If you had loved me, really loved me, we would have been married *before* this child was conceived. Now, I ask you again, because I'm not strong when you're around—my mind gets fuzzy with too many emotions—please, Mike, leave me alone now."

Mike dropped her hands in a fury, stalked away from the sofa, and stood looking out the window. Finally, he turned, and in the coldest voice she had ever heard him use, said, "What you want then is a limited partner, right? Someone to put up the money, support the business, but have no say in how it's run."

"Mike!"

"What else? You have Jim Winburn sending support checks for Max and Maggie. Now you'll have mine. Get enough out of me and you'll be able to live pretty nearly as you wish. All the benefits of being married, none of the responsibilities."

Now as angry as he, Virginia interrupted him in a near-shriek. "Good God, is money everything to you? Is *that* what you think I want from you—or ever wanted from you? Does everything in your life come with a price tag? If that's what you're thinking, then why walk in here proposing marriage at all? Get right to the deal. What you want is the child, not the mother, and she's a reasonable woman. Make her an offer, Mike, make her an offer."

"Whatever you say it's worth." He said the words very slowly.

They made her crazy. If she had been looking for final punishment from him to convince her she was right, she found it. "It! It! This is not an 'it,' Mike. A child, a person, a he, a she—not an 'it.' A soul, a mind, a human being, and there is no price for 'it.' Money enough hasn't been coined to buy this baby." The veins on her neck stood out as blood rushed to her face.

Her words whipped him to a towering rage. Crossing toward her, lips pulled back against his teeth, grabbing her shoulders in a mean grip, he shook her as he talked, less to hurt her than to restrain himself from hurting her more. His words did that. "Money didn't make this child, God damn you, I did. It's my child and will be until it dies, and your stiff arm holding me off doesn't push away the reality that I—AM—ITS—FATHER. Hear it! Get used to it! If you can't deal with that simple statement of fact, then the courts will teach you how. Get ready to fight, lady, because I want what's mine, and every lawyer in town I can buy with my dirty money, every string I can pull, every pressure I can bring to bear until you understand that, I'll use against you."

Neither of them—two decent people—was quite human. Virginia jerked herself free. "Get out of my house, Mike, and take this with you. This is *my* baby, mine alone. You will never see him grow up. Never hold his hand, never teach him to catch a ball. He will never follow you into your professional world, never collect your riches or your power. He will never, if I can help it, ever hear your name. As for your courts, for all the women through the ages who were desperate for help, whose lives were ruined by liars who looked judges in the face and said, 'Your honor, I never saw that woman before in my life,' count on this, Mike: for all those women who couldn't prove the paternity of their children, I'm going to look your judge in the face and say, 'I never saw that man before in my life'!"

Mike threw her hard into the chair in order to move past and stalked to the door. Halfway there he stopped, turning toward her again. Instinctively she braced, physically afraid of him for the first time. He saw it and stayed his distance.

"You. The high-minded one. Who sets values and priorities and insists that others live up to them. Where is honor now, and fairness? Where is just knowing what's right, and doing it?" He wasn't listening for an answer. "And why is what *you* want all that matters?" He reached for the door. "You think you're prepared to fight for this child? Keep your gloves on, lady. This is just round one."

Virginia knew what it meant to be alone and lonely, but had never before felt alone and beleaguered. Fury receded rapidly into fear, then welled again to unadulterated anger—at him, at Shelby, at herself for arriving at such a preposterous position. In an instant her life-enhancing, optimistic plans were perverted; her energies drained into an acrimonious duel with the one person in the world she felt least equipped to fight.

At least she had a scapegoat, a target on whom to detonate the emotional bomb pounding in her head.

"Shelby Anderson, please."

"Sorry, not here," the mechanical voice sang out.

"Ask her to call Virginia Winburn, will you? Tell her it's urgent."

First she would dump her angry feelings of betrayal, her aggravation at the unnecessary complications her friend had caused—and then she would reach out for counsel and the solid support that had seen her through other crises. God knows, Shelby knew what adversity was, she almost thrived on it. She was like the dandelion, tough and hardy as it struggled for space in the grass, defying efforts to eradicate it, but unable to prosper when farmed in neat rows, lovingly furnished with fertilizer, carefully tended to produce a crop of greens.

Trouble, actually, had brought them together. Jim Winburn and Ned Anderson, fraternity brothers at Washington and Lee, drank and clowned their way through the other's wedding as boutonniered groomsmen celebrating the southern flower each had picked as bride. Bound by circumstances, Virginia and Shelby accepted each other as instant friends, becoming acquainted—even close—as they followed their husbands into freezing duck blinds, football stadiums, and weekend house parties.

The Andersons lived nearby in Newman, Georgia, a town known for having more money per capita than any in the United States, a dubious distinction perhaps, but the reason their early years were not marred by financial insecurity or social problems. Their life was greased, also, by knowing and being accepted by those who were known and accepted; and though there are no guarantees in such an environment, the future is often generous, barring natural calamities, acts of God, or such outrageous behavior that even a tolerant social order cannot make the necessary excuses.

Their marriage withered from the latter, and the unacceptable actions were Shelby's. To understand her then and why she did what she did, you have to know what she was not: She was not particularly brave or adventuresome, though she was impish and spontaneous, whether eating a hot fudge sundae just before dinner or planning, packing, and departing for a two-week trip in a morning's time. She was not an intellectual and no more than moderately informed on national issues, though she read widely, if randomly, and learned the complete skeleton of a subject if she fell in love with the leg bone. She was not strong physically or particularly well coordinated, though she was well built and drew on a deep well of enthusiasm which passed for energy. She was not outlandish—not even "different"—and was never considered a character. Indeed, outside of the South, she would have been thought square by avant-garde standards. She was personally conservative, rather demure, and not at all concerned with her appearance, preferring casual dress even at stately moments. Her arresting face always made her the woman in the room the stranger wanted to meet, but she was not so sultry or so devastating that other women guarded their husbands. She was simply a spirited, attractive young woman.

In reciting other things she was not, the list must include: She was not domineering, or inflexible, or boring, or often quiet. She was not unfair or unkind, dishonest or insincere. Her mind was not narrow, her acquaintances and friendships not limited, her ideas not preformed, and her beliefs not closed to reevaluation. And she was not easy to forget.

For Ned Anderson, she was also not easy to handle. As the divorce bill read (which preceded the two-day trial in the white-columned courthouse), he was chagrined, generally unhappy, and certainly embarrassed because her political preferences differed from his own (she actually considered working for Robert Kennedy's presidential campaign); her taste in literature appalled him (she read Betty Friedan, even the radical Simone de Beauvoir); her social philosophies caused him great agitation (she called the black woman who ran the local Head Start program "Mrs. Johnson"); her friends were distasteful (she suggested asking Julian Bond to a gathering); and her religious beliefs were beyond understanding (she stopped attending church altogether and even asked permission to hear a visiting guru discuss Hinduism when he appeared in Atlanta).

More repugnant than any overt action, however, it was her opinions, ranging from people to the theater, he could not stomach.

The judge agreed with Ned Anderson and found cause enough to give him what he asked: a divorce on the grounds of cruel and inhuman treatment. Though throughout the testimony of numerous witnesses who attested to her strange ways she was never suggested to be a disloyal wife or unfit mother; and though she was never alleged to be abusive in language or spirit, sexually seductive or unresponsive—in short, a model wife in almost every respect—she was guilty of cruel and inhuman treatment by Georgian community standards because her thoughts and beliefs were not consonant with the thoughts and beliefs of her husband. The wife had sinned and would be punished.

Virginia sat through the trial at Shelby's side in spite of the tension it caused with Jim Winburn, who insisted "they should stay out of it altogether." She was aghast at the testimony and stunned by the decision, and by the end of the trial reached two indelible conclusions: one, that she and Shelby were destined to see each other through whatever came their way, and two, that she would resist with all her strength ever allowing a court of law to arbitrate her personal disagreements.

By late afternoon Virginia was tired, but her life was reasonably well organized—at least on the surface. She had checked again on her father's progress, and had spent some time catching up on the firm's business with Stanton Rutherford, who was more concerned about the anxiety she had been through than his untended clients. About once an hour she placed another call to Shelby, who was strangely unavailable. She even tried to track down Albert Arthur, who lived with Shelby— when they were getting along—but he was neither at the apartment nor at her house in the Hamptons, where he preferred to write, especially in the summer. Giving up on the telephone, she walked to the greengrocer in the next block and brought home a sack of fresh fruit and vegetables, some milk for coffee, and an evening paper. As she turned into her building she almost ran into the outstretched hand of a process server.

"Mrs. Winburn?"

"Yes," she said, unsuspecting.

"This is yours."

She had to shift the grocery bags in order to take what was thrust at her, and didn't realize until she saw only the back of him what he had come to deliver. She pitched the papers into the top of one of the bags, and flushing deeply because the doorman had witnessed the exchange, hurried to the elevator and to privacy to discover what they meant.

She had never been a fighter. She avoided conflict and pain even when it did not pertain to her. Long ago she gave up television specials where slaves were whipped to death and teen-aged girls raped with broom handles, and brutal films where prisoners of war were tortured and live animals slashed to death in bloodthirsty rituals. Oh, no, not for her. She opted for tranquillity over thrills, preferring books and music to provide quieter excitement. She would have gladly given up reading the news of the day if she could have avoided it without feeling guilty, and was jealous of an eccentric friend who barricaded himself from the hurly-burly of the world behind stacks of papers which he perused thoroughly and at a leisurely pace—his only requirement that they be at least two years old, so all the kidnappings and assassinations, the maniacal killings and murderous fires had become soundless footsteps in time's parade.

Now she found herself at war—isn't that what the paper before her meant? A "temporary restraining order granted ex parte enjoining the abortion of Virginia Winburn until such time as the plaintiff can bring evidence to bear on the paternity of the child of said defendant." Virginia covered her eyes with her hands to shut out the reality of what was ahead, and remained in that position until she became madder than she was paralyzed.

"Shelby Anderson, please."

A familiar secretary's voice paused. "Is that you, Miss Winburn? Didn't you know? Shelby's not here anymore—hasn't been for almost a week."

"No. I've been out of town. What do you mean—not here anymore?"

"Perhaps she'd better explain. Why don't you phone her at home—that's where I'm directing her calls. And tell her the place is bathed in tears, will you?"

Virginia's hard-working friend, ordinarily available only through long-distance operators in remote locations difficult to spell and impossible to pronounce, was finally reached at home at six-thirty on a Thursday evening.

"For God's sake, what's going on?"

"I quit. Last week. Shoved it up Renfield's ass and left."

"Christ, what have you done?" It wasn't fair. Just when Virginia needed to concentrate on herself she discovered Shelby also was in trouble. Shelby solved the dilemma.

"I'll bore you soon enough with the gory details. First, how's your dad?"

"He's going to make it—I may not."

"What's the matter? You sound tight enough to explode."

"An explosion took place all right, not of my doing, though I have to handle the fallout. Shelby, for God's sake, what did you tell Mike?"

"The truth—that he's pregnant. I know, I had no right. And honestly, I had no intention. I went to see him on business after Renfield became intolerable and I quit the network. Just once I wanted to do the smart thing as well as the right thing, so I took him a sensational idea which would give Matterhorn a marketing edge and put *petite moi* into the bucks too. He loved it—I'll give you more on that later—and we were having a fine old time matching our futures to our aspirations when he suddenly asked what *your* fondest dreams were. It somehow didn't seem fair that I was plotting my course to a higher star, and Mike was reaching further than most men can see, and you were going to start slipping backward . . ."

"That's what *you* think!"

"That *is* what I think! Anyway, I blurted everything out, just told him flat out about the baby, and told him you'd chop me up for gull meat when you found out."

"How could you do that to me?"

"Easy. Gin, you should have seen him. At first he didn't believe me, then he was in shock trying to absorb what I'd said, then finally—now we had consumed a couple of drinks, so alcohol may have played a part—tears started splashing down that perfectly controlled face. I had to look away until he got his handkerchief working. Whatever accommodation you want to work out now is up to you; that man can be had as easily as deposits in an unattended bank."

"He's suing me, Shelby." She spit out the words.

"*What?*"

"I don't read legalese well, but if I'm not mistaken I'm holding a petition to the Family Court of New York to establish paternity rights over my child."

"I don't believe this . . ."

"In the meantime I'm enjoined, according to another lovely piece of paper, a temporary restraining order, from having an abortion until we talk this matter over before a judge. A week from Tuesday."

"Good God."

"Bank vaults are never left unguarded."

"But how does a man go from benign happiness to punitive action? You were as sacred as the Virgin Mary three days ago. I thought you'd have me canonized for bringing you two together."

"I goaded him into it by being less than receptive to a business proposition he called marriage."

"Since when does a man who is proposing have an injunction in his pocket as well as a ring?"

"Mike plans for all eventualities—it's called 'hedging' in my business."

"Only if he's scared or desperate."

"Two adjectives one never applies to Michael Strange," Virginia said curtly. "Listen, spare me the lay analysis of his underlying motivations. I just needed you to confirm the fact that you're responsible for this maelstrom. Why you two couldn't have worked out your futures without destroying mine . . ."

"Gin . . ."

"Don't stop me. Now I have the unenviable probability of an ugly, bruising legal battle, with gossip columnists and *Daily News* photographers recording every moment of an embarrassing trial. . . . Me! On trial! My baby—talk about auspicious beginnings! I can see the headlines now: 'Did he do the dirty deed?' and 'Defense claims Immaculate Conception'!"

"Gin, don't get hysterical."

"The only thing I'm going to get is a lawyer—first thing tomorrow. My other option is what neither he nor I want, but what he's driving me toward, and that's an abortion. If I think about that I *will* become hysterical."

"What lawyer?"

"The Edward Bennett Williams of paternity cases, if such an animal exists. Can you imagine the legal machinery Mike will crank up against me? He's never even lost a proxy battle, and unfriendly take-overs are his specialty. He fights for what he wants with any means at hand, and I'm not ashamed to say I'm feeling mighty small, mighty alone, and mighty scared."

Once in bed, the room dark, and only pictures in her mind moving, Virginia admitted she had been less than honest. As she cupped her hands across her still-flat stomach she felt not alone at all.

Friday, August 15

Virginia got to her office early, the better to begin the inevitable sorting-out that neutralized even the most relaxing holidays. Not surprisingly her desk was an accumulation of internal memos, daily call sheets, and a stack of recent annual reports. Otherwise the office was as neat as usual, strangely impersonal, in fact, for a woman of such markedly individual tastes—it might have belonged to a person of any age or sex. The only adornments were a Boston fern hugging the window and a double picture on her desk holding shots of the children clowning in the left-hand frame, their faces hidden in a huddle, backsides to the camera, then throwing themselves exuberantly at the viewer in the right. It was the office of someone not quite sure how she had gotten there, or how long she might stay.

Before putting away her bag, still standing at her desk, she dialed the internal number of Stanton O. Rutherford, chairman of the board and chief executive officer of Peabody Slocum, who, after her four years with the firm, was also a friend.

She expected to find him in. No employee or partner worked longer hours. He attributed his success to unrelenting diligence, and explained to her once why he arrived two hours before anyone else. "There may be some who are one hour smarter than I am," he said, "but nobody's two hours smarter."

Virginia liked the man. If his emotional reactions were pinched, reflecting an eastern upper-class background and a life of quiet pleasures and understated tastes, he was essentially a kind man who believed in the intrinsic goodness of people and an optimistic man who used his prodigious energies, when possible, to right wrongs of the present by reflecting on inequities of the past. Like most men of his age and station, his personal knowledge of women was limited to dealing with his wife, with whom he shared a devoted relationship, and secretaries. Over them all he ruled benignly but with an authority as total as was their dependence on him. He was puzzled by the new breed of professional women, and uncomfortable around them—his biases ran deep—still, he was ultimately too fair-minded to allow his discomfiture to retard their progress and sought out, when there were almost none to be found, women who could be trained in the intricate world of high finance. In this way he met Virginia when she was graduating with honors, at the age of thirty-six, from New York University's MBA program as a finance major specializing in investments. She was a *rara avis* among women students because of her age and interests. A Peabody Slocum recruiter brought her to the attention of Rutherford as a reasonable way to begin to redress the glaring imbalance of sexes within the firm. She knew she was a token, but was proud of it and relieved by the salary, which, far from grand, was more than she had dreamed of making—wasn't woman's work generally unpaid labor?—and which offered respectability as well as the necessities of living. Rutherford saw in her a woman he could understand and relate to—she was of his kind. She found him a man to admire personally as well as professionally, so the vaccination took for them both. She was protected from the strangeness of a foreign environment, he from a sex he could not fathom; and she prospered in his employ, moving through levels of responsibility as quickly as she mastered the subject matter.

Rutherford shielded her from jealousies her unnatural presence in a masculine enclave might have engendered by letting it be known that her superiors would themselves be judged by how rapidly she assimilated information and techniques. With their rewards tied to her advancement, she was pushed along with corporate winds at her back and a minimum of resentment from her managers. At the same time she provided Rutherford with a private learning experience, for, having made the decision to include the strange sex, he was determined to increase his understanding of it. In doing so he came first to admire and trust her, then to stand as her mentor in a business sense and her protector in a personal sense. The combination worked for them both and she was grateful.

Rutherford's secretary had not arrived, so he answered his own telephone, welcoming her home with affection. Could she see him now? Of course. He made interruptions sound scheduled.

The walnut-dark paneling and ancient Bessarabian rug formed a den for the financial king of beasts that was a natural habitat, for he belonged in surroundings of age and taste. Seated behind his fine English partner's desk, he bespoke at once the gentility and power of the street that ruled the planet's capital. He rose as Virginia entered, adhering to patterns the modern business age would never erase, and touching her gently at the elbow, led her to a chesterfield sofa that dominated the end of his cavernous corner office, murmuring concerns about her father as they went. She felt the softness of a touch that, she knew, had never held a tool or instrument heavier than a fish knife and glanced sideways at a face so unmarked it seemed unlikely to have known either inclement weather or great joy—or even a strained moment in the bathroom. He was not a man who pursued the outer limits of emotion, or one who engaged in self-indulgence. Not until she was seated on the deep red leather was she, in a flash, aware how exotic, how alien her message would be.

"I've news, Stanton, but it's not about my dad. It's very personal. I need your help." She was stammering now, looking down, fingering the heavy art books on the coffee table, finding it more difficult than she had imagined to tell him. There had been another day when she sat in this chair, nerves zinging. He had hired her then after a long conversation about her professional goals. She had been so sure about what she wanted. In clear and specific terms—so unusual for her—she had articulated what she was and what she saw herself becoming. As she talked, firing him with her determination, she became almost transported by the predestined certainty that she belonged in this company, and would succeed here beyond his dubious projections, beyond her fiercest hopes, beyond the fledgling opportunities offered any female recruit to the world of money. She asked him, impassioned by the combination of fortuitous and hard-won circumstances that brought them together, to take a chance on her, and he did. Now, she forced herself to continue . . .

"I'm going to have a baby—not for a long time, but I *am* going to have a baby." She looked up at him directly and met the unchanged face she expected. "Being pregnant won't interfere with my work, you can be sure of that." She threw her hair back with a shake of the head and tried to smile. "I was always my strongest when I was pregnant. Besides, I'd never let you down, you know that—but there may be other problems. You see, I'm not going to marry" . . . she wanted to get out quickly answers to questions he would not allow his expression to ask . . . "and I'm afraid there may be some legal complications."

"Do you mean from the father?"

"Yes." Virginia hurried to avoid further details. "They're unwarranted, actually, but I may have to face a court action, so

I'll need the best counsel I can find. If I'm lucky he'll keep me out of litigation and away from any permanent trouble. Of course, I'll do everything within my power to spare the firm—or myself—embarrassment."

What could he say? She was giving her trusting friend almost no information, yet asking for total understanding. He was too much of a gentleman to intrude into her privacy. During her pronouncements he had shown neither surprise, confusion, nor consternation.

"What do you want of me?"

"Just your patience. I'm not quite sure what's ahead, but if . . . any inconveniences . . . keep me away from the office, they'll be temporary."

Rutherford nodded slightly.

"Also, I'd like your permission to ask Clarkson Franklin to represent me, for a couple of reasons. First, I've been impressed with the way he handles our legal problems, he's tenacious and tough—I may need that. And second, I like him as a person, and that's important. This matter is more than a little touchy, as you may imagine. I'll need some empathy from my lawyer as well as my friends."

Rutherford's eyes never left hers. His body remained motionless, legs crossed, elbows resting on chair arms, fingertips lightly touching. Was he reliving another day more than two years earlier, when he had summoned her from the research department? She sat across from him as she did today, bright-faced and eager, too pretty to be quite so intelligent, and he rewarded her dedicated efforts and incisive reports with an opportunity—unheard of!—to train as a security analyst. Was he remembering her flush of excitement, lit by the fires of challenge and competition? And was he tasting again, but sour now, the pleasure of playing God in another's life, making the improbable possible by offering her a position women were traditionally excluded from holding?

He answered evenly, "Of course, call Clark. He's an excellent choice, particularly if there's litigation involved, though I warn you, the only winners in head-to-head court battles are the lawyers. They're hideous experiences."

"And the last thing I want to deal with," she said.

An uncharacteristic sigh escaped him. "The entire situation is difficult for me to comprehend—raising a child alone, at this point in your life." Rutherford pulled his gears out of reverse, back into neutral. "But then I don't know the whole story, do I?"

He stood as he spoke, bringing the conversation to a close. "Do what you must, and call me if I can help. I just hope you know what you're doing."

When a face is inscrutable, can it become even more impossible to read? There was a moment during the brief conversation when Rutherford's impassive expression tightened further, when his eyes moved even further away. On the surface Virginia had completed her mission, informing him frankly of her plans but in a manner which suggested her continuing employment was a given. His acceptance had been perfunctory but polite—again, what she had wanted. So why the jangling anxiety as she returned to her office?

She knew—because of the questions he hadn't asked: Does your future here count for so little? After all my grooming, teaching, pushing toward partnership, with your time and energies diverted can you possibly succeed now? Haven't you at last proved your critics within the firm correct and me unrealistic to think you wouldn't, at some point, react like a woman instead of a professional? One doesn't have a personal life at Peabody Slocum. You leave that on the coatrack along with your umbrella, and pick it up again on your way out. The rules are clear; everybody abides by them. What makes you think you're different?

I'll work it out, she repeated to herself over and over as she

walked the long hall to her office, fists clenched against the battle, I'll work it out.

As she turned the corner by the conference room, cool and
semi-dark now in its emptiness, another day suddenly came to
mind, a day of thoroughgoing, boundless joy. She hesitated,
remembering, then on impulse slipped inside the room, shutting the massive door behind her. Matching chairs, so neatly in
place now, were pushed back from the table in disarray that afternoon, a year ago, when she had thought herself walking into
a routine meeting only to discover, in surprise and then in
shock, a gathering in honor of her new position as security analyst. A roomful of dark-suited men stood as she entered, champagne in hand, calling her name with interspersed cheers.
Rutherford moved from the head of the huge oval table and,
handing her a glassful as the room hushed to quiet, announced
her full promotion to security analyst. All the Miss Americas
receiving crowns and titles, all the lottery winners with numbers newly drawn, all the Olympic athletes bowing heads for
gold medals, all the elected politicians rejoicing over victorious
projections, all of them combined, she was sure, could not have
equaled her exquisite delight at that moment.

Rutherford's toast, flattering and welcoming, paraphrased,
she remembered, President Kennedy's inaugural address: "So
let the word go forth, from this day forward, that the torch has
passed to a new sex . . ."

She had responded, picking up his theme, and thanked him,
laughing. "I'll ask not what my company can do for me, but
what I can do for my company . . . and I'll pay any price, bear
any burden, meet any hardship to assure the success of Peabody
Slocum . . ."

She had meant it. More than the title and the responsibility,
more than the substantial earnings, more than the respect of
her colleagues and the satisfaction of breaking tradition's hold
on a hold-out industry, she had reached a goal even she
thought unlikely, scrambling up a narrow rocky path, condi-

tioning herself as she climbed, learning the tough lessons of stamina and perseverance, and acquiring the ability to pick herself up when she fell. She was able to do it because she was good—and because she paid the price.

Virginia saw the pride of that day vanish from Rutherford's eyes this morning. She walked back into the corridor, and then into her office. Had her indomitable determination also disappeared?

No, by God, she would work it out. The telephone. An appointment. With Clarkson Franklin, the financial community's fastest gun for hire—the Street was littered with the corpses of his opponents. Because they had worked on a recent case together, and because she insinuated that Stanton Rutherford suggested that she call (using his name with more freedom than he had offered), he agreed to an appointment on an emergency basis that afternoon.

The world operates on contacts; that was lesson one in life outside the home. She learned it late but learned it well. It is whom you know, can get to, and who will fight on your side that carries the day, not necessarily the merits of your cause. The rich and powerful grow richer and more powerful by trading insiders' knowledge, special offerings, tips, and favors the way women bake an extra pie and drop it off next door; just acts of friendship in the informal circle of the very successful, that's all, merely taking care of one another and expecting nothing back—except reciprocation.

Virginia was trading on her connections now too, thankful for the warmth of the corporate fire she sat close to. For the first time since Mike banged out of her apartment yesterday afternoon, the blood stopped beating behind her eyes and resumed normal circulation. Able to work again, she churned into the heaps of papers before her like a country jalopy scattering chickens, moving them competently and expeditiously into her out basket and wastebasket. When the phone rang, shortly before her appointment with Franklin, she did not know it signaled the fire was dying out.

"Rutherford for you on line two," her secretary sang out.

"Yes, Stanton?" She was still warm and comfortable.

"It appears we have more of a problem than I thought this morning when we spoke."

"Yes? What's that?" The onset of a shiver.

"I've just received a call from Mike Strange. Perhaps you'd better come back to my office."

Walking through his door she felt a decided chill. "Sit down, Virginia." He waved her to a chair close by his desk, then seated himself again. "This may not be an easy conversation for either of us." His perfectly manicured nails pushed papers an inch or two away, then he continued. "Strange tells me he's preparing litigation to prove the paternity of his—your—child." Seeing the distress that crossed her face, he added quickly, "Of course, he asked me to keep the information absolutely confidential, and I intend to. But he indicated he was prepared to wage a protracted legal battle, if necessary, to get what he wants. That puts me in an awkward position, to say the least. The publicity that sort of action attracts when a man of his prominence is involved is simply unacceptable for the firm. Even beyond that, though, there's the matter of the eight-hundred-million-dollar debenture sale we are bringing out for Matterhorn next month, and though he didn't say so directly, he strongly indicated that he expected me and the firm to support his efforts. I tell you this only because of my personal affection for you, Virginia. Frankly, if this preposterous situation had developed with any other female employee in the place, she'd have found severance pay in her check and that would have been that. But you know my concern for you goes beyond the professional. I haven't had time to think through all the ramifications of the situation, but one thing seems clear. I can't allow you to use Franklin as counsel, his conflict of interest would be too great . . ."

"But, Stanton, you don't know my position in the matter." Virginia leaned forward as if her body could stop the words hurtling at her now, but he cut her off.

". . . And I don't *want* to know any more than I do. I cannot, will not, jeopardize the bond offering—or our connection with Matterhorn Industries—because of your personal problems, as cruel as that may sound. Nor would you if our circumstances were reversed. From what you've told me, I'll be honest and say I'm more than a little concerned about your judgment. But this is your affair to handle as you will—as long as you don't tarnish the firm's name or alienate us from one of our largest clients. In fact, in order to keep us strictly in the clear I think it's advisable for you to take a leave of absence, with pay of course, until the case is resolved."

"But, Stanton, my work . . ."

". . . Will simply have to wait. Simmons can take over your retail companies and Davis the industrials. As for your lawyer, surely there are many others capable of seeing you through the litigation, and you can return when it's over."

"Really? Can I?" Virginia knew she had lost; the extent of the loss was all that was left to discover. "Concerned as you are with the *future* of your relationship with Matterhorn as well as the present, how can I ever come back?"

Rutherford was silent. He bent his thin, elongated face over his hands and nibbled the ends of his fingers. "That's difficult to say. I wish I could answer you quickly and say, 'Certainly we'll take you back.' But now that you raise the question, since neither of us knows how the case will be decided, with what antagonisms and hostilities, I suppose we'll have to wait until it's resolved. If you lose, *you* may not want to remain since Strange is a major client. If you win, *he* may decide to take his business elsewhere as long as you're in the house. Either way, it'll be a perplexing situation, won't it?"

"For the sake of my professional career then," she said, "I

must lose the case; but for my personal life I need desperately to win. Hobson should have to choose."

"If you'll forgive my saying so, it seems to me the choice you ought to be considering would endanger neither your professional nor your family life. Now if you'd like to discuss that . . ."

"No, Stanton, thank you. It's kind of you, but if you'll forgive *my* saying so, I don't think you'd understand. This isn't one of those clean-cut decisions one makes because 'it' is always done this way, or because 'they' say it should be done such a way. It may sound melodramatic, but there's more at stake here than one woman's professional standing, or one firm's profit line. There's another human being for whom I am temporary spokesperson and custodian." She rose and stretched out her hand for his. "I'm grateful for your frankness, even though I think you're being unnecessarily protective. I'll let you know what happens."

What a fool she had been to think her friendship or her strategic position within the firm would stand up against Michael Strange's power. She walked stiffly back to her office without seeing the way, past her secretary, who followed her with a worried look. Brushing aside the paper work on her desk, she picked up the phone as she dropped the children's picture frame into her handbag. She found Shelby again at home.

"Seems I've lost a lawyer and a job all at the same time," she began. "Of the two, at the moment the lawyer's more important. Any ideas on a Friday afternoon, when half of New York's already on the Long Island Expressway?"

"Yes," Shelby answered quickly, "let's join them. Bert and I are leaving within the hour. If we can beat the traffic to the tunnel before three we've a reasonable chance of being at my place before tomorrow. I've been calling your office for an hour —didn't you get the messages?—to say we were going to kidnap you if necessary and take you along. It's one forty-five now. If you shoot home immediately and pick up some gear, I'll collect you at two-thirty and we'll be off."

Virginia's sigh was from such a deep inner place it almost muffled her words. "I have to find a lawyer, Shelby, not a beach. Don't you understand? I'm fighting for my life—or my way of life!" Tears formed under her eyelids and were reflected in her voice.

"I know, babe. Take it easy. I have more than a weekend suntan planned for you. Remember the story I did on the first successful female partnership in New York? The women who argued the abortion case before the Supreme Court and won?"

"Just what I need. A bunch of ranting feminist lawyers."

"Don't jump to conclusions. They're some of the soundest minds practicing, and more important for you, they know the law that pertains to paternity cases. Paula Seibert heads the firm. We've already had two conversations about you today, and I was planning to drive from Sagaponack to her house in Quogue tomorrow to talk further. She very kindly offered to advise me about your situation on an informal basis. Why don't you come along and listen? You'll still have time to contact other counsel, and if you have to, you can always ask for a delay, everybody else does. So, don't argue, and for God's sake hurry. The LIE is already bumper to bumper all the way to Patchogue."

"You talked me into it. I'm walking out right now."

"Great. By the way, my news stinks too. I've lost my second job in one week. Mike canceled the plans we had—guess why?"

"Me?"

"Sure. He's playing for keeps, putting all the pressure on you he can. I'll explain later. Now, hurry."

There was little enough to gather for the weekend. Shelby's two-hundred-year-old farmhouse in the potato fields of Sagaponack, halfway between grander retreats in Bridgehampton and East Hampton, stood as a deep, cool well for the world-weary, beckoning biological and psychological systems burnt out by urban pressures to refill and refresh. A pair of jeans to wear out there, another pair of whites for evening, a couple of T-shirts, a bathing suit, and a sweater for a nocturnal beach walk and she was ready.

Shelby's bright blue Rabbit pulled up to the apartment house at exactly two-thirty. Bert Arthur jumped from the front seat to lift her sailcloth tote into the rear and opened the rear door.

"Bertie!" They exchanged double-cheek kisses, then a solid hug. "How are you? You look wonderful."

Not just words in Bert's case. He was a lithe, spare man, approaching fifty more slowly than his peers because of a body held taut by long-distance running. Clear blue eyes against a perpetual tan and an easy smile made him one of the handsomest of men. No one judging by his face would recognize his Jewish origin; almost no one hearing his fast conversation would miss it. With an IQ that equaled his good looks, plus discipline and a considerable capacity for hard work, he should have been successful too. He wasn't. Perpetually on the cusp of great victories, he seemed to possess the Midas touch in reverse —everything he touched turned to alloy. His screenplay was almost produced, but lost financing at the last moment when the Rank Organization quit film-making. He wrote a soap before soaps became a national phenomenon, then embarked on a detective sit-com just as the networks began quashing sex and violence. He was constantly living on the proceeds of what might happen, but didn't, so he was generally a dime or two away from debt. Wondering at the apparent ease of those whom he considered less talented, he became embittered along the way. His quick mind and easy quips often had an edge that made others uncomfortable, and pushed them away. He and Shelby had spent several years together, building a deep affection for each other, but her success was an obstacle for them both. She had never been able to give up an inculcated belief that a man —her man—should be the provider, the strength, the support of

a couple. Though she was perfectly willing to share whatever
she had—her apartment in the city, her house in the country,
her friends, her professional connections—something in her felt
they should not be all hers, and something in him resented her
for having them. Now they spent time together less and less,
both trying to find new relationships that suited them better,
without success.

Bert slammed her rear door, then walked around to the
driver's window. "Slip over and talk to your friend. I'll steer us
out of here. Takes a madman to deal with Friday traffic."

Gratefully, Shelby swung her legs over the gear stick, turning
to face Virginia. "You'll have to cover your ears, but his driving's better than his language, and he won't interrupt while
he's yelling at *them*. Tell us what happened today at the
office."

While Bert bucked the Rabbit through midtown traffic,
weaving into nonexistent holes, jumping through yellow lights,
pushing through pedestrians at corners, Virginia outlined her
two conversations with Rutherford. Then in the steaming, almost motionless lines of frustrated motorists at the Thirty-
fourth Street tunnel, while some of New York's most recent
immigrants peddled dripping ices door to car door, it was
Shelby's turn to bring Virginia up to date.

"First let me take you back to my meeting with Mike, when
I originated all this trouble. I called him for an appointment
because I'd had it with Renfield. The fucker made his first pass
and his last mistake with me, after a long boozy lunch with
someone else who must have turned him down. Maybe all
femaledom is wise to him now, but he took it out on me,
mashing me up against a wall while we were looking at some
outtakes, and it made me crazy. I haven't wrestled a guy since I
parked at the gravel pit in high school, and I'm too old, too
tired, and too rich, as the saying goes, to start again. Once I untangled myself—no easy doings—and got back to the safety of

my office, I wrote a letter of resignation, put it in an interoffice envelope, and walked out."

"A pretty hotheaded response, wasn't it? You have a contract which doesn't include extracurricular. Why didn't you call him to account with the head of TV News or . . ."

"Because, to tell you the truth," Shelby jumped back in, "I'm sick of the whole outfit. I'm tired of doing the same thing over and over, just in different forms, and I'm tired of being only a reporter and calling other people's plays. Let them send someone to cover my touchdowns for a change. Besides, I've been nursing along a sensational idea—which is why I went to see Mike."

"Goddamn asshole, no you don't!" Bert sped up the car suddenly to prohibit a lane changer from nosing in, then smacked his brakes to avoid hitting the car in front. Both women were thrown forward, then backward in a snapping motion.

"Jesus, Bert!" Shelby yelled as she recovered a sitting position. "No one in four lanes of traffic is going any better than five miles an hour. Give us a break, will you, and save your stunts for the open road."

Snakes of cars rolled slowly eastward as far as one could see, first one lane moving, then another. During the intervals some drivers stood on one foot outside their automobiles, peering through the curvy waves of heat rising from the hoods ahead, looking for, praying for movement.

"There must be an accident. It's too early for this kind of a tie-up," Bert growled. "Shit, where are the fucking police when you need them? Off giving tickets to people lucky enough to be speeding. If we could ticket *them* when we drop below fifteen miles an hour, there'd be some justice."

"So what's your bright idea?" Virginia brought Shelby's attention back to the conversation.

"There's going to be an electronic explosion in the eighties, we know that. Video discs, video cassettes, video recorders and players—consumers will be able to buy almost everything and everybody to play on their tubes at home—except themselves."

"What do you mean?"

"Just picture the families out here." Shelby waved her hand in the direction of the Great Neck community they were crawling past. "They have stately homes, two Mercedes in every drive; they ski in the winter, go to Europe in the summer, and have almost everything, except aristocratic ancestors and—you tell me what . . ."

"Hell, I don't know," Virginia said impatiently. "Happy marriages."

"Celebrity. They're rich, but they aren't famous. Never will be. And they'll never see themselves on television."

"Why should they?"

"Because everyone wants to. Haven't you noticed, whether you're watching Olympic ski jumps, a World Series, or a mayoral news conference, everybody tries to get into the picture. The most sophisticated people I know become adolescents around a television camera. Look at game shows—they turn sensible middle-class Americans into clowns—anything for a shot on the tube. Well, I aim to give them a way to immortalize themselves while they turn me into entrepreneur. I want to form a company called Personal Statements, a service which will make average people instant television stars. I'll take cameras, professional makeup and lighting, teleprompters—all the equipment—right into their homes, and with all the tricks I know as a broadcaster, teach them how to make a decent presentation . . ."

"But to say what?" Virginia interrupted.

"Whatever they want. Maybe a woman's getting on in age. She's still healthy, looks fine, but knows she hasn't too many years left. She might make a personal statement to her family, saying certain things to her husband, to each of her children, maybe another message to her grandchildren. She records a cassette, which she then puts away in the safety-deposit box, along with her will, as a permanent reminder of what she thought, how she looked, how she wanted to be remembered, and all *before* she ends her days in a hospital with tubes sticking out in every direction."

"Isn't that a bit morbid?"

"We take still pictures of each other now, cherish them, and pass them on to the next generation. Why not talking pictures with messages? And it doesn't have to be sad. What about a family on the east coast that can't join the rest of the clan on the west coast? We come in, gather the group around the tree for a big chorus of 'Jingle Bells,' the kindergarten kid recites a Christmas poem, Mom sends love, and Dad says a case of booze is on the way. Presto, a cassette's in the mail to be plugged in at the other end. Cheaper than airline tickets! Or what about the corporate executive who can't be in Europe and at his northwest sales meeting at the same time? We provide the service, he sits comfortably in his office asking everyone to meet their quotas, the cassette goes to Seattle and he goes to Paris. I can give you a hundred instances how the service might be used. Believe me, its time isn't coming, it's here."

"Interesting. But why did you see Mike?"

"Because his new video recorders are going to be Sony's biggest competition. When he comes out with the capacity to record in stereo, he'll have only a short time before the Japanese catch up. I suggested that he incorporate this service as a promotional device for new customers, offering them a Personal Statement as a come-on for initial purchase. He thought it was almost as brilliant an idea as I do. We were both counting our fortunes there for a while. That's when I put my size nine right into the middle of your life, for which I will be forever miserably sorry."

"You and me. But how do you stand with him now? What did you mean when you said you lost your second job this week?"

"Rutherford wasn't the only one who received a Strange phone call today. Very curt. He put all our start-up plans, the marketing research, the cost projections, everything into abeyance until, as he put it, his difficulties with you were resolved favorably."

"He added 'favorably'?"

"Certainly did. Tying my good fortune to his, of course."

"And to my misfortune."

"I doubt he's thinking much about your well-being."

"What will you do, Shelby?"

"I'm not worried—now. Maybe by Monday I'll sober up and see what I've done to myself. But I really wanted out of broadcasting. It's no accident that most of the people you see on the tube are young. It isn't a grown-up's game, except for a few Cronkites who tell us the way it is every night. It's time for me to move on, to find a way to spend the next twenty years. I was looking for a way out, now I've got it. If the Personal Statement idea is sound, I'll find another way to launch it. When was anything in this life easy?"

Shelby was like the male fiddler crabs that roamed the Hamptons' beaches, first waving their long right claws in the air to attract the females, then rapping them on the sand to lead them into their burrows. If there was a troublesome encounter with another crab and one lost a good right arm, he simply marked time, impatiently, until his tiny left claw grew to the size of the amputated right and he was back in the fray again, waving and rapping. She too was indomitable. Virginia envied her grit, and the confidence that promised success, however far down the beach.

The open road broke before them like the sun after a summer storm. As if released from gloom, Bert danced down the highway, flipping the car gracefully from one lane to the other. Automobiles and passengers seemed to drop the burdens of the city and fall into the first full moments of the weekend's respite. Pine trees and beach roses banked the roadside in place of billboards and gas stations. The fetid air which had followed them from the city seemed degrees cooler as the balance between man-made and natural fell more favorably toward the wild. No longer afraid of stalling out in stop-and-go driving, Bert ordered the windows up, started the air-conditioning system, and turned on his favorite entertainment medium—an untrained but remarkable tenor voice. For a man who could sing his way across the United States and never repeat a song, the trip from Islip to the Hamptons would be merely a warm-up, barely tapping his repertoire of beloved show tunes.

The women became quiet, hypnotized by the speeding landscape, the sweetness of his singing, and their reveries. The miles slipped under the car as they retreated to their private thoughts, listening, Shelby mulling over the turning points in her life, which had, until now, been an amalgam of ambition and accomplishment. The long road from Georgia housewife to network reporter had been a straight line from south to north. She had lifted her boys out of the town that rejected her and in which she no longer felt comfortable and had driven as far as she could without getting the regional bends, which was Washington. There, thanks to intervention by the liberal connections for which she was so thoroughly censured at home, she took a job, the first paying job in her life, doing the only thing for which she had some training—talking. With almost no women appearing on the television screen in the sixties, and before the stampede from journalism schools which took place in the seventies, she was able because of her striking good looks and smart mouth to insinuate herself into a local news operation. She did not find the work difficult; indeed, the greatest obstacle she encountered was learning to say words which the southern tongue had almost no way of forming correctly— "dimacratic" slowly gave way to "democratic," "sinator" became "senator," and ultimately even "umbrella" lost the accent on the first syllable. Ned Anderson's money put the boys in private schools and hers began to provide a level or two above the necessaries. Men came along often—Shelby believed in denying herself nothing—delighted by her sassy ways and lack of de-

mands. Her life became so full, and was such a turnaround
from the earlier unhappiness, she actually debated whether to
accept the summons to New York; but, like all who climb lad-
ders for a living with their chins pointed permanently in a
heavenward direction, she had no choice but to move up. *The
Today Show?* An evening news anchor position? All seemed
possible at first, and all desirable, especially as she graduated
from local news to network documentaries, amassing awards
and developing a recognition factor. After her last move to
Renfield's highly rated program, her goal seemed plausible as
well as possible, for she was one of the two or three most competent women on the air. So why the discontent? she asked herself. Because she and Bert had not worked out as she hoped?
She knew that had been a long shot from the start. Because she
was disgusted with television as a medium? Not really. There
was too much opportunity for too great an impact; she knew
that. And knew also she could have handled Renfield with a
breezy line that would have held her job, his ego, and their
relationship intact. No, to be scathingly honest, boredom was
the cause—it had all become too easy. The dandelion was with-
ering from cultivation and needed another patch of thick un-
yielding grasses to struggle through.

Virginia, less able than Shelby to cut through to an admis-
sion of weakness, dealt more with feelings than facts, and
relived the inexorable chain of circumstances that led to her dilemma. Mostly she wondered how she had moved so far from
Mike, the only person in her life whom she had completely
trusted and unqualifiedly adored, that she could contemplate
meeting him in pitched combat. The scene in Rutherford's
office today was in sharp contrast to one last fall. Mike had had
his own session with Rutherford, discussing the blossoming future of Matterhorn Industries and the possibility of a new public offering. She had rushed through touring new manufacturing facilities of one of her retail accounts in order to be back

at Peabody Slocum before he left. He was there, doodling on a piece of paper at her desk as she burst through the door.

"So this is the way industry moguls spend their time, Mr. Strange," she said, divesting herself of handbag and briefcase and dropping into his lap. She kissed his forehead, nose, and cheeks, and slid across to his mouth.

He slipped his hand under her skirt and up along her thigh. "Actually I'm hard at work, Mrs. Winburn, trying to arrange a merger. Maybe the most profitable of my career."

With her arms still around his neck, she leaned back and looked at him. "That has such a strange sound, doesn't it?"

"What's that," he said, reaching to nibble her lips.

"Mrs. Winburn." She kissed him back, talking between their connecting mouths.

"Not to me."

"Does to me," she said, breaking away. "A name with no reality. I'm not a 'Mrs.,' Winburn means nothing to my life now, and there's another Mrs. Winburn now who deserves the name . . ."

"Why didn't you go back to Cargile when you divorced?"

"Wasn't smart enough, and I thought it would be unseemly leading two children around with a different name."

"Oh, you proper southern women." He began kissing her again and moved his hand higher, where it ordinarily went only after business hours.

"If I were all that proper," she said, feeling the familiar thrill he aroused so easily, "I'd move that hand away."

"But you don't want to, do you?" Both had passed the point of no return and knew it and surrendered to their feelings. "Besides, the name's no problem. We can change that easily enough . . ."

God bless Mary Jennings, loyal guard dog of the door.

After Mike had gone, and she had subdued her disheveled hair into respectable curves and splashed water on her flushed face, she rang Rutherford's office to request a moment's time. As she walked the long hall her mind flashed back to another day when she entered her father's study, pulled up a footstool to sit at his feet, and told him of her engagement. Something in her then desperately hoped for an argument, some inescapable reason why she should not do as she had planned, but Everett Cargile touched the cheek of his untried, unformed, twenty-year-old daughter who had only begun to live her life and said, "Anything you want, baby." Today, she thought happily, she wanted no argument.

"Stan," she said, hardly able to contain herself, "I want you to take me off the Matterhorn account."

"Oh, yes?" His eyebrows lifted in surprise. He motioned her to a fine Chippendale chair at right angles to his desk. "There's no trouble there, I hope."

"No, Stan, no trouble. I've just become very involved with Michael Strange—on a personal basis. There's no way I can be objective when it comes to him, and that has to affect my judgment about the company. One more laudatory report from me, and if that stock runs up five or ten points, we'll have some justifiable questions to answer."

"I see your point. Well, give me your recommendations as to who should handle it, and . . . well, Virginia, I couldn't be happier for you, you know that. He's a good man. Take care of him and he'll take care of you."

It's life's little turns that lead you to unpredictable destinations, not the huge intersections. It's the small forks where a road sign is obscured or nonexistent that can move you, unsuspectingly, away from your goal. Rats in mazes push their noses first in this direction, then that. Why aren't we allowed, Virginia wondered, to make mistakes and retrace our steps to take another path? No, run it out, run it out . . .

Bert's singing broke through her daydreams. He had made his way through Gilbert and Sullivan to his favorite Iolanthe, and to the Lord Chancellor who promised as a very young man to go to the Bar with an original plan and who, among other unusual attitudes for lawyers of the day, would never perjure himself as a matter of course . . . The suggestion of lying in court, plus the overhead highway sign marking the exit to Quogue, abruptly roused Virginia from her stupor. "Talk to me about Paula Seibert."

Shelby, mesmerized by Bert's music, raised her head sleepily from the backrest. "I think she's tops, really an impressive woman. She's accustomed to setting precedents—you know about the abortion case. She also changed the law in New Jersey, arguing that couples who've lived together with only an oral contract between them still have to divide property when they split—that works for men and women, of course. She's not your prototypical barricade-climbing feminist from the sixties. She's been married for twenty-three years to a terrific guy. She has a couple of the nicest kids you'll ever meet, twins, in college, and she's a leader of national efforts to pass the ERA. Besides, she knows family law as well as anyone in the country."

"When can we see her?"

"After her Saturday-morning tennis game, around noon. Perfect timing—I'll just be getting up."

Shelby's energy and graceful frame belied the care she gave her body. Her last regular exercise had probably been phys. ed. at college; walking for the mail was a major effort. She smoked too much, binged on junk food, and drank enough at parties to grease her tongue at night and wreck her head in the morning. A bad back periodically laid her low and she tired easily, becoming grouchy and at times mean-spirited. Still, her body seemed to gather no years, her legs and arms firm as a twenty-year-old's. She vowed she would escort health fanatics like Virginia and Bert to their graves.

In contrast, Virginia did not know how to be indulgent. She seldom ate between meals—her mother's cry, "You'll ruin your dinner," still knocked snacks from her hand. She gave up cigarettes on her thirty-fifth birthday, the year of her divorce. There were so many parts of her life out of control she was determined to regulate that which was within her power. She kept regular hours, slept soundly, and could wake without an alarm. She read labels to avoid food additives, took megavitamin doses, ran or swam three times weekly, and for the life of her, never thought she looked as healthy as Shelby—and never believed she had as much fun.

There was as little chance of Virginia becoming intemperate as there was of Shelby developing self-discipline. Determining patterns locked in when—in childhood? in the womb? In fact, neither chose to be different. The character change both would have welcomed, had it been possible, dealt with their capacity for competition, or the lack of it, and here they were similar. Both felt their ability to fight for causes, for friends or children, was boundless compared to the extent they could do battle for themselves, or engage in self-promotion. "If you can't sell yourself, how do you expect others to do it for you?" Virginia's father asked. The question was valid but pointless. She could no more verbally extol her worth than she could react aggressively when she was unfairly judged or bullied.

The women spent conversational hours hunting the cause, searching for the Delilah in their lives who sheared their strength away when they needed it most. Shelby claimed it was their southern heritage which expected women, niggers, and mules to follow orders automatically. Virginia tracked backward to a different reason. Watching young Maggie competing on the boys' swim team because there was no girls', driving her slim body through grueling practices two hours before school and two after, pushing her small frame to match boys with denser musculature and longer reach, Virginia realized she herself had never seriously participated in sports, nor was she ever encouraged to by her parents, peers, or educators; she learned the subliminal message that there was no value to be gained by developing her body. Slimming it, yes, and dressing it carefully,

but her body was to be seen, not to be functional. Later she realized men think of themselves as solid packages of muscles
and bone, organs and skin, but women view themselves as hol-
low, consisting only of surface areas to be painted and polished,
shaved and plucked, bleached and perfumed, but not to be
used.

There were strange new imperatives for young women now.
When Maggie joined the swim team, her traditionalist father
asked if she realized how extensively swimming would develop
her shoulders, and how unattractive they would be in later
years when revealed in evening gowns. She answered him with
disdain. "I'm not living this life to be looked at."

Maggie was living her life to win. Fighting for her team
forced her to pay attention to tactics and strategy; she learned
to search out an opponent's vulnerability and plan a killing
blow. Training for meets taught her to push herself past endurance to increase her strength, and past pain when time came
for the ultimate effort. She learned to lose while her world
watched, and patch herself together to try again. And she
learned to win and to hold on to the thrill so she could position herself positively for the next match.

How Virginia yearned now for Maggie's confidence that winning merely depended on carrying the strongest forces into the
field. If only she could wear brave intransigence as a shield and
purity of purpose as a sword. How she wished she could be beg-
ging for battle, eager to attack, to wound, and to return with
victory. That was Mike's state of mind at the moment, she was
sure of it, while she was quaking and trembling, dreading the
approaching confrontation. The most she could hope to do
would be to anoint another, without her fears and trepidations,
to defend her.

A fast series of traffic lights, a left at the Southampton
corner, and the frazzled threesome turned gratefully onto the
last leg of the highway. Flat potato fields winged out on either
side of the car. The ocean, a mile to the right, out of sight and

hearing, made its presence felt by cooling and cleansing the air. Through the tiny village of Water Mill, guarded by its ancient brown-shingled, broad-beamed namesake, past Bridgehampton's watering holes where the summer set sized up each other's tans and house guests, the Rabbit held its place in the endless line of cars moving toward the eastern end of the Island, taking turns veering off country lanes and side streets toward final destinations and strong alcoholic drink.

When his turn came to wrench free of the other travelers, Bert whipped toward the ocean onto Sagg Main and suddenly they were alone with nothing around them but the oblique rays of the evening sun welcoming them back to the land.

If June is the lushest month in the Hamptons, rich with the burst of new green, eye-blinding with the pink and purple of azaleas, mountain laurel, rhododendrons, and dogwoods; and if July is the most satisfying month, the summer neither just beginning nor almost over and steady in its parade of glorious days; then August is the most tranquilizing, like a sleepy afternoon after a midday Sunday feast. Potato plants, having exchanged their blossoms for underground tubers, lie heavy in the fields, offering first bite of the coming harvest to crunching nematodes. Grasses, inspired by sprinklers, struggle to hold their ground, but are exhausted by the effort. Geraniums and petunias, pinched back by canny gardeners in July, bloom bravely in the August heat, but roses, almost audibly panting, produce only occasional blossoms as reminders of their former glory.

Humankind, too, reduces its efforts on the East End. Earlier exertions of frenetic tennis games and cocktail gatherings which mingled old acquaintances and new aspirations as summer began, melt into a gentler program of the convenient and the possible. Heat puts a lid on the summer pot.

Shelby's house had fended off deep summer heat and the inevitable mildew, absorbed from walls and rugs into dispositions, since Revolutionary times, when British soldiers were quartered in the area. Humble in origin, it had weathered along with its kindred into the most desirable real estate, more valued than contemporary gables—those arching eyebrows gazing toward the ocean—more sought after than spacious village houses surrounded by lawns and neighbors. An anachronistic need to rediscover the elemental, to set store upon the simple, and to revere that which has endured turned dirt farmers' shelters into sanctuary.

A refuge realized, or so the house seemed to the weekend travelers whose drooping city spirits began reviving at the sight of it like house plants after an overdue watering. Cheerfully unloading the car, they carried bags and boxes across the tilting porch into silently waiting rooms.

Shelby was an acquirer. Never quite comfortable on Sundays when the stores were closed, she accepted the job of making purchases as a second calling, and devoted to it almost the effort she expended in making a living. The results were evident. Rooms were not so much furnished as accessorized, the all-white sofas and chairs merely backdrops for colorful quilts, paisley shawls, piles of pillows, and hooked rugs underfoot. Wicker tables alternated with country pine chests around the old plaster walls—again white—and held half a lifetime of pictures of her children, kings and presidents, colleagues and friends. The rooms were so full of her they did not require her actual presence to bring them to life.

The bedrooms were neat, expectant. Virginia's assignment, the first left at the top of the stairs, was at once comfortably lived in and pristine. The white iron bed, banked with eyelet pillows, covered with a pale pink and green antique medallion coverlet, begged her to stay, now, even before the appointed time to sleep. She was dissuaded not so much by the hour as the sound of the refrigerator door opening and shutting, and Shelby's and Bert's voices discussing the first of the evening's fare. A bottle of chilled Mâcon was open by the time she walked into the ample kitchen, and a platter arranged of salami, Greek olives, and feta cheese, all remainders from the preceding weekend.

"You don't really make ice out of Perrier," Bert challenged.

"You'd rather drink Temek along with your wine?" Shelby filled the last squares of the tray from the chic green bottle and replaced it in the freezer. "So, it's extravagant. I can't stop the farmers from poisoning our wells, and it's cheaper in the long run than chemotherapy."

The disappearing sun sucked in its excessive heat along with its light while changing the horizon before them to shades of pink, then lavender, then deepest purple. Talking quietly on the western patio with ancient grapevines twisting overhead and birds calling farewells from the huge protective trees at the sides of the house, the trio were stunned again, as if for the first time, by the awesome sky they had come so far to find.

"If you think this is something, wait until later tonight when the Perseids shoot—it's the Big Picture Show in the Sky," Shelby said.

"That's what we used to call heat lightning on summer evenings in Atlanta," Virginia remembered, "before air conditioning brought everybody indoors. All of us children took quilts and lay on our backs in the grass watching the most incredible bursts of light, like explosions, hopping from cloud to cloud, that always meant rain and a break in the humidity. I haven't seen them since. I know a little about stars, but what are the Perseids?"

"A hailstorm of meteors, crashing toward the earth. If there's no moon tonight, and you look in the direction of the constellation Perseus, you'll see an unbelievable display of shooting stars, as if God were holding a Roman candle. Every forty or fifty seconds another one will arch across the heavens. Some look as if they'll drop in your lap."

"How do you know it'll happen tonight?" Bert asked.

"It happens every year at this time in August, just for a couple of nights. I think the earth passes through some cosmic debris. Just proves that perspective is everything, doesn't it? What's garbage out there is a miracle here. I was all set to do a story on them, complete with new infrared camera equipment. Well, hell, I'd rather be here watching it with you two."

"Really? Was that spectacular—not to mention well-paying —job so easy to give up?" Bert asked.

"Leaving the network wasn't hard, but holding on to the idea that I'm a competent person capable of making a living somewhere else is like holding water in my hands: it's gone before I can raise it to my mouth to drink."

"What's the worst thing that could happen to you now, Shelby?" Virginia asked.

"Short-term? That I couldn't support myself and the children. The ultimate worst, of course, would be admitting I'm a failure at what I do. My sense of myself is so tied to my work that I can't find me anymore without my employee identification card. What's the worst that could happen to you?"

"That I would lose this child, or control over it, though I don't know which comes first. As much as I want it, sharing it with Mike is more punishment than I can imagine, yet the alternative, not to have it at all, is too terrible to consider."

"Aren't late pregnancies dangerous?" Bert liked Virginia and was as concerned about her decision as Shelby.

"Yes, for the child, not for the mother. But when I'm four months along—four or five weeks from now—I'll take a test and find out if the baby's all right. It's called amniocentesis . . ."

Bert grimaced. "Is that when they use the big needle"—he held his hands a foot apart—"and stick it . . ." He looked like a Japanese committing suicide with a sword.

Virginia laughed at his squeamishness. "A piece of cake. The miraculous thing is you know right away if the baby is normal."

"Suppose it isn't." Shelby had been listening attentively. "Would you . . . ?"

"Have an abortion? Sure. I wouldn't wish the life of a mongoloid on my child—or me."

"Why," Bert interjected softly, "is having another child, at forty, such a consuming passion when you already have children?"

"It's difficult to imagine, isn't it, Bert, and as a man I doubt if you'll understand the explanation, but much has to do with the fact that I *am* forty. It's a productive age for men, just when they begin to roll. But for us it's when *what we do best* begins to stop. Our chief mission on this earth, regardless of what else we may do along the way, is almost over. It's as if one half of you dies, yet you have to carry the carcass around for the rest of your life. Do you know that women are the only animals that go through menopause? All the others know it's time to die, and do once they're past bearing babies. In many parts of the world women still die around forty. Thanks to our knowledge of nutrition and disease control we get an extra thirty years."

"Surely you're not arguing," he said.

"No, Bert, I just want to live those thirty years with this child at my side. Funny, there's an undeniable voice deep inside crying, 'One more time.' At the same time I know I can't manage half a child. You know, it was just a few years ago that I discovered what the word 'autonomy' meant. Before that my father had the last word on every decision in my life, then he passed the torch to Jim Winburn, but now I have it. I've found out how heavy it is and how hard it is to keep it lit, but at last I'm responsible for my own light and I'll be damned if I'll give it up."

"Christ." He shook his head. "The rest of America is looking for a sugar daddy, a welfare check, or a rich uncle to die and leave them fixed and you . . ."

"Give up. Don't try to figure me out. What about you? The worst thing that could happen to Albert Arthur."

"That he would die tomorrow of Temek poisoning," Bert said immediately. "Both of you are so ready to cave in. You, Shelby, if you can't continue to work. You, Virginia, if you can't have another child. Your identities lie in what you have or what you do. As long as the sun keeps coming up after it goes down, I'll take my chances on what happens in between. Don't you know it's *how* you live and work and meet your responsibilities that counts, not what they are?"

"Isn't it amazing?" Shelby broke in. "Here's a man estranged from a bitter wife who for four years has refused to discuss divorce and who barely allows him glimpses of his children. A man who's had one unlucky break after another, who can't pay his last tax installment, and all he wants is another tomorrow." She looked at Virginia and threw her hands wide. "Men! Where do they get the confidence? The staying power? *How are they so sure of who they are?*"

"The only thing they're sure of is they get hungry when the sun goes down." Bert smiled. "C'mon, let's go to Sam's for a pizza. Let the big strong man take the two weak little girls out for a feed. That is, if you're up to pizza, Virginia. How's the digestion?"

"Perfect. Strange, but when I'm pregnant I feel, look, even sleep better than any other time. Course, I eat twice as much but I'm sure the big strong man can provide."

For two people resolved to take new directions, Bert and Shelby were singularly attached. Though they did not touch in public, their emotional connection pervaded the small group at dinner. Virginia was not surprised when they pled fatigue at an early hour and climbed the creaking stairs. Their departure left her the sole spectator for Shelby's Big Picture Show in the Sky, but then she was accustomed to solitary pleasures. Armed with an Amaretto, a reclining chair, and a sweater against a chill the ocean seems to provide even after blistering days, she stationed herself at the garden's edge with her back to the few remaining lights in the area and tuned her eyes to the darkness.

The moon, considerately, had resigned the sky, now an awesome stretch of black velvet strewn with diamonds. Cygnus the

Swan soared boldly overhead, eternally determined to overtake the brilliant Vega, her long neck leading a white starry cloud down the long side of the galaxy. Behind at some distance, the Dipper hung on the wall of the sky as solidly as on a hook beside a stove while Draco the Dragon meandered restlessly between it and its smaller clone. Cassiopeia's vivid W led her eyes eastward, where, having exhausted her camper's stargazing lore, she relied on luck alone to find the brave Perseus, son of Zeus, elevated to the heavens because he slew the monstrous Medusa. The first shooter confirmed his location, propelling toward her so violently she expected an accompanying noise like thunder or gunshot. A second chased after it halfway down the width of the sky, then a third, only seconds later, and before its long white tail disappeared another burst into a fiery suicidal plunge. At first she counted them on her fingers, then stopped as their numbers mounted, and transfixed, lay motionless letting the quarter hours slide by while the heavens played.

The balance between the increasingly uncomfortable night air and the wondrous spectacle before her began to tilt toward the dark friendly house, though each time she resolved to move, more celestial fireworks held her back, till at last she tired of even the incredible. Fumbling with the door, bumping blindly into the kitchen table, she made her way upstairs to sleep, as usual, alone. She was accustomed to it now, God knows, though she still slept so gently on one half of a bed she could make it up in the morning without walking to the other side. Perhaps she was symbolically waiting for the other half of her life to be occupied, or perhaps she was just lazy and didn't like cleaning up after herself any more than necessary. She was always the subject of her muddiest thoughts.

She changed in the dark, unwilling to break the spell of the magical night and lose the contentment she had felt under the restless sky. There had been no feeling of insignificance, of cosmic unimportance. In the very sight of infinity, unable to comprehend its universal vastness, she nevertheless felt a natural relationship and a destined right to be part of the whole. Why then such feelings of estrangement from much of her daily world? Why not the clear certainty of connection with human company that she felt with stars or autumn winds, mountains in the snow or Beethoven sonatas? (Her hand moved familiarly, comfortingly inside her nightgown across her breasts, knowing from experience that a connection with herself was an antidote to loneliness.) Mike had been such a bedful when she had slept with him, large and protective. He generally had fallen asleep quickly after they had made love, yet held her as at other times completely within his power, breathing softly across the top of her head. Even when he was unconscious she could not move from his grasp. (Her hand moved smoothly to her inner thigh, and she spread her knees slightly, but willed her mind to take no notice of what she was doing.) Their long forms had fit together naturally, unlike their minds and personalities. If only they could have slept their lives straight through, or met when time for sleep was near, when their insecurities dealt with sexual performance or who had too much of the blanket—both minuscule problems. (A mild electric current zinged through her back teeth as she rolled her nipples between her fingers, but continuing her game of denial, she refused to allow herself to move or to react.) They had untangled more than arms and legs when they left each other's bed. They rose as individuals determined to restate their uniqueness, their differences—their stubbornness. Some rebellion in Virginia forced her to stand ground she really did not care to defend; was she still battling the overweening control of her father and her husband? Once when Mike's business schedule changed, suddenly, aborting a short but carefully planned vacation, she refused to readjust her days away from the office and took her children on a holiday. To demonstrate her independence? To underline the distance between them? He said little when she told him—was she secretly pleased with the effect?—but something hardened behind his eyes. The next weekend on the boat he did not refer to the incident, but spent an uncommon amount of time joking with the captain and picking through various kinds of gear in marine supply stores. At dinner, in an unpretentious restaurant overhanging a dock, with a paper bib beneath his chin to catch the lobster butter, he launched an impersonal diatribe against liberals' approach to government. As she sat silently listening to his vehement arguments which had no pertinence to their being together, she recognized retaliation. He did not make love to her that night in the tight space they shared belowdecks, and though she knew the impasse should not go unresolved, she let them go to sleep without reproof. True, he was a master of the indirect attack, but was her liberalism directed only toward political issues? Where was the flexible, generous, compassionate approach to their relationship that she valued so highly in government? What unjustifiable distrust or insecurity so corked up her passion for him that it disallowed a free flow of honest emotion? (What was that surge, that thrill of feeling moving up from the midst of her? Whatever, she would not recognize it, most of all she would not move to its insistence, would not allow it to possess her.) Why must she be pursued, conquered, *forced* to turn over her emotional sword? And why was she willing to do it only when pinned down by another's superior strength? (No use. No more resistance. An inexorable sensation took over, forcing her knees together, her hands into the deepest part of her, blood in her ears drowning out the quiet, eyes shut against the darkness until it was over.)

God damn. Even celebrating aloneness, defending against isolation, he was there. She knew, though, he did not hold her against her will; she was the one who refused to let him go.

Saturday, August 16

Blessedly, the heat did not return with the day; fresh morning winds had chased off the low-hanging humidity. Virginia found Bert in the kitchen before eight, dressed for his daily run in shorts and the old-fashioned, underwear-shaped T-shirt that serious runners favor to differentiate themselves from amateurs. He was pouring water into the coffee machine and trying to fit the grounds container into place, without success.

"It's against my principles, but let me do that for you." Virginia bumped him aside good-naturedly. "And hand me the milk. We'll have café au lait."

"Too strong for the tummy as is? A widdle morning sickness here?" Bert asked in baby talk.

"I told you. Not a pregnant symptom."

"Then you're making the whole thing up. Just grandstanding for, for . . . attention."

"Did you almost say sympathy?" She put the lid on the pot of milk, lowered the flame, and laughed. "Don't feel sorry for me, Bert. If ever in my life I was sure of what I wanted, it's now. No one's holding my feet to the fire to have this child."

"Listen, I'm on your side. How about a run if you feel so terrific?" His tough slimness would have inspired Buddha to abandon his sedentary perch and take to the track.

"But you walk faster than I run."

"So warm me up for a couple of miles—I'll do knee lifts to get my blood going."

"You're on. But first, let's join the birds."

Every leaf of the weeping willow between them and the sun was outlined by the early rays, a thousand shades of green waving gently before them. Borders of impatiens, refreshed by the morning dew, surrounded the old brick patio, inviting them to sit awhile and drink their coffee.

"Is Shelby as unconcerned as she appears about losing her job? Or is she playing brave again, Bert?"

"She's terrified. Her confidence is intact. She knows she's a professional, as good as any around. But she doesn't know where the next dollar is coming from. She's the real support of those kids, you know. Have you ever heard of a guy with as much money as her husband had who left his wife in worse shape? That's what she got for wanting out of a marriage before it was fashionable. She always thought each paycheck would be the last—though you'd never know it the way she throws money around—and now she sees herself halfway to the poorhouse."

"That's an insecurity most working women I know carry on their backs—or in their wallets."

"Perhaps, but with Shelby it's a neurotic obsession. She just needs time to outline her options, and she'll have plenty of them—she's too resourceful not to. Her major self-recrimination at the moment comes from ratting on you to Strange. Pretty tough to forgive, I suppose."

"Wish I could dredge up some self-righteous anger. If I were completely honest, I'd admit something in me wanted him to know—I'm not quite sure why, though I damn well better figure it out. Maybe I'll do that on our run. Do you solve problems on the road the way other runners claim they do?"

"Just the big ones—like how to stretch out my hamstring; why my metatarsal is acting up . . ."

Bert ran Virginia to the beach—where they gawked like inland tourists seeing the monster ocean for the first time—and back again, twice, then pranced off smartly to his own pace. Slipping out of sandy shoes on the porch, she dripped perspiration onto the kitchen floor while she filled a large glass of orange juice and ice for herself and poured Shelby a cup of coffee.

"I like it straight and late," Shelby often said.

Ten o'clock was not at all late for Shelby. She enjoyed her bed too much to leave it without reason. When her hardest times came, she was wont to stretch out until resolution arrived, or depressed spirits revived. The Lying-Down Disease, she called it—a sickness that brought along its own cure.

"Groan, groan, if I weren't feeling so guilty, you wouldn't see me until afternoon," she said as Virginia waved the coffee under her nose like smelling salts.

Virginia sipped her orange juice curled in a chair by the bed, as Shelby unwound from her fetal position and made halting motions toward the bathroom.

"It's confession time," Virginia said as her friend began to regain consciousness. "I'm not proud of this, Shel, but I must admit to strong reservations about seeing a woman lawyer. That may sound fatuous, and it's an unbecoming statement from a strong supporter of our sex, but I'm looking for strength I don't have, and to me that spells m-a-n."

"No faith, no faith," Shelby sputtered through toothpaste.

"That's right. I have a blind spot. I won't end up in a female obstetrician's office either, without a major change of mind."

"Well, you're dead wrong, but it's understandable. How

many women did you ever go to when you were in trouble? Only one, and she said, 'See your daddy.'" Shelby turned the water off. "How do you feel about corporate executives who tell Rutherford they don't want the advice of a woman analyst?"

"I think they're ninnies. I *know* I'm better than anyone else in the place."

"Think that one over, pal, while I get dressed."

"Would you vote for a woman president? I'm serious, Shelby."

"Of course. Every guy who's held the office in the last twenty years has fucked it up. Why not? Of course, I'd insist that she be brilliant, capable, experienced—and vote as I do." She leaned out of the bathroom, hairbrush in hand. "You're the girl who doesn't trust a man enough to share your life with him, yet doesn't trust a woman enough to deliver your baby. Who's left?"

"Me—and you, I suppose."

Shelby walked to shelves in her closet, lined with numerous sweaters, shirts, shorts, shoes. "Perhaps if you trusted yourself more, the apparent authority of your deliverer would matter less." She stuck the legs of a teenager through short shorts, pulled on a T-shirt, scuffed into sandals. "Look. We all come by our prejudices honestly. Ask me how I feel about blacks."

"How do you feel about blacks?"

"Don't ask. Some are friends—close friends. Some are colleagues, for whom I have enormous respect. I've voted for blacks, supported their causes. I've slept with a black man." She looked for the shock on Virginia's face, found it, and hurried on. "But there's a lesson I learned somewhere back in the cotton fields that says we aren't the same. I'm not proud of that either."

"But white and black represent a hundred eighty degrees of the racial spectrum and two cultural heritages with an ocean between them. That's more understandable—and forgivable—than not trusting your own sex," Virginia argued.

"You're generalizing from the specific. You've never gone to a woman lawyer. Your other babies were delivered when you most probably didn't *know* a female OB. And how many women have you had the opportunity to vote for on any elective level? Give yourself—and us—a break. And Paula Seibert. She understands the struggle we've had to find a place for ourselves in this crazy age, caught between what we are and what we want to be, and explains it situationally, without hostility. You may not use her professionally, but you'll learn something from her."

Shelby was a competent driver except in the tangled mix of town traffic, where she became a public hazard checking out the latest additions to Bridgehampton's antique stores. Eyes more on shop windows than the road ahead, she spotted a quilt and wicker chaise that would be sure purchases on the way home. Local shopkeepers adored her. She knew them all by name, which she discovered mainly by writing checks. They were accustomed to her impulsive buying, in minutes skimming the best objects of the shop. They admired her sharp eye and unwillingness to haggle, and saved their favorite acquisitions until she saw them first. It was good business for both sides.

Virginia often accompanied her. It was relaxing, strolling from one place to another, talking over small problems, discussing the foibles of mutual friends and their own. Her purchases were chary compared to Shelby's, but then, their economic philosophies were different: she bought only when she had the money, and when she needed the object; Shelby bought what she wanted, then found a way to pay. In the same spirit she kept her refrigerator full, prepared to handle the uncounted and unexpected, even if food was eventually thrown out. She always preferred to have more of what she needed, whether it was food, things, friends, places to go, or temper tantrums. The only thing spare about Shelby was her waistline.

They found themselves virtually alone on the Saturday highway, traveling back in the direction from whence the city horde had come. Shelby took the Quogue exit, and immediately, as was the way with rural villages situated on the East End, they were in the heart of town. A few blocks down the main street, a turn toward the ocean, they were again surrounded by deepset fields with trees suspended like huge umbrellas deflecting the summer sun. Bullrushes marked the almost hidden entrance to a tiny lane. Several drives later they turned into the Seibert property, and before the engine was off were greeted by its owner.

"No trouble finding us, I hope." Still in tennis clothes, a white band around coal-black hair and a smile as bright as her lipstick, the strongly built woman, thickening around the middle, waved them out of the car and inside. Introductions and glasses of iced tea moved them from the kitchen through several comfortable rooms out onto a deck shaded by an awning. The lawn sloped to a pond of some length from left to right, but the width was shallow, so the thickly growing water lilies seemed to form a bridge to the other side. Virginia looked at the peaceful sight and longed to walk across. The conversation they were about to have was the opposite of the scene's harmony; it was about nature's forces out of kilter.

"I brought you the two documents I received Thursday," she began.

"From Strange?" Paula asked.

"Yes. A temporary restraining order prohibiting abortion and a petition to establish paternity—at least I think that's what they are."

Paula glanced at them quickly, nodding her head in assent, then placed them beneath the yellow pad on the table before her. "After you called, Shelby, I made a cursory search of the law to give you a rough idea what's happening here. It's a complicated field—paternity law—and a muddy one. For example, a lot depends on where you happen to live. If you were a resident of Brooklyn, Mike couldn't sue at all because fathers there have no standing to initiate proceedings."

"Well, it's too late for us to move her," Shelby said, "but suppose she just went away for a while."

"No good," Paula answered. "The putative father, as he's called, can bring a case like this any time before the child's eighteenth birthday."

"Jesus. Will I have to fight this for years?" Virginia asked.

"Oh, no. At least, as long as the judge thinks he has enough evidence to make a decision now. But let me go on," Paula said briskly. "The Family Court has jurisdiction over these cases. If yours goes to trial, it'll be heard by a judge without a jury who can also, by the way, exclude the general public if he or she wants, so you can expect some privacy."

"Thank God for small favors. But, Paula, suppose I don't respond to the petition at all, what could really happen to me?"

"That wouldn't be smart. The judge would issue a warrant directing the respondent—that's you—to be arrested and brought before the court."

Virginia sighed. "O.K., then what does the petition actually ask?"

"He's claiming to be the father of your child, and he's asking you to show cause why the court should not enter a declaration of paternity in his favor. Ordinarily, the petitioner asks for an order of support as well, but that's usually when the petitioner is the mother. In this case he states he's ready and willing to provide support."

"Would the amount of support make a difference to the court?"

"Well, the court has the power to award custody of an illegitimate child"—Paula saw Virginia's grimace and slowed, but did not stop—"to the father, if that's in the child's best interests, but it won't award him custody simply because he has more material advantages than the mother."

"Is there any possibility—at all—that I could lose complete custody?"

Paula smiled gently. "Anything can happen in a trial, you should be aware of that before you get into one, though I suppose it's unlikely in your case. Of course, the court could order visitation at specified times, or perhaps joint custody. Fathers are getting a more sympathetic hearing today than they have in the past."

"But how does he prove his case?" Virginia was fearful of the answer, already experiencing the confrontation.

"The first issue is whether he had access to you." She saw another moment of discomfort on Virginia's face. "Sorry. That's the law's term, not mine. It means whether there was the opportunity for the two of you to have sexual relations. Then he will have to present evidence that relations took place about the time of conception. That may be difficult to prove if he doesn't know exactly when the baby will be born, or, I suppose, exactly how far along you are in the pregnancy. Still, he can ask the judge to order an examination by a doctor for a professional judgment, and proceed from there."

"How does he prove access?" Now Virginia began to be interested by the process, apart from her personal involvement.

"Oh, pictures, calendars, testimony of friends. Headwaiters, hotel clerks, apartment house elevator operators, whatever evidence he can pull together. He has the burden of proof to show that access was possible. You either prove it wasn't, or show there were one or more other men who could also be the father. The evidence must be absolutely clear and convincing in his favor before a filiation order will be awarded."

"Mike always thought he was sterile. He's had any number of tests over the years, and all the results said he couldn't have children."

"Impossible to have children? Or unlikely that he would?"

"I don't know. I never asked for a detailed readout."

"Of course, you can ask to have *him* medically examined, too. If the tests prove sterility beyond a doubt, then he has no case, but my guess is that a report would show him less likely than the average man to father a child, but wouldn't deny the possibility, however remote."

"Suppose I *do* take the stand?"

"And deny he had access? Then it's your word against his, and the credibility of your witnesses against his, and the judge will decide. There's one more possibility. Usually the court will either dismiss the petition or grant the order of filiation. However, most of these cases take place *after* a child is born, and as a routine matter the judge orders a blood-grouping test to determine the possibility of a man being the father. It's possible the court may put off its decision, if the evidence is too contradictory, until after the birth so a blood test can be made on the baby."

"Then this could drag out for almost a year!" Virginia was clearly aghast.

"Well, usually paternity cases aren't brought until after the baby is born anyway, unless a woman wants the father to bear medical expenses."

"Can a blood test positively identify Mike as the father?"

"No, nothing is as certain as that. However, it can say if he definitely is *not* the father. If it comes out positive, it means he *might* be."

"So, then I'd have a fighting chance on the strength of the evidence . . ."

"Right. And you can make him stipulate now the date or dates when he thinks he got you pregnant."

"Singular. Just one date."

"All the better. Then if the baby is born either early or late, in relation to his date of conception, there's even more evidence in your favor."

"But that's a long shot."

"True."

"So what are my chances?"

"Hard to say without knowing more of the facts, and what he might allege, but in the past it has been terribly difficult for women to win paternity suits. The courts have been reluctant to name a man unless the evidence is overwhelming, because it means twenty-one years he has to support the child. I suppose a judge will be just as slow to force you to accept his paternity if you insist it isn't true. But you must deny it, strongly, and be willing to bring all kinds of allegations against him to win the case."

"Like what?" Defending was a situation Virginia could handle; attacking was another.

"Like strong evidence as to his sterility. The numerous other relationships he has had without issue. A detailed enumeration of the times the two of you had intercourse without using contraception. The methods he has used in the past to force his will—business deals, that sort of thing. Anything that makes him out to be demanding and tyrannical, a man who takes what he wants. And any kind of evidence that would prove him to be an unfit father . . ."

"But he wouldn't be."

"You can make a person seem like almost anything in a law court. For example, witnesses who have seen him drunk, or in fits of temper. Or women who could testify to his having had a number of affairs."

"But it's all so ugly."

"Well, remember, anything you can do to him he can do to you. Listen, Virginia. Before you start thinking about the outcome, you'd better think about what your position will be. I don't need to remind you that you will be under oath, as will the witnesses you present in your defense."

"Any off-the-cuff advice?"

"Sure. Stay out of court. This is one of those personal tangles better decided quietly, between the parties. That may be ex-

actly what Strange is looking for, a way to force you to reach a
private accommodation. Believe me, trials of this kind do no
one any good. They're expensive, can be lengthy, attract exten-
sive publicity—especially when one of the protagonists is as
well known as he—and generally deteriorate into embarrassing
petty wrangling. Have you tried talking to him?"

"Unfortunately, yes—and those were the results." Virginia
pointed toward the legal documents. "There's no accommodation possible with Mike short of acknowledging him as father and arranging some kind of joint custody and control."

"And you can't handle that?"

"Emotionally? No. With the child or without, I cannot deal
with him in my life. Suppose I make a run for it, just leave the
jurisdiction?"

"You can be arrested even if he *thinks* you are going to
leave. Once you're gone you cannot return without the arrest
warrant being enforced, no matter how many years later—
unless, of course, he drops the suit."

"But Mike would be the type to find you wherever you are,
kidnap the child, bring him back to New York, and force you
into court," Shelby said. "You can't run far enough from a man
like that."

"Is he vindictive?"

"No, Paula." Virginia's eyes saddened, she swallowed to clear
her throat. "And he's not mean. But he's used to having his
way. He's a decision maker, an activist. If we agree that men, in
general, run the world, and that just a tiny few of them make
the major decisions, then you understand his power—and his
attitude. Presidents ask his advice, don't you see? Charities seek
his support. Political parties vie for his attention, foreign gov-
ernments for his business. The media want to record his words
and his pictures, socialites fight for his attendance at their
affairs. Even without his looks and charm he could crook an
index finger and lead almost any female to bed. Now I have
what he wants . . ."

Paula nodded in agreement. "The ability to procreate is the only unique quality women have over men—those who *can* father children. For those who apparently can't, having a child must seem like the ultimate power. Since he's habitually in control, he may see this as a two-sided battle, to establish dominance over you and at the same time get his child."

"*My* child, Paula. No other possessive pronoun, please. Mike's the kind of person for whom relationships are spelled out in pronouns. My women, my wife, my child. Intimacy isn't the foundation of his associations, ownership is. If he used feelings as a basis for personal connections, he'd have to drop to the equal of the dependent, the weaker, and abandon his power position. He can't do that. Though he'd be the last to admit it, or even understand it, Mike's an emotional inadequate." Virginia, ready to conclude the session, pushed away her tea glass. "Back to the legalities. From what you've said, either I make myself out to be a loose woman, as we used to say, with various potential fathers in and out of my bedroom, or I prove he's sterile, or we let the court decide which of us is telling the truth."

"Without closer examination, that's the way I see it. Now if witnesses are willing to testify to having relations with you around the time of conception, you almost certainly have yourself a victory, and an easy one. Otherwise you may be in for a punishing trial whether you win or lose. Who is more fit to be a parent, and why, as presented in evidence by psychiatrists, relatives, friends, and accountants, can be a tawdry circus, and the principals too often look like clowns."

The women drove a number of miles toward home without speaking. Shelby's methodology for solving a problem was to talk it to death, attack with feelings, parry with honest revelations about the weakness of her position, and vanquish it utterly by the force of her arguments. Virginia, instead, inwardly rolled over her obstacles, searching out any flimsy understructure, hunting routes around or under which would negate the need for a frontal confrontation. Once Mike had taught her a lesson about finding a difficult solution. Overly simplistic, it was a short question: What do you want to happen? Followed by another question: Then what is the shortest line between what you have and what you want? It worked for Mike; he ordered his life by it. She applied it now, staring at the horizon, her knees jacked up against the dashboard. What *do* I really want? I want to have this baby, and I want it wonderfully, happily, pleasurably to fit into my life. What's the shortest line between where I am and what I want? The answer floated to the top of her mind as in the inky liquid of the mysterious black balls of her childhood which she turned over and over to answer profound twelve-year-old queries. "Compromise." She said the word out loud.

"What?" Shelby asked.

She repeated, "I've got to compromise. Give in. There's no way I can paint myself out to be a harlot." She laughed. "I'd have to hire actors to perjure themselves. It's been so long since I was with anyone but Mike, I can't remember what's the back and what's the front. That's the smart thing to do—why can't I do it?"

"Perhaps you need to wrestle Mike, to grapple with him in mortal battle to work him, finally, out of your mind."

"If only I thought I could."

"You never did respond to Paula's suggestion, you know, that perhaps he's trying to establish dominance over you. Maybe *he* needs to spit the bone of you out of his throat too."

"No, Mike always *had* control—I handed that over like my handbag to a purse snatcher. Ridiculous as it may sound, I believe I'm trying to prove my supremacy *over him*. It goes like this: The dumb ox wasn't smart enough to know that we were a golden couple, wasn't steadfast enough to hold on to the one person who could have shown him, taught him love. He traded me in for shinier models that will never go the distance. So how do I get back at him? By producing the only trophy he really wants, only I don't let him join me in the winner's circle. Isn't there power in that?"

"But, kid," Shelby said, staring too long for safety across the front seat, "quelle price! Sure, queens had their heads chopped off when they couldn't deliver babies, but just because you *can* doesn't make you royalty or give you any real power. And think what you give up for your Pyrrhic victory. Being a mother's terrific and all that, but motherhood by its nature requires denying the importance of *your* identity, *your* connection with the outside world."

"But," Virginia retorted, "isn't avoiding motherhood—which we'd agree is central to women's lives—acquiescing to the male world of power where thinking and doing are more important than feeling and giving? I refuse to do that! Men live their lives for their individual accomplishments. I'd rather be a member of the sex that has a broader concern for the human condition."

"Not all men."

"Oh yes, all men except those who opt out of business and political and professional pursuits—the power fields. Some few become writers and artists and clergymen, but they have to assume 'feminine' qualities to do that, like compassion and sacrifice and devotion. Look at those who make up the liberal leaders in this country. They're cloistered academics and philanthropists who never enter the lists; they're artists and intellectuals who'd rather have ideas than possessions. Now who are the conservatives? They're people who analyze and strategize, who build dreams into realities, activate systems, and compete for material rewards. Now I'm not ranking one above another," Virginia said quickly, "we need both, but who's to say that feminine qualities like endurance, selflessness, tenderness— more apparent in the quiet world of motherhood than in any other activity I can think of—aren't just as valuable as characteristics that make you successful in the great big outside world?"

"O.K., O.K., our mothering skills are considerable, I'll concede that, but the fact is that our society doesn't value them as highly as you and I do. They are totally unpaid. A woman can put in a lifetime of work at the hearth and cradle and not earn a penny for her old age. What man would work so hard for so little?" Conversations like this made Shelby angry; she put her foot harder on the accelerator as she talked. "Nine out of ten men who leave their families for whatever reason never give them any support. Why does our society allow that? Why don't other men, who are in positions of power, call them to account? Because the women who were abandoned are doing jobs that are unimportant to them, that's why. Men care about women mothering children *only when they want the children*. Remember those pictures of children in Vietnam orphanages? Perfect little GI Joe faces except for the slanted eyes. Why haven't their fathers claimed them? Why don't they care?"

"I know, Shelby, I know. And I know the price you pay when you devote yourself to another human being's welfare, and the inward direction motherhood forces your life to take, and the sublimation it requires to live through another's potential instead of your own. I remember, all too well, how your daily life is trivialized, how you give up adventure and opportunity. My head knows all those things, but what can I do? Once a child starts growing inside it changes your perception of reality. This one's already a solid part of my life and my future . . ."

"And Mike isn't . . . ?"

"Mike's like those soldiers who left Vietnam who had more important families to go to. Do you think for a minute he'd be putting up this fight if he had children of his own? It's just another possession for him, another achievement. I make no difference one way or the other, so how can I include him in my life?"

"You're not wavering, even a little?"

"Sure I am, like a pendulum, swinging first to one side, then the other—for two reasons. Because I hate my petty motives for revenge and because the idea of a trial paralyzes me. But I love this child, Shelby, with the same fierceness I feel toward Max and Maggie and I simply have to have it, though to tell you the truth, it's easier for me to think about not having it than having Mike around playing father."

"You'd actually prefer an abortion?"

"Prefer is the wrong word. I keep telling you, I have no choice. I'd lose my sanity around him all the time—having him but not having him. I'm somewhat suicidal now, every day. Doing away with myself and the baby at the same time is one way out of this."

Shelby turned from the road again to look hard at her friend. "You don't mean that."

"No, not really—though maybe I do. I'm not sure of anything except that I want out of this."

"Well, if you do yourself in," Shelby said dryly, "and you have any years left over, I wish you'd leave them to me."

A party in the Hamptons is just different. The quality of the food is unimportant, though clever cooks of both genders grouse on the way home if only minimal effort has been made. It scarcely takes more than that with the nearby heavy harvests producing vegetables Cézanne would have painted, and local specialty shops dizzying the senses with crusted breads, pâtés, and cheeses whose smells alone are worth the golden price. No, food is immaterial; flowers too. God's Garden overflows in such abundance that arranged additions are superfluous. And as if in recognition of Nature's gayer dress, clothes attract little attention. Oh, there are some partygoers self-consciously imprisoned in jump suits and golden chains with tousled hair and four-inch heels, but they are not the artists and agents, writers and film-makers, the broadcast types, publishers, entertainers, and print reporters who gather clannishly together—and they would not be welcome. For these people—politically too democratic to join clubs which restrict blacks or Jews or women—unofficially constitute a blatantly discriminatory group with nebulous but rigid membership requirements based on public acclaim and recognition; and this amorphous, ever-changing group is the central focus of the Hamptons. As if wearing horse blinders, it does not remark on Southampton's black-tie dinners; it does not report on East Hampton's matches on the grass courts at the Maidstone Club; and the sexy swirl of singles who stalk partners on Amagansett's Asparagus Beach, greased to glowing between their bikini parts, might as well sun at Coney Island. It is concerned only with itself and expects others to be also—and they are.

The trio in white pants and pastel shirts, with sweaters knotted casually around their shoulders, left their wineglasses in the kitchen and headed toward the car in the first still moments of the evening. They had been to many such gatherings before, Shelby in a starring role, Virginia supporting, Bert holding himself in the background, perennially complaining about the arrogance and egotism around them. Having neither the wealth nor the celebrity that follows from acceptance by a greater public, he sublimated his own feelings of inferiority by grumbling about others' superior attitudes. He had a point—but he missed theirs, for they were genuinely talented people whose ideas were their fortunes, and who sought each other out for several reasons: they understood the warmth that flowed from having a hit or writing a book that sells, and the cold of failure that could just as easily freeze them out the next time around; they enjoyed the affirmation of status by being around those whom they also admired; and they, quite simply, liked to be with people who could talk.

"Is there an occasion tonight?" Bert asked as he backed into the roadway. "Or is the crowd meeting for the usual celebrity picture-taking session for the Bridgehampton *Sun?*"

Shelby tried to ignore his barbs, though inwardly she winced and filed them under "incompatible." "Tony splurged and took the same house he rented last year, though it's more than he can afford. It sits on Mecox Bay and probably he wants to show off the sunset. Besides, he's had a tough year, splitting up with Annie, and you know how he loves those kids—to the point of being an unnatural parent—I think he wants to prove to them that life goes on as before. Anyway, he's the cook in the family, so the food should be terrific."

"He's the nosher in the family too, if you can judge by the girth," Bert muttered.

"Wait till you see the *new* Anthony Salenger, darling of the nation's editorial pages. He's lost a hundred and sixty pounds this year, and only a hundred and twenty of those were Annie. He's looking quite svelte. I had him picked out for you, Gin, till you decided to expand *your* middle—just as he got his under control."

"Well, don't give up the idea," Virginia added in good humor, happy to be away from her problems for a few hours. "What makes you think pregnant isn't sexy? Besides, look how convenient I am. Anyone I sleep with doesn't have to worry about getting me pregnant."

"Is that why we're putting ourselves through this group torture, to provide Gin with a little sex?" Bert asked. "If I'd known I'd have handled her needs at home and we'd be boiling lobsters this very minute."

"Anything for a friend, right, Bertie?" Shelby reached across to rub the back of his neck. "We're going because Tony's a sweet guy who needs some support right now—and because Stewart Banner surprised me with a call while you two were at the beach. He'll be there and says he wants to talk about my future."

Bert and Virginia looked at Shelby in surprise. "So ABC knows you're free!" Virginia exclaimed. "What's he offering? Are you interested?"

"I don't know to both questions," Shelby answered. "Guess everybody knows I'm loose—we aren't called the communications industry for nothing. If I get any offers from the other networks, they'll come within a week or not at all, so I'm not surprised to have him tap me on the shoulder. Let's wait and see, though, if he signs my dance card."

Bert parked at the head of the car-lined driveway without even a pass at closer access to the party, acknowledging their late arrival. The women balanced on their toes during the long walk to the house, holding their heels above the soft ground, Virginia matching her mood by falling behind Bert and Shelby. Usually she was genial by nature, and extroverted, stimulated by the prospect of meeting people, curious, even eager to vacuum-clean a roomful of new information. As a rule. Since her break with Mike, though, and her ordeal of loneliness began, she found herself less inclined to seek, and more uncomfortable accepting, others' company. Now the hum of the house, growing louder as they approached, beat down her former enthusiasm. As if chained to Shelby, bound and forced to follow, she moved reluctantly ahead. When they reached the front door, and the chatter rose to din level, she closed her eyes, inhaled deeply, and willed herself inside. Was the loss of one person, the opportunity of one connection, so killing that it destroyed forty years of habitual vitality?

"Overreacting again . . . self-indulgent martyr . . . wallowing in self-pity . . ." Virginia forced a smile and froze it, muttering self-reproach as she pushed into the party, placing tiny cheek kisses around like a mama bird returning to a nest full of outstretched necks. Playing by the rules, she moved robot-like toward the bar on the wide veranda that promised a strong shot of alcoholic courage and a view of the tranquil pond. The old song arrived in her head unbidden, at first barely making itself heard. ("What did I have that I don't have? What did he like that I lost track of?")

She brushed it away to make her social contribution, talking animatedly while she waited for a drink, but Alan Jay Lerner would not leave her alone. Even as she spoke, the tune came back with its devastating questions. ("What isn't there that once was there? What have I got a great big lack of?")

How would she keep from crying standing in the late sundown amidst unsuspecting friends who had come for conversation, not a display of neurosis? The song was undeniable. ("I'm . . . just a victim of time . . . obsolete in my prime . . . Out of date and outclassed, by my past.")

Goddamn you, Lerner, she thought, you're not invited to this party. But the words kept coming. ("What did he love that there's none of?") She broke off abruptly, knowing she had failed the experiment, and almost rudely slid away from her group.

The combination of flight from inadequacy and eyes blurred with tears made recognizing the body she bumped into difficult.

"Tony, it's you! How really good to see you!" It was. The thinned-down face was flaccid still but showed promise now of a definitive jawbone, the slightly protruding eyes more interesting than when surrounded by fleshy pudding, and the hug was genuine. They held each other at arm's length and performed the unusual act at a party of looking deeply into each other's eyes.

"Shelby says my ESP is improving. I picked the only weekend you'd be around—lucky me."

"Lucky *me*," she said suddenly, meaning it, and following it cheerfully with chatter buoyed by the presence of a person she really liked, warmed by his response to her. Her gloom melted as rapidly as the ice cubes in her wine.

Tony had looked for and finally located her in the crush. Tired of playing host, he had no intention of sharing her. In a manic mood, he said, "Come, lovely one, we'll leave these lost and perverted souls and join the swans." Waving an arm airily in the direction of the water, he encircled her waist with the other.

Still small, she thought—thank God. As they strolled toward Mecox Bay she remembered the condolence note she had written last summer when his marriage died. He must have been looking out from this very spot when he answered with words of the saddest sound: "I stand at the point from which Gatsby gazed across at that which could never be his, and like him, am oppressed by the impossible. I watch and wait for the light to go out and take it with hope, and I wonder if I will ever care again."

Unlike most, who kept their emotions hidden, Tony's soul showed like a petticoat; it never embarrassed him, particularly in the demonstration of affection toward his children and, once, toward Annie. He reminded Virginia of the native toadfish swimming in the shallows around them, fish almost hideous, half head, half body. They frighten all but female toadfish, who, heavy with eggs, search anxiously for a place to deposit them. Like Tony, the territorial toadfish is a nester, guarding a tree stump, a submerged boot, a tin can. At night he grunts a love song, so weird and insistent it can be heard above the surface far from the liquid mating grounds. It is the signal that guides a transient female toward his plebeian nest and beguiles her into dropping yellow eggs at his fin. Duty performed, the female darts to other watery pursuits, but the loyal father, relinquishing even food, guards the eggs until they are hatched, then continues his vigil at nest-side until the hatchlings are free swimmers, some six weeks in all without sustenance.

Tony's love call had produced his Annie, graceful daughter of Broadway, spawned in the theatrical world by a father who stamped his taste upon it and her. She remained in his nest long enough to leave her young, then answering the wilder, more familiar call of adventure, abandoned her ugly toadfish to raise their offspring alone.

Only Tony was not ugly now. He was not handsome, far from that, but certainly physically appealing, Virginia decided, looking sideways. Suddenly, as they spoke, the song was back. ("Where . . . do I go to repair . . . all the wear and tear?") Ah, Lerner, I've got it yet, she thought, the old girl hasn't forgotten all the music. And she marveled how easily it came back, the ingratiating smile, the gentle look. Her soft exclamations of awe, the can-I-feel-your-muscle? approach. She watched him arch to her stroking like a cat; verbally she ran her fingers down his spine.

The sun dropped into the water while they talked. "If we stay here any longer," Virginia said, "your bartenders will pass a hat for their pay."

"You're right. I should go back and take credit for throwing this lavish affair, but we must finish our conversation—when? tomorrow night? I know, let's have a picnic on the beach and burn our hides or finish the *Times* Acrostic, whichever comes first. Or let's fight the weekenders for a bar stool at the Laundry or . . ."

She ducked the invitation without really considering it. "Can't, damn it. Got to get back to the city early and attack some major problems."

"Then don't go home now. Stay till the last sodden guest leaves and pick up dirty ashtrays with me. We'll finish what's left in the bottles and tell drunken secrets."

"But Shelby . . ."

"Will never miss you. And I'm lonesome, so you'll get points for playing Good Samaritan."

Lonesome—he said it. The word she had come to think of as her middle name, a perpetual condition to be endured but never overcome, a destiny without deliverance. Tony too? Others suffered the disease? How selfish of her to forget, but her loneliness produced a kind of isolation. It drew down a curtain between her and life's audience, forcing her to play out her desperation on an empty stage without the reaction of fellow sufferers.

She had eyes that melted on loved or steady faces, and a smile that preferred to give pleasure than hide regret. They combined to answer him. "Tony, it's a perfect offer," and she held his face in both hands as she kissed his lips lightly. "On to the ashtrays."

And to a connection, however brief and however wrong for her in the longer view of time. She knew, walking back to the house, stumbling in the dark over unfamiliar terrain, that she was probably doing the same thing emotionally, but the short-term gain of relief from pain and the pleasure of lifting another's despair discounted the future.

She passed the final hour of the party in high spirits, delighting again in being wanted, catching Tony's eye occasionally as he circled among his departing guests, smiling with him in collusion as he fanned them out the doors. Except for Shelby, whose last look was an over-the-shoulder smirk, his friends were unaware of how appreciated their departures were.

As if a puff of wind pushed the last ones out and slammed the door behind them, they were suddenly standing alone in the debris of plastic cups on windowsills, crumpled napkins filled with half-eaten bits of pâté and cheese, pillows spilled from sofa perches, cigarettes still smoking and smelling foul as they died. Virginia stubbed out those nearest her, stacked the first batch of disposable cups, and looked around for a place to throw them.

"Tony, why don't you empty the last of the ice, find a large plastic bag for the pail, and we'll dump everything in one spot."

"Good idea," he said, heading for the kitchen. "A bag and a bottle of wine, not necessarily in that order."

By the time he returned, victoriously waving a newly opened Chablis and two wineglasses, she had gathered the flotsam in the living room and screened porch, had righted lampshades, straightened pictures, and generally smoothed away the crowd's effects. The dining room's destruction lay ahead but Tony stopped her, turning her around at the door.

"Enough. I need your company more than your help." He placed a glass in her hand, filled it with the light-gold liquid, filled his own, then tipped it to touch the edge of hers and said softly, "Lovely to see you."

It did not take him long after they were seated on the porch sofa, sipping their wine and laughing about some of the party's glossier moments, to move naturally toward her mouth and cover it with his. There was no hesitation in her response. She simply cleared her mind and accepted the sensation, kissing him back with an abandon that comes from either passion or a hunger for it. She gratefully welcomed the warm hand that slid under her blouse to hold her softest side, and even helped the fingers that moved to the side opening of her jeans. No warning flags went up, no yellow caution lights blinked behind her fast-closed eyes. She listened only to her breath against his face and felt only the relief of having his hand between her legs. Gratefully she slipped her legs around him and took him into her for the satisfaction of feeling whole again. His weight and warmth was a simple elemental pleasure, like eating a candy bar when famished, or finding a fire when terribly cold. When his muscles contracted for the final surge, he shot life into her again, and though she had not come to the height of her own feelings, she lay in the quiet of his in a kind of peace. She ran her hands from his shoulders to his waist, patting him down from heavy gasps to even breathing, and relished the momentary connection to a man for whom she felt not the slightest affection.

"Thank you," she said evenly.

Tony raised his upper body to look at her face, half afraid she was mocking him. "Are you serious?"

She pulled him back to her. "Sh-h-h. No response necessary, I'm just happy to be here."

But why? All her life she had pushed hands away: awkward sweating hands of boys in the front seats of their fathers' cars parked at drive-in movies, while more sweat formed on the six-pack on the floor, and still more formed under her arms in dread that the hands would fight their way to her chest and discover her padded bra. Later she decided her small bosom in the Age of Monroe had been more responsible for her virtue than her morals, but together they kept her virginal.

Even during her engagement to Jim Winburn, with both of them puffing on the sofa in heavy petting exercises, she limited the activity of his hands and other parts. Her mother, periodically blinking the hall lights from an upstairs switch installed for just that purpose, was added restraint. Most in control of her actions, though, was her father, who delivered a mighty message to her at the age of fifteen. Striding unexpectedly into her room as she sat cross-legged on her bed studying, he smoothed her bangs and said, as if the moment could not pass without her knowing, "Every man wants his wife to be a virgin, Virginia, I want you to understand that. Regardless of what he may do himself or ask you to do, he'll feel cheated if he doesn't marry a virgin."

The sermon was completed as quickly as it began. Having fulfilled his parental duty of sex education, he left her. His message did not. It never occurred to her later to disappoint him or the man she would marry, and girdled in the chastity belt of his expectations, she wore the white of an honest bride.

Breaking the rules of marriage was no more tempting. She discouraged southern hands when the young men in her crowd spent long weekends with football and Bourbon, and years later eastern hands of more sophisticated men on terraces between waltzes or by fires after hearty days of skiing. She simply was not interested—perhaps not strongly sexed? She did not dwell on the answer. Being with Jim Winburn was enough for her, sexually, even when most of their other bonds had broken down. When she found herself single again, the need to experiment—or the pleasure—was no more a part of her than it had ever been and she found herself still brushing the hands away. Except for Mike's, of course, from which she never defended herself.

Tonight was different. Tony was a man for whom she felt nothing except a sort of sweet friendship and gentle pity, and from whom she wanted nothing, least of all a phone call in the morning, who would probably present her with difficulties as she moved away, and she would certainly move away, but to whom she was deeply grateful, for he affirmed what she was desperate to know and unable to discover alone, that she was still normal, functioning, alive.

"Just, thank you."

Tony deposited her in the driveway at her insistence. She was determined to walk into the house alone, more to declare her independence than to avoid waking Shelby and Bert. She passed through the front of the house and, disregarding the late hour, went again to the back patio and the chaise from which she had seen the incredible stars, but tonight they were lost to a rising moon which spotlighted elongated striations of gray poufs moving across a faint Milky Way. The night was as cloudy as her mind, which wrestled with unanswerable questions: Had she desecrated her child with the sperm of a man not its father, and had she soiled herself? Was her need so great, or so paltry, that it could be satisfied by the body of a mere acquaintance? Would he have found her as desirable if he had known she was pregnant? Why did she care so little, and why, dear God, didn't she—somewhere, anywhere—hurt?

Sunday, August 17

Morning brought no answers to the self-mutilating questions. It did bring the telephone call from Tony, which she did not want, and a need to sort her feelings out with Shelby, which she did. The call came first; it was as kind, as touching as the man who made it, with expressions of concern for the late hour of their return, remonstrances that she had returned at all, an appropriate amount of humor about something he had said, and she had done, and then—she waited and it came—a request for more: more of her, more time together, and the unspoken implication with which serious people open lines of communication, the possibility that she might be for him and he for her the personal link both were missing, desperately, in their lives. A drowning man pushed a life preserver to another swimmer in trouble; she tapped it back.

"I really can't stay over another day. I'm knee-deep in legal troubles and have to be looking up lawyers in the yellow pages tomorrow." She heard the disappointment before he spoke.

"Not coming back anytime soon?"

"No plans at the moment." She was turning away a caring, compassionate man, worthy of attention anytime, but even more so when she herself was needy. Why? She bit her lip and backtracked. "Do you have any plans to be in the city?"

"None as long as the weather holds. Actually, I'll have to see my agent soon. If the clouds roll in, I'll call, all right? And use him as an excuse to see you."

It was as if her loneliness were too frightening to share with anyone else. She dropped the phone in its cradle with the relief one releases a heavy package. The ghost of Jim Winburn danced around her, sticking out his tongue, mocking again in a singsong what he had said shortly before their separation: "No man will ever want you, because you won't want any man." Michael Strange's ghost was more dignified, in control. "You set the rules, baby. Independence is what you wanted; independence is what you get."

Not fair, not fair. She shook the ghosts away. So I'm a woman who doesn't give up the dead easily, she thought. Yes, it *is* harder to see the future when your eyes are blinded by the past. But where do you put memories when you want to retire them? What safety-deposit vault holds thoughts, hopes, connections, so you can sign in once a year, check them for changes or deterioration, and lay them to rest again? God, let me rent that magic box.

The familiar onset of depression, so recognizable from its many previous visits, was no surprise. She had come to know its symptoms as a victim of migraines knows when the edges of consciousness are first nibbled, then attacked in giant bites. She felt her spirits begin to decline the way miners, depicted in movies, climb into crowded elevators and, wooden-faced, realizing there is no deliverance from their preordained duty, descend into blackness. With the same foreknowledge, she knew she would return to an acceptable level again—at least, she always had.

She needed Shelby. The conversation would be difficult—

Shelby disliked Virginia when her optimism faded, her mouth turned down and held. Nor did she understand her. Shelby's own powers of recuperation contained ingredients of verbosity and wit, a physical exuberance that dared enemies to attack, and dispersed them with sheer bravado. Mostly she did not understand Virginia's hopelessness, and the despair her flawed relationship with Mike had produced, but sitting at the bleached pine table in the comfortable kitchen, still sleep-heavy and thick-voiced, she stirred her tea in absentminded circles and tried again to divine the crippling insecurities.

"So you slept with him, big deal. Who are you, Original Virtue? What do you have that's so precious it can't be shared, or given away? And don't give me your mother's sermon on reputations again. A reputation isn't something you own, it's what others think of you."

"Don't belittle this, Shelby. I can rationalize the physical part of last night without beating up on myself. What consumes me is my inability to come to terms with my future—aloneness made permanent. I don't care anything about Tony —never will . . ."

"How can you be so sure?"

"Hell, I know. I always know. I see a man across a room, and know. The way he smiles, how his eyes look at me, how correct his grammar is, how long his pants are, whether he wears ankle socks . . ."

"Jesus, all that before you know his bank balance?"

Virginia laughed. "Come on, pal. You size men up the same way—and they do the same to us. Tony's too soft, too flabby, even too considerate—he borders on submissive. I knew he wasn't a realistic possibility for me, but I slept with him anyway. Now screw my mother's concern for my reputation, Shel, I'm not proud of myself for dropping on a couch with a fellow I have no intention of spending any time with—regardless of what a sweetheart he is. The worst of it was how good he felt. How welcome to feel his weight on my chest, to be wrapped in strength again . . ."

"And to be wanted?"

"Of course, that's the most seductive element."

"So?"

"So I'm reduced to finding that comfort like a two-bit hooker. Listen, when I was growing up in Atlanta, do you know the one girl that any guy could have? She was a deaf-mute, rather a pretty thing, but an object of derision most of the time—till one of the fellows got horny. Then he'd call her parents and take her out, just long enough to screw her in the back of his car and drop her at home again. She was the most desperate human being I've ever known, frantic for some kind of connection with people her own age. She'd do anything to get noticed, and she did. I find myself thinking of her now. I recognize a similar desperation, and an inability to change my situation. I have no doubt that one reason I feel I must have this baby is not to take Mike's place, nothing could do that, but to be a repository for my affection, and to give it back."

"You scare me, Gin. Remember the story I did last fall on the thirteen- and fourteen-year-old children who are getting pregnant and deciding to keep their babies? Their lives are so miserable—crowded into squalid rooms, three or four in a bed, filthy clothes, ignorant parents, and worst of all, no prospect for change in their lives. Suddenly they're pregnant; they see an escape. To a place of their own, with something to love, and their own welfare check every month, and a possession they don't have to share, which will love them back and make them feel special. Little do they realize, of course, that within a short time they'll reproduce the identical living arrangements which they thought they'd left behind, two babies in every bed, and each day bleaker than the next. Those children decide to have babies for all the wrong reasons, and they're not too different from yours. In reality, what are *you* doing but guaranteeing yourself the very world you need to get away from—a closed-ended arrangement which almost entirely precludes any responsible grown-up man from becoming involved with you? Shoot, Gin, *husbands* feel left out when their wives have babies, how's an outsider going to get your attention? Just when you say you feel your most desperate about rebuilding your life's house to include someone else, you fire the contractor."

Virginia's face became, visibly, older and more tired. "If you're suggesting I choose between this baby and Tony Salenger, I can tell you now there's no contest."

"I'm suggesting no such thing." Shelby's voice became sharp and snappish. "I'm suggesting you're closing out your options just at the time you should be enlarging them, and you're allowing the easy natural affection one can lavish on a child to substitute for the more difficult relationship with a man your own age. You're copping out, Gin, giving up, caving in." Shelby stood; her voice rose with her. "You said yesterday you think about killing yourself—what is this but another form of suicide? Only, it's death the long way, the way outlaws were killed, Dodge City style in the Old West. When the judge found someone guilty, the posse rode the condemned man out to the hanging tree, where ropes were still swinging with the bones of the last victim. They'd throw the noose over the neck of the latest one, bound and helpless and blindfolded. Then, while the poor bastard waited for the slap on the horse's rump which would send him to his Maker, he'd hear them, instead, slowly riding off into the distance. At first he always thought he was reprieved, they'd let him live after all! But slowly, slowly, the terrible truth dawned on him—that he was to die all right, but he wouldn't know when. When his horse decided to mosey over the hill for some grass? When night fell and a coyote came by and frightened him? When he simply got bored with standing around and headed to the barn? All the while the guy waiting, waiting, terrified to move, not knowing whether to yell for help and take a chance on scaring the horse, dying small deaths every minute while he waited for the big one to come. That's what you're doing, Gin, only *you* put yourself on your horse, and *you* slipped the noose around your neck. You'll spend nine months preparing your life, and by the time you

free yourself up again, you'll be safely past the point when anyone will be looking your way, unless they're particularly partial
to gray hair and bridgework."

The telephone interrupted Shelby's tirade. Virginia's eyes,
staring at her friend, followed her as she answered it. She reen-
tered the room almost immediately and hissed through
clamped teeth. "It's Tony—who wants to drive you into New
York tonight. Now, goddamnit, tell him graciously that you
will, and open yourself to the possibility that life just may not
be over after all."

Virginia was confused. Shelby knew too much, bored too
deeply, touched her sorest places. She had a disturbing habit of
finding her out, as her brother had years ago on various Hallow-
eens, when regardless of her attempts to disguise herself with
ingenious concoctions of paint and cloth, he would seek her
out in a crowded room of noisy children, raise her face mask,
and say, "You can't hide from me; I'll always find you."
Meekly, she walked to the phone and obeyed Shelby's directions. A half-smile flitted around her mouth as she returned.
"Now if he were just six-two, and gorgeous, and very powerful . . ."

"Sounds like you're describing Strange."

The smile disappeared. "Doesn't it. The irony is that the at-
tributes I find most appealing in a man are those guaranteed to
require a prince's homage. My mother used to say a smooth
dancer and a handsome face doesn't make a loving husband.
Jim Winburn proved she was right, and Mike almost did, and
here am I still hunting a good-looking date for the ball. When
I grow up I'm going to learn to look for more than broad shoulders and a Pepsodent smile."

"Start with Tony Salenger."

"I'm still a kid. But I'll drive to town with him—and thanks
for hearing me out." Virginia reached across the table and
touched her friend's cheek. Shelby unabashedly kissed the hand
as it slid by.

"And do some thinking about your future as you go, will you? You know what they say: 'So many men, so little time.' "

Virginia laughed with real energy. "I will. Now about yours. What did Stewart Banner have to offer?"

Shelby stood up from the table and stretched, lifting her short lacy nightgown high upon her thighs. A smug look of pleasure took over her face. "A job, that's all. Just a major network spot."

"Hey!" Virginia raised a closed fist in salute. "What's the show?"

"ABC wants an answer to Charles Kuralt's *On the Road*. He sees me crossing the country picking up human interest stories, doing pretty much what I choose, with some stories assigned by New York. But that's just the half of it. I'll also co-anchor the Sunday-evening news show *Wrap-up* that starts in January, a half-hour live program of, hopefully, provocative people who can express ideas and make predictions, who can provide what's missing in television—intelligent conversation."

"Sensational! The money's good, I take it. Did you accept?"

Shelby slumped again to her chair. "Not yet, but I'm afraid I will. I have a history of taking the easy way out—and Christ, it is seductive to be sought after. Not to mention the fact that women on television ordinarily are like day lilies—they don't bloom at night—so this is a milestone. But it's really just more of the same, Gin, glib talk and hype mixed with a little news—is that any way for an adult to make a living? Watching the overnights to see if you still have a job? Packaging the common to appear special, homogenizing the uncommon to make it palatable for twelve-year-olds? That's the mentality television programs for, you know. Jesus, back to that . . . I don't know. Maybe it's time I did something that others could report on."

"Like what?"

"Like the idea I gave Mike. Or maybe I have a book in me. Or perhaps I should take on a worthy cause and pay society back for being good to me."

"You? The girl who spends like a princess and wants to live like a queen?"

"That's true—I'm a prisoner of my salary check now. Once there was a time when I would have paid to be able to work; I'd look at my paycheck with a kind of wonder, half expecting to be 'found out' and have it taken away. Finally I began to accept my own value and, by God, learned to ask for more, but I sold my options at the same time. I know myself—habit and patterns are my friends, innovation and risks just acquaintances. Sure, I took a life-blow losing that job, but it might be an opportunity in disguise and I need to think hard before I make a decision."

"And see if Mike comes around on the Personal Statement project?"

Shelby looked up from her teacup and shrugged her eyebrows. "You never know. He might."

"Poor baby, I ruined it for you, didn't I?"

"And I for you. But who knows, maybe Buddha has bigger plans for us. Now, since you've gotten me up at this ungodly hour, let's get to the beach so I can go back to sleep."

Driving back to New York from the Hamptons on Sunday night is to join an endless funeral procession traveling single file down Montauk Highway, mournful cars regretfully going away, doggedly going toward. Leave-taking is difficult after weekends of such splendid light that days turn into giant advertisements for Kodachrome film, late afternoons into landscape paintings, and evenings into topless tents of blackest clarity. As cars pitch first into a two-lane highway, then spill faster into three, air becomes thicker, heat rises, congestion roots out calm, and senses brace for the city's assault. Sealed in air conditioning, Tony and Virginia rolled with the tide of ongoing automobiles, talking quietly, exploring each other's past and filling in personality blanks with the kind of conversation that a generation ago would have been considered too personal but now is as acceptable—indeed as expected—as the question "What do you do?" Former mates and lovers, legal quagmires, feelings of guilt and loss are stated as matter-of-factly as symptoms of physical illness. Intimacy is the new alchemy which transforms strangers into golden friends.

They passed understanding and advice back and forth like a box of chocolates. Tony spoke of his roving Annie, eyes already on her next companion as she sat with him in a crowded restaurant drawing up a separation agreement, asking no more from him than what he least wished to give her—her freedom. He remembered his need to "handle" the arrangements, helping her make travel plans, pulling down her suitcases, binding up cartons that contained the remnants of their marriage. He opened the door for her as she left, then sat by the phone like an anxious parent waiting to hear she had started her new life safely. Virginia marveled at his lack of acrimony, recalling the tempestuous discussions which had ended her life with Jim Winburn, when each required a lawyer at the table as a peace-keeping force before they could pry their lives apart. She recounted the battles, once they could no longer wound each other's psyches, over college expenses and orthodontia and summer camp, and the fury she had felt when in the limbo between marriage and divorce, Jim had allowed bills to accumulate which she had no means of paying, like school tuition for the children, maintenance charges on the apartment, and long-overdue department store accounts. He knew her vulnerability: embarrassment when dunning telegrams in contemptuous yellow envelopes slid under her door; humiliation when the telephone was shut off. He wrung her out like a washcloth, squeezing till her immediate anxiety was more to bear than the prospect of bearing the major part of the children's support. "I don't want you ever to live better than I do," Jim had said in a moment of honesty. He saw to it; she signed the hateful papers which indentured her and set him free.

Why was Tony, abandoned and let down, optimistic about

another start, even eager to begin, while she was still bitter about the past and reluctant to trust again? The traffic rolled relentlessly toward the city lights.

They spoke of children, his young still and uncomprehending victims of their parents' preferences, therefore whiny at the deprivation of first one, then the other. As if with mirrors Tony tried to insinuate himself within each of their days to cover the loss, dropping by the apartment to deliver repaired skates or throw a ball in the park for a quarter of an hour before dinner. The autos moved in unison now, every space in every lane occupied, forcing all to the same determined speed. Ahead was the tunnel which would lead the mechanical herd down and through and back to the real world just the other side of the river.

Virginia talked of Maggie, so insecure about her father's affection after he left that she washed windows in his new apartment, cleaned his oven and refrigerator, and prepared special treats for his return home from the office. If he noticed, it did not induce him to increase past one their number of telephone calls or add time to the one afternoon a week he set aside for them. Max tolerated the loss well on the surface, though his conduct reports labeled him a sudden bully at school and he became disruptive in class without enough to hold his attention. At home his concern for her never diminished, nor did their mutual affection. If anything, he put on long pants as the man in the family well before he should have. The demarcation lines between parent and children fuzzed, sometimes they caring for her with the focused concern she reserved for them.

As Virginia talked she pictured their faces looking earnestly to her for direction with expressions that reminded her of their dependency and her responsibility. Their images were perhaps the reason she did not immediately see the white rear lights of cars ahead change to red and begin to veer off in oblique zigzags; the air conditioning shut out at first the screaming tires, the heavy thuds.

Only seconds passed before the danger rippled back to them. Tony braked hard, reaching his arms across her chest as he anticipated their inclusion in the line of dominoes crashing into each other with no time to escape and no place to go. Their turn came—impact! then a millisecond later thrown against the dashboard with sounds of human screaming, maybe their own, mixed with splintering glass and cracking steel, and the automobile behind socked them again, buckling the front of the car a second time and bouncing them off to the side. The noise continued at a distance now as more automobiles piled into each other, turning the Long Island Expressway, westbound, into a scrap-metal yard.

For a brief moment all noise and motion stopped while the stunned and hurt and mortally wounded grabbed for reality. Then moaning began, and crying, and creaking of metal as those who were able opened doors and began to pull out other passengers.

Tony and Virginia were in no condition to move. Toward the front of the crash line, they had taken some of the heaviest blows. Virginia's head, hammered against the window, swam in and out of consciousness just long enough for her to feel the steering wheel in her abdomen and Tony's bulk beneath her own. Vaguely she heard his voice but could not make out his words—blood perhaps was in her ears. She knew it was in her mouth.

They were still lying in the same position when faces appeared at the window and hands began grinding open the door handles, and when she heard as if from a great distance one voice, maybe more, asking if they were all right, she wiped the blood from her lips on a wrist that did not seem to belong to her in order to say, before completely blacking out, "Tell the doctors I'm pregnant."

Monday, August 18

Long before Virginia was able to open her eyes, she lay immobile, taking measure of the pain. Her head—was that the worst? —seemed encased in an iron cap too small for her skull. No, it was the chest, the chest. Sharp stabs of fire there. And what below, and where—her leg? her knee? Hot spots of torment spread unlocalized down the length of her. As if her hold on life were too precarious, she dared not move or open her eyes. Silence made her feel absolutely alone, but that did not matter. Nor did it matter *where* she was, only *that* she was. The same woman who yesterday considered giving in to death early, she thought in one of her more lucid moments, was thankful to lie in broken pieces.

She knew she was in a bed because she could feel the sheets, and by the weight of bandages which held her down like anchors, understood she had been cared for. Pungent medicinal smells made her think the pain would get better, for surely there was a hospital staff close by. They would make her well again, she would be . . .

"My God, the baby!" The words came out of her with such force they lifted everything that would move, wrenching her right arm out of a restraining contraption she saw as her eyes briefly opened, then closed when white heat struck her ribs and threw her back on the pillows.

"It's all right, honey, be still now, it's all right."

She knew it was Mike speaking but was too weak to respond.

"You must not move—do you understand?" He spoke slowly and firmly. "You've torn the intravenous needle out of your arm. I'll get the nurse to fix it again, but you must not move."

"Mike." Tears washed across her eyes but they increased the pressure in her head, so she fought them back. "Where . . . how did . . . what happened to . . . ?" There was not enough strength to ask and she wanted so much to know. "The baby . . ."

"Lie still. The nurse is here to help."

Virginia slipped back to her dark world, feeling somewhere jabs in a forearm, but they were inconsequential compared to the rest of the torment. A cloth passed across her forehead and wiped her eyes. She opened again to the sight of the face, bending over her now, that she saw in her mind every morning upon waking and every evening before sleeping.

"How much do you hurt?" he asked.

"Terribly."

"Where?"

"Everywhere. Mostly my chest."

"That's the broken ribs. How's the head?"

"Exploding." She could barely talk for the pain. "Can they give me something?"

"The doctor's due soon. He hasn't wanted to because of internal injuries, but he should know more by now. You've been out almost twenty-four hours."

"And the baby . . . ?" She tried to raise her arms toward his face.

"Don't, honey, you'll pull that thing out again. We—well, we don't know for sure yet. So far, so good. Another couple of days will give us a better idea."

The relief was so immense she fell back and let the pain, as if released by a giant irrigation system, flow through her head. "Thank you, God, thank you . . ." she said silently, gliding away to the world of black.

Wednesday, August 20

Shelby slipped around the partially opened door, craning her neck to see inside.

"Come in, pal—I need you, or what's left of me does."

"Well, I knew Tony would put some excitement into your life, but this is ridiculous." Shelby leaned over the leg with the cast, glanced worriedly at the bruises along her face and neck, and looked deeply into her eyes in open thanksgiving. "This is the first moment they'd let me in. You'd think there were classified secrets in here the way they guard you. How are you, babe?"

"Better. Not hurting so much now—the morphine helps— the doctor says I'll keep the baby, too, though we'll both have withdrawal symptoms when we leave."

"I know. Mike told me."

"Mike?"

"Sure. He's been a veritable command post, staying in touch with me, the doctors, your family in Atlanta. He ordered your parents not to come—said your father wasn't strong enough to make the trip—but he has Mag and Max coming in to-night . . ."

"No!"

"Yep. They insisted, and he said they were right. He's flying them in on a Matterhorn jet."

"Good God—they'll never want to come down." Then, remembering suddenly the constant details of her life, she said, "I don't have anyone at home to take over."

"He's arranged that, too. His housekeeper is opening the apartment, ordering groceries, fixing dinner for them. Mike says he'll have someone else there tomorrow to stay on until you are operational. When will that be?"

"Soon, I hope, maybe the first of the week. The concussion wasn't as severe as they feared; the internal bleeding has stopped. My ribs will take several weeks to mend, and the fracture somewhat longer, but I can get out of bed probably tomorrow, and leave when I get some strength. Tell me, what about Tony?"

"He left the hospital yesterday. His collarbone's broken and his right shoulder's wrenched and pretty sore, but he wasn't hurt as badly because you were thrown in front of him by the first impact and shielded him from the dashboard when the car plowed in behind. He's at home mending now, and waiting for them to connect your telephone, so he can call and say 'sorry.' "

"Wasn't his fault. And he did everything he could to keep me from hitting the dash. Did he say anything about the baby?"

Shelby hesitated. "Of course. That was a surprise—naturally he's been concerned. You'd better know that the baby is no longer secret information. With medical reports being what they are when people call to inquire, your friends found out rather unexpectedly that you were pregnant."

"Well, they had to know sometime."

"I suppose."

"Yes."

"Umm-m." Shelby bit at a cuticle.

"Well, what was the reaction?"

"What you'd expect. A few minutes of argument over whether you were passing through mid-life crisis or simply crazy. Mike, of course, has announced to everyone that the baby is his."

"Shit fuck piss crap suck cunt screw." Virginia, who seldom swore, had a string of expletives which she reeled out always in the same order in moments of frustration. She pounded the bedcovers with her one free fist. "He didn't do that, tell me he didn't."

" 'Fraid so, though he's restrained himself from passing out cigars. Listen, Gin, he's the proudest—and the most relieved—man who ever turned father. And I don't know any man who's ever been as concerned about anyone as he's been about you—worried, nearly frantic."

"About the baby, Shel, not the mom."

"That's not fair. You should have seen him pacing these corridors. He was here almost at dawn Monday . . ."

"How did he know?"

"The authorities called the *Times* when they found Tony's press card. They assigned a reporter to track down your identification. He called your apartment and heard the recorded message on your machine saying you were with me in the country. I got the good news about four in the morning and . . ."

"You called Mike."

"I did. You'd think I'd learn, wouldn't you, but hell, I was three hours away and you were unconscious in God knows what shape. I was afraid you were dying. They moved you to New York Hospital, and I thought if anyone could get the best doctors, the fastest emergency treatment, and nurses round the clock, it would be Mike, and of course he did. All it took was a few well-placed calls to members of the board of directors and the chief of staff, and not since the Shah of Iran, I promise, has anyone gotten such attention."

"He relishes taking charge in an emergency that way, staying cool, outthinking everyone else—like the quarterback who runs the ball on the fourth down before the whistle blows to save the game."

"Why so tough, Gin? Most can't play the game at all. Whether he derives ego satisfaction or not from doing it, at least you got the finest medical help possible."

Virginia turned her head to hide the tears forming and saw the flowers Mike had ordered for her bedside daily, as well as a stack of glossy new books which she was too weak to read and a box of delicate nightgowns and bed jackets which she could not pull over her bandages. "Tough? It's just a cover. I wish he were doing it for *me*—and I know better."

Shelby moved toward her bed. "Don't cry, pal. I didn't mean to upset you, but just once can't you believe a man is taking care of you because he loves you?" Shelby smoothed the hair on the head turned away from her, kissed her temple, and left the room.

Before the elevator doors closed she knew he was on the floor again. His walk was brisker than most, more purposeful. She heard him gleaning information and gathering adherents as he came until he had swelled to a retinue outside her door. Reports in, he summarily dismissed his flock, who were alternately awed and charmed by his attention, and broke into her room as if there were a strong wind at his back.

With the customary brush of a kiss on her forehead he swung his eyes around the room to take in any changes since he had been there last and patted her arm in approval.

"Better, you look better," he said, pulling out half-glasses and reading the nurses' comments on the chart, "and the doctor says the swelling in that big head is finally going down, though I told him not to ask medical science for a miracle."

She only half laughed in deference to the constant pain in the same head. "He also said if there's no more internal bleeding when I get up tomorrow the chances are I'll keep the baby."

"Yes, thank God," he said, leaning against the windowsill. The sunlight lit his eyes like neon. "We're damned lucky."

They had always hypnotized her. It required an effort now to shake them off. "Not we, Mike, *I'm* lucky. But from what Shelby tells me I'm forever in your debt."

"That's ridiculous. Anybody would have . . ."

"But everybody didn't. You did. And I'm terribly grateful."

"Let's don't talk about it." He dismissed the topic. "Now when do we get you out of here?"

She was dogged. "I *want* to talk about it, because whatever the future brings I know the fast action I got made all the difference in keeping this baby."

Suddenly on guard, Mike straightened up and took his hands out of his pockets. "What do you mean—what the future brings?"

"Well, we're adversaries, remember?" She said it softly, even now finding it difficult to believe. "You're taking me to *court*, for a ridiculous soap opera drama—unless, of course"—and she was newly hopeful—"you've decided to leave us alone."

"How can you call us adversaries? Aren't we in this together?"

Virginia allowed the words to cut through her just as she had late yesterday afternoon, when for the first time in eight long months she had called his office, daring to believe again because of his extraordinary thoughtfulness that she had been elevated to his chief concern. His attentiveness had been the culprit, transforming her from securely self-reliant to reveling in the weakness his hovering presence produced. She actually regressed chronologically, feeling physically smaller when he was there, and safer, as she had when the bomb exploded on their first day together. His great size contributed, but it was more

than that. He was the promise of *protection*—what only her father had been before—the purest expression of a man's love she
had ever known. It wasn't as if she required protecting—intellectually she knew she could take care of herself—it was
something almost primeval, the contentment that sprang from
watching her man watch beyond the campfire where the wolves
prowled. As her emotional dependency increased, she began unwittingly to resurrect the dreams so forcibly buried when it became clear his attention had been diverted: the romantic image
of the two of them standing against the world, his encircling
arm symbolizing the greatness of his feelings for her.

The dream was fragile; it dissolved from no more force than
his secretary's response. "Sorry, Mrs. Winburn. He's gone for
the day. I believe he's having dinner at the hotel."

For the first time since the accident the pain she felt was not
physical. She knew—too well—what a dinner at the hotel
meant for Mike. Blindly hoping she was wrong, she tried him
later at the Carlyle, but the desk clerk intercepted the call just
as he had for them in the past, and she remembered—too well
—the activity that prompted Mike to turn off the phones when
entertaining at home.

Remembering now made her strong. "The only thing we're
in together," she said sharply, ignoring a hot flash through the
back of her head, "is the ignominy of open court—next Tuesday, while the world laps up juicy details of my private life and
a black-robed stranger decides my future." Her fury rose as she
remembered. "I've lost my job and I'm hardly in terrific condition to find another; I'm spending money I don't have in a
legal battle I don't want, and the person responsible for the
fact that we're 'in this together' tells me how lucky we are."

His face had not changed though his eyes had lost their
shine. "I thought you might feel differently, having come so
close to dying. That you'd have a new perspective on what really matters. I suppose it was ridiculous to think you'd move an
inch after taking a position."

"This isn't a buy-or-hold market decision, Mike—this determines how I'll spend the next half of my life."

"God damn it, and how I'll spend mine"—he spoke in half time, underlining each word—"and I want it to be with my child and its mother. Why do you think I'm here anyway, out of duty? Or to see that nothing happens to the baby? I can handle that over the telephone. What are you afraid of—that you'll have to deal with someone who cares about you? Or that you might have to forfeit some of that stubborn independence?"

"*Cares* about me! Is that what you told Deena Woodard last night?" By registering nothing on his face he confirmed everything. "If you *care* anything at all about me—and I suppose that's as close as you'll ever come to the word 'love'—it's because, thanks to this"—she waved an arm down the length of her—"I'm completely dependent on you and you're completely in charge. You *care*, aside from how you feel about Deena Woodard, only when I'm helpless and I need you."

"Let's leave Deena out of this. We've been . . . friends . . . for some time, and I needed to explain some things, that's all. As for wanting to be needed—is that bad?" His eyebrows lifted the lines in his forehead almost to his hairline. "Listen, the word 'love' to me means doing for someone, taking care of them. In the providing is the pleasure, and the reward." He began to pace around the sides of her bed. "Yes, and I want to be thanked for it, and missed when I'm gone, and waited for and welcomed home. I still have juvenile fantasies about going away to war with my girl at the station when the troop train returns; or I'm a sea captain hunting giant whales for months at a time, with my wife circling the widow's walk on top of the house, staring at the horizon and wishing me home. It gives me a hard-on just talking about it. And the fact is that this is the first time I've ever been able to be of use to you. You've asked my advice, on occasion, but always made your own decisions. You've fit in to my schedule when it was convenient for you, but only then. There was nothing I could do for you that you didn't handle better yourself, and fuck it, Ginny, I need to be a hero! I have to be in charge! There's an African country where a young boy reaches manhood on the night he can stand still and allow a lion to attack him. He can't move, he has to plant the butt of his spear in the ground and force the lion to jump him in order to kill it; from that day on he's a man. Hell, maybe if I'd done that once I wouldn't need to continually prove myself—or maybe I would want to repeat the stunt every time my girl was around to see the look on her face."

Mike walked again to the end of the bed, hands in pockets, head down, then wheeled. "Am I so different from other men? I was trained to win on playing fields—for the sake of the old school. I flew a fighter in Korea—to save my country for the women and children we left behind. I built a business, then a conglomerate, not just for money, but to hear crowds cheering." Mike stopped. "But most of all, Ginny, what pushes my adrenaline level up and away is the applause of a crowd of one" —he said it as if he thought of it for the first time—"and I've never heard you cheer."

Virginia spoke quietly, twirling the ends of her hair between the fingers of her free hand. "In the fourth grade, more than anything in life, I wanted to be a cheerleader. The boys' school where my brother went had a football team, babies I suppose, at the age of ten, but they seemed like brutes to me. The team chose four girls every year to wear the official colors—a navy blue pleated skirt, a turkey-red sweater, white socks that stood up on the leg, and shiny brown penny loafers. The rest of us were still in turned-down socks and oxfords and no sweater we owned could compete with theirs with the big letter on the front. Of course I wasn't chosen—I was taller than most of the players and not the cute, kissable type for Saturday-night spin-the-bottle games. That's the last time I ever wanted to be a cheerleader."

She looked at him directly. "I'm a whole human being,

Mike. I care about accomplishments, too, and I, too, need to hear the clapping. Sure I make my own decisions, because I have a brain and my judgment is good. Do I have to suspend critical thinking, or pretend to have a lobotomy, to feed your ego? It sounds as if the only way you can get it up for me is to have me permanently incapacitated. Don't you remember? That was your wife!"

Virginia raised herself from the pillow with difficulty. "This is what *I* need, Mike. Someone who cares about me, *loves* me, because he thinks I'm wonderful, not because I'm helpless and dependent. You think I'm wonderful only when I'm telling you you're wonderful."

"Aren't we saying the same thing?" Mike asked. "That we each want more than the other has been willing to give? And isn't there room for negotiation?"

"We aren't a package deal you make through compromise, giving in here, adjusting there. You'll never find me really acceptable because I'll never want you to be totally in charge."

"You mean *I'll* never measure up to what you want, but then who will, Ginny? What do you see ahead that's any better?"

"That's the worst of it, nothing," she admitted, falling back on her pillow. "Every man I meet I weigh against your standard. And everyone fails. Even if I found someone as special, I would probably transfer my problems with you over to him. I'm not alone, you know. There's a whole generation of women like me who've had to learn survival techniques late in life but who've been able to make it on their own. That builds pride, and confidence. And it's unthinkable to give all that up, or pretend to, in order to make some man feel dominant. This must sound so childish to you and to men of your level of success. I can picture all of you stifling the urge to pat us on the head and send us out in the yard to play some more, but don't you see? For those of us who had no expectations other than being someone's wife, what we've managed to do is a miracle!"

"But look at the price you've paid. Every endeavor—like every business deal—should have a cost-benefit ratio."

"Yes, a terrible price," she agreed. "Paid in skin and blood, and most of all, the loss of hope of finding someone who'll understand. But if you've been starving, there's no price on a piece of bread. And if you've lived in a form of captivity, there's no sacrifice you won't make for independence."

"And where is happiness in your newly discovered freedom?"

"I suppose, at least I hope, in our daughters' lifetime. I'm afraid my generation of women has marked our value up to what we think we're worth, but it's beyond the inclination of most to pay."

Mike started for the door. "I'm sorry for you, Ginny, you and your unhappy hard-nosed bloodless band. I'd rather take care of you as my wife, but I'll fight you as an equal if you insist. Just remember, the game is hardball—softball is for girls."

But happiness isn't an absolute, Mike, an item on a menu to order up. Or a recipe, add a little of this, subtract a bit of that. Virginia knew it to be instead a relative measure of your present condition compared to what you hoped for. She watched blind people tapping up subway steps on their way to a nearby therapy center and marveled they were not permanently depressed, but they weren't. Nor were prisoners, or paraplegics, or the retarded; they had their downs, but they had their ups. Even the poor, as long as they weren't hungry or without life's basic necessities, had a capacity for happiness as great as the rest of the population. Whatever one's situation, Mike, happiness comes from attaining one's expectations, or rescuing oneself from anticipated misery or defeat—or not reaching beyond what's possible to have. Which is what she had done by hoping a man would accept the fullness of her powers, her intuitive intelligence, her strong-minded ambition, and let her be. But maybe it's honestly beyond you to do so, Mike, born when you were, brought up as you were with a one-dimensional view of women. Men who'll make women like me happy, she thought, are probably fourteen now, or fifteen, the products of an up-bringing by mothers with a separate identity of their own, so their sons won't find us alien, or undesirable.

Understanding the gulf between them did not make it bridgeable; she knew what she had to do. Since she couldn't have him under conditions she could accept—all of him loving only her—then she had to get past wanting him at all, and as in removing a dead tree, sawing it down isn't adequate. You must dig out the stump and smooth over the earth so new grass can grow. In the most fundamental way she needed to exorcise him from her life.

She also knew her intelligence and judgment were greater than her will; she would have to have help to move him from the center of her attention and now, as in the past when she looked for allies (though she was concerned that she placed too much pressure on them), she turned to her children.

Perhaps the struggle to have and keep her baby, this impossible baby, was in large measure due to the contentment Maggie and Max had brought her. They were the only people she loved without reservation, and only through them did she occasionally discover the satisfaction of selflessness. They were her only accomplishments which required no defense, not because they were special but because they were hers.

Oh, they had imperfections—no one knew them better than she—and she often wished there had been a training course for motherhood before practicing on her favorite people, she had made so many mistakes. Maggie had filched a hand-held calculator when she was much younger, took it from her office with the same boldness with which she later denied the theft, and the same impassiveness with which she masked her inner terror. Virginia found it later hidden in an underwear drawer, and with sternness approaching cruelty forced her to return it to the office and apologize. But she didn't let the matter rest there. At home again she cut the child's long hair against her protests, shearing away the first hint of adolescence as punishment. As Maggie stared into the mirror, her tears had fallen silently, but later they spoke to Virginia, saying, "Wrong, wrong, your self-righteousness will hurt us both"—and it did. It was months before the child returned to a habit she had developed as a toddler, of lying full length on her mother's form, Virginia putting aside her book or paper to lift her into a prone position where she could kiss the top of the heavy head and run fingers through hair smelling faintly of sweat and playground dirt.

But mostly she was gentle with them and kind; they paid her back with open affection and brought her their troubles, which were few in number—lucky children, lucky mother. Probably far fewer than if Jim Winburn had remained to share their rearing because there was just one undiluted voice of authority in the house, and because with uncommon understanding for such immaturity, they realized she was anxious about her ability to hold them all together. They seldom baited her as children do, and refrained from foolish, life-threatening escapades. She was even spared the fear of their taking drugs, less perhaps because of her lectures than the personal tragedies of others. Max and his friends experimented as all children will, but one classmate was rendered comatose for months from an overdose and one became schizophrenic halfway through high school. Another sensitive boy, a near-genius, saw his mother walk into the ocean on a frigid winter night after combining drugs and alcohol. Torn between two impulses—to rescue her from the waters himself or to call others stronger than he who would have a better chance of saving her—he did neither and watched her drown. He would never recover, but Max would never play around with drugs. She would have preferred to shield them from such misery, but knew those experiences made them stronger; and, as though tending kites which catch the wind and begin to soar, she unwound the string and watched them climb away from her, certain their connection was irrevocable.

Now they were coming home. Almost three weeks and the

threat of death made her half mad to lick them with her eyes as mama cats do with tongues. Her silent world had palled and cried out again for their confusion, their incessant radios tuned to different stations, even for their disorder. My God, I really miss them when I'm lonesome for their mess, she thought, watching from her hospital bed as the clock brought its hands around to their arrival hour.

Then they came, bounding down the hallway, noisily competing to find the room first, push through the door first, be at her bedside first. There. Thank God, home. Arms around shoulders, avoiding bandages, looking, exclaiming, hugging tentatively, touching, then retracting anxious fingers that wanted to know and hoped to soothe.

"Jesus, Mom, how many times have I told you not to drive with a guy when he's had too much to drink." Max perfectly imitated her singsong rebukes. "That's the last time I want *that* fella around the house."

"Who was he anyway?" Maggie interrupted. "If you had just married Mike you'd have been in a limo and it would never have happened, and we'd be flying a DC-8 the rest of our lives. You should have seen that plane! Jesus Christ . . ."

"Maggie!"

"Sorry, Mom, but is that a neat way to get around, all the cassettes you ever wanted to play, little envelopes of hand cream in the john, taco chips and cashew nuts . . ."

"Passed by a stewardess," Max broke in, "with arthritis." He held his hands in front of his chest, crooking in the fingers to represent what must have been an impressive chest.

"Mo-mm." Only Maggie could drag the word into two syllables, and only when her brother infuriated her. "Do we have to listen to that?" Maggie's breasts were not as large as her brain, and never would be, but she didn't know yet that she had gotten the better deal.

"Jealous, jealous." Max knew when not to quit.

And Virginia knew how to break them apart with diversionary tactics; she had been practicing them for years. "What's this about forty-foot dives off a bridge into the Colorado River?"

They were too easy. "What a bummer. Dad only let me go off three times." Max never stopped moving, looking, touching things as he talked, her television controls, the contents of the table drawers, cards on flower arrangements. Virginia watched and remembered the little fellow in knee socks and short pants whose energy so outlasted the rest of the family that she often suggested at the end of a long day that he run around the block. The child who had never known a sullen mood would light up as if offered a present and streak away.

"Even Maggie jumped off once—but then she was doing a number on the lead paddler and wanted to get his attention."

Maggie was as impassive as her brother was hyperactive—a rock by a willow tree—and her perfect features, more remarkable than her mother's, needed no animation to be appealing. If she had been cast in stone, she might have—like Nefertiti—been admired for a thousand years, yet she had no idea of her beauty or how to enhance it, an attitude her mother approved of. Virginia had known at first hand the demoralizing effect of being brought up to capitalize on one's looks, and knew too well at the age of forty the fear of losing them and relying only on what was left when they were gone.

Maggie smiled broadly at her mother. "Some hunk."

"Knowing your addiction for good looks, I'm surprised you came home."

"Only for you, Mom." Maggie's confidence was supreme when it came to attracting young men. She never understood her mother's doubts about herself or her pessimism about initiating new relationships. The child would sweep away concern with the back of her hand and tell the adult it was all a game—you just have to know the rules.

"But stop getting away from the subject," Maggie said. "Seriously, how do you feel? How badly are you hurt?"

Even Max stopped wandering for the answer. She described the broken and the merely bruised parts, and as her indulgences were generally emotional, not physical, dwelt more on the healing process than the extent of the injuries. The crash itself was more interesting to them, their eyes widening at the details she could remember and those she had heard after the fact. She told the story vividly enough to elicit an unexpected "Yuck" from Maggie as she described blood from her head wound blinding her, and a preppie "Intense!" from Max as he imagined the queue of ambulances necessary to cart away the wounded. She decorated the narrative with a myriad of details, less to tell them everything than to avoid telling them all—but the time finally arrived.

"What frightened me most was the possibility of losing my baby, because, believe it or not, your old mom is pregnant." (See shock register on the faithful son, disbelief on the trusting daughter.) "Quite a surprise, I know, but a happy one, isn't it?" (Why was she perfectly content with her decision until she had to explain it to someone close to her?) "And the doctors think the accident won't have any permanent effect, though I may have to spend some time in bed letting you two wait on me." (How else could they accept this information, contrary as it was to every expectation they had about her, contravening as it did the principles she insisted on for their own lives?)

Max recovered first. "A baby . . . ? Why are you having a baby?"

"Well, I didn't choose to Max, it just happened, an accident."

"But do you want it?" he persisted.

"Sure I do, the same way I wanted you and Maggie, because you were mine and because we'll be a family together for the rest of our lives."

"But we aren't a family," Maggie interrupted, "at least, not the kind that has babies. You need a father for that."

"Yeah, for godsakes, who is the father?" Shoving his hands in his jeans pockets, Max looked suddenly betrayed.

(How do you tell a boy-child somewhat in love with his mother, and decidedly her protector in his mind if not in fact, that a man exists of such consequence that she would lie with him, and bear his child? How do you tell children who have been the single-minded focus of your affection that their love will be diluted, that they must share? How do you name a person intimate enough to father their brother or sister, and tell them concurrently he will never be a part of your life? The situation was clearly fatuous, the game unworthy, her actions untenable, her motives impugned. Virginia began to shake outwardly, visibly, and knowing her control was tenuous, begged for time.)

"Look, sweetheart, this news is a blow to you. I would never have told you like this if it hadn't been for the wreck, the doctors' fear that I might miscarry, and the fact that you might hear this from someone else . . ."

"Fuck someone else." Max was furious, his face flushing as the rage boiled up. "Just give it to me straight, Mom. Who's the father of this future brother or sister? Stop horsing around and tell me the truth, will you? Or do I have to wait and see who it looks like when it grows up?"

"Don't yell at Mom, Max, she's hurting." Maggie rose from her seat at the foot of the bed and moved toward her mother as if to protect her.

"I'm not yelling, I'm asking"—his voice rising even further—"now who's the fucking father . . . ?"

"Max!" The authority in Virginia's voice, developed through years of consistent application, stopped the outburst.

He moved away from her and leaned his forehead against the wall. "Sorry."

"Come here, son. Help me, I need you badly." She held out her hand. Slowly he turned back, accepting a seat at the side of her bed—"Watch the ribs, now"—and his position as her chief support.

"I just haven't the foggiest what you're doing, Mom." Even as a little boy, his eyes seemed oversized for his face, his blue pupils swimming above the lower eyelid. Filled with tears now that acted as magnifying glasses, they seemed enormous.

"Have we ever told each other anything but the truth?" Virginia smoothed the thick brown curls with her fingers. He was almost too handsome, she had often thought, and was grateful for the Roman hook in his nose, late in developing, that gave character to his face. "But this is difficult for me, I need your patience and understanding. I can tell you exactly what happened, and what the situation is, but I can't tell you exactly how I feel, because that changes every hour. Mag, pull your chair up to the head of the bed so that I can see you both at the same time. I'll start at the beginning."

Mother and children, relying on each other, finding their way together, customarily shared their secrets, their problems. Excluding specific sex, which Virginia felt was inappropriate subject matter, there was no limit to what they discussed, so in natural fashion she reconstructed the story. They had known the strength of her connection to Mike, had felt her hurt, had seen pride mask unhappiness when he backed away from her, and especially dreaded answering the question, when she returned home after an evening out, if there had been any calls, knowing she meant *him*. But they were children, absorbed in themselves at an age when no emotion lasted longer than a day, so there was no deep understanding of her loss or the depression that followed.

Rapt now, they heard her explain that Mike had thought himself unable to have children, that he—and she—had never thought precautions were needed, that pregnancy was unthinkable, impossible. They listened as she described her fear and disbelief to find herself pregnant, her initial indecision, then slow acceptance and determination that the three of them should raise the child together. By the end of the recitation, the team was intact again, all playing on the same side.

"Mom, can I ask you a question?" Maggie had a directness she did not inherit from her mother. "If I were pregnant now, what would you advise me to do?"

"At eighteen? About to go to college? With your life hardly begun? I would make an appointment for you at an abortion clinic, and hope you'd let me help you through."

"Why me, Mom, and not you?"

The child wanted logic and Virginia did not have it to give. "It's complicated, baby. For one thing, I have the two of you, and know what I'd be losing. I have unresolved feelings about Mike, too. And remember, you and Max will be off on your own soon—who will be around to mess up the house when you're gone?"

Maggie would not be diverted. "Does Mike want you to have the baby?"

"Oh, does he. I had hoped he wouldn't know, but now he insists that he wants to raise it too."

Max's natural belligerence when his territory was threatened bubbled up at the thought. "Yeah? What does he want to do, stop by and give the six o'clock bottle on his way home?"

"No, dumdum," Maggie inserted. "He really wants to *be* the father, doesn't he, Mom?"

"That's crazy. And live with us?"

"Actually, Max, he wants us to live with him. He wants to marry me, if you can imagine that."

"Hey-y-y, excellent! Jets and limos, and Park Avenue—doesn't he own a house in Gstaad? No kidding, we'll be rich—Mom, you hit the jackpot!"

Virginia looked beseechingly at her daughter. "There's nothing quite as rewarding as passing along value systems to your children."

"Christmas in the Bahamas, steak twice a week, no more clothes on sale . . ."

"Enough, Max, you'll make us all crazy." Maggie's soft voice covered her brother's. "What about it, Mom, will you marry him?"

"No. If I hadn't gotten pregnant, there would be no discussion of marriage. In other words, it's not me he's after, the dolt, it's the baby. But babies don't hold existing marriages together if there's no solid foundation to begin with, so there's little hope ours could make it. I'm afraid there's worse news to come. Mike is now exercising his 'legal rights' with a paternity suit . . ."

"What's that, for godsakes?"

"Max, will you watch your language? That's a headache—a giant one. I'm to be in court next Tuesday to explain why he shouldn't be allowed all the privileges of a real father."

Stolid Maggie again framed the inescapable. "And why shouldn't he?"

"Mag, picture a man walking down the street, opening oysters, eating them, and throwing away the shells. He hands you one of the many in his sack as he passes. You open it and find a pearl inside. Can he turn around and claim it, just because you have something now that he wants?"

"But this is a baby, Mom, not just a silly pearl."

Virginia put her hand on her stomach. "God, if you give me another one as smart as its sister, I'm in for a heap of trouble."

Maggie would not be mollified. "It seems we're all in for a heap of trouble. . . . What are we going to do?"

Thanks, Mag, for making the subject plural, but it's neither your problem nor within your ability to frame an answer.

Virginia listened to their chatter until the elevator door chopped off the sound, knowing they wore her affection down the hall like perfume just as she would feel their arms around her long after they were gone. Her children weren't exceptional —long ago she gave up the idea of rearing a genius or a future president—but they were unique and definitively formed. They

could exist easily now without her, for she was merely a traffic
cop giving occasional directions when they asked, and orders
when they didn't. Stop, slow down, go, watch your drinking,
check your companions, mind the curfew. She passed out
money and homilies, remained accessible when they chose to
check their impressions against hers, and watched, bemused, as
they walked away from her. There was little left to do but love
them from a distance and applaud, though there was much
they did for her—gave her purpose and companionship, and ter-
minated thoughts that dying might be preferable to a depressed
state of mind.

Once she too had possessed a characteristic she saw in them.
It was an inability to imagine anything but victory. When her
seventh-grade teacher offered Elvis Presley's autograph to the
student with the highest semester grades, didn't she *know* it
would go home with her? When the votes were counted senior
year, didn't she sit confidently at her desk, straightening her
No. 2 pencils and bringing out her Waterman fountain pen to
ink in her latest boyfriend's initials on her loose-leaf notebook,
certain of her election as student body president? When Jim
Winburn and the other swains left their architectural drawing
boards, their moot court preparations, their cadaver dissections,
and their daddies' cotton offices to converge upon the latest
crop of Atlanta debs, wasn't she *sure* he, the handsomest of the
cocksure young optimists about the business of reproducing
their parents' lives, would ask her to dance and then to marry?

In those days she never questioned success; victories became
harder to win as she grew older. An objective referee would call
the score decidedly in her favor: healthy, bright children; a loving family group; a professional standing enviable by either
gender; and an income which allowed for leisure and aesthetic
pleasures. But no matter how often she listed them on her
mental yellow pad—thanking heaven for each blessing—she
toted up the score to a minus, and worse, thought her powers
defunct to change it. At some point confidence slipped from

her shoulders like a summer tan in the first days of September. She knew (though did not often admit it) that even in the earliest, most euphoric stages of their love affair she never fully believed that she and Mike had a chance for "happiness," as he put it, and the fault lay with her. Behind her was a major defeat and a broken promise, with a man who had lashed out with fists and words, who had called her unloving and unlovable, and who had taught her to depend only on herself. Breaking up her marriage, like contracting leprosy, rendered her ineligible for future closeness and forced her to look to herself for solutions.

No, Maggie, bless you, this is my problem. It belongs to a migrant in an emotional desert, to a woman in no-man's-land, who's not quite sure how she got there, but who's unwilling to stay, and wants desperately to find a way out.

Weighted down as she was by bandages, turning the top half of her body was difficult, dialing the phone almost impossible.

"Paula Seibert, please. Virginia Winburn's calling."

The voice, so strange several days before, had the familiar sound of an old friend. "Well, hello! How's the patient?"

"Better. At least the body's mending. I'm not sure about the spirit."

"As if you didn't have enough trouble . . . though this certainly lets you put off the return date for that petition."

"No, that's what I'm calling about. I know I'm supposed to appear too, but under the circumstances, can my lawyer go alone?"

"Sure, if that's what you want."

"That's what I want. And if you'll take me on, I wish you'd see this through to the end."

"All right, I'll be in court for you on Tuesday. When will you get out of the hospital?"

"The first of the week sometime, but I won't be strong enough to go with you, that's for sure. Still, I don't want to delay this, so push for a hearing date as soon as possible, will you?"

"Any particular reason?"

Virginia paused to gather strength for the inexpressible explanation. "I'm almost three months pregnant. Any decision I make has to be made soon." She could not actually say the words.

"You mean, if you decide not to have the child."

"Yes." Her answer was almost inaudible.

"I see what you mean. I may have to say that to the judge in order to expedite the hearing."

"Mike will be there when you do, won't he?"

"Yes, he's required to appear," Paula answered.

"Well"—again there was a long pause—"he has to understand that abortion's a possibility, so say what you have to."

After hanging up the phone, she continued lying in the same strangely contorted position, half facing the night table. What divine wisdom, she thought, that we should grow our young deep in our most central parts. Not under our armpits or in sacks at the end of our fingertips or somehow attached to our backs. But tucked under our ribs, close to our hearts, in the midst of all the systems that make us work. Except our brains, she realized—but then if we gestated babies near our brains, we might get rid of a lot more than we do. No, they belong there, in the middle of us, a part of all we do and feel.

That's why she thought the baby knew—had heard—and why she felt now she had to soothe its terror. If fetuses knew pleasure and pain, jumped at loud noises and kicked their way out of uncomfortable positions, could they not also perceive the misery of a mother's indecision?

"Once there was—a little kitty . . ." The words swam back to her mind, unsung and unremembered since Max was tiny. She had heard them as a toddler herself, and so had her mother and grandmother, and God knows who before that. "Long time ago." The song was always sung softly, just above a whisper, so as not to inhibit sleep's approach, and very, very slowly. "And in the barn he used to frolic, long time ago." She sang it again now because it was appropriate, the most natural thing she could do. "Two white teeth had Mr. Kitty—all in a row." She swayed slowly to the rhythm as if she were in the old wicker rocker at home that had lulled her babies' night fears on so many occasions. "And when the kitty bit the mousey"—and she made the gesture with her teeth which she had made, and her mother and her grandmother and God knows who before—"the mousey cried out Oh-h-h-h-h." This was the point when they had all held their babies closer, rocking gently, telling them with the motion and their arms and the silly words that it was going to be all right.

"It's going to be all right," she said out loud, then sang the song again.

Thursday, August 28

The sunlight blinded her as she was wheeled from the dark hospital corridors toward the waiting car.

"Sure you wouldn't prefer an ambulance?" Shelby slammed the driver's door and came around to help the attendants lift her into the back seat.

"No, I can manage." Virginia puffed a bit, first resisting the move, then going with it as six hands raised and arranged different parts of her. "Besides, the price is right."

"Reasonably comfy?" Shelby half turned to check her patient as she drove into the avenue. "Try that extra pillow behind your head."

"Stop fretting, just watch for potholes, will you? And tell me about the world of the living. What did you decide about ABC?"

"You're looking at the latest dropout from the unemployment statistics—I sold my soul and ass yesterday for a great deal of money . . ."

"They're damned lucky to get you."

"Of course. If they don't realize it, I'll remind them this afternoon at the production meeting. I start work officially Monday, but we discuss my first assignments today." Shelby swung wide onto the Seventy-ninth Street transverse, taking care not to jiggle her charge.

"What about the idea of your own business?" Virginia asked.

"Shelved. My partner and I fell out permanently. Mike Strange is sending one of his high-priced lawyers to take my deposition."

"Your *what?*"

"He wants my testimony for the paternity suit."

"But you weren't under the bed. How can *you* testify to *our* sexual conduct?"

"Oh, they'll be very clever. They won't ask me if you fucked, or where or when; they'll simply use me to set the stage for probability and possibility. Remember when we went to Nassau and the Exumas on his boat? Where did I sleep, where did you and he, that sort of thing . . . where you were the week the children stayed with me . . ."

"When we skied in Europe?"

"You've got it."

"That was so long ago who can remember? And what has that to do with the first of June, when I got pregnant?"

"Nothing and everything, Paula says. They'll establish you had a close sexual relationship through innuendo, then use other witnesses to prove you were together around that time."

"What witnesses?" Despite the heat, her hands were cold.

"According to the children, the elevator men and doormen were sworn and asked to identify pictures of Mike, then asked if they'd seen him in the building in the last couple of months."

"And I'm sure his driver has been questioned, his help at the apartment, and the headwaiter at our usual restaurant. The man has his bloodhounds out sniffing through the town while I'm prone on a hospital bed without a single defense strategy decided."

Shelby recognized more than a touch of panic in Virginia's voice as she slowed before her apartment building. "Call Paula over this afternoon, the children need her too. They were served with summonses this morning. Seems Mike wants them on the stand."

"Shit fuck piss crap suck cunt screw."

"That again? If nothing else, my darling friend, maybe this case will enlarge your repertoire of profanity."

"So why does he want us?" Max was uncharacteristically morose. His lank frame was draped across a chair by her bed, sideways.

"He doesn't really. There's little you can add he can't find better witnesses to say. He wants to put pressure on me by subpoenaing my children, the bastard, and he's doing it. He knows that the idea of you on the stand, testifying about my sexual conduct, is enough to make me give in."

"Is it?"

"Close. Not only is it embarrassing, it's tacky. I hate it and so will you. How did the process server get upstairs?"

"The doorman said there was a delivery for you. A surprise."

"I'll say."

Max read from a paper he had shoved in his pocket.

" 'Mike Strange, plaintiff, against Virginia Cargile Winburn. The People of the State of New York, to Max Winburn, Greeting: We command you, that all business and excuses being laid aside, you and each of you appear and attend before one of the Justices . . .' "

"Max, spare me."

"Why did the guy give me five bucks?"

"That's from the judge, for your time."

"So it shouldn't be a total loss?"

"I'd give a thousand if you didn't have to go."

"So would I, Mom."

Mother and son sat together quietly, sharing the misery of the moment. Max's leg swung mechanically from the chair arm.

"Maggie lucked out. She was at the store, you know, so she didn't get hers."

"He'll be back."

"But Maggie won't. Says she'll hide out so he can't find her."

"No! Where is she?"

"Don't know. Said she'd report in."

"That's crazy. She has to come home. Tell me when she calls, O.K.? Promise?"

"Sure."

As if Raggedy Andy's toe had been cut open and the sawdust dropped out on the floor, Max's energies drained away.

"What other cheerful news do you have?"

"Old man Rutherford called."

"Yes?"

"He's to be a witness, too. Wants to talk to you about it."

"God. There's no end to it."

"Why does he have to be there?"

"I suppose because I took myself off the Matterhorn account when Mike and I began to see each other seriously. And again because it puts more pressure on me."

The boy bounded from his seat in a fury. "Shit, Mom, let's just don't go. He can't make us." He smashed a fist into his open palm. "Let's just leave town and tell him to go f . . ."

"Honey, hang on."

"But it sucks, Mom, the whole business sucks. Do we really have to go through with this?"

Virginia looked through her son into unexplored territory for the second time. "I don't know, Max. I don't know."

"Are you really all right, Virginia?"

She could picture the honest concern on his controlled face, pinching vertical lines between his brows. "Yes, really, not to worry. A few weeks of mending and I'll be fine."

"And the baby?"

"Both of us, just fine, thank you, Stanton." Now she imagined a shadow across the patrician face as if they disagreed on what was the best of news, so she moved the conversation forward. "I understand you have to testify at the hearing."

"Just a deposition. The lawyers are coming tomorrow to the office."

"I'm so sorry—you know that."

"Can't be helped." He sounded sincere. "And all I can do is tell the truth as I remember it. It's not a difficult position for me, I just wish it weren't happening to you."

"And I." She could not suppress a sigh.

"I'm having your checks mailed directly home."

"That's very thoughtful . . ."

"But I'm concerned about your immediate financial position, with the hospital expenses, the lawyers and all. If you need a personal loan . . ."

"Bless you . . . I don't now, but if I do, you'll be the first call I make."

"You know you can count on me."

She also knew he had not offered a draw against future salary, or a loan against Peabody Slocum funds, because he did not expect her to return. And he felt rotten about it, but not nearly as bad as she. Irrational maybe, beyond reason, in fact, her inordinate fear of not being able to support herself; after all, was she not a valued, known commodity on the Wall Street People Exchange? With a reputation and a track record? Was not that translatable to another position in another firm? The truth was elusive: Yes, if ability to produce counted. Not necessarily, when you consider the continued bias against her sex, the cloud under which she was leaving the firm, and the lack of positions available in a down economy when layoffs were accepted business economies. She tried not to let her mind slip to adding up the sums in the money-market funds, the present value of several stocks and some tax-free bonds whose price was so low they were unsalable, yet add she did, and sucked in her breath. Barely enough for five or six months the way they lived now. But retrenchments could be made, let's see, drop the maid to once a week, skip the trip this Christmas, no department store bills—but hell! savings aren't income! What would they live on, count on? And suddenly, thinking that, she realized she meant the three of them, the living, the *family*. An addition that would suck away resources and energy and her ability to provide was not included.

"Thanks for coming. Not many lawyers make house calls."

Paula Seibert moved unselfconsciously, with a minimum of motion. Conservative in more than dress, there were no loose edges about her. She walked straightaway into the living room with her hand outstretched. Virginia sat in a crowd of pillows, her foot propped on the coffee table.

"Feeling more comfortable, I hope?" Paula asked.

"Much. There's not much I can't do now—except dash for a bus. Sit here, on the sofa. Max is creating in the kitchen—his favorite pastime. Shall I ask him to bring you a drink? Coffee? A soda?"

"Thanks, no. What's the master chef concocting?"

"God knows, but it'll be as incredible as the mess he leaves behind. Speaking of mess, let me bring you up to date on mine so we can make some plans."

"You sure you feel like going through this now? Any judge in the country would give you an adjournment considering your condition."

"No postponements! Jesus, my personal life's in chaos, so's my professional status, and the kids are bearing up but they're under enormous strain." Virginia shifted to a more comfortable position. She had lost weight in the hospital and pain had left its fingerprints on her face. Her hands shook slightly as she folded her glasses and laid them on the book she was reading.

"I've been thinking about the options you outlined. As I remember, my defense is either that there was another man or men around me at the time of conception—which would be a lie—or that Mike and I didn't have sexual contact. That would be a lie too. The remaining possibility is to have him examined medically and hope to heaven the tests will prove he's incapable of fathering a child. But that's not likely since I'm living proof he can."

"Only you can decide, though, what you want to say about the first two."

"But what about the question of proof? If I named another intimate partner or two, wouldn't they be put on the stand and questioned?"

"Probably."

"No one's about to go through that without reason, so the first option's out. As for the second, if I claim not to have been with Mike, I'll have to perjure myself. If I get around my morals, I'll have to bring off a public performance and I tremble like a tuning fork when I lie." Virginia paused a moment, remembering. "Ever since I stole a quarter from my mother at the age of six and ran to the corner and bought five Baby Ruth candy bars. I squatted in the garage and swallowed them as fast as possible—I'm sure I didn't chew—but she discovered the money missing and called me in. I fibbed and said I hadn't taken it—she knew perfectly well I had. I ran back to the garage and threw them up. I'm still not sure whether I was ill because of the candy or the lying, but ever since I have given up both."

"Well, if you're sure . . ." Paula said. "Without contesting the evidence, I think you'd make a mistake to let this go to court. Perhaps you'd better consider stopping the proceedings and negotiate some kind of agreement with Strange that you could live with, one that holds his participation in the child's life to a minimum."

"Knowing Mike, that means I'd see the child every other weekend." Virginia shifted again, in visible distress. "But that's not the last course open to me." She strained to control her voice. "What I want to explore—must explore, mind you—is what freedom I have at this point to have an abortion." Virginia's arms, crossed and hugging her body, seemed all that was holding her erect. She looked directly at Paula for an answer.

The change of tactic surprised Paula, and touched her. She reached over and patted Virginia's one good knee. "It's a terrible time for you, isn't it?" she said, but seeing that sympathy would break her client's tenuous hold, stood abruptly and walked out of the room. "I changed my mind about that drink. I'll have Max fix something for both of us."

She returned from the kitchen, a wineglass in each hand. Virginia stuffed a Kleenex down in the pillows and said, "You must think I'm a jackass. You've dedicated your energy for years so women can have abortions when they need them and here I am . . ."

"Feeling the same misery most women suffer when they consider abortion. Do you think anybody enjoys it? Go to a clinic sometime. Look at the women waiting their turn, then watch their faces when they leave. Believe me, there's no rejoicing. I've known people to grieve after an abortion as if a living child had died; I've seen others mourn for years. Maybe there are some women—and opponents of abortion would like us to believe this—who go through it with no emotion, but they're a callous bunch without depth or sensitivity. Women who're able to have children aren't those who end up in abortion clinics—it's those who can't, and damn it, they deserve our compassion."

"Thanks, Paula." She was honestly grateful. "Now tell me how much force that injunction has against an abortion if I decide to have one."

"Ordinarily I'd say not much at all; as a matter of fact, it wouldn't even be issuable. The Supreme Court has said that a woman's right to privacy and to determine her own reproductive life supersedes any rights a father may have. She doesn't need anyone's consent for an abortion. States have tried to write laws to change that, but they've all been struck down."

"Even a husband has no say?" Virginia asked.

"That's right. The Court's thinking is that if a father had the right to prevent an abortion, then he might also have the right to force his wife to have a child, or compel her to submit to an abortion. He can't even stop her from sterilizing herself."

"Don't fathers have any rights in the matter?"

"It's murky. The Court says a married couple isn't necessarily of one mind, but is a union of individuals. Since it's the woman who physically bears the child, she's more directly affected by the pregnancy, so her interests outweigh her husband's. But the Court also says the right to privacy isn't absolute; for example, a woman was forced to have a blood transfusion against her religious principles for the sake of an unborn child's health. Vaccinations are compulsory—that's another example of the state's intrusion into physical privacy. And blood tests are legal for evidentiary searches. So a woman's right to privacy prevails *unless* there's a compelling interest which outweighs her own."

"Well, is there, in my case?"

"That's just what Mike wants to argue. Before I left the office I called his lawyer, Gilbert Fenway, a tough litigator. Now, I had no idea you were contemplating an abortion, but for my own satisfaction I wanted to know why an injunction had been issued on a matter on which the courts are in such agreement. The answer is that Mike's determined to have his paternity acknowledged, and Fenway convinced the judge that an acknowledgment of his right and ability to procreate—which is guaranteed in the Constitution—overrode, even if only temporarily, your right to an abortion. The judge granted an injunction, for just a few days, and reserved all your rights at the same time, but he did say Mike could have a hearing before any abortion took place."

"But what made him think I would even consider an abortion?"

"He probably didn't. That's what you hire first-rate lawyers for, to think of things you might not. But you see where this puts you. Even though you have every right to an abortion, you're in contempt if you disregard the injunction. The court is saying, in effect, you *must* appear whether you want to have the child or not."

"Then, Paula, what would stop me from going to court, acknowledging his paternity, and *then* going for an abortion?"

"You can do that; it's absolutely within your rights, though I'm sure he'll use every possible argument to keep you from carrying it out once his legal interests in the child are established. Remember, this body of law is so new it's still being written. More to the point, I imagine Mike will use the hearing itself—which is certain to be a cause célèbre and the focus of a lot of media attention—to pressure you into backing down quietly and negotiating an agreement. Fenway almost said as much. Still, if you can take the glare of the hearing, you can have an abortion immediately afterward."

"With the press following me to the operating table. God, Paula. It's one thing to go through a court procedure in order to keep the child—I could deal with that—but in order to have a public abortion!" Virginia began a kind of mechanical head-swinging. "I ask myself a hundred times a day, how did I get into this?"

"Well, hold on. We've only discussed this from their point of view. Actually the burden of proof—which is usually on a man to prove he is *not* the father—in this case is on Mike to prove he *is*."

"But all his lawyer has to do is put me on the stand . . ."

"Oh, no. You're not required to testify if you don't want to."

"I'm not? But doesn't it make me look suspect?"

"Absolutely not. The respondent—again, through the ages it's usually been the man—the respondent's neglect or refusal to testify doesn't raise any presumption against him."

"Can they make me take a lie detector test?"

"No, it's not admissible evidence. Nor is a blood test in most cases unless it proves conclusively that the baby could not be the father's—in this case it would have to prove conclusively that it *is* his, and with the current state of the art that's not possible. Mike's evidence must be so clear and reliable that a genuine belief is built up in the mind of the judge that he's the father."

"Hey," said Virginia. "Suddenly it doesn't sound like such a cinch."

"Far from it. He'll be building a house on the sand and trying to make it look like the foundation is poured in concrete."

"Can he do that?"

"He'll certainly try. By constructing circumstances and probabilities, by demonstrating his reputation for trust and veracity, by impugning yours. And he'll call your own people to testify. For example, who told him about the baby, wasn't it Shelby? He'll have her repeat that conversation. He'll find a way to question the kids without edging into hearsay evidence. Maybe he told other people you and he were having a child . . ."

"Half the town."

"Of course, and don't think it was self-congratulation. It was on advice of counsel, you can believe that. He may have set up a trust fund for the child, or an expense fund for the pregnancy, I don't know. He'll go to any lengths—including submitting to fertility tests, and presenting expert psychiatric testimony that his health will be harmed unless his interests are acknowledged. I know it sounds extreme for a man in his position, but that's what the case requires—so much personal information, in fact, it makes me wonder whether there's an underlying need to punish you."

"Perhaps not to punish me as much as to beat me. Mike likes winning. It would be too difficult to walk away from this without a judgment or a hearing." Her head began moving slowly again from side to side. "How did I get into this? I'm not painted into a corner, but a circle."

Paula lit up with the flush of anticipated combat. "Not at all. He may never get the chance to call a witness. I'm prepared to ask for a summary judgment on the grounds that whatever evidence Mike can produce, he won't be able to establish a prima facie case that he's the father. And further, that any evidentiary examination into access to you, or lack of it, by others around the time of conception is a violation of your right to privacy—'the special intimacy of the sexual decision,' as the Court puts it, which must be protected from intrusion by the state."

"Will the judge accept that?" A part of Virginia was mesmerized by the realization—incredible!—that the discussion was not abstract, it applied to her. Another part of her listened, entranced by the process, the reduction from passion to legal skill, from loving fact to manipulation of legal precedent. Where were the miserable participants in cases past whose torturous situations had become the subject of legal tomes, whose identities had been resurrected as Roes and Does, whose misfortunes and dangers had paved the way for hers?

"I can't say for sure," Paula answered. "This case has earmarks of first impression—which means we're cutting new ground. What's uncertain, too, is how heavily the judge will weigh Mike's interests. Up till now, neither criminal nor tort law has been particularly concerned with protecting a husband's interest in the fetus, and even less concerned with a natural father's, which is Mike's legal identification—but times are changing. A landmark case held that it was unconstitutional to disregard the interests of a father who wanted to retain custody of his illegitimate child instead of allowing it to be placed for adoption, and do you know how he won his hearing? On the

basis of the equal protection laws in his state—the equivalent
of a local ERA. He argued that the state wouldn't suspend his
driver's license without a hearing, or deprive him of a welfare
check. Why should it deprive him of a son or daughter without
a hearing just because he was a man?"

Virginia found herself rubbing her eyes; she really wanted to
be rubbing her ears to block out the sound. Paula marked the
frustration.

"I'm not trying to confuse you, Virginia. I'm simply explaining how fathers are getting a fairer hearing today, and why you
can't predict how the court will respond."

"And all this goes on with the *Daily News* taking down
every word?"

"I'm afraid so. This case would make the papers even if you
weren't a Wall Street presence, and Mike weren't one of the
most visible CEO's in the country, because it epitomizes the
struggle to reshape the balance of power between the sexes on a
sociological basis as well as a legal one. It brings the national
debate about man's world and woman's place down to two individuals—precisely the kind of juicy story that news editors
long for."

A sigh rose from the deepest part of her. "One last question.
Suppose, I don't show up at all?"

"Do you mean for the paternity hearing?"

Virginia nodded.

"You're in contempt and the judge can fine you or put you
in jail, or threaten any other punishment he might decide
would make you appear. But it's strange, when you think about
it. Your best tactic would be to have an abortion *before* the
hearing, because judges have been unwilling to bring any proceedings against women who go ahead and have them—what
are they going to do, put them in jail until they are pregnant
again? Or put a dollar value on a six-week-old fetus and ask a
woman to pay the fine?"

"Weird, isn't it? By doing what I don't want to do—have an

abortion—I can beat Mike in court, though we both lose what we want. If he goes through with the paternity hearing and wins, and forces me to have an abortion, we both lose again. And if I win the paternity hearing and the right to bring up the child alone, then he loses another way. With the outcome so much against him, why is he striking out at me this way?"

"Stubbornness, I suppose. And a determination to have his way, and the firm belief that he's in the right. The same reasons you're holding out against him. I told you once that no one wins in these tangles."

A late sun slanting through the windows outlined dust particles temporarily suspended in their course through time and space. Eventually they would settle and be wiped away, but for the moment their uniqueness, their mission, was undeniable. Virginia tried to fix on one, but competing motes tricked her eye, causing her to lose sight of the chosen.

Like the specks of dust drifting by, much of Virginia's life seemed beyond her control. She did not logically decide significant matters, not the major ones. She reserved her observation and acuity, her reasoning and rationality for such matters as chicken vs. pot roast for dinner, or a week in the mountains against a week by the sea. She brought her intellect to bear on recommendations to increase holdings in technology issues or consumer cyclicals. She solved the problems of her friends and children with inductive and deductive thinking. But when it came time to marry, or take a lover, or divorce—or now, to have a child—she could only reach beyond what she knew and, like a lightning rod, accept a message when it struck, coming from an unknown place, arriving in its own moment.

"I'll have to live with this a while longer, Paula. But I want you to proceed with the idea that I'll defend the paternity suit with—and for—everything that's in me."

Before spearing the chicken Kiev, she averted her head. Butter spurted obligingly. "You're easily the best cook on the

West Side. You'll make some lovely young lawyer or stock broker a terrific wife."

Max was pleased. Chin about six inches from the plate, he shoved rice and chicken onto his fork with the back of his thumb, indicating he knew better than to use his fingers but was more interested in moving things rapidly from plate to mouth.

"No sweat, no sweat. And there's mass chicken in the kitchen. I fixed some for Maggie too, before she split, so we'll have leftovers for the weekend."

"Are you kidding? Unless you've cut down from your usual six meals a day, we won't have any leftovers by midnight."

"Just a growing boy, Mom." Max unfolded his shapeless six-foot frame, which resembled nothing as much as a giraffe's neck. "In fact, I'll reduce the supply right now."

She had never known him lackadaisical or lacking in enthusiasm though his interests were unpredictable; he was hardly the All-American boy. Football held no magic for him, though he occasionally lay supine eating his way through a pro game. And girls were a part of his existence but they came and went like minor snowfalls, providing entertainment for short periods, then melting away. (She came upon his stash of *Playboy* magazines when he was still a pup, and gave him a flat refusal last Christmas when he asked for a subscription to *Penthouse*.) He passed through a smoking phase, pretending to take long showers while the smoke, seeking cooler air, curled under the bathroom door and she and Maggie stood outside laughing. There was enough regular boy there to put him within the "normal" range of kids, but intimations of his manhood were surprising. He took an unabashed delight in food—eating, cooking, shopping. He preferred to sing in groups and stage productions rather than listen to records or the radio. More music ran through his head than Maggie, with her vast record collection, would ever hear. But perhaps his chief pleasure came from scrutinizing the stock market, planning financial coups with the few hundred dollars he had earned, and discussing with his mother the effect of government actions and international events on investors' inclinations. Because she was in the business? Not entirely. He was thrust into the role of only man too young, and shed his childish skin before it was time.

Soon after the divorce, when still a little boy, he drew the house he would live in with his wife and four children, two stories of deluxe accommodations surrounding a swimming pool, with a wing planned perpendicular to the main house just for her. In the crayon drawing he placed a slide under her second-story bedroom window so she would have easy access to the pool. Now, at sixteen, he worried that his impending graduation and start of college would leave her alone. He sized up every man who walked in the apartment as a possible mate and shoved her toward the more promising with a pushiness matched only by the most ambitious mothers marrying off their daughters. It made her laugh, but she also winced at the possibility that she may have driven his childhood away, so almost with relief she watched some adolescent traits hang on. He would forget to relay the most important telephone messages; his clothes wrinkled in piles on the closet floor after "unpacking" a suitcase; and she had not yet devised the reward or command that would induce him to run an errand in the neighborhood. Yet they seldom passed unpleasant words. She would make a demand that he would acknowledge, then forget. He would overlook her shrill unreasonableness in moments when she was pressed. They loved each other fiercely.

Max lifted one leg over the seat of his chair and dropped into it, his nose to his plate again before he hit the cushion. "Mom, I gotta level with you."

"Yeah?" A warning bell rang dimly. "Meaning what?"

"About Maggie. She isn't going to call back, she's really gone."

Virginia placed her silver carefully on her plate. "Gone where?"

Max's mechanical jaws disposed of the forkfuls as rapidly as they came. "When she left today she made me promise not to tell you until she had plenty of time to get away. She didn't want you chasing after her to bring her back."

"But where has she gone?" The warning bells were plural now; they were making a racket inside her head.

"Can't tell ya. Made me promise. She doesn't want to testify at the hearing. So she skipped out. Took some money and beat it. Don't worry, though. Old Mags is tough—she can handle herself."

"Max! She's barely eighteen and she's never traveled alone. Where did she get the money, and what in hell's name is she doing?"

"Hit her bank account. Wants to get pretty far away so there's no chance of anyone finding her before Monday."

"Is she going to Atlanta—to your grandparents? Is she going to your father? Talk to me, Max!"

"Nope. Someplace where she can be alone. She says she doesn't know when she'll be back. If she likes it well enough, she may try to get herself in a school, wait tables on the weekend. Probably won't, though. She's too big a chicken to hack it for long. Bet she's home in a week or so."

"Mygod. What a dumb thing to do." Virginia dropped her head into her hands, shoving her plate away. "That's all I need, God. The other plagues weren't enough. Now send the boils and the locusts."

"I knew you wouldn't like it. I told her."

Virginia swung toward him as much as her foot, propped on a stool under the table, would allow. "Now tell me, Max. It's nighttime, no telling where she is or what's happening to her. Unless you want to see a grown woman become hysterical before your very eyes, tell me where she is!"

"She's someplace she's been before—it's not strange territory, so she knows her way around. And it's pretty safe, so . . ."

"Nantucket. Of course. She's in Nantucket." Sometimes Vir-

ginia knew things about her children with such certainty they
did not require confirmation. "She knows the island, and she's
been in enough of those restaurants to feel comfortable asking
for a job. Nantucket, right, Max? Sure, not far away, but iso-
lated. She's hiked all those roads, knows every inch of the
place. And being August she probably assumes some pals will
be there. All she has to do is get out to Cisco Beach and look
around for them." Virginia struggled to her feet, reaching for
her single crutch. "Come, Max, you'll have to get her and bring
her home. You'll know where to look, the town is tiny. We'll
get you on the next plane, find you a place to stay, or maybe
the Griswolds are still there and will put you up, but no, that's
embarrassing, better we should . . ."

Virginia hobbled down the hall, talking over her shoulder at
Max, who was scraping the last mouthfuls from his plate as he
stood bending over to finish and to leave the table at the same
time.

"You don't know where she's actually staying, do you, Max?
I could call and talk some sense into her . . ."

Max loped down the hall after her. "But, Mom, suppose she
won't come back with me?"

"She will. You'll manage. Or you'll get her to a phone and
I'll convince her. Jesus, a runaway—kid stuff! Oh, God, why do
I have to handle this now?" The hysteria was retreating but giving way to pressure up the back of the neck which would graduate into a full-blown headache.

The next hour was organized chaos. A direct flight at the
height of the season was an impossible dream. She routed him
instead to Boston, then transferred him to a small inter-island
plane which would put him on the runway shortly after eleven.
She alerted their long-time friends the Griswolds that a mini-
emergency existed, without going into details, and arranged to
have him transported to their house at Quidnet. She dug
emergency money out of her jewelry box, kept on hand "to get
one of you out of jail someday," and packed him off with

enough to bring them both home. She told him to call her as
soon as he landed in case she had heard from Maggie, hugged
him hard, and thanked him. He was gone before she realized
how frightened she was for him as well as Maggie, and how furious she was at her own helplessness.

Was that it? She stared at the leg stretched out in front of
her. Or was it her competence? She knew she would get past
this, she always did. But something in her resented that she
could. Wished instead for inadequacy and dependency, longed
to lean on a stronger arm for physical and emotional support,
yearned to share the problem and listen for a better way.

What you really want, she thought, is another kind of
crutch. You've never learned that life isn't a string of warm
days in the Georgia sun with Daddy watching over you till the
cool nights come. Or that, ultimately, everyone has to provide
his or her own answers. You've never learned it because you
don't want to accept it, and because you don't really want responsibility for yourself. You're a phony, living a lie, preening
independent feathers, posturing cock-like in front of the world
while you secretly dream about sitting on a nest waiting for the
eggs to crack.

Virginia looked down at her arms crossed protectively over
her stomach and through them to the living symbol of her am-
biguity. She turned her mind to "off" for protection. Sometimes she understood herself too well.

When the phone rang late, she was certain it was Max. Too
worried to waste time, she grabbed the receiver and asked immediately, "Are you all right? Do you have any news?"

"I'm O.K.—but are you?"

It took her a moment to realize the voice belonged to
Shelby, who added, "And I do have some news."

"Sorry, Shel. I'm expecting Max to call from Nantucket. I
sent him off to retrieve his sister, who decided dropping out
was easier than showing up at the hearing next week. Crazy

kid, she left to avoid the witness stand and I'm off the deep end worrying about her."

"Just what you need."

"Don't sympathize, I'll cry."

"All right, then I'll add to your troubles."

"Must you?"

"Unfortunately. Seems the story of you and Mike has pretty well made the rounds. It was first up for discussion at the producers' meeting this afternoon."

"I don't want to hear it."

"Yep. They're going to do the story. They see it exemplifying the way men are asserting themselves in domestic matters these days. It'll lead the show on the new September lineup— if it's as good as they hope. Mike has already agreed to any interviews they might want, and they'll add various judicial and legal talking heads, feminists, child psychiatrists, that sort of thing."

"Christ, Shelby."

"I knew it'd make your day. And listen to this: I have to produce it."

"You! But you won't—you wouldn't!"

"Yes, I will. As a matter of fact, it's better this way. Look, babe, *they are going to do the story*. I did everything but threaten sabotage trying to talk them out of it, and at first they even wanted me to be the reporter. No way, I told them, not only because of our friendship but because I've been subpoenaed for the trial. That persuaded them I couldn't be on camera, but then I made the suggestion—and it surprised them at first—that I produce it instead."

"But what's the point?" The day had brought too many dizzying complications; her mind lurched now from point to point, requiring elementary explanations.

"If they use one of the fellows, well, you know how they love public hangings. Maybe, just maybe I can tone it down, present it less sensationally with some protection for your side. By God,

I'm going to try. All I know is, you're a hell of a lot better off with me on the story than off."

Virginia was silent.

"Hey, talk to me."

"I know you're trying to help, and I'm grateful. But I was just remembering a night many years ago. Jim and I were newlyweds, and I was very young. I went to the window just about dark, reached for the shade pull, and happened to look outside. There, just inches from the screen, was the outline of a man's face—a peeper—who must have been watching for some time. I screamed and jumped away, but by the time Jim got there he was gone. Every time I came near that window—for days—I trembled, and he was just one person looking in. Now the world's outside, there's no shade to pull and no one to call for help."

Monday, September 1

"The worst part, sometimes, is the waiting." Paula led her group up the steps to the Family Court building, through the marbled doorway, into a hallway crowded as a Bloomingdale's aisle the Saturday before Christmas. Except for the lawyers, probably everyone there wished they were somewhere else. Uniformed guards directed reluctant adversaries, witnesses, plaintiffs and defendants, their families and entourages toward banks of elevators, while priests of the unholy mysteries—denizens of the Bar—walked God-like among their people.

"I'd wait a lifetime to avoid this," Virginia answered, her voice tight.

Maggie and Max walked on either side protectively, bumping her shoulders every several steps. They were apprehensive and nervous—unusual emotions for them, but they were beyond their own fears when it came to their mother, whom they were there to support.

"Hey, really, Mags. You know you wouldn't have missed this

for all the hunks on the beach." Despite his nervousness Max was not below enjoying himself. He had not met a day, yet, he didn't like.

"Do I still have the choice?" Maggie had returned, but not happily, for she could not imagine being a part of any testimony which would damage her mother. She would have fought Mike Strange bare-handed given the chance—wasn't she a match for most of the young swains who bent elbows to her in arm-wrestling matches? She had not an ounce of fear of any opponent, and the sight of her mother trembling before the ordeal of a public trial was beyond the understanding of her idealistic young mind. Having now been convinced that running was not only not possible but also not helpful, she had turned her combative nature to standing firm behind her mother's shoulders. "You're ept, Mom," she was saying with her presence, "and if you aren't, I am."

"Ah—it'll be a gas." Max doubled a fist to raise an early biceps and jabbed the air. "Just wait till this tough macho dude takes the stand . . ."

"Yeah?" His sister interrupted his theatrics. "And the first time you say shit or fuck to the judge they throw you in the slammer, right, Mom?"

"Will you two stop?" Virginia asked, following Paula into the elevator, where she finished her admonition in a whisper. "Haven't I enough to worry about?"

"Sorry, Mom," they said almost in unison. Max hung his head. Maggie reached for her hand and held it like a little girl.

"I hope you never get near that witness chair, Max," Paula said over her shoulder, stepping off on the fifth floor. She tucked her briefcase under her arm. "The waiting room's to the right."

Through tall oak doors they saw a square room capacious as a warehouse with line after line of chairs already filling with noisy groups of people. Whole families were present, speaking a babel of dialects and languages, often in loud voices. Children squirmed in arms, or chairs, and around their parents' legs, unwittingly the cause of many of the disputes. Most were not people of substance, far from it, or even education, and few had any real understanding of the system through which they would pass; still, their reality was the same as Virginia's: they had encountered troubles unsettleable by ordinary means, so all the previous weeks and months and, in some cases, years of competition and jockeying for position, all the screaming matches and crying fits, all the advice of friends and legal counsel, all the hopes for resolution and desires for revenge, brought them finally, this diverse group of wretched combatants, into the room at one time for one purpose—arbitration and disposition by the state.

The four found seats in a less occupied part of the maelstrom and huddled together, feeling out of place—and they were. Their strong faces and controlled intelligences, their emotions reined in tightly, contrasted sharply with the tumultuous folk around them, many of whom were haranguing their companions, pleading aggrieved positions as if one more restatement of the facts would guarantee the rightfulness of their cause.

The racket made them quiet. "I'll report to the court officer that we're here," Paula said, patting Virginia's shoulder as she walked away.

"This sure doesn't look like courtrooms on TV." Max was awed by the spectacle.

"It isn't." Virginia was relieved to be able to teach and explain. "Cases in Family Court are usually short—you don't even have to have a lawyer—and they aren't important to anyone except the people who bring them. They usually involve separation disputes, financial support, that kind of thing. Sometimes out-of-control kids whose mothers are having them put away."

Max's eyes were big. "You mean like reform school?" She

nodded to him. "And their *mothers* send them?" She nodded
again. "Bum me out . . ."

"So take warning, big shot, your time is coming." Maggie
began to enjoy the uniqueness of the morning in spite of her
indignation. "Will our case be over fast too?"

"There's no telling." Virginia looked up as Paula returned.
"We're not even sure when it'll be called."

"Looks like Strange's influence has been at work," Paula said
in answer, taking her place again.

"Which means we're first on the calendar, right?" she asked.

"Well, first or second," Paula responded. "We've been assigned Luis Cabrerra—good Catholic, father of six kids."

"Swell! More of his doing. Can you really fix which judge
you get?"

"It's not as sordid as that. Lawyers who practice regularly
down here get to know the clerk and ask for favors. And it
would be hard not to find a judge who isn't from one ethnic
group or another. These are political appointments, you know,
and the city's full of Irish, Italians, Hispanics, you name it.
Only ten percent of the city's WASP, so you're not going to
find many judges named Smith or Jones."

"Still, he's calling the shots, isn't he?"

Paula acknowledged the truth with a shrug of her shoulders,
and Virginia's stomach, already curdled on a morning cup of
coffee, cringed again. Authority bums me out too, Max, she
thought. The summons to the home room teacher when she
was twelve. The cop writing her first speeding ticket. Facing an
IRS audit. In every confrontational situation, subliminally she
saw her father's taut face and heard his threatening words,
coming back from childhood: "Don't talk back to me, young
lady." What was she afraid of—that the belt that beat her
brother would be used against her? She cowered in the glare of
first his, then others' disapproval, and developed a healthy fear
of men in general. She also learned to duck. She walked down
the back stairs when her father was coming up the front; she

became afraid of her brother's virulent attacks and avoided them and him in time; was terrified when Jim Winburn's red-faced rages urged her to throw objects at him or beat him back; and shivered like a kite's tail when an angry manager called her to task. Innocence was no armor against attack; virtue no protection. If she had been judged in provocative situations by her demeanor, she would have been found consistently guilty, for the very suggestion of blame made her quake. And it made no sense trying to explain her ability to cope alongside her unwillingness to contest, thwart, defy, oppose. She was, when facing an authoritative man, almost a coward.

Suddenly, adding to the din but not overcoming it, a working group surrounding a television camera backed into the room, clearing a path for the object of their attention, and it was Mike. Lawyers to the left and right, reporters and photographers following, it was enough of a spectacle to stop toddlers in mid-wail. All necks craned to see the personage, and temporarily a hush replaced the constant clamor, which resumed in even greater volume when flashbulbs began to punctuate the moment.

"Hey, it's our case—why aren't the photographers over here?" Max complained.

"Just try to keep them away," his mother said, shrinking in her seat.

"Be natural. Don't avoid them, and don't answer any questions," Paula advised. "They can't come in the courtroom itself, so this won't last long—if we're lucky."

As if on cue, an officer of the court across the wide room called out in a bored voice, "Strange vs. Winburn, Part A. Strange vs. Winburn, proceed to Part A."

Virginia pulled herself up with difficulty. It was not because of her still-bandaged leg and ribs, nor was it the fault of Maggie and Max, who, leaning in to support her, added to the drag. Like answering a call to dental surgery, or as soldiers respond when ordered into fire, she went, but only because of a lifetime of taking orders.

Looking for movement in the crowd, the press recognized their prey and rushed to intercept her. The minicam, however, remained stationary and, pointing itself in her direction, let her walk into its picture. What it recorded was the entrance into Part A of the Family Court of Manhattan of a perfectly contained, perfectly confident, successful, and well-regarded New York businesswoman—on the outside.

Shelby's blessed face materialized from the pack. Waving her crew away first, she hugged her friend hard.

"Have you seen that platoon of lawyers?" Virginia hooked a finger toward Mike, entering ahead of her.

"Hell, you hold all the cards—and the baby. A gross of lawyers won't change that."

"My poor kids, they're terrified," Virginia whispered as the children moved through the door.

"And you, Gin?"

"I've been in better shape." She wobbled her hand back and forth, thumb to little finger.

As if hearing the conversation, Mike disentangled from his legal gaggle and came toward them. "The children won't be asked to testify, Ginny."

Her eyebrows shot up. "No?"

"They weren't meant to get subpoenas. Overzealous lawyers. Sorry about that."

Even at a time like this he made her remember why she had cared. She looked into the bottomless eyes for the old connection. "Want to call this off?"

"Yes. And find a little Italian restaurant and make some plans."

"And Mrs. Woodard. Will she mind waiting in the limousine?" Virginia could not help tonguing the sore tooth.

"I've let her go, Ginny."

She allowed his cruelty to register and felt, for the first time, no jealousy for her successor. "But then all relationships are expendable, aren't they, Mike?" She turned away from him for the last time and found her place next to Paula. Shelby sat between the children in the front row, holding their hands. Their faces looked young and vulnerable to her.

Judge Cabrerra thumbed the papers before him once, then again—in disbelief? Hundreds of cases came before him where distressed women demanded of resistant men greater participation in their children's lives, and battled for just enough financial and emotional support to endure the burden, and here was a woman who wanted only to be left alone . . . She imagined his disdain.

Gilbert Fenway, next to the judge the most comfortable person in the room, and next to no one the most elegant, rose tall and lean to address the Bench. His three-piece suit mocked the summer heat. "Your honor, the plaintiff, Michael Strange, asks the Court today for nothing more than what is his already by virtue of the laws of this state and the rights of humankind; he asks to take his place as the rightful father of his child . . ."

Where did this all begin, she wondered, except in hope and love and passion—oh, God! the passion? And where can it end now except in disillusionment and unhappiness? And why didn't she have the power, or control, or dedication to make what she wanted come around? First Jim Winburn, then Mike. Love seemed a fight ring where she took punches as well as threw them and from which she emerged eternally bruised. And she had once called *Mike* an emotional inadequate . . .

". . . The most basic human emotion that exists," Fenway continued, "is the love between parents and children. The Court will notice I said parents, not just mother. Is there anyone in this room who would have preferred *not* to know his or her father? Who is *not* richer for the relationship regardless of the length of time it existed or the conflicts it endured? And is there any one of us so wise or so prescient that we would, even before a child is born, declare that baby better off never to know its father . . . ?"

What *am* I doing to this child? she asked once more. Either I allow it no father, or I give it a life filled with polarization— or I give it no life at all. Better off! What's better off?

". . . This hearing could be a short one, your honor, regardless of our list of witnesses prepared to testify in my client's behalf . . ." His words jerked her back to reality. Short! Didn't she wish! "Because medical science is now able to do what a conflicted human being can't: tell the truth." Virginia cut a glance at Paula, frowning slightly but composed as usual. "A conflicted human being who is more concerned for her own immediate welfare than for the future of that most innocent of victims, a newborn baby."

Fenway paused, sucking thoughtfully on the arm of his glasses, then directed his universal question straight at one Judge Luis Cabrerra. "Let me ask the question again, this time another way. Is there anyone in this room, fortunate enough to have had children, who would *not* have had them? And is any one of us so cruel that we would wrongfully deny another the joy and fulfillment we ourselves have known? By his own testimony, by the subjective testimony of those who know him best, by the disinterested testimony of experts, and, your honor, by the latest miracle in the world of scientific medicine, we will prove Michael Strange not only is the father of this child, and destined to be an adequate one, we will prove him a potentially remarkable one. He asks no more than the right to try."

Fenway turned toward Virginia after the last of his remarks, but she was looking at her hands. Paula moved quickly to dispel his mood. She began her opening remarks crisply, standing almost motionless before the judge.

"Your honor, my client categorically denies the plantiff's allegations. Instead, she asks the Court to consider the grave injustice that a hearing of this sort causes because of its unconscionable invasion of privacy and accompanying public embarrassment. The Court knows that allegations in a filiation proceeding must be supported by clear and convincing evidence in order to establish paternity. *No such evidence exists in this case.* Indeed, the very relationship under discussion doesn't exist, having been permanently broken off more than eight months ago. If it were ever taken seriously by Mr. Strange, and that too is open to question, it certainly is without validity now—one hardly reads a newspaper that doesn't chronicle his social appearances with other women."

Paula was swinging hard early, fighting to have the hearing dropped. "And if there ever was such an occasion, as the plaintiff suggests, when he and Mrs. Winburn had relations, the possibility that he might have fathered her child, on that one night, is so remote as to be impossible. How many people, and for how long, have known this man was sterile? He and his wife of over twenty years were unable to have children though he had every test and procedure known to medical science. The results? All negative. The test we asked the Court to require of him before this hearing—just days ago? Also strongly negative. And during the year that he and Mrs. Winburn dated regularly, was there any use of contraceptives? Of course not. He knew there was no need . . ."

Those nights, she thought, really quite wondrous. And not because she wasn't concerned about getting pregnant. They were so *filled up.* There was nothing she wanted that she didn't have then, nothing that felt incomplete. She would lie next to him, absorbing his strength and relishing it—then spend the days running from the control that accompanied it. But those nights . . .

Paula's determination was fierce—at least one woman was unafraid of battle. "He is absolutely unable to make a prima facie case that he is the father. Even the most complete obstetrical examination can't pinpoint when a child was conceived—estimates can range over a period of weeks. So in order to refute the pitifully weak claims of an almost sterile man, Mrs.

Winburn would have to disclose her sexual activity over the entire period of time when she *might* have become pregnant. That's an intolerable invasion of privacy given our constitutional guarantees.

"If Mrs. Winburn were the one seeking the filiation order, then a discussion of access would be pertinent and reasonable." Paula said the next words very slowly, very distinctly. "But— she's—not. So she does not intend to take the stand and engage in what would be for her an odious situation. But my client asks that you consider this, sir. If she knew Mr. Strange was the father of this child, would she be in this proceeding at all? She's the mother of two children whose relationship with their father is one she's nurtured because she knows the importance of a father in a child's life. Is she not just as concerned with the best interests of her third child? If you consider only his ability to provide, wouldn't she be foolish not to accept him? . . ."

Wouldn't she be foolish indeed. So why hasn't she—one more time, Virginia, put it into words—why hasn't she? *Because he doesn't want me, he wants the baby.* And why is she able, in full view of God and the press, to plead a patently false position? *Because I want him to leave me alone more than I want to admit the truth.* How well she understood men who had sat in her place before her, denying babies rightfully theirs to avoid the women who bore them.

". . . But no amount of money guarantees a loving father." Paula wanted to wrap it up. "Once the baby is born and does *not* resemble him, or share his interests, or even—because of the bitterness a trial like this engenders—does not want to be around a man with so little connection to its mother, then will having forced this false relationship be in its best interests?

"There's no limit to psychiatric proof that children are ill served when there's no rapport, or even worse, hostile feelings between the caring adults." Paula had been facing the opponents. Now she directed her steady gaze again at the judge. "Michael Strange does not belong in the life of this child. Obviously, he holds no place in the life of its mother. What she asks from this court is what every mother deserves—the opportunity for a serene pregnancy, a trouble-free birth, and the chance to bring up her child without the unfair and intolerable interference of others."

Unfair? Not really. But intolerable? Oh, she's right there. Survival itself insists that she be free. If she could not be with him totally, she must be alone together with her own. She was shaking free now. A slow, torturous process, but she was getting away.

"Call your first witness, Mr. Fenway," the judge ordered.

Mike walked determinedly to the stand. If nervous, he did not show it. Fenway led him through preliminary questions easily, then brought him slowly to the facts.

"To your best knowledge, when was the child conceived?"

"I know when the child was conceived, the night of the second of June."

"What happened that night?"

"Mrs. Winburn had dinner with me at Orsini's, then we went to my hotel."

"And did she spend the night?"

"Mrs. Winburn never spends the night." Was a smile working at his mouth? Her refusal to stay over had always been a source of contention between them. "She always insists on going home—but we had sexual relations, if that's what you mean."

"Why do you think you are responsible for Mrs. Winburn's pregnancy that particular night, Mr. Strange?"

"I'm certain of it." He looked at Virginia as if daring her to deny it. "First, her best friend, Shelby Anderson, told me . . ."

"Objection, your honor." Paula stood abruptly. "No one has the perfect intimate or medical knowledge available to make such a statement, not even the closest of friends."

"She's awfully well known for accurately reporting the news, ma'am," Mike interjected, smiling, before the judge could speak. He *was* having some fun at this, the bastard. But then he always smiled at trouble.

"Isn't Miss Anderson a witness for the plaintiff, Mr. Fenway?" Judge Cabrerra asked.

"She is, your honor."

"Sustained. We'll hear her testimony directly."

Fenway turned again to Mike. "What else makes you know the child is yours?"

Mike became solidly serious. "The way a parent knows a child after decades of separation, or a brother knows a brother. In the gut. And in the heart. But before you object again, Miss Seibert"—Paula was already on her feet—"also because Mrs. Winburn told me it was mine. If she'd be willing to take the stand she'd say the same thing."

"Objection, your honor. Mrs. Winburn is not on the stand and will not be taking the stand."

"Sustained."

Mike was undaunted.

"And because Mrs. Winburn isn't the kind of woman to sleep with just anybody. She'd have to be all wrapped up in someone and I'm the only man who has been in her life for a long time."

"Ob-JECT-tion." Paula's voice was raised. She was clearly angry. "The witness has no information about Mrs. Winburn's personal life."

"I must ask you to confine yourself to the facts," the judge said severely. He appeared exasperated. "Sustained."

Fenway moved his witness away from danger. "Have you ever had children of your own, Mr. Strange?"

"Unfortunately, no."

"Have you been examined medically to see if you were capable of having children?"

"Yes, on more than one occasion."

"Why more than once, Mr. Strange?" Fenway was not going to miss an opportunity.

"Because my wife and I desperately wanted children. We'd have done anything to have them."

"And what did the tests tell you?"

"That there was no reason why we couldn't. My wife seemed perfectly normal. My sperm count was somewhat on the low side, but no doctor ever told us we couldn't. They just said keep trying."

"Did you?"

"We did until my wife became ill with multiple sclerosis. That was about ten years after we were married."

"And did you 'try' with Mrs. Winburn?"

"We never used contraceptives, not during the year we were seeing each other regularly, nor in the six-month period afterward, when we were together occasionally."

"Why, Mr. Strange?"

"Because having a child with her would have made me the happiest man in the country."

Paula was on her feet again, demanding the judge's attention. "Really, your honor, this is going too far. We are all aware that paternity in the state of New York must be proved 'to the point of entire satisfaction,' but what have we here? A man who *wishes* he could have a child, one who has been trying for years, who, by his own testimony, has a less than normal possibility of doing so. Now, we can feel compassion for him and wish him well in the future—he should marry and have a houseful—but this flimsy testimony—he knows it 'in the heart, in the gut'—is it enough to put Mrs. Winburn through the stress of this proceeding? Your honor, I ask you to dismiss the hearing on the basis of little to no evidence supporting Mr. Strange's claim of paternity."

Judge Cabrerra took off his wire glasses and, using the edge of his robe, wiped the lenses, then slowly hooked them over each ear. He was perplexed by the strange people before him with their stranger motives. Most of what he knew was God-ordained, particularly the crowded house in the Bronx he would return to, divested of the robe that made him daytime different, and the multi-children who had turned his receptive nut-brown bride into a lumpy, shrill companion. They were all simply, unarguably, his. His to be responsible for, his to support with the $51,000 his appointed position brought him— more money than he had ever expected to live on, yet so little to go so far. He was an accepting man, even when he felt put upon by his lot and demeaned by a public which believed his time was spent returning teen-aged murderers to the street. Such foolishness, he thought, for people so blessedly trouble-free to bring on themselves. "Will the parties and their counselors join me in chambers?" he asked, sounding weary.

The foursome assembled awkwardly in a robing room at the rear of the main courtroom while the judge repeated the act of cleaning his glasses. If not swift, he was a deliberate man. When he spoke his voice was almost inaudible.

"I don't know what you nice people are up to, but I know this case doesn't belong in my court." Mike and Virginia both looked as if they'd been sent to the principal.

"Well, we certainly agree with that," Paula broke in, but he silenced her with an upraised hand.

"Please. Obviously you two had an intimate relationship and there's good reason for Mr. Strange to think he's the father of the child. No one ever brings these suits unless there's some basis. But the law requires clear and convincing proof, Mr. Strange, and that's hard to come by. And whatever her reasons are, Mrs. Winburn doesn't want to talk. Now, you are decent people. Seems to me you ought to thrash your problems out in private. Anyway, there's no live baby yet and I can't adjudicate without one." Solomon washed his hands and waited for a response.

Mike shoved his hands into his pockets and toed the frayed carpet with an expensive Italian shoe. "If people can't settle their problems with words, they either come to blows or to court." Virginia followed the pattern he was tracing on the floor as if it were a profile of their past. "We've tried, believe me, your honor, but I haven't been able to say the magic words to convince Mrs. Winburn that since we made this baby together we belong together bringing it up."

"Do you mean," the judge interrupted, "that you're interested in not only being with the child but also the mother?"

"Sure am. That's a man's role, isn't it? To head up a family, take care of the mother, provide for the children?"

Through thick glasses, Judge Cabrerra's four eyes sought Virginia's two. "Is that a possibility?" he asked, and received a sharp negative shake of her head as answer. "Well, Mr. Strange"—shaking his own—"it seems what you want is beyond the power of a court to convey. She seems determined to head up her own family, take care of herself—whether you are named father or not. About all you can hope to win is the duty to support the child for twenty-one years and some minimal visiting privileges. Is the fight worth it?"

Mike looked at the floor again, rocking back and forth on his heels before he spoke. "I'll get more than that, your honor. A validation of my existence—proof that I came along this way, something to leave behind when I go."

"Then endow a hospital, for God's sake," Virginia blurted out before Paula could stop her, stung again by his implied indifference to her and his egocentric view of parenthood. "I'm going to have a baby—not a ticket to someone's immortality."

Mike remained impassive in the face of her fury. "I can build a hospital—that's easy—but I can't love a hospital and it won't love me back. I can't teach it things or hold its hand to keep it from falling. And I can't spend Christmas Eve with its mother filling a stocking and setting up a train."

The judge was beginning to decipher the hostility between the two. "Seems to me, Mr. Strange, you'd have done better to say the last first."

Mike smiled and scuffed the rug again. "Well, your honor,

they say good judgment comes from experience, and experience comes from bad judgment. I'm just learning as I go."

Judge Cabrerra made one last attempt at mediating. "Mrs. Winburn, a child's an expensive burden today what with doctors, schools—all that. You sure you can handle it alone?"

Even in the split second before she answered, Virginia knew her response would separate her forever from what a part of her wanted to be—vulnerable, dependent, *feminine*. And make her forever unattractive to the only type of man who appealed to her—sure, powerful, protective. The price, goddamnit, the price you pay to control your destiny. "Your honor, did you ever consider not having one of your children because you couldn't afford it? I may not be able to give it everything I want to, but how many can? Yes," she said quietly, almost sadly, "I can handle it."

"Sure she can," Mike broke in. "That's her problem, she can handle it too well. But, Ginny"—he looked at her, one side of his mouth smiling in the way that could always break her heart —"I can give it something you can't—a father. Not to mention a name and respectability. And all the love that's been locked up for years because it's had no place to go."

For the last time Virginia listened for what was missing in Mike's proffered contract of support and affection, heard its absence, and for the last time rejected the neat arrangement. More as an affirmation to herself than to the judge, she repeated, "I can handle it alone."

The judge's attention flitted briefly again to his wife of many years, who by contrast was suddenly so much more desirable, more *controllable* than the inflexible woman before him. He reminded himself to buy some flowers at the shop in the subway station on the way home, something he had not done in years.

"Well, that's that," he said, resigning his brief role as peacemaker. "As I said, there's nothing more I can do until the child is born and there's more definite proof to act on."

Virginia knew his words meant anxious months of uncertainty; for Mike, who generally took what he wanted when he wanted it, they represented an unnatural, frustrating delay; Paula was concerned about the strain on her client and the judge was more than a little tired of the willfulness on both sides. Of all the people in the drab little room, Gilbert Fenway was the least disturbed. "We expected you'd feel that way, your honor, but the fact is, there *is* more accurate proof available. In fact, one hundred percent accurate proof."

Paula and Virginia were immediately on guard. The judge looked quizzical. "Yes? What's that?"

"A simple blood test, your honor."

"Blood tests prove nothing really—except who *isn't* the father, you know that, Mr. Fenway."

"Not this one—it's brand-new. It's been in use in Europe for a number of years; UCLA's School of Medicine has just introduced it here. It's called the Human Leukocyte Antigen test— HLA for short. What's different is that it doesn't just allow for the possibility of paternity like the old tests, it *proves* it." Fenway riffled through his briefcase, extracting several xeroxed pages.

"How certain did you say?" The judge skimmed the article as he talked.

"It's called perfect, but if you want to be conservative, say ninety-five percent. Cells are taken from the baby and the father. If the chromosomes match, the child is his—as foolproof as matching fingerprints."

After the smooth progress of the hearing, Virginia was unprepared for the unexpected. She wanted to ask Paula what it meant, but was quieted with a look.

"Interesting," said the judge. "Here, Miss Seibert, are you familiar with this?"

"No, I'm not," said Paula, reaching for the material.

"So what are you suggesting, Mr. Fenway, that we lay over this hearing until the child is born and a test can be made?"

"No, sir, better than that. I'm suggesting that Mrs. Winburn have the test done when she goes for amniocentesis several weeks from now."

The judge leaned back, clearly interested in the possibility. "The test can be made on a fetus?"

"It can, your honor. The head of hematology at Mount Sinai Hospital is waiting outside to explain how that's done."

"With no danger to the unborn child?"

"We're told the fetus is always at some risk during the process, but it's minimal. So minimal it's considered routine now for women over the age of thirty-six."

The judge looked at Virginia. She felt his age counter going, and knew it had climbed over the thirty-five mark. "Do you plan to have amniocentesis, Mrs. Winburn?"

She was flustered. "I'm not sure, your honor. I mean I've made no plans, I . . ."

Paula jumped in to cover her indecision. "Whether Mrs. Winburn has the test or not must depend on consultation between her and her doctor. Certainly the Court would not order a medical procedure which in any way threatens her child."

"You're right, of course, Miss Seibert. Still, it's an interesting proposition. Mr. Fenway, why don't you ask your medical expert in to answer a few informal questions?"

The doctor's information confirmed the certainty of the new test. Later, going home, Shelby was to say to Paula, "What? No more sweet young things ripping off rich boyfriends? No more groupies accusing rock stars of fathering their kids? What will lawyers do to replace those huge fees for sticking it to wealthy playboys?"

And Paula was to answer, "You're right. A lot of cases will never come to court now. Just think, if we'd had the test in the old days Oedipus would have known who his father was. How would Freud ever have named his complex then?"

And Virginia was to say, "Swell. I'm pleased you're so entertained. And doubly pleased that a lot of guys are going to have to start supporting their babies for a change, but would you two concentrate on me? What am I going to do?"

Paula had been correct. The judge refused to force a procedure that could endanger the child, but after conferring with the doctor, who always advised amniocentesis for older women to be certain the fetus was developing properly, he made it clear he expected her to have it done—voluntarily.

"Since you are so certain Mr. Strange isn't the father, the test will be convincing proof of that, won't it? I think the Court would find it strange if you didn't avail yourself of such easy evidence. Of course, if you choose not to have it done at four months, the Court can order it when the baby's born." He looked at the man who was winning the day. "That all right with you, Mr. Strange?"

"Not really, your honor. I don't really want to be an absentee parent." He rocked on his heels, his arms folded across his chest. "I don't want to get a birth announcement in the mail. I want to know how the pregnancy is going, and to be consulted about medical care. I want to be there to time the pains and shake the doctor's hand when he comes out of the delivery room. I want to be a full-time father, so I'd rather you order the test done right away."

Swaddled to his thick neck by the enveloping robe, the judge looked like a turtle brushing the suggestion away with his flippers.

"Can't do that. Have to wait till the baby's born. But maybe by then you people will have resolved your differences. Certainly hope so. This case doesn't belong in my court."

What *was* she going to do?

"You know, if there hadn't been a blood test like that, he'd have invented it." Virginia was not surprised, but she was disconsolate. Paula told her the case was far from lost. That she could attack the integrity of the test, even though results

proved positive, and also the integrity of those who administered it. That the law would require strong corroborating evidence even with a positive test. That in the last analysis it
would be used only as a judicial tool, and the credibility of the
parties would still be paramount.

But Virginia knew she was whipped. There was only a certain amount of truth-dodging she was willing to do, and only so
long a time she could uphold her fiction. It was getting late
now for a decision. She sent Paula back to work, and to cases
she could win, with a promise to consult as to the next step.
She shipped the kids out for a pizza and a movie—something
horrifying to quiet their nerves. And she blessed Shelby again,
for being where she was needed.

"The only pleasure of the day was watching the crowd at the
courthouse drop to its knees when you came in with the camera crew. Doesn't all that attention make you nervous?"

"Are you kidding?" Shelby slung her bag over her shoulder
and stopped at the door to say goodbye. "I love it, and need it.
It's almost that I have to see other people's faces react to mine
—and know that they *know*—to affirm who I am. Don't you
ever want that?"

"No," Virginia said, "the spotlight embarrasses me and
makes me shy. But I know what you mean. Some people let
their bank balance define them, or their professional success—
men, mostly. Women use their shining houses and homemade
bread to tell the world who they are. I suppose the luckiest of
both sexes are defined by a God if they believe in one."

"That's it, but for me, let them know who I am when I hold
out my hand—before I give them my name."

Virginia sorted through her options quickly. "I suppose I use
my children to define me. It's what I'm smug about—conceited
really. When others measure the kids' sharpness, their intelligence, smile at their humor, appreciate their looks, *then* I remember who I am."

Her seriousness brought Shelby back to the imminent decision her friend had to make. "So now what?"

"Let's don't talk about it."

"What can I do?" There was no need to talk, Shelby knew.

"Come by tomorrow and get the kids for a while, if you can."

"O.K. A two-hour brunch. That should hold Max until lunchtime anyway." She reached to hug her friend, then held her at two arms' length. "I'm right there with you."

"I know, honey. Thanks."

Then she made a telephone call and received one. Hers was perfunctory; it established an appointment. But the one that came in was as old as the ages because it was blood protecting blood.

"How did it go?" Ev Jr.'s voice was far away. She talked to him so seldom she was not quite sure, at first, it was he.

"Not good for our side," she answered almost brightly, then caved in, stumbling through her tears. "Matter of fact, it was rotten. Doesn't look like I'll get what I want after all."

"I don't believe that, not from the Indomitable One. You know what Dad says, 'You can't keep a squirrel out of a tree.'"

"Oh, yes, and what's his other favorite? 'That's no hill for a stepper.' Well, this hill and tree are both over my head. By the way, how is he—still talking all right?"

"Perfectly. The doctor says that artery is good for another eighty years, but back to you—what can I do to help?" Even during the worst of the childhood years when his cruel teasing reached its zenith, he reached out for her when she was in crisis. It was Ev who had gone out to find her when darkness turned the way home into a mystery; Ev who swam after her raft when, terrified by swelling waves, she had abandoned it beyond the breakers.

"Just tell the folks, will you? I'm not up to explanations now."

"That's easy. Want me to come up and hold your hand?"

"No, Ev. What I have to do now only I can do. But I'll need you later. Can I call then?"

"Anything you want, little sister. Anytime."

It was a long time before she moved from the phone at all. Then, sitting at her desk, she began sorting out and throwing away old memoranda, bits and pieces of last week's tasks and last month's problems. It was an old pattern: if she wasn't able to straighten out her life, she would straighten out her drawers.

She did not allow herself to think because she couldn't face the logic of her situation. Instead she cleaned out envelopes holding bank deposits and salary stubs, and organized her current tax information. It was mindless work which kept destructive thoughts at bay as long as possible.

She reached to the back of the bottom drawer to discard painters' and plumbers' estimates from the last time she had the apartment done, and pictures clipped from magazines to help her with the decorating. She gathered letters and notes from the children, meaningless to keep, really, but impossible to throw away. She bound her past in rubber bands to read in the future.

The desk was straight again, and she was sorry. The task had kept her from taking her ultimate decision to bed. The closet beckoned beyond, but she was too tired and her fractured leg too shaky a support to consider a further delaying mechanism.

With resignation she pulled her nightgown from the bathroom hook, brushed her teeth, and washed her face. There was no escaping now. She turned off the last light and lay in the dark listening to the air conditioner working against the heat of the night and wondered how to begin.

"We do what we have to do," she said out loud, and realized there was no decision to make; it was over. For beyond her personal choice and ethical beliefs, in spite of her strength and determination, her will crumpled before the essence of what she was—a predictable woman.

She had tried to change the patterns, and some indeed had given way; the changes had brought a sense of freedom. Little things, like not wearing a slip anymore or colored nail polish or deciding not to dye her hair, to let the gray come through. Or no longer calling herself Mrs. Winburn on the telephone with tradespeople, and wearing heels that made her taller than a date and not minding. Or buying lunch for a man, and occasionally asking one out. And sending a dish back to the kitchen when it was badly prepared. But the changes were minor, rather like nips and tucks in an old garment to bring it into style. What she had tried to do in having this baby, believing she could raise it alone, in the face of the opposition of some and the pain of others, was too radical. And the extreme design, no matter how delightful to contemplate and how contemporary, when she pulled it around her shoulders produced an unmistakable effect: on her it was inappropriate, for she was, after all, a predictable woman.

"We do what we have to do."

The night would not be long enough; there was so much living and learning to do. She would begin and then compress the luxuriously long process of knowing and nurturing through the tending years into pitifully few hours.

She knew the beginning, for her babies looked alike—this one too: large-headed, with a fuzz of blond around the ears, and eight pounds of stout body grown fatter during the extra week or two in the womb she always seemed to provide. A quiet baby, born with a connection already established, a natural bonding. It would take about three months to settle in, to separate night from day. She would feed it whenever there was a hunger cry—and she'd know. She recognized baby noises as if they were a second language. She pictured the baby pulling at her breasts, heard the tiny smacking sounds, felt the peace.

The pictures in her mind changed; the night dream moved on. A fat, happy babe, less helpless now, gurgled in high chair, banging a spoon in anticipation. She opened and closed her own mouth as she spooned in the porridge, as much slipping down the chin as the throat. Later the limp head lay heavy on her shoulder, drugged from warm milk, as she rubbed a welcome burp up the small back.

She watched herself stuff fatter, stronger legs in snowsuit and held out a finger to be grabbed in a tight fist. They walked for the first time in the winter sun. People turned to watch the flat-footed steps, splaying out in snow-white shoes whose polish came off against your clothes. She took the smallest steps of her life, matching her companion's.

She saw the terrible times too. When even a mother's perfect knowledge of her child can't say why the fever rages, and where the pain comes from. She watched the vomit spew out like a projectile leaving a cannon's mouth, and wondered again how fast they get sick, and how quickly well. She felt the burning cheeks spotted pink like a clown's face, listened to the tortured breathing, and begged God to let her baby understand as its first intelligible sentence what it means to blow your nose. And she knew again the reward of responsibility, when another's life and safety depend upon your vigilance and the need is total—and the night passed on.

Touch the mental kaleidoscope, see the pictures change: The baby at her feet on the kitchen floor, streaming drool (why always and only the first two fingers in a teething mouth?), then chest to cabinet pull-ups using the door handle as a brace, wobbly now, but walking alone, hand outstretched, sounding very much like a duck asking for a cracker. Gratified, the body plopping full weight on thick diapers, gumming soggy pieces of giraffe or elephant. Animal crackers, reindeer Christmas cookies, chocolate rabbits at Easter. She would introduce the animals of her childhood to another generation and feel the comfort of continuity.

Birthdays, of course. Celebrated first for the family's benefit before the child understands passage of time. How old? "Free," with four fingers held aloft, or two. Learning slowly, imperceptibly moving to understand that unhappiness comes from other than a lack of dryness or an underfed stomach and involves conforming to others' demands or schedules or comforts. Eyes hold tears impossibly long before spilling over when bedtime comes and others are allowed to remain behind. She takes the resisting child down the hall, holding the exhausted body close, crooning songs that come automatically to mind after years of lying dormant. Slats on the rocking chair crack, the words become a hum, she continues rocking long after weariness triumphs over young determination. Contentment passes from child to mother. The warp of time stretches almost to still.

Virginia roused herself from her thoughts and pillows piled high behind her back to light the lamp and find the aspirin bottle and water glass beside her bed. Careful to avoid drugs and coffee, even others' smoking since her pregnancy began, now she tossed her head back sharply to let three tablets ease her discomfort. Priorities gave way to priorities—how swiftly they changed. It was relief from physical pain she wanted; the mental pain she sought again, doggedly, clicking off the light, sinking again into the reverie of what might have been, as one reaches to finish, after unwillingly awakening, the end of a special dream.

It was more difficult now. The child was older, features hardening into shape. The sexless body was demanding gender characteristics. She turned the child around in her mind to avoid the necessity of a face and watched the miniature blue jeans, gathered in the back by belt, rolled above shoes to add extra months of wear, tear across the playground toward a climbing gym and struggle up among the bars. She circled nearby, resisting the need to be in close, gasping each time the hand reached a higher rung, then suddenly gave in to fear as the curly head rose above the topmost square and moved underneath to cushion any fall. The accidents would come, if not this time. Teeth biting through a lower lip in a bathroom fall, concussion when a bike bucks its inexperienced rider, illness invading a defenseless body so the only hope remaining is in prayer.

She had always worried—often unnecessarily—about her children's health. She tried to memorize drawings of tracheostomies after hearing every mother should know where to cut a child's throat in case of choking, then never could remember whether the cut should be lateral or vertical. She read antidotes for toxic substances and tried to keep in mind which poison one should induce vomiting for and which one should give milk for after swallowing, but the very extent of her nervousness blocked her memory. She imagined her toddlers falling into abandoned mine shafts though none were in the area, and dreaded their climbing into abandoned iceboxes though she had never once seen that particular debris.

Virginia shook away remembered and imagined terrors and moved to times of joy, seeing first a Christmas tableau with animals approaching the manger. Her child, hidden beneath headpiece of "the sheep with the curly horn who gave his wool to keep Him warm," was followed closely by "the donkey, shaggy and brown," and "the dove from the rafters high." She sat in the audience on folding chair and in the midst of holiday madness found the peace that Christmas promised. Then she watched stubby hands making brushstrokes at the kitchen table and wondered why every child saw spokes of sunshine sticking out from a yellow ball. She folded away the painting in a pile of early efforts, most marked "To Mommy" which rendered her unable to throw them away. The trunk also held a baby's cap, worn and useless now, an early pair of shoes, a hand-knitted crib blanket. Snapshots and a silver cup. Considering the time and care involved, there were few remains of childhood. Most carried what they were into adulthood. Not this time.

Where, tonight, were the negative feelings she had known

with her other children? the weariness? the loneliness when cut
off from an active world? the relentless repetition, the constant
demands on her time and patience? She looked under the
stones of her memory, turning them to check the darker side,
but did not see what she chose not to find. She could not
afford to diminish what she had so little of. Not this time.

The nighttime clock pursued a laggard's pace, but realizing
its deception, she increased her own. She pushed the swing in
the park high, then higher. Readied the small sled with its
bundled burden and pushed it off. Ran beside the two-wheeler
until with a steady course it moved away on its own. Held the
wobbly body between her legs while tiny skates bent side to
side upon the ice. There was too much to teach, to do. She became exhausted in her bed, less from the efforts made than for
those for which there was no time. At last, mercifully, against
her will, fighting the release which would deprive her of her
own, she slept.

Tuesday, September 2

She awoke slowly, quite early, and reluctantly let the real world assert itself, lying on her side imperceptibly rocking back and forth. One hand around her abdomen, she begged moments more in exchange for a promise to rise at their end, then broke her promise and asked for even more. She held their last communion through the placenta of her mind, offering the sacraments of love, accepting absolution in return.

When finally she rose she was calm and purposeful. She bathed her face and body as if for surgery, then repeated the motions, comforted that the flush of her skin proved not all her senses were numb.

She dressed simply, cotton pants and shirt, tying a sweater around her shoulders in spite of the heat. She brushed her hair back hard until it fell straight to her shoulders. There was no need for makeup. She packed her handbag, adding extra Kleenex and money from the emergency supply, and chocolate confiscated from the children's rooms. There would be time for food and coffee later; she needed to get on about the day.

The cool air outside was a surprise. Sometime during the long night currents from the north had swirled over the city dropping temperature and humidity to a point unknown since spring. It was a day of promise and renewal. She signaled a cab to the curb and sank into the buckled plastic seat. Laying her head back, she watched the giant apartment houses slide past the corner of her eye, marching like soldiers down the avenue, their residents sauntering in search of the morning paper and a Danish. To her left, runners made endless loops through the park. Unconcerned, carefree people on an uneventful morning. If we were all in pain at the same time and to the same degree, she thought, God would have a rebellion on His hands.

The taxi ticked its way through early streets still free of the usual midtown traffic and stopped at the designated corner. Virginia paid the fare and walked to the graystone entrance—a place she had never known and would never know again, but the best, the safest facility in town—her own doctor had assured her of that. With steady stride she walked into the elevator, scanned the overhead information, and pushed the appropriate floor. A large waiting room directly off the elevator, even now, this early, was filling up with quiet people who had nothing left to say. She heard her steps on the cheap vinyl floor as she walked to the center desk to leave her name and cash. She was handed a receipt and forms and returned to find a chair. Like men in a porno movie who choose to be where they are but want no one to know them there, the women in the waiting room spaced themselves apart, finding solace in solitude. Faces were averted, or bent close upon their chests, but she could see they were mostly young—she might have been the grandmother of the group, she thought, and found it the only reason to smile. Some men had come too, and were seated alongside their companions. They had a slack-jawed look, as if unaccustomed to helplessness. Their shoulders hunched like little boys in a corner, being punished by their teacher.

Names were called from time to time. She watched absentmindedly as girls moved impassively to the desk and disappeared behind the adjoining door. She heard hers twice from a long way off before she jerked in response and walked stiffly through it too. Another waiting room, with benches along the wall. Forms in hand, she sat in line, as silent and detached as the others there. One young woman paced a tight ten-foot circle; no one asked her to sit.

She was called again, this time by an attendant, not much older than her Maggie, who asked the prescribed elementary questions almost apologetically. Are you certain this is what you want? Would you like to speak to a counselor? Will you return for a checkup? Do you understand the basics of birth control? Here are the signs to look for later, the timetable for repair.

She waited again, again was called, and led to a makeshift cubicle. A detached voice explained the drawstring bag for her clothes. Alone, she stripped them off and tied the front-opening gown around her chest.

Another call—the last. A room empty of people with one long table its only furniture. A face without features led her in, helped her up and back onto the flat surface. She rested her arm protectively against her forehead as if to ward off the purpose of being there. She would never be in this place again, or see this face, yet a part of what she was would end here, in minutes, without a dirge of drums or lamentations. No one here would raise a voice, no one would care.

A needle came, more welcome now than feared. She heard the nurse's instructions as she felt it in her arm—no turning back. She could not see the doctor who walked into the room, because of her tears, so he will be faceless too, she thought— appropriate. But she heard him say that she would feel nothing for fifteen minutes. I will feel everything for the rest of my life, she thought, and so she said it.

"Don't."

"What's that?" The doctor turned around from a supply of

surgical materials where he was stripping gloves onto his hands.

"Don't do it, Doctor. It's wrong—I'm wrong, listen, I'm getting fuzzy . . ." She tried to raise herself on her elbows. The nurse and doctor were at each side, bending over to be certain what she was saying. "But it's a mistake." She slipped down again, the powerful sedative taking her with it. "Oh, hell, I'm going out . . . don't, please don't . . ."

She awoke later, on a cot, covered by a thin blanket. She looked down the darkened room at beds lined as in the dormitory of an orphanage. The hulks were silent, immobile, till one by one they rose, forms without energy, young backs bent with heavy burdens. At last she did the same, swinging her legs over the side of the cot, sitting still till her head cleared. An attendant, gentle as the rest, pointed the way to juice and cookies, but, too dazed to talk, she shook her head. What children are given at recess, she thought, when their work is done.

Desperate to find someone who could tell her, someone who knew, Virginia was gathering herself for the effort to rise when she saw the operating room nurse coming down the dimly lit hall pushing a cart. A towel had slipped out of place over the cart's contents, and for a moment, before the nurse automatically readjusted the cover, she glimpsed its sloshing red liquid, containerized for disposal. Virginia signaled her as she passed.

"Did you? . . . Am I?"

The nurse leaned close to her ear, slipping a protective arm around her shoulder. "We did not do the abortion. You've just been sleeping off the sedative," she whispered. "Would you like to talk to someone—one of the counselors?"

Virginia had an overwhelming desire to whoop in relief but was too weak. Instead she buried her face in the nurse's neck.

"Thank you, thank you," she repeated, the words barely audible.

"Is there anyone . . . ?"

"No, no, nothing now, nobody. I just want to go home."

Like Virginia, the day had changed its mind during the hours she had been inside. The morning's purity was replaced with thick, heavy air, made murderous by a sun heating the cemented city with a fury. It ricocheted off the sidewalk into her face, reinforcing her woozy feeling. She leaned against the building while searching for her sunglasses and when she put them on she saw him at the curb. Just as he used to wait for her. Chauffeur quiet, immobile in the front, he with papers spread, half-glasses on the end of his nose, seeming to completely occupy a space designed for several. He was out of the car coming toward her before her hands left her temples.

"Is it over?" His face was dark. He looked as if he had not slept. Virginia braced as if to ward off blows.

"How did you know I . . . ?"

"I knew. Come, get in the car."

"But how . . . ?" Then she realized. "You didn't have me watched *again!*" She pulled back against his arm leading her to the curb.

"Stop, goddamnit . . ." His face went tight and he hissed between his teeth. "I said, get in the car. If you don't want me to take you home, then go alone and send the chauffeur back for me. You shouldn't be on your feet."

Suddenly meek, she let him lead her to the car, where she ducked inside and moved to the farthest corner. Mike followed, sliding the plastic barrier closed between the seats after directing the driver.

"Mrs. Winburn's, Joe."

The limousine rolled soundlessly for several blocks before they spoke.

"You all right?" he asked almost reluctantly.

"Um," she nodded. "Been waiting long?"

"Since about eight-thirty. Takes longer than I thought." He did not look at her but brushed ashes from his shirt.

"All that time? But you could have . . . why didn't you try to stop me?"

He was like a man who had taken a whipping. "God knows. I thought about it enough. Been expecting this—even alerted the court so a warden would be ready." He took a deep breath.

"But . . ." she prompted.

"By the time my man called this morning . . ."

"You did have me watched!"

"Of course," he said with annoyance, "but by this morning I had sorted out a few things."

"Yes?" He was uncharacteristically hesitant, mumbling rather than speaking forcibly. He was not in charge and did not seem to care.

"Mostly I came to realize that I wanted this child because it was *ours*. I asked myself how I would have felt if I'd gotten a stranger pregnant, or someone I didn't particularly like." He cleared his throat. "The truth is, I wouldn't have put up a fight. Don't get me wrong"—he faced her abruptly with a sudden fierceness—"I think abortion is wrong, dead wrong." He dropped his eyes again, his chin almost resting on his chest. "But I would have let whoever she was make that decision . . ."

"With no guilt attached?"

"Damned little, to be honest. It would have been her load."

He was quiet once more. They both looked out their windows and saw nothing going by. Finally he spoke again. "So I had to admit that our child was something special. And being its father would be special. And bringing it up with you was something I wanted to do. Like crazy."

The response in her head was so loud she was sure he could hear it: That's what *I* wanted to do—like crazy! But don't you remember? How unimportant I was? You threw us away like yesterday's newspaper . . .

But those words were too dangerous because they were honest, and left her open to more pain, so instead she repeated evenly, safely, "Then why didn't you stop me?"

"Well . . ." She had never heard Mike sigh before. "When

you fall out with your partner the business is bound to suffer. You might as well fold it up. We'd have been lousy parents with all this going down between us, and the kid the cause of it all. Everybody would have been miserable—and that's not the way I wanted it, ever."

"Or I." The emotional hemorrhage of the long night and the longer morning began to tell. Virginia's hands shook in her lap. She felt as if her bones were beginning to collapse toward the center, as if she needed a substitute backbone.

"And I realized that as long as the child was the source of our troubles, you and I had no way of working things out. After the wreck, when that call came in the middle of the night, I have to tell you my first thought wasn't about the baby. I didn't want *you* dead. Or crippled. And I wanted to be the one to make you well again."

For the first time she heard *her*, without the baby, with no conditions imposed. *Her*, in first place, a belief she had once held close but was forced to recant. Now here it came back again, redeeming itself by the act of being uttered. But wait . . . believe him again? And disregard the consequences of placing her faith in the glittering idol of superficial feelings? Forget the punishment true experience delivers?

Virginia tried to shake away the spell by forcing herself to remember his cool heart was like a fire short of kindling—it was a hard blaze to keep burning; still, she felt her center of gravity shifting toward him despite her reservations. Wasn't this a vulnerability he had never shown before? Wasn't this movement, however hesitant, toward what she had hoped for? And if he could step away from his extreme position of favoring loose connections, hadn't she enough flexibility to move away from hers of total commitment? She couldn't see him for the tears. Nor could she see that his eyes were filling, too, as he went on.

"I knew you might go for an abortion—'You do what you have to do' you always said. At first I intended to stop you—at least as long as I legally could. But that was just a power play, and what kind of satisfaction comes from forcing someone to do what you want? I tried that. I took you to court, and well . . . victory wasn't sweet. Winning by decree is demeaning somehow. Like wrestling someone fifty pounds lighter. And I knew as soon as I let you up you'd do what *you* wanted to anyway."

"Yes, ultimately I did what I wanted to do." For the first time in a long time, inside, and even slightly on the outside too, Virginia smiled. "Would you mind terribly holding me up for a while?" she asked as she leaned her head against him.

He turned sideways on the seat to better accommodate her weight, and put an arm around her shoulder to draw her in. "Sure. Rest now. We can talk later."

"Yes," she said. "Later. So much to talk about," she said. "Thank God."

HEYWOOD BOOKS

TODAY'S PAPERBACKS
– AT YESTERDAY'S PRICES!

Heywood Books is a new list of paperback books which will be published every month at remarkably low prices. It will range from glitzy, up-to-the minute women's novels to compelling romantic thrillers and absorbing historical romance, from classic crime to nerve-chilling horror and big adventure thrillers, presenting an outstanding list of highly readable and top value popular fiction.

Look for this month's new titles:

THE CANARIS FRAGMENTS	*Walter Winward*	£1.75
PERAHERA	*Julia Leslie*	£1.50
HERE LIES NANCY FRAIL	*Jonathan Ross*	£1.50
RAMILLIES	*Barbara Whitehead*	£1.50
SEEDS OF THE SUN	*Vicky Martin*	£1.75
ALONE TOGETHER	*Sherrye Henry*	£1.75

FICTION

One Little Room	*Jan Webster*	£1.50
The Winnowing Winds	*Ann Marlowe*	£1.50
The Root of His Evil	*James M. Cain*	£1.50
Criss-Cross	*Lee Jordan*	£1.50
Lovenotes	*Justine Valenti*	£1.75
Perahera	*Julia Leslie*	£1.50
Alone Together	*Sherrye Henry*	£1.75

SAGA

Daneclere	*Pamela Hill*	£1.75
Making Friends	*Cornelia Hale*	£1.75
Muckle Annie	*Jan Webster*	£1.75
The Windmill Years	*Vicky Martin*	£1.75
Seeds of the Sun	*Vicky Martin*	£1.75

HISTORICAL ROMANCE

The Caretaker Wife	*Barbara Whitehead*	£1.50
Quicksilver Lady	*Barbara Whitehead*	£1.50
Ramillies	*Barbara Whitehead*	£1.50
Lady in Waiting	*Rosemary Sutcliff*	£1.75

THRILLER

KG 200	*J. D. Gilman & John Clive*	£1.75
Hammerstrike	*Walter Winward*	£1.75
The Canaris Fragments	*Walter Winward*	£1.75
Down to a Sunless Sea	*David Graham*	£1.75

HORROR

The Unholy	*Michael Falconer Anderson*	£1.50
God of a Thousand Faces	*Michael Falconer Anderson*	£1.50
The Woodsmen	*Michael Falconer Anderson*	£1.50

CRIME

Here Lies Nancy Frail	*Jonathan Ross*	£1.50

NAME ....

ADDRESS ....

....

Write to Heywood Books Cash Sales, PO Box 11, Falmouth, Cornwall TR10 9EN. Please indicate order and enclose remittance to the value of the cover price plus: UK: Please allow 60p for the first book, 25p for the second book and 15p for each additional book ordered, to a maximum charge of £1.90.

B.F.P.O. & EIRE: Please allow 60p for the first book, 25p for the second book, 15p per copy for the next 7 books and thereafter 9p per book.

OVERSEAS: Please allow £1.25 for the first book, 75p for the second book and 28p per copy for each additional book.

Whilst every effort is made to keep prices low it is sometimes necessary to increase cover prices and also postage and packing rates at short notice. Heywood Books reserve the right to show new retail prices on covers which may differ from those previously advertised in the text or elsewhere.